MASTER PIECES
Misadventures in Space and Time

*An unofficial charity anthology in aid of The
Stroke Association*

Edited by Paul Driscoll

Master Pieces
Published by Altrix Books in 2019
Edited by Paul Driscoll

Cover Design by Ginger Hoesly.

DOCTOR WHO, TARDIS, DALEKS and CYBERMEN (word marks and devices) are trademarks of the British Broadcasting Corporation.

PUBLISHERS NOTE
This is a not-for-profit limited edition release, raising funds for The Stroke Association. If you acquired this copy second-hand please consider making a donation.

Acknowledgements. Special thanks to Scott Claringbold of Red Ted Books for entrusting me with the project he began in 2016, Kara Dennison - my partner at Altrix Books, Ginger Hoesly for such superb artwork, and all the contributors for their patience, professionalism and generosity.

In memory of

Terrance Dicks (1935 – 2019)
Barry Letts (1925-2009)
Edward Brayshaw (1933-1990)
Roger Delgado (1918-1973)
Peter Pratt (1925-1995)
Anthony Ainley (1932-2004)
William Hughes (1998-2018)

Table of Contents

Bandages
Chris McKeon

I.

The dark cocoon hung at the end of a dry string of stardust beneath a necropolis of hollow stars. No flicker of stellar fire, nor whisper of solar wind disturbed the dark cocoon's tethered balance above the boundless abyss of infinite emptiness. Inside the dark cocoon, the being slept.

Remember…

The small voice burst the silence of sleep. The being awoke. Its eyelids pulled apart. Eyes gummed in dust swung across the dark strings constricting its vision. Its mind scraped questions across raw thoughts: who… where… why? The being struggled to move, to turn, to breathe. A weight pressed against its chest. The being sensed the surrounding ebony weave compressing against the surface of its brittle skin; felt the strands tightening closer. The being's jaw tugged loose, a sliver of air hissed in effort as the being strained to shift its limbs. Then the light ruptured the darkness.

Remember to…

The small voice spoke again, this time louder, but the being paid little attention as the sudden light volleyed a shockwave of brilliance through the immobile dark. The light enflamed the frozen graveyard of stars. The disinterred stellar system exploded into prismatic supernovae. Celestial quakes spun the cocoon around and around in the ether, like a dark pulsar twisting in a melting firmament. The being within the cocoon tensed with dread from the unknown terrors of the light outside.

Remember to wrap…

The small voice spoke a third time, with greater strength. The force of the voice engulfed the cocoon. The words burrowed deep into the being's ears and reverberated through its hollowed mind. The words held no meaning, no context, no sense. The being's mouth wrenched wide. A raspy howl shredded its throat. Summoning all its will, the being at last spoke with a weak voice. "Remember to wrap what?"

The strong voice answered.

Remember to wrap yourself before you hit the bottom.

The light brightened to blindness. Brilliant shafts pierced between the dark strips of the cocoon. Then, with a sharp, snapping crack, the stardust tether holding the cocoon in suspense fissured. The cocoon dropped. The descent

7

gained speed, faster and faster. The blind of the light flooded the cocoon, bleaching the being's sight. The being shut its eyes, tore its fingers against the weave of its containment. Its hands breached the surface…

It saw itself, twisting in energized air, screaming. It saw itself, packaged into cloying darkness, suffocating

… and the impact shattered the cocoon. Its dark strands flew wide and disappeared into the white light. The being felt itself hovering, weightless, above empty, silent space. Just before losing all sense, the being looked down and saw a face standing directly below and looking up in wonder.

With its limbs flung wide and tethered by the black strands of the unravelled cocoon, the being hung senseless upon the feeble wisps of an ancient wind, rocking gently upon the chilled, whispering flow. For a moment, the being almost remembered everything. Then all memory fled, and it slept.

II.

The person awoke with a shudder. He was lying supine with his arms by his sides and legs outstretched upon… something, something that he could not feel. The person lifted his head and opened his eyes. He felt his neck strain for leverage against the movement, as if his skull was weighted beneath the anchor of eternity. After moments of effort, his leaden lids split and unsealed. A white corona burned the edges of his sight. The brightened edges poured towards the centre and filled the person's unfocused vision. The ubiquitous light was quite unwelcome.

The person beheld an endless void of white. There was no other colour except the ragged edges of black bordering his vision. The person tried to lift his hands towards his eyes. The movement was difficult and painful, but he endured the strain and eventually his limbs rose and came into view – the person froze in revelation when he saw them.

He witnessed his hands, wrists, and arms. He dropped his gaze and struggled to lift himself at the waist. He exerted tremendous effort to accomplish the task; his arms shuddered and shook to brace against the weight of his own body, a weight so heavy he felt as if his spine, ribs, and skull were sure to burst backwards through his pain-screaming skin.

At last, the person's torso balanced upwards. After the exercise, exhausted and in agony, his eyes were shut tight for what seemed to be several minutes. Then the person unclosed his eyes and studied the rest of his body. What he saw carved his consciousness hollow with dread.

Every surface of his flesh was wrapped, bound, and buried beneath thick strips of midnight-coloured bandages. The gauzy bands were tattered and torn with frayed, fibrous ends, and the fibres intertwined and interwove together to restrict the person's mobility to near-paralysis. With stiff, numbed movement, the person reached upwards and touched his head to feel the rough, misshapen exterior. It was the same everywhere.

He was trapped within his own body, underneath a ragged skein of darkness.

The person's breathing quickened. The hiss of rasping air circulated warm within the cranial, concrete containment. At that moment, he felt his arms shake and bend, their feeble strength finally buckling under the extra weight of the bandages encasing his frame. The person's upper-half fell backwards to strike whatever surface upheld his ruined body. He lay there, staring into the endless, encompassing light. A heavy, blunt pain weighed into his chest.

The person tightened his lungs and throat to stifle the sounds and sensation of fear surging within. Swallowing, he summoned his voice, which escaped through dried lips as an almost inaudible, dust-thin whisper.

"What... happened... to... me?"

A face appeared, consuming the person's sight. It was the same face the person had seen when he had fallen from the stars.

"Oh, there is an answer, my good fellow."

The face was familiar, it was the face of –

The face smiled sadly, and gave his answer.

"You died."

III.

The gargantuan orb of white light held dominion atop a desert sky. Beneath the reign of the light, rose the cracked crown of an arid hill marked with the petrified remains of an ancient tree. The tree was stained with light and scarred by dust. Thick knots of light-charred growth cankered the trunk. A crown of spindly branches burst into the air, as if to block the blanching fire of the sky's shining tyrant. Each branch curved back towards the scorched earth, baked by futility. The fallen branches released a seared shower of scarlet leaves, which formed a crust upon the heat-split ground. Against one side of the tree the leaves entombed a shape. The shape was a corpse.

The white orb in the grey sky beat its heat through the scarlet tomb and seeped into the black shroud of the corpse. The heat buoyed the corpse's sleep and enlivened his dead dreams. He heard the earth cracking, the leaves crunching. A swath of light banished the darkness and the corpse awoke.

9

Something was brushing the leaves clear from the corpse – no, someone. The corpse saw:

Dirty coat, torn trousers, scuffed shoes, crumpled shirt, dangling bowtie, lumpy hat. It is the Clown. As always.

The Clown's chalk-pale skin and glass-grey eyes bounded the corpse's vision. The Clown smiled.

"My dear fellow, you really ought to live a little. You don't want to face death lying down. It's rather undignified, you know. You've done nothing but sit against this tree for ages now."

The corpse exhaled to clear his airway. After a sufficient struggle, he managed to open his throat.

"If I do nothing but sit, then it is by your design. You were the one who placed me against this tree."

"Well, if I hadn't, you'd still be blinded by the light, now, wouldn't you? And that reminds me."

The Clown gazed upwards towards the white in the sky.

"The light's seen enough by now, so it's time to announce our presence!"

The Clown brandished a long, striped tube. He raised the rod to his lips and piped a light tune. The Clown lifted his heels and hopped from one foot to the other, churning plumes of dust with each note and step. The Clown played. The corpse watched. He found the sight disquieting.

"Why don't you join me?" the Clown called to the corpse between musical phrases. "I'm having the most fun I've enjoyed in ages!"

"I have no mobility," the corpse responded. "I can only sit and watch your ridiculous performance."

"I suppose, then, it's for the best. It means you can't run when they come for you. And they are coming now."

A weight pressed into the corpse's chest.

"What are you babbling? Who is coming?"

The Clown ceased to play and pointed towards the remote horizon.

"The ones you murdered."

The corpse followed the Clown's finger. He saw several figures with faces of whirling, enflamed dust racing towards the hill. The white orb in the grey sky closed to black.

IV.

The effigy saw the soldiers mount the hill. They shifted without sound. Their uniforms were stained and rotted; their parched faces were webbed in dust; and

10

their eyes were empty. The soldiers shuffled towards him. The effigy felt himself lift into the air amid a swarm of cinder. The dust swarm spun the scarlet leaves surrounding him into thick, sharp-surfaced ropes coiling around his wrists, ankles, and chest. His heavy, bandaged limbs could offer no self-defence, no escape from the bondage. His weakness, his helplessness, boiled his flowing frustration – he bellowed hot rage! Then he felt a leafy cord ensnare his neck and tug upwards. He impacted against the tree…

The effigy awoke to darkness. A ruddy glow shifted at the bottom of his vision. The effigy slid his eyes downward and saw, several feet below, the horde of dust-soldiers slouching at attention, their empty eyes fixed upon his hanging form. Each held a flaming torch in their crumbling hands. The effigy laughed at the macabre sight.

"You rabble are actually intending to immolate me? How provincial! And for what purpose do you empower yourselves to destroy me?"

There was a snapping rustle in the branches above. A single stalk bent low before the effigy's rope-fastened shape. With legs encircling the dry branch, the Clown balanced himself in the air. His upside-down, chalk-pale lips curved downwards, and a dark twinkle danced upon his eyes.

"For justice, you insensitive scoundrel! You died as a murderer after all, and these are your victims, the ones you stole from their proper places to serve your endless, senseless slaughter!"

"I have no memory of these… creatures. They mean nothing to me."

The Clown brandished his musical rod before the effigy.

"Well, then you haven't changed at all, because they meant nothing to you before you killed them! But your death means everything to them now."

The Clown straightened his legs, dropped from the branch, and spun in the air to land before the dust-soldier horde. He spun towards to the torch-wielding company and raised his arms and voice to the midnight sky to bellow an off-key refrain:

Upon this night
Unleash the light
And with its might
This effigy – burn bright!

The soldiers' dusty craniums lifted to the sound of the Clown's cry. Their eye sockets filled with violet flame. They shuffled forwards. As they approached the tree where the effigy hung, a low, moaning wail diffused from between their grime-locked jaws. Their moaning increased with each step. They lifted their torches towards the tree.

11

The effigy beheld the company's advance and felt a great weight compress against his chest. His ragged breathing quickened. He strained his limbs against the scarlet ropes binding him to the tree. He would not burn here, not like this! He felt the bandages encasing his body tighten –

Remember to wrap before you reach the bottom…

The voice! It was…

Something heaved the ropes that bound the effigy and he smashed through the hollow trunk and fell into the darkness.

V.

The carcass jolted awake. He remembered falling, free-falling, crashing through a thick mesh of …? There his memory ended. Now, he opened his eyes to see. He beheld nothing, not even the close wrapping of darkness. He felt nothing, not even a wisp of wind. No, there was something, some slight tug upon his chest. The carcass felt himself rocking lightly, as if he were hanging by –

A thread? Indeed, you are, my good man. By several threads, in fact.

"Who are you? What do you mean? What threads?"

These threads. Observe.

White light roared downwards and cleared the darkness surrounding the carcass. Through the light the carcass saw himself entangled within a veiny system of tendrils embedded into the heavy wrappings upon his chest. The carcass realized: he was –

You are ensnared within the roots of the same tree where you were hung to die.

It was the same voice that had spoken to him before his fall from the stars, and before his fall into the tree. A voice of resolution. The carcass enjoyed the sound; it reminded him of –

It reminds you of what, my dear fellow? I am quite interested to know.

How the voice knew his own thoughts the carcass could not understand, but he felt compelled, even eager to answer: "Of my purpose, my presence, and myself."

Of course. How flattering. It is no surprise, however. Greatness begins with – Wait! Listen.

The carcass listened. Through the hollow casing of the root-laced, earthen mound, he felt the thudding vibrations of rapid footfalls. A muffled, frantic voice wailed.

I know, I know! All is not well; all is not prepared. But I shall find him soon! I swear it!

"The Clown. I know his voice too well," the carcass muttered, "no thanks to all our recent time together. But despite the undesirability of this enclave, that fool can hardly hope to find me."

12

A swift strike of air breached the hollowed hill. Through the opening issued a large, smooth-curved metal blade. The blade retracted. More footfalls, circling to the other side of the outer hill. Another swipe, another strike. The blade carved the void once more; its tip balanced precious few meters from the carcass's bandage-bound face, spewing dusty flakes into his eyes.

"A scythe?" the carcass muttered in disbelief? "He doubles roles as Father Time?"

His season shall end soon enough. But we have little time. With the light unleashed, the Clown shall discover us shortly. Now, I can lead us to safety, but you must trust me.

"Where are you?" the carcass asked. With great effort, he turned to see what lay below him. The carcass saw only a pool of viscous, black silt. Then a black, leathered hand pushed upwards through the muck. The carcass recoiled at the sight. Then he heard the Clown's footfalls racing, nearing. The carcass made its decision, strained against the clinging roots. His arm broke free and reached for the hand. The leather hand dragged the carcass into the mire.

VI.

The body drowned! Dark slime filled his throat and nostrils. He choked on the putrid ooze. He tried to swim, to flail, to move; but the weight of the deep crushed his limbs to his sides. As the body dropped, he felt the hands of the spirit clinging onto his back, dragging him deeper into the depths of the pit. The spirit wrapped its fingers around the body's shrouded throat and pulled back his head.

Listen to me, listen! There is no more time. Recall what I said when you fell from the stars. Remember to wrap yourself before you hit the bottom. Now is the time!

Rage inflamed the body as he tore open his mouth and bellowed. Slime and stench expelled through his bandaged face as he screamed his desperate, wretched reply.

"WHY?! When I'm already lost?"

This is not the bottom. This is not your end. Wrap to control the bandages that bind you.

The liquid darkness poured into the body's mouth, eyes, ears. He saw no more, heard no more. But he willed himself to endure a moment longer as he listened to the spirit and spoke one more word.

"How?"

Be true to yourself. Remember who you are. And become the darkness.

The body understood. Without knowing how, except knowing that he must, the body ceased struggling against the weight of the dark and embraced it, received it, imbibed it, consumed it – the darkness sank into the body's

13

bandages, loosened their binding. The body moved, at last he moved! Howling with joy, the body raised his arms and clutched at the gnarled roots stuck in his chest. With his full strength he plucked them loose. Then, with roaring rage, he tore the roots downward.

The earth moved. The surface breached. The tree dropped into the chasm. The Clown plunged into the void.

The crater in the earth was deep, dank, and dark. At the bottom of the crater lay the shattered shell of the tree. Strewn about the fallen tree were the tattered and torn remains of numerous military uniforms caked with red stains. Save for wisps of dust, the lonely clothes were empty. Footsteps echoed. The body, with new-found mobility, walked towards the fallen, crumped shape of the Clown, who lay on his back upon the wet earth, impaled upon his scythe. The body warmed himself at the sight of the Clown's pained writhing as his chest dropped and last breath stilled.

"You shall sing and dance no more, Clown. And my life shall be the better with your blessed death."

The Clown's dulling, glass-grey eyes stared upon the body. He released a laugh and whispered one last sentence.

"But… whose… life… will… be… yours?"

It is mine, where I must be, where I will myself to be, always. The body is mine. At last!

The body spun around. He saw the dark shadow of the spirit rushing towards him, his leathered hands outstretched. The spirit struck the body and entered! The body felt himself tear apart.

VII.

With absolute confidence securing his posture and countenance, the Chief entered the scarlet-walled War Room and gazed upon his favoured domain. His black-armoured Guards sounded his welcome return with full-throated cheers. The Chief snapped his fingers to cut the Guards' cry to silence.

"The games of war are ended, and victory is ours! All the races of the Galaxy have fallen beneath the shadow of the War Empire. Soon the Empire shall march across all of time and space to gather every galaxy within the Cosmos! And then, I present you, my children, with eternal dominion!"

The Guards' bellows of approval thundered throughout the War Room and swelled like a majestic symphony within the Chief's ears. Then the Chief heard another sound, some distance behind him: a shrill, strained voice ranting in the corridor outside the War Room. The Chief smiled as he heard the blunt sound of a blow striking against flesh and the shrill voice shrieking in shock and pain. The Chief addressed his quieted Guards once more.

"But first, we must sweeten our triumph with a final purging of disloyalty. Bring forth the traitor!"

A group of white-suited Scientists carried into the room a small, trembling man dressed in bloodied, crème clothing.

"Arise, carrion," the Chief commanded. "Arise, and kneel before your Superior."

After several moments, the broken man managed to lift himself to a kneeling position. The Chief sneered upon the wretched shape, crumpled and bleeding beneath him.

"You were my chief of security, my second-in-command. You could have shared in our approaching glory, and yet you dared to attempt a fallow rebellion against my person. I cannot imagine why."

The traitor lifted his haggard face and revealed haunted eyes sunken with sickness and hate. He opened his mouth to speak his voice, which was a sound the Chief had always found most annoying.

"You are an outsider! An alien! And we shall not trust aliens to lead!"

The Chief chuckled. Then he kicked the traitor square in the face, who wailed as he fell backwards.

"And yet your people were once known as aliens! And without me, unknown aliens you would still be! Only through my leadership has your race's potential become fulfilled. Of course, *you* were always a disappointment, allowing resistance to fester among the experiments, and always challenging my authority. When I came to your people I was promised efficiency and cooperation."

The Chief lifted his gloved hand and gripped the golden medallion that hung around his high-collared neck and rested with heavy pride against the centre of his chest.

"Without the knowledge *I* have, this complete venture would be impossible."

The Chief paused, shuddered. The medallion weighed heavy upon his chest. He turned and looked to the near wall. In the scarlet shine he saw his face. It was not his face!

This is my life now. You must not return. No!

The Chief felt his chest tear open and dark bandages streamed from the wound.

VIII.

An unfurled silver flag swung across the bronze-fire sky visible through the ragged cleft of the vaulted canyon. The casualty lay upon the rough surface of the canyon bed, waking from the dream of warring delights. He lamented the return to consciousness; he had enjoyed the vision of his triumph.

The casualty winced as he rolled onto his side. He looked down to the source of the pain – and froze. Blood poured from the large hole in the centre of his bandaged chest. From out of the gore a golden circle protruded, the same as the medallion from his dream!

It was no dream, you fool, nor is this a flag above you!

The casualty heard the echo in his mind, the same from the vision, the darkness, the stars. He looked upwards, saw the stinging shine of the silver sword swiping downward! The casualty spun away from the arcing strike of the blade. He rolled along the slippery stone bed and twisted to face his attacker.

It was the Clown, and he was dead. His ghostly face with glass-grey eyes was submerged beneath a murk of shifting darkness. The turbulent brume surrounding the Dead Clown's face billowed around and through his misshapen clothing like a vengeful storm heralding undying determination. The Dead Clown brandished his long, narrow sword towards the casualty and his enlarged voice reverberated within the wind-swept chasm.

"Traitor, Criminal! Now you remember the guilt of your crimes of war! You bear the seal of your shame upon your breast!"

Beneath the mask of his bandaged face, the casualty sneered and mocked the Dead Clown's declaration with a scorning laugh. He gripped the bloodied medallion jutting through the torn bandages of his chest.

"This is no mark of shame, but the symbol of my greatness! And I remember no guilt or crime. At last, I remember myself, and the ultimate objective I designed to achieve: the glory of absolute power over all life in the Cosmos through the engineering of my armies."

The casualty extended his arm and pointed his finger to the Dead Clown.

"And I remember you, and all you did to foil my destiny! For that I hate you, and shall destroy you here and now, once and forever!"

The Dead Clown bellowed with laughter. The sound chilled the casualty's core, as the imprint of an older memory trembled in his mind, the laughter of another, hated figure, one he could not quite recall. The Dead Clown spoke again.

"You design to destroy me, but I imagine you shall destroy yourself first. Have you noticed the shape of your shadow?"

16

The casualty paused and looked to the stone bed. There, in the lurid light of the white orb in the rusting sky, he witnessed the cast of his shadow. It was the misshape of two beings, raging and tearing against one another. The casualty shouted his terror, turned, and fled into the chasm. The rising laughter of the Dead Clown followed his flight.

IX.

The exile manoeuvred himself through the convolution of tunnels. He had been exploring them for some time, ever since discovering their entrance nestled within the chasm walls. The frigid passages were narrow and interwoven, like the layout of a fossilized nervous system. The weather-hewn walls were overlaid with such quantity of moist, pungent moss that the stone had discoloured to a green-blue tint. And yet, somehow, the exile felt increasingly at home within the deepening fathoms. From a distance behind, he could hear the rising echo of the Dead Clown's voice, shouting warnings and condemnations. The Dead Clown was overtaking the exile's descent. With each passing step, the exile struggled and strained to move beneath the wretched bandages constraining his body.

The body is no longer yours alone, and it shall soon be mine.

The haughty tone of spirit forced a tremor of fatigue and sickness through the exile. He clung to a wall's mossy barnacles to keep upright; and in the low, gangrenous glow from stone-adhered morass he witnessed the changes writhing within his form beneath the bandages: His arms and legs were heavy, bulged and gnarling, and he could feel his head deforming into some grotesque, elephantine mass. And most arresting of all was the thundering thumping emanating from all sides of his chest, as if many hearts were pounding deep inside, as if –

"I am splitting myself asunder!' the exile whispered through an agony-warped jaw.

"Precisely," the spirit spoke – to the exile's horror, though his own voice – "and I am sprouting from within your rotting shell. Soon I shall emerge and claim my right to exist in your place."

"Why?" The exile retched and wrestled control of his voice. "Why are you doing this? Why are you consuming me?"

"Because it is my right! And it is the only way to correct the vision that you failed to achieve."

The exile growled in rage and pushed from the wall. He surged forward through the passageway towards a close, pitch-dark portal.

17

"Very well then! I know that my objective foundered, but it happened because of the interference of squabbling, paranoid insects who dared to defy my authority and plotted against me."

The exile reached the shadowy threshold and turned back in trembling rage.

"And most of all I fell because your interference, Clown! And now I will have my revenge upon you! And I claim that vengeance first!"

The exile breached the shadows and entered a chamber choked in dust and entombed in silence. At the centre of the chamber was a chair encased in stone. The exile flung himself towards the chair. He gouged his hands through the bandages and tore the spirit from within himself. The spirit screamed at the extraction, its dripping darkness spitting in the open air. The exile flung the spirit against the chair, and then with a tortured shriek he ripped the golden medallion from his torn flesh and struck the gleaming circle against the spirit. Sound exploded. Light blinded. The exile roared.

X.

The survivor opened his eyes and saw the rough-sculpted stone chair before him. It was empty, save for a pair of black leather gloves resting upon the golden circle of his medallion. The survivor reached forward and fitted his hands inside the gloves. Then he saw the dark outline of his shadow cast upon the chair. It was his own shape, restored to its full strength and stature. The spirit was gone, but not forgotten nor dismissed.

The survivor looked upon himself and saw, with deep satisfaction, that the bandages were gone. In their place was an elegant, midnight silk jacket with scarlet and gold lining its high-collar, creased midnight trousers, and dark boots. The survivor inhaled and felt his breath pass with ease through his strong chest, which resonated with the strength of his double-heartbeat.

"I am whole," the survivor declared with calm certainty.

He looked down to the golden medallion resting upon the stony throne. He lifted the circle and peered into its gleaming surface, as if to perceive some remnant of the spirit he had bestowed to his future. There he saw only his reflection, a face covered in tattered weaving – the survivor's other hand snapped to touch his face. It was still covered beneath the bandages!

"Well, my dear chap, it seems you're not quite as complete as you might like to think."

It was the Dead Clown, standing in the portal's boundary with his sword straight and outstretched. Beneath the gloomy mist surrounding his body, he had changed even more. His now hawkish frame was longer and leaner, his clothing fit well with various shades of reds, greens, and blues shining upon the coat, and his hair had transformed into a vast tuft of light.

The survivor placed his hands behind his back and addressed his enemy.

"Perhaps not yet. But I am determined to be free of this burden soon, after I dispatch you, of course. And you seem to have dispatched yourself since we last met. I can hardly classify you as a Clown anymore, living, or dead."

"Quite right, too. I rather fancy myself as becoming more of a Dandy in the future. But your future ends here, sir. At least you'll die well-dressed. One question, though: What happened to your medal?"

"The symbol of our people? It became a millstone around my neck, and a reminder of past shortcomings. Now, I no longer require a symbol of my grandeur; I am my own greatness. Nevertheless, if you seek my medallion, you may have it. Here!"

The survivor flung the medallion towards the Dandy, who swung his sword to deflect it. The survivor lunged forward, ripped the sword from the Dandy's hand, and plunged its shaft into the Dandy's chest. The Dandy became the Clown. Then he disappeared. The survivor exhaled.

"Of course, you were never here, because whatever your appearance now, you still live. The one who is dead is whom I must destroy to become myself again."

The Grandfather.

XI.

At the heights of the southern mountains there was a house, overgrown with wood. Inside the main hall of the house there was the Grandfather, overwrought with age. The Grandfather paused and turned to the wood-wrapped fireplace beside his high-backed chair. He gripped a long, iron poker veined with fibrous, wood tendrils and struck the glowing embers of flaming charcoal smouldering in the stone pit. The Grandfather replaced the poker in its vine-infested sheath and considered one of the light-coloured, wooden game pieces arranged on the white and black checkerboard before him. He chose a course and moved the piece from a white square to a black. Then the Grandfather settled into his chair and smiled.

"You have endured a long journey, a very long journey indeed, one fraught with danger and hardships; and it has finally brought you here, to my house. Your move, young man."

Across the dust-grimed table was another chair gripped and bound in wooden vines and flowing dust. There, the rival sat wrapped in shadow and

19

silent obsession. A black-gloved hand emerged from the darkness and gripped a dark-coloured piece to move from a black square to a white. The rival leaned forward, and the firelight revealed his face bound in the midnight shroud.

"And what is your move, old man?"

The Grandfather leaned forward and rested his withered hands upon the head of his splinter-flecked cane. The flares from the pit reflected in the intensity of his glare.

"Kindly refrain from addressing me so! I may be ancient, but I am not old. More importantly, however, I ask you if know why you are really here."

The Grandfather shifted another piece upon the board. The rival outstretched his glove to set a countermove before answering.

"Perhaps simply to resume our amiable contest. When we met before, we played a game much like this, in a place much like this. So many wondrous things were happening then. Such glorious chaos."

"Yes, and as I recall you hid your face then, as you do now, to cover your intentions, I imagine."

"I hide my true intent, old man? Am I always so disingenuous, even to my oldest friend, my own—"

"It is your nature, you villainous renegade! And what we were, we are no longer!"

The Grandfather grabbed a game piece and struck it against a new square. The rival calmly moved a piece as the Grandfather straightened his cane before the rival's bandaged face.

"I have watched you since your fall from the stars through my eye of light, and I have beheld the darkness of your determination. You have no remorse for your destructions, no compassion for your victims, and no desire for forgiveness."

"Then there is no sin in destroying you and everything that you are!"

The rival cast the board into the flames. He lunged forward towards the Grandfather, his hearts and hands longing to kill. The Grandfather shouted. Then the house caught fire.

XII.

The Grandfather's house was dying in flames and screaming its agony across creation. Inside the centre of the fire, locked in bodily combat, were the Grandfather and the monster. And the monster was winning.

"You are old and useless! Your will is weak, and your spirit is frail. Submit your will to me and die quickly!"

The monster was screeching through the bandages surrounding his face. His breath rushed hot and hateful. Through the dark gauze, he saw his hands wrapped around the Grandfather's throat, saw the old man's bulging eyes, saw the tears streaming through his eyes. Tears?

"A tear? Why are you crying, old man? Is it the fear at the end of your existence?"

The Grandfather gripped his hands around the monster's crushing wrists and pulled a fraction free.

"No, you wretched, selfish creature! I weep not for myself, but for you! I weep for you! What will your horrid, base desires, your lust for power, for chaos, for destruction – what will it profit you?! Why seek after these things?"

"Because I want death!" the monster bellowed as he tensed the totality of his muscular strength to bear down upon the reed-thin throat of the Grandfather, who gasped and grappled for air. "Death brings power, and power brings me meaning, the meaning of my life."

The Grandfather was fading, his eyes dulling, his voice whispering, but still he spoke.

"Then... you... live... for... nothing..."

"I live to be myself," the monster exclaimed. "I live to destroy you. Here, and outside."

The Grandfather exhaled a small whimper, and then slumped. The monster hissed a breath of joy at the sight and let the old man's body fall to the burning floor. The monster watched the Grandfather lay there, broken, bruised, bleeding, and already long dead. Then the monster looked to the enflamed heavens and laughed.

"Yes, I know that he is dead, and that he already was dead. He died long ago, in the ice of Earth's southern pole. How I wish that I had been there, to kill him myself. Well, now he dies in the flames of his home. And in flames, I am reborn. For only within a dead mind can a living mind be remade. And that is exactly what you, my people, have been trying to accomplish. You knew that I was nearly dead, when you found me on the planet of the War Games. You saw my regeneration was aborting, that one life and the next were held in balanced abeyance. And you sought to control me in my weakness! Well, you have merely unleashed my truest self! I am..."

The monster felt the house uproot and heave itself over the mountain cliffs in one last effort to destroy him. The monster laughed and tore the bandages from his face, revealing his image: crème skin, emerald eyes, a black mane of hair with a centred streak of grey, sharp-cut side burns, and a long, thin beard. As the monster fell, he named himself.

21

"The Master!"

XIII.

"The Master is loose. You will report, Recorder."

The Recorder looked with fear towards the First's towering figure. The Recorder demonstrated the devastation and a litter of shrunken bodies. At the destruction's epicentre was a melted cocoon connected with sentient cables to a suspended network of glowing orbs. Within the shredded container was a mass of charred, midnight-hued filaments.

"Somehow, the Master awakened during the mental re-structuring procedure and…well, overloaded our instruments. He tore free and went mad with rage, killing everyone. I only survived because–"

"The Master desires an audience as much as he craves escape. He will be in the capsule decommission centre, trying to requisition his space-time machine."

The Tribunal departed without a further word. Simultaneously, the Tribunal arrived within the decommission centre. They avoided the shrunken corpses scattered across the chamber floor. The Tribunal reached an alcove occupied with a large, green metal box. A doorway into the box was open. From within, the Master emerged.

"The Tribunal. Your august presence is a great honour."

"Master," the First replied. "You appear well-preserved, despite our most meticulous efforts."

"Yes, your attempt to re-engineer my future has failed. My next life will show his face in time, but for now, I am the Master. Now I must depart. I have an old friend to destroy."

The Second's patience exhausted. "Enough. You shall come with us now or – AHHH!"

The Master had blasted the Second with energy from a small, hand-held tube. The Master smiled and pocketed his weapon. The Third hurried to bathe the Second with light from his eyes.

"His condition is grave. A regeneration may be required to maintain him."

"Take him," the First commanded. He kept his eyes fixed upon the Master as the Third disappeared with the Second's glowing form. "You cannot escape, Master. Your feeble machine barely functions. It is far better to surrender yourself to our organization. You may yet find a place and purpose among us. Consider your position, and your future, very carefully."

"I have fixed my purpose and my future is my own, now and forever. As for my machine, you are correct that it no longer performs as it should, but my true ship is as capable as ever! Behold!"

The Master snapped his fingers and the green box disappeared. In its place, a black cube manifested. "My TARDIS emerges from its hiding place. As do I." The Master opened a portal to his TARDIS and half-entered. "Farewell, Goth. Seek me again, and I shall destroy you. Oh, and if you see my opponent before I do, please do inform him that I live. And I am hunting to kill."

The Master descended into the darkness. His TARDIS whispered its departure.

Left alone, the First sighed and pondered. "Poor fool. Even now he is ignorant of our influence upon his ship, and his destiny. And while we see fit, he shall not encounter his rival. Not until our purposes for both have been fulfilled."

The House on McQueen Street
Scott Claringbold

For as long as I can remember there has been a house at the bottom of our street that looks… out of place.

Our house was built back in the seventies on fields on the outskirts of town. It's one of those houses with the orange-coloured bricks and white wooden panels. Our little village is surrounded by fields. It's like we're in our own little bubble living here. Separate from the rest of the world.

Our estate is a snaking road from the top of a hill right down to the little stream at the bottom. About two hundred houses, all packed together like some child's play town. Visitors sometimes have to pinch themselves to believe what they're seeing. Mostly the neighbourhood is pretty friendly, I know just about everyone in our street. Except the bloke who lives in the creepy house at the bottom of our road. Well, I think a bloke lives there – it's hard to tell. I've seen several different people come and go from that house.

Usually the visitors are men in suits, but sometimes it's a woman who dresses like someone forgot to colour in Mary Poppins.

The house is a big old Victorian-type house. Thick and sturdy looking. It sits back behind a large garden – that looks very well kept despite the fact I've never seen anyone in there.

***

I had gotten up early that morning, the sun was streaming in through my bedroom window, even at this hour. I decided to take my bike and head out on an adventure. I was thirteen at the time and, of course, I had friends, but sometimes I just wanted to be alone with my thoughts and not have to get into arguments about which football team – or sci-fi film – was the best. Mum and Dad were still in bed and I could hear my sister, Alison, playing in her room. It was my room when we first moved here. I was six and had this big room all to myself. About six months after we moved here, Mum told me she was going to be having a baby. Dad wasn't too thrilled with the news, saying 'Why did it have to be now?'

Not long after, Dad had to convert the garage into a downstairs bedroom/living room for me. It sounds great but it was pathetically small.

I made myself a mug of tea, switching off the kettle before it whistled and woke up my folks. Next, I packed everything in to my rucksack and headed out to the shed. My blue Raleigh Grifter sat there waiting for me, my Christmas present the year before last and my pride and joy. The bike gleamed as if it had just been taken out of a shop window.

***

I wheeled it up the drive and set off on my journey. The morning was bright and warm, the birds sang in the trees. I free-wheeled down the road and was aware of a blur to my left.

Then the world tipped upside down and went black.

When I awoke, someone stood over me. A tall, thin-looking boy – maybe only a year or two older than me. He had a vacant expression on his face and made no attempt to speak to me. I tried to move and felt a pain in my ribs. The boy took something out of his pocket. It was at that point I noticed his odd clothing, a black and white tunic and matching trousers that gave him a look of a monk.

He waved a silver wand in front of me and it made a screeching noise, "You have a cracked rib but you'll live."

"What happened?" I asked. My bike lay on the other side of the road, the front wheel buckled and the handlebars twisted. I had been knocked off by a car.

The boy bent down and placed his arms under mine. He yanked me to my feet and I was surprised that it didn't hurt me. The boy began to walk me over to that scary house across the road.

When he opened the door, I wondered if I was concussed or hallucinating because it seemed far too big. The living room was a huge library, stacked top to bottom with books of all sizes. A winding staircase led to the ceiling with a gantry running round the middle of the room.

In the centre of the room was a strange four sided plinth, covered in dials, switches and knobs. It was like nothing I had ever seen before.

"What's your name?"

The boy looked at me from under his old-fashioned haircut. "I am the Master."

I laughed at that, more out of nerves than mirth. I soon stopped when I saw the look he gave me.

He led me to a chair and handled me, roughly, into it. "Did you see who, or what, hit me?"

26

The Master shook his head, and a smile slithered across his face. It scared me a little. He crossed over to the plinth and began to flick switches and turn dials. There was a loud groaning sound, and a light flashed up and down the column that connected the plinth to the ceiling.

A second later, the Master said, "Why don't we go and find out?" For a moment I was confused, but then I realised that he was answering my earlier question.

"What? How…?" I stammered, but the Master was already stalking toward the front door. "Great, I'll just get myself up then."

I struggled toward the door, the pain making me stop to take a breath. I stepped out of the front door and it appeared to be the same time of day as when we went in. I glanced over the road and, to my surprise, my Grifter had gone. "Hey, some sod's nicked my bike."

The Master grabbed at my arm and pulled me behind the tall, imposing hedge. "Shush, we have a small window to play with here. We mustn't run into ourselves."

I looked at the boy before me and wondered if perhaps he had been dropped on his head as a baby. The things that he said, and the things that had happened since I met him really made no sense to me. "Eh…?"

The Master pointed towards my street. I peered out and thought I could see someone with my bike. I was about to shout, when I noticed that it was… me! Well, that stopped me in my tracks, but then it slowly began to dawn on me – a thick fog dissipating in my brain. The house was a time machine.

The other me cycled down our road and for a moment closed his eyes. A blue boxy car came round the car and collided with me… the other me. And then… and then the bastard drove off without stopping.

The Master pulled me to one side and at that the moment the other Master stepped out of the front door and made his way over to the other me.

"Did you recognise the car that hit you?" The Master asked me in a hushed tone.

I nodded. "Yeah, it was that cranky old git, Mister Sanders. He used to keep our footballs if they landed in his garden, and sometimes he put a screwdriver through them."

The Master grinned. It really was the most evil thing I have ever seen in my life. "Fancy paying him back?"

I gingerly touched my ribs, "Yeah, let's sort him out. How, though?"

The Master held a finger to his lips and pulled me down the side of the house. Our other selves went into the house. "Ok," The Master said. "Let's time this right."

27

We waited a few minutes and then the other Master crept over the garden and the other me followed. We watched our counterparts talking for a moment and then dashed back inside the house. The Master made me sit in the armchair, and he danced around the plinth in the centre of the room.

There was a flash and groaning noise, a sound that I could imagine a constipated elephant making. The Master pointed towards the front door. I pushed up out of the chair and made my way out. It was dark outside – night-time dark. The view was different as well. Our street had gone, and when I looked back at the Master's house it was now a delivery truck. I thought I had hit my head in that accident and my brain was running riot.

"A chameleon circuit," the Master said, by way of explanation. "Disguises my TARDIS."

I nodded feebly, as if I really understood what the hell he was talking about. He took out that wand-thing and waved it about. It emitted a high-pitched squeal and he stalked off towards a nearby building.

We were walking towards a fish and chip shop. The wand – which I found out later was called a sonic screwdriver – seemed to screech louder the closer we got. The front door was locked shut and the lights in the front of the shop were switched off. Even in the dark I could see that the paint was peeling off the shop-front.

"This is the early hours before you accident. Do you understand?" I didn't, but I nodded anyway.

I turned suddenly at a noise behind me, a prowling cat was chasing something across the road. I winced at the pain my side. A thought struck me. "If this is before my accident, how come my ribs still hurt?"

The Master looked at me as a disappointed parent must look at a naughty child. "This is still the same timeline, the accident has already happened – we've just hopped back a bit to see how."

"Oh, I see," I replied. In truth, I still didn't get it. I was only thirteen!

"The heat signature of your Mister Sanders shows that he is in here," the Master said, jerking a thumb over his shoulder at the shop.

"How do we get in?"

The Master held up his wand/screwdriver and it began to squeal at the lock. Moments later, my new friend was letting himself in through the open door. I followed like an obedient puppy.

We heard voices coming from a room at the back of the shop and we crept forward to see what was going on. There was a lot of smoke, and it took all my willpower to stop myself from coughing. As I peered round the door frame, I could see five men sat round a table playing cards. One was Mister Sanders. Not only was he smoking, but he was drinking a golden liquid from a glass. Whiskey.

The old bugger was drunk when he hit me. A rage washed over me – he could have killed me!

The Master pointed back into the corridor, and we made our way further down. "Do you want me to teach him a lesson?"

I did. I wasn't usually a nasty or vindictive person, but at that moment in time I wanted that old man to suffer. Later, when I thought about it, Sanders hadn't really done much damage, but the sight of my mangled Grifter really made me angry.

We headed back outside and The Master suggested we should look up and down the street to see if we could find Sanders' car. I found it a street away, and we waited for Mister Sanders to come back to it. It was cold this early in the morning and I was wishing I had put on a jacket. The Master didn't seem to be afflicted by the weather.

About two hours later, Mister Sanders waddled his way along the road to his car. He swayed as he walked and tried hard to stay quiet, but was failing miserably.

He reached his car and the Master jumped out of our hiding place and placed a hand on the back of the old man's shoulder. Sanders shrieked, jumped on the spot and swore loudly as he dropped his car keys.

"Excuse me, sir. Have you just come from the illegal gambling den in the fish and chip shop?" The Master asked in an authoritative voice that scared me. There was something about the way he fixed Sanders with a menacing stare that worried me.

Sanders scratched his chin, contemplated lying and then shrugged. "Yeah, so what?"

"We're staking the place out. Any minute now, several of my men will break in the door and arrest anyone on the premises."

Sanders seemed to think about this. I sat in my hiding place wondering how the old bloke could be duped by someone who was clearly not even old enough to have a weekend job, never mind be a policeman. But he was fooled.

Sanders began to stammer an apology and seemed anxious to be away from the Master. "Listen, I could make an exception seeing as you weren't on the premises. How about you hand over your winnings and be on your way, and we'll say no more about it?"

Sanders jumped at the chance to get out of any trouble and handed over a roll of tatty looking notes. As he bent down to pick up his car keys, the Master grinned at me and waved the money in the air.

Sanders clambered in to his car. My ribs still ached, so I knew that nothing had changed – he was still going to run me over.

The Master reached my hiding place in the shadows and stuffed the roll of notes into my hand. "To fix your bike, or get yourself a new one."

"He still runs me over, though. My ribs are still cracked." I snapped, feeling really annoyed.

"Ah," The Master said, nodding knowingly at me. "You need total retribution?"

"I do?" I asked, uncertain. My new friend, however, took my response as a sign of approval. He whisked out a small gun-like object, which seemed to have a small radar antennae fixed to it. Aiming at the car that was now driving away, he pressed the trigger. To my total amazement, the car began to shrink, until it was no bigger than one of my Tonka toys.

My mouth fell open as I witnessed this. The Master walked over to the car and picked it up. "Here you go."

I held the vehicle in my hand. Inside, was a tiny Mister Sanders sitting behind the wheel. My brain was struggling to comprehend what had happened. "Is he dead?"

"Dead as a Dodo." The Master grinned, and clamped an arm around my shoulders. "Anything for my new friend."

I wasn't quite sure how I felt about seeing Mister Sanders shrunk to the size of an action figure. "Does it wear off?" In hindsight, that was probably a really stupid question.

"What? Death! Ha-ha. Oh, I like you. What did you say your name was?"

"Oh, it's Roger." I held out a hand and the Master grasped it with two hands and shook it, quite violently.

"How about we take a little trip in my TARDIS?"

The house, time vessel, was a machine that could travel anywhere and anywhen. That description alone was enough to pique my curiosity.

We travelled together for months, visiting lots of weird and wonderful alien worlds. I can say that we taught each other lots of new things. The Master was keen to know more about humans and earth.

I suppose it should have come as no surprise to me that the Master was from an ancient alien race.

Mister Sanders' car sat on the TARDIS console. Every now and again, the Master would pick it up and whisper obscenities at the little figure sat behind the wheel.

Then, one day, a pang of guilt gripped me. "Can we restore him?" I asked the Master.

"Why would you want to?" the Master asked, and it hit me that he didn't really feel any compassion for the old man.

"I didn't want to kill him." I said.

The Master shrugged. He played with some switches and the house/TARDIS began to groan. Seconds later, a sullen face looked at me and waved towards the door.

I headed towards the door, knowing that I was never going to see my friend again. I stepped outside without looking back. It was daylight outside, and I hurried along the path and down the garden. Peering through the trees, I could see the earlier me pushing my bicycle up the drive. Was it my bicycle or his? And why was I thinking about myself in the third person? Time travel could be so confusing.

The other me cycled down the road and I saw Sanders' car hurtle around the corner. I raced along the pavement, and as the other me reached the end of the road, I screamed, "Look out!" Just in case that wasn't enough, I ran into the road.

The car slammed into me. The other me winced at the impact, and I could see the look of shock on his face as I crumpled to the ground. Sanders jumped out of his car this time and began to mumble incoherently.

It hurt. The pain that lanced up and down my body, really hurt!

The other me didn't know what to say, he/I just stood there with a shocked expression. I guess seeing yourself get run over would do that.

I was aware of another figure joining us... the Master. He's going to make everything right again I thought.

But he just looked down at me and shook his head, tutting. "Looks like he's had it."

I tried to speak but all I could manage was a gurgle as blood filled my mouth. I had saved both the earlier me and Mister Sanders, but had managed to get run over twice by the same car!

And then I understood. I was going to die. Well... this me was.

I wondered if the Master knew this was going to happen. Perhaps he was showing me a bit of the universe, knowing I wasn't going to be in it for much longer.

He knelt down next to me and placed a hand over my heart, "Such a fragile thing – the human heart. You all get so upset and sentimental over the silliest things."

I tried to talk again, but it was no use. Mister Sanders was across the road banging on the front door of the nearest house, asking if he could use the telephone.

31

The Master picked me up and moped off towards the house.

And that was when my head filled with all these weird visions, of alien civilisations, of the past, of the future, of watching him walk away with another me, dead in his arms.

I'm not quite sure what happened that day. The memories in my head belong to some other me, but they are there as a reminder that I should take each day as it comes and live my life to the full.

And that's the story of the day I watched myself die.

The house at the bottom of the street is gone now.

I appear to be the only one who can remember it.

Everything He Ever Wanted
Mike Morgan

Engines screaming, the time machine materialised. The Master was too busy checking readouts to pay attention to the plebeian details of where exactly his Ship had set down; knowing which world he was on would be enough.

"The planet Jendall. Sufficiently industrial it seems, judging from the atmospheric pollution."

Satisfied with the results of his scans, he straightened from the console and, pausing only to pull on his black leather gloves, he strode to the opening doors of his control room.

A raucous crowd greeted him beyond the doors of his TT capsule. There were at least fifty mauve-skinned humanoids with rodent-like facial features thronging about his vessel, shouting and gesticulating wildly.

He blanched momentarily before pulling himself to his full height. He was the Master; he was not afraid of a superstitious rabble terrified by the appearance of his Ship. They would soon bow to his will.

But they were not shouting at him in hate, he realised. They were cheering.

***

The Master wasn't sure how to react. This wasn't the sort of welcome he was accustomed to.

"It is him!" cried one elated soul.

"It is as the stories say! His vessel is a blue box that forms out of nothingness!" called out another.

The Master cast a glance at the capsule at his back. It was true that it was cuboid. Currently, his space-time machine was modelled after a large, chunky, light blue computer bank, common to research laboratories on Earth in the 1970s. He'd forgotten to reset the chameleon circuit.

Wait, did they think…?

Had tales of his arch rival reached even here?

Less than a second passed before the Master raised his hands for silence, once again in full control of the situation.

"I crave your indulgence, gentle townsfolk. You are quite correct in thinking that I am… Ah, but I dare not say. I am travelling incognito for the time being, due to events I would not dream of boring you with. If you would do me an inestimable favour, I ask only that you refer to me using some alias, some *nom de guerre*, and refrain from any mention of, well, anything medical, shall we say?"

One of the townsfolk stepped forward. He wore a chain signifying high rank. "Of course. We understand completely. You fight evil throughout the universe. There must be times you need to hide from your enemies."

"That is true. I can see you are familiar with the problems I face."

The Jendallian nodded. "I am Uthwren, elected mayor of this city. We have heard of many of your kind who take on assumed names. The female scientist that experiments on innocents for her own cruel purposes, the hooded one who interferes in history for the sake of the chaos it causes, the one with the snake painted upon his skin who seeks only thrills and diversions…"

"Quite." The Master paused. "Not to mention the most famous of them all."

The alien mayor looked confused.

"The Master," prompted the Time Lord. "The brilliant renegade possessed of the most ingenious mind in the universe."

Uthwren shook his head.

With considerable effort, the Master held back from shooting the idiot with the tissue compression eliminator stashed in the pocket of his mandarin collared Nehru jacket.

Not recognizing the danger he was in, the alien asked his fellows, "What name should our visitor choose for his assumed identity?"

Their ignorance of his reputation rankled, but it did afford him with certain opportunities. He was on Jendall for a reason, and with this turn of events his aims would be easier to achieve than he'd dreamt possible.

Urbanely, the Master suggested, "Why not refer to me as the Master? I'm sure he wouldn't mind, and it seems no one in these parts knows him well enough to penetrate the deception."

They agreed willingly.

Seeing the humour of the situation, the Master smiled.

"Excellent. Now, if you will excuse me, I have much to do."

The townsfolk cried out again before he could walk away.

Uthwren spoke for them all. "Please, gentle… Master, we need your help!"

"My help?"

"Yes. We are at war."

"Are you?" replied the Master carefully.

"We are cruelly attacked, Master, with millions of our people dead. There was no warning, and so we were unable to prepare. In truth, we are losing. We implore you, aid us in this, our most desperate hour!"

They were expecting an answer.

34

"Oh, yes, I'll save you." He smoothed his goatee. "That is what I do, isn't it?"

***

Uthwren explained how Jendall had found itself unexpectedly at war. Without any warning, just a few hours earlier, dozens of warheads had been fired from their neighbouring world, Ghastion.

"The missiles struck major population centres. The devastation was terrible. Even now, rescue teams are digging survivors from the rubble." Uthwren gestured at the Master. "We prayed for help, and you came. The traveller who brings succour to so many throughout the universe."

The Master inclined his head. "I did not know of your great suffering. Had I but heard of it sooner, my arrival would not have been so delayed." He stepped closer to Uthwren. "But tell me, how can warheads reach you from another world in your planetary system? Are your weapons so advanced?"

"Normally, it would not be possible. But our two worlds are almost at their closest. Due to the orbits of our respective planets, they draw near to each other every five hundred days. In another month, we will be past perigee and Ghastion will pull further away. Interplanetary strikes will then become impractical again."

Glancing upward, the Master saw Ghastion through a break in the tangerine coloured clouds. The adjacent world was close enough to be seen with the naked eye. Smaller than the Moon when viewed from the surface of his rival's favourite planet, perhaps, but still quite the spectacle.

"The solution is clear. You need only hold out long enough for Ghastion to continue along its orbit and for your world to be outside of its effective attack range."

"I am not certain we can last that long."

Playing the part of his eternal enemy to perfection, the Master said suavely, "Then I pledge to save your beleaguered race from extinction. I will find a way to protect you all from these missiles."

He winced inwardly at the saccharine nature of the vow, but it was just the kind of tripe that his old college 'chum' would spout. And the Master needed to put on a good show in order to get what he wanted. There was no way that dull-witted poltroon of a crusader would abstain from aiding such plucky, democracy loving, all-round good eggs if he were here, and for the Master to remain convincing in the role he would have to play along.

35

"All I need to save you," he continued, oozing charm and certainty, "is a common ore found in the mountains near here. I realise this sounds strange, but believe me. The ore can be refined into a tremendously rare substance – Quavek."

"Quavek?" The mayor's whiskers quivered.

"That's right. It can be made into excellent shielding. You Jendallians can use that super-shielding to protect yourselves from bombardment."

Uthwren looked intrigued by the idea. "It will be difficult to make enough of it to defend everyone."

"A trifling matter, I assure you. I can construct machines that will weave vast domes of Quavek over your cities."

The mayor seemed convinced. "I should have expected such a stratagem from you, um, Master. It is a peaceful solution. Your preference for avoiding violence is legendary."

Somehow, the Master stopped himself from letting loose a bark of derisive laughter.

If he hadn't been playacting at being his old friend, he would have never suggested such a nauseatingly pacifistic plan, but it had proven convincing. These primitives were completely taken in.

"Trust me, my friends. The shields will be so strong, no attack from Ghastion will get through." He clapped his hands. "Let us start! We have much work to do."

***

To the Master's wonderment, the Jendallians wasted no time in starting the mining and processing operations. He graciously accepted accommodation in the planet's capital city, in a suite in the president's own palace. All the better to coordinate the planetary defence, naturally, and not because he took joy in the finer things of life.

He had the natives bring his ship to the palace, needing it close at hand. They found a large hall in which to place it, reverentially. The hall itself was refurbished to house the Master's proposed device for turning the processed Quavek metal into thin strands that would be shipped out to the cities and woven on-site into the dome shaped protective barriers.

Each day, the simple-minded buffoons of the Jendallian government brought him progress reports from the mines. The work advanced smoothly, with tons of ore being extracted from strip mines dug with indecent haste. There were casualties from the mines, given the speed of the excavations, but the Master assured his hosts that the sacrifices of the brave miners were worth it.

He even attended one or two commemorative services for the dead miners, in a show of solidarity and compassion. Virtually, of course; he wasn't going to miss any of the banquets at the palace by travelling to the mines in person.

Sipping at the finest wines the planet had to offer, the Master smirked privately. The Jendallians were executing his plan for him, little suspecting that he had a very different purpose in mind for the Quavek.

***

A second week passed, seeing the official opening of the Quavek processing plant. Since the natives were throwing themselves into the endeavour, the Master found himself at something of a loose end.

The president, a white-furred, hunched-over fellow named Flerrot, took to consulting the Master on various matters unrelated to the interplanetary assault. This made sense to the Master; obviously the president should seek his wisdom on all kinds of issues, for the Master was an expert in everything.

It would have been absurd for such an advanced being to feel flattered by such unrelenting respect and awe; the Master merely thought Flerrot was being sensible.

"My dear chap, put all your affairs in my hands. I will find the solutions to the problems you face."

When more warheads struck, this time annihilating the temples of the salt flats on the southern continent, the Master organised the fastest and most efficient relief effort the Jendallians had ever seen. The president happily took the credit in public and turned ever more to the Master in private.

Most of the issues the Jendallians regarded as intractable were nothing of the sort to the Master. Famines and droughts were simply the result of ineffective resource allocations – trivial matters for the Master to resolve, and the carbon pollution of their air was childishly easy to remove with nothing more than bioengineered sponges.

As the primitives relied on him ever more to decide the running of their world, the Master mused that they had essentially granted him absolute power over their futures. All he had ever wanted was power, and here it was, handed to him on a silver platter. He hadn't needed to grapple for it, to assassinate or murder his way to the top; all it had taken was the pretence of morality.

He felt nothing but scorn for their gullibility.

37

Months passed. The stockpiles of ore grew, and the processing plant thundered ceaselessly, night and day, smelting the ore into sheets of indestructible metal.

It transpired that the Jendallians had a poor early warning system. The unsophisticated sensor array only gave a few minutes warning of the enemy strikes, and that was too little time to attempt to intercept them. The Master scribbled down plans for a better warning system on the back of a napkin. Flerrot could hardly speak, he was so grateful.

The Master interspersed his advisory meetings with the Jendallian leaders with walks in the palace's ornamental gardens. He enjoyed the rigid lines of the pruned bushes and the straight paths between the flowerbeds.

The children and families of the planet's leaders often played in the gardens. Although he preferred solitude in his walks, the Master instantly adopted a pleasant, even avuncular, manner when their paths crossed his.

In this way, the daughter of the president came to like him. Her name was Whinn and she was a delightful child, with bright button eyes, soft whiskers, and a wet nose.

Bumping into him one day by the central fountain, as she frequently did, she asked, "Why do the people of Ghastion hate us so?"

"The Ghasts? Who can say? The universe is full of terror, child, and evil does not always require a reason." The Master allowed a half smile to grace his lips. "But do not worry. I am here to keep you safe."

She took his hand, her tiny digits slipping between his longer fingers, and whispered, "I thank the gods for you, every day."

He patted her hand gently. "My only desire is to do what is right."

***

That evening, the Ghasts launched the largest missile assault yet at the planet.

More than a thousand missiles with thermonuclear payloads rained down through the stratosphere, heading toward the densely populated regions of the northern continents. There were too many to shoot down, even with the new sensor array. Almost a billion lives hung in the balance, and the promised shields were not ready.

The Master borrowed some electronic parts from the storehouses of the palace's guards and cobbled together a jamming device. With a flick of a switch, the Ghastion assault was ended and the huge interplanetary rockets rendered inoperative.

They fell from the sky, most of them crashing, lifeless and unable to detonate, into Jendall's oceans. A few struck unpopulated areas, and the armies of Jendall hurried to clean up the radioactive debris.

Flerrot was amazed by the Master's swift intervention.

"A minor countermeasure," he demurred. "It was your quick implementation of the enhanced early warning grid that gave me the time to build the jammer. Your part in this triumph should not be overlooked."

The old Jendallian looked like he might explode with pride.

Uthwren was there in the palace's Crisis Room, representing his city. He raised a paw to get the Master's attention. "Now the crisis has passed, may I ask a question?"

The Master nodded graciously.

"The city astronomers have been working on getting a closer look at Ghastion as it approaches absolute perigee."

"Have they?"

"Yes, they have. And they report that the planet appears very different to how it normally looks. There are thick clouds where before there were none, and when we do glimpse below the cloud cover there are signs of extreme volcanism."

"That sounds peculiar, I agree."

"Do you have any explanation for this sudden change?"

The Master spread his hands wide, all innocence. "My dear chap, I hardly–"

"The astronomers also estimate that Ghastion is as much as a degree off its normal orbital path. If that is true, it's an unprecedented perturbation."

"My knowledge of the universe is extensive, but there are some mysteries that even I have not yet solved. Come, Uthwren, let us consider these puzzles another day. For now, let us concentrate on our defence."

Uthwren seemed reluctant, but his concerns were forgotten as an aide rushed in. "My president, my lord Master, I have wonderful news. The processing plant informs us that the required quantity of Quavek metal is now ready. We are able to proceed with building the shields."

∗∗∗

This day had long been prepared for. Crews were standing by on the outskirts of every major conurbation, ready to receive the metallic fibres that would be woven together into an impossibly lightweight but unbreakable mesh.

First, the uncountable stacks of Quavek sheets had to be transferred to the hall where the Master's TARDIS was housed, in order to be put through the special machine that would turn them into strands.

Lorry after lorry deposited bundled loads of Quavek sheets outside the hall. The outer doors of the echoing chamber were flung wide and toiling crews of workmen transferred the metal inside on rumbling forklifts.

Nodding sagely, the president and his aides gestured at the huge bulk of the Master's completed device, designed to stretch the metal into fibres. So strong was the Quavek after the initial smelting, reforming it into other shapes was beyond their technology.

Nearly six months I have wasted here, thought the Master.

"My friends," he called, from an overhead gantry. "I beg you, leave me in peace to complete this quotidian task. It is but mere manual labour, dull to observe. And I wish to finish it as quickly as possible, without distractions."

The assembled dignitaries assented, as keen as the Master to get the Quavek strands on the road, out to the waiting city work crews.

Whinn had accompanied her father, the president. As she trailed after her white furred parent, back to her rooms, she half turned and waved shyly at the Master.

The Master closed the heavy double doors after them, and then he smiled. But there was no laughter in his eyes this time.

***

Reworking the metal into the impossibly slender strands he required was an automated process. The Master had finished preparing his production line days earlier. Now it was running, he was free to focus his attention on more important matters. For a start, he had half of the Times crossword left to finish.

Alone in the cavernous hall, with only the susurrations of his machine and the almost inaudible hum of his ship thrumming through its open door as company, the Master began to read out a clue. "Four down, six letters, 'Student of philosophy, law, or medi—'"

He was interrupted by the crackling of a message coming through on his TARDIS's communications panel. The words were hard to make out. Curious, he stalked over to the cuboid exterior of his vessel and walked through the open entranceway.

Entering the control room, he still could not make out the content of the message. "A cry from Ghastion, perhaps," he murmured. He adjusted the levers on the panel and the hisses and pops faded, leaving the frightened voice of a cat-like Ghast, clear as a bell.

"Help us!" implored the voice. "Oh god, you must help us. We're all dying."

The Master nodded and turned off the speaker. It appeared the Ghasts were reduced to emergency power. He doubted the Jendallians possessed the means to detect such a faint transmission from Ghastion. That was just as well. If they heard the pleas, it would raise some awkward questions, precisely as his plan was coming to fruition.

In the silence left by turning off the speaker, the squeaking of a sandal on his control room's floor was unmistakable.

The Master turned and saw Whinn.

She had snuck back, no doubt eager to see what her friend was up to. He considered for a moment that, perhaps, he should have closed the TARDIS door.

"What did they mean?" asked Whinn.

"You should be getting back to your family," chided the Master. "They will be worried about you."

"They sounded scared, not angry."

"They are Ghasts. Who knows what emotions they have?"

"But I thought they'd be angry. I thought that was why they were attacking us. We must have enraged them, in some way. But that Ghast didn't sound angry at all."

The Master turned his back on her, concentrating on the controls. "Not angry with you, no. Not angry with Jendall."

"What... what is going on?"

He paused, for a second, thinking of her cute button eyes and the red undertones of her fur.

"You want to know what this is all about? Very well, I'll tell you. It's not as if you can do anything to stop me now. The Ghasts, as you so correctly surmised, are not warmongers at all."

"How do you know that?"

"Because I came directly from Ghastion to Jendall. I know the Ghasts well. I had their confidence too."

"What are you saying?" He could tell from her voice her heart was breaking.

"The Ghasts were not as trusting as your people, so it took longer to persuade them to mine and process the Quavek on their world. But they fell for it in the end and that's all that matters. They gave me what I wanted."

The Master could almost hear her thinking.

"I saw outside. You've turned the Quavek into metal string?"

41

"Yes," he replied. "Just as I promised I would. Just as I did on Ghastion."

"Why? Why do you need metal string on both worlds? It doesn't make any sense."

"It makes perfect sense. You're just not in possession of all the facts and so you are unable to see the meaning of it." He finished at the controls and turned to face her. "The 'metal string', as you call it, is going to be attached to the core of this world using a short range interstitial shunt and a dimensional anchor."

He waved away her incomprehension. "You are a child. Of course, you do not understand. Trust me when I say this is very easy for me to do, because I am the product of a civilisation that plays with quasars in the way you play with a spinning top."

"You're tying the string to the centre of our planet?" said Whinn slowly. "What about the string on Ghastion?"

"Ah, you are not as dull-witted as I'd thought. Yes, the unbreakable, energy storing, high capacity Quavek cable I made on Ghastion… Yes, your suspicions are accurate, I tied that to the Ghasts' world too, in much the same way. Let's see, that was about six months ago."

He saw the look in her eyes, eyes that he supposed many would regard as adorable. "Oh, was that shortly before the Ghasts attacked Jendall?" There was a soft beep from the console, confirming the cable anchoring had been completed. "Why, it's as if the two events are connected."

He strode to the far side of the console and opened the lid of a carved wooden trunk. He doubted Whinn had noticed it, surrounded as she was by the larger-on-the-inside majesty of his TT capsule. "Don't let appearances deceive you, this is no ordinary trunk. This is where I'm storing the other end of the cable anchored to Ghastion."

Dragging the thick metallic rope behind him, the Master moved purposefully to the outer doors. "Come with me. I have one final task left to perform."

"You're doing something wrong. I don't know what it is, but I know I've got to tell my father."

He pulled the tissue compression eliminator from his jacket's pocket. "I don't think so. Now, outside. You are about to witness the obliteration of your insignificant planet. It would be such a shame to miss it, on account of being dead."

***

It took only seconds to connect the trailing end of the Ghastion cable to the loose end of the Jendallian one. "Deadlock sealed," observed the Master smugly. "There's no pulling them apart. And the clock is ticking."

"Clock?"

"The Doomsday Clock, my dear, ticking away the seconds until Armageddon."

Whinn's eyes were bigger than ever. "You've got a cable running between the two planets. If the cable can't break… and if the two ends can't come free… then… that means, as the worlds move along their orbital paths, the cable will go taut. My world, Ghastion too, will be pulled out of orbit. We could fall into the Sun!"

The Master grinned satanically. "Matters are far worse than that."

Next to them, the cable sat on a massive drum, a cylinder that towered over both their heads. On it, the strands began to thrash. The noise made Whinn put her hands over her mauve skinned ears. The cable was unspooling, feeding through the open door of the Master's inconceivable vessel.

"Imagine you are viewing Ghastion from space. Imagine you can see the cable emerging from a warp portal on its surface, stretching out, out, out into the darkness between worlds. Then, imagine that cable vanishes roughly halfway to Jendall, through another warp portal. Do not concern yourself yet with the other end of that cable. Focus your thoughts instead on Ghastion. See the planet rotate on its axis. See the world pull that cable around itself in a tightening noose of indestructible wire."

He stepped closer to the girl child. "The wire cuts deeper and deeper into its mantle, scoring the surface, whipping one way and then the other as the planet turns. Imagine the scale of the devastation upon that surface. Vast volcanic eruptions, mountains sliced apart, the structures of the Ghasts torn asunder."

"You're a monster! You're supposed to be a hero, why are you doing this?"

He ignored her plaintive question. "I told the Ghasts I was coming to Jendall. That's why they attacked. They were attempting in their pitiable way to break the other end of the cable. A futile tactic, since that end was safely stowed inside my space-time machine, far beyond their reach. How desperate they were."

"They were trying to stop you, before you could complete your plan."

"And they tried reaching out to your people, to enlist your help. Begging your aid, begging you to kill me before it was too late. But the planetary upheaval was too much. They could fire a few missiles they had sat around, but that was all."

He waved the barrel of his weapon at her, taunting her. "That 'tightening noose', by the way, is now happening to Jendall too as it rotates on its axis. One

43

end of your cable is anchored to your planet's core. It emerges from a warp portal in this very chamber, just over there." He indicated the far side of the cable factory room. "And then it travels along this chamber, onto this gigantic spool, and into my TARDIS."

"Aren't you worried about your ship?"

"I'm doing this for my TARDIS," he sighed. "Your two worlds will not fall into your Sun, you may rest assured of that. There won't be time. Both worlds will rapidly wind their cables around and around their surfaces until there's no more cable left. Then, they will collide. The annihilation will be utter."

Clearly taking great delight in the horrified expression on Whinn's face, the Master allowed her a moment to protest.

"Why? Why are you doing such an unspeakable thing?" howled Whinn.

"To charge the cable with kinetic energy."

She shook her rodent-like head in dumb incomprehension.

"Unspeakable is an apt word in this context," continued the Master. "The quantities of kinetic energy that can be harvested, and then redirected, from harnessing the orbital mechanics of two planets are truly unspeakable. That is energy I need."

"Need?"

"To power my TARDIS. My ship was damaged, you see, in a recent, squalid little argument with a god who wouldn't listen. I find myself needing to, ah, revitalise my vessel."

"You're killing billions of innocents... for that?"

He was rather taken aback by her failure to see his logic, and simply shrugged. "What more reason do I need? The fulfilment of my desires is all that matters. Ghastion and Jendall were simply the nearest available worlds with supplies of Quavek and gullible populations who would mine it for me."

Sobbing uncontrollably, Whinn threw herself at the Master, punching wildly.

Not bothering to shoot, he swatted her feeble form aside and re-entered his TARDIS. He was done with Jendall.

***

The Master pocketed his weapon, smoothed a crease in his suit jacket, and flipped the dematerialisation control. The engines sounded terrible.

"Soon," he promised the Ship. "Soon, you will feel better."

He'd resisted the Jendallians' requests for him to move his ship closer to the processing plant, forcing them to transport the Quavek sheets to the palace instead, precisely because he hadn't wanted to risk many more short hops, not

44

until his ship was restored. The fools had swallowed his fabricated reasons, without once asking why he wouldn't pilot his TARDIS such a short distance.

He watched the effect of his departure on the scanner screen. It wasn't only the case that his TARDIS was moving, it was leaving the Quavek wire behind, no longer being the funnel through which the strand was held steady.

The cable in the factory chamber whipped viciously upward. Its far end, the part that led out into space, phased fully into sight. All the warp portals that had heretofore obscured its true form were removed.

Faster than the eye could track, the room was torn apart. Tons of debris collapsed in billowing clouds of dust. The Jendallian cable was becoming a planet encircling noose.

Whinn's arm was barely visible, poking out from under a mangled heap of twisted roofing beams.

The Master checked a dial and, idly, switched off the screen.

"The energy banks are charging nicely. It shouldn't be long before I have all the power I need." He thought of Flerrot and Uthwren, and how they had so willingly thrust upon him the entire control of their world.

He snorted. "As if I could ever be satisfied with dominion over one measly planet. There is an entire universe for me to dominate. Soon, I will once again bestride infinity as a Colossus. I am the Master. It is only right that the universe trembles before me."

For the briefest of moments, he thought he saw the reflection of bright, button eyes in the glass of his console's time rotor.

But then the ghostly image was gone, and he bent his mind wholly to plans of conquest.

Master Chef
Lee Rawlings

The muse. Who waits for the muse? Harrumph!

You wait for years and then five ideas hit you at once. No, no, no. If Master is stuck for an idea then Master needs to poke his brain with a red hot mind probe and winkle one out.

A flare for the dramatic has taught me one way to jog the wretched grey matter – simply trying on new outfits! One always thinks that if the suit fits then the character comes along and shakes one's hand. From there the idea forms.

Of course, occasionally one can come up with a plan that requires no dressing up at all, but where is the fun in that? Besides, one must always dress for the occasion – isn't that so, Master?

Indeed it is, Master!

Do you remember that marvellous Auton plot? What a wheeze it was with plenty of urban masquerading – a performance that would put the Great Draminski of the Rimmel Trinket Rep to shame and he had three heads and two bodies to play with! Oh, I did enjoy playing the colonel though although that was a simple suit with added and obligatory charm. But that telephone engineer just some overalls and a generic low life's face? Genius. I played that to the spot. Just missing the applause. We had such a splendid time until that repugnant cosmic squid turned up and the… Doctor spoiled the party by pointing out that it just might eat me too. I do hate it when he points out the obvious.

The Doctor.

Such a meddling fool.

Anyway, no time to reminisce, Master. Time waits for no man let alone a Time Lord. Well perhaps maybe, occasionally, now and again.

So to destroy the Doctor!

TARDIS: Play Hot Chocolate.

Outfit time!

Now where did I put that 21st century American President's skin? Ah here it is. Well it needs a bit of a nip and tuck and that hair, what a mess! Oh dear, it's falling off.

Not even authentic! I should have known, it is always the same with these wealthy narcissists.

And look at that, a monstrous tear in the inner thigh.

TARDIS! Find Sewing Machine.

TARDIS! Wait a moment!

What is that revolting smell? Oh dear, there are bits of brain still attached, how very disappointing. I suppose it must have starting going off in the living host before I got to it. Never mind. Maybe I will give the Prime Minister of Great Britain a shot one day.

TARDIS! Open rubbish compression eliminator.

Au revoir, Crump or whatever your name was.

Perhaps I could dress as a monk… no, no, no, been done! Perhaps a crazy fortune teller, an aircraft pilot, a TV evangelist show host a… oh, what is the use?

Today is simply *not* a dressing up day! Back to the drawing board!

TARDIS! I need something to help me think. Perhaps some moist Moon Monkey strips and a fine dry sherry. The one I stole from Mother Theresa.

One Week Later.

Well Master, it has been a week now and what dastardly audacious plans have you come up with to pique the interest of that sanctimonious do-gooder – the Doctor?

1. Inflating Corgi dogs and injecting them with rabies to eat Britain's royal family. Pitiful.

2. Possessing clowns in all of the Butlins holiday camps in Britain to attack beloved grannies. Dull.

3. Encouraging the hideous Cropigals to release its fungal spores and instigate racial wars. I do like that but Earth seems to be already infected. Pointless.

Maybe I will try on a few more outfits?

No.

Outfits no more.

Is this it?

Has the Master finally run out of ideas to crush his most hated rival? I really need somebody to worship me again. I miss that.

Think. I the Master will be revered and worshipped by all of the Doctor's foes, for annihilating him completely!

Oh I like that.

But how? HOW?

Ouch. I must stop thumping the control desk without my gloves on. And where is that antibacterial fluid?

TARDIS? Space wipes please.

Mmm, better.

Wait a moment. How could I possibly forget! The first time I wore gloves was after I came back from that diabolical schism field trip and fell into some wild Vortesaur dung on the way back to class. Horrified, ill, disoriented and a head full of schism, I immediately felt not only the need to cover my hands from future grime and filth around me, but also an intense desire to rid myself of the filth of the 'good', the 'happy' and the 'helpful' in the universe.

The Doctor being one.

I wrote down a plethora of ideas the morning after. Maybe my youthful exuberance produced a forgotten piece of innovative gold?

TARDIS! My academy notebook!

Yes of course! A fruitful time of wild ideas and untamed imagination, a highly creative phase where unbridled machinations were caught within the pages of a simple notebook. I was a genius even then, was I not Master? Yes you were Master.

TARDIS! Cigar. Regius Double Coronary I think. And some crackers with Slap Butter from the Mountain Goat limpets of Drogo 9.

Only the very best for Master… *The* Master.

One Hour later.

Page 24.
Assign The Doctor with a companion born to kill him, one made with part Time Lord DNA.

49

What an imagination! But no, not keen on all of that training a Time Lord assassin from birth. Oh, and babies? All of that care and attention? Not to mention the day trip to the schism to really turn it nuts. Brrr. No thank you. Mind you Master, I just might sell that idea one day. What a good thought Master.

Ah! Here we are…

Page 42.

Mmm.

Well that is complex and could take a long while to set up, but why not! I have nothing else to do and the plan is incredibly devious, outrageous and very Master. And Master will need to get outfits, plenty of outfits!

TARDIS!

Open up Journal of Plans / Book 5.

Audio connection on.

Huuurum! Hurrum! Lalalala. Brrrrrr. Redlorry Yellowlorry. Blah blah.

Jowls and voice nice and loose and…

Record!

Knowing the Doctor's weakness for fine dining and drink I think I have the perfect idea from my young mind. From my very own academy notebook a plan so cunning yet amusing I think I shall allow myself a little chuckle before I start properly… He-he-he! Ooh! Come now, TARDIS! Keep the ship steady!

Pause Recording.

My Louis Cannes mirror nearly fell out of its roundel! That is my dressing up mirror you know! I do not wish to thrust my sonic probe into your Eye of Harmony circuits again TARDIS, but I shall! Initiate the stabilisers! Oh, forget it. I'll do it.

Thank goodness for that big red button refit.

Easy as pie. Mmm pie.

No, pie can wait.

Anyway Master where was I? Ah yes.

Killing the Doctor in a dastardly fashion.

Resume Record.

From the notebook there are many small and deadly games ready to play out, I will simply tie them all together into one long game. I just need a connecting theme. Something so hidden it will be a perfectly delicious end for my most hated enemy.

Pause Recording.

50

Time for a Brandy and a think.

TARDIS! Brandy and Pie. Napoleon's own stock and one of those crispy fruit and penguin pies, immediately!

Ten Minutes Later.

It will be a slow poisoning! Over multiple planets and time zones! I shall use a deadly mercurial metal and watch the Prydonian fop slowly go mad, losing all of his precious memories, over the space of a year. I would need a vast selection of disguises so that I could get a front row view of course. He would never suspect until I reveal myself at his final phase of demising. Doctor and madness? It is almost there. The plan is missing something..

Wait a moment.

What is this scrawl in the back of the notebook?

This isn't my handwriting, what does it say?

'Unravelling Time Lord DHA with a chemical compound?' DHA? No... DNA! Unravelling Time Lord *DNA* with a chemical compound. What a magnificent thought!

Scribbled in by... the Rani! What a vicious genius she is!

But what is this next to it, alongside two badly drawn hearts?

'I love the Doctor.'

Harpy!

A Few Hours Later

TARDIS!

Journal of Plans/Book 5/entry 2.

Audio connection on.

Harrumm, Barrrum. Twenty Cats upon a Hat, twenty Catz upon a haaat. Ssss. T T T T. Meeeeeeeow!

Voice warmed up and...

Record.

So to lay the baits; I will set up scenarios and situations that the Doctor could never ignore. His pompous arrogant blood will be drawn to every perfect scenario; a war game controlled by one person, me, the Master!

51

Spanning the galactic cosmos across planets, star cruisers, space stations and Ark fleets, I will set up his slow death like a giant deadly treasure hunt. I weep at how easy this will be, yet so utterly fulfilling.

Poison the Doctor as he eats and drinks! A killer sandwich here and a murderous ginger pop there. Simple really and deliciously disturbing to watch.

Pause Recording.

TARDIS!

POISONS – TIME LORD – DNA.

Oh, and a glass of port while I wait.

What kind of glass is that, you imbecile? Looks like something you would hold a Goombur's specimen in! Wider, deeper and crystal!

That's better. Master needs to appreciate the complex array of tones before the liquid impresses a wild dance upon the taste buds of Master's tongue. You can only drink a mouthful of Pantonic fireflies from Rigel 1 with pure crystal you know; the mouth becomes a stage; balletic and gentle at first but then becoming dangerously edgy and as sharp as Puffer fish pin!

Glorious.

Look at this port Master.

Yes, I see it Master.

What an exquisite colour. Like blood. I wonder if the old Vampires take as much time admiring their choice of tipple as I do?

That scent; warm, delicate, a tease of oak and deeply sunned autumn fruits, with a hint of primitive Earth gunpowder.

Now to taste. Ah, there it is.

The surprise splash, like a wave of dark chocolate and brandy crashing against basalt rock with a light note of stazer discharge.

Bamplummian Owl Port, 200 years old.

The best in the universe. Now, where is that poison information?

TARDIS?

Am I going to have to find my Sonic Probe?

Yesss. About time!

So, Time Lord DNA unravelling poison contains… Oh, are you sure this is correct?

Bamplummian Owl glands?

I presume that the master port makers of Ergon 6 know what they are doing. Being still alive, one must assume they do. Maybe they just make the port from the beaks?

TARDIS? Did you wait to see if I would be poisoned? Mmm? Ha-ha. Very good. You have a wicked sense of humour darling!

TARDIS! Display the recipe for this despicable poisonous cocktail that will end that sanctimonious weasel, the Doctor!

Thank you. I shall read aloud.

Audio connection on.

Barrumm. Ya Ya Ya. OOOEEEIIOOUU. Mouth and throat warmed up and..

Record.

- 1mg of Bamplummian Owl gland (handle using gloves).

I shall have to use sterile plastiskin – I cannot have my black leather gloves stained with mammalian organ juices.

- A small stamen of the Gannymedian orchid – Frozen Blue.

A bit of a hunt, but perhaps the trading quadrant in Beloise Sum 3 might have a back street blagger selling a bag or two.

- 2gms of Sugar.

I presume to hide the taste of the bitterness of the orchid, which I believe tastes of old Draconian scale flakes.

- 330ml Standard Water.

Obviously.

- Edible glitter.

Now why would anyone invent that such a ridiculous garnish? I think we can leave that out, it isn't a children's party!

Although, one day... Now, come on Master! Mind on the job. You can ponder future silly trifles when your arch nemesis is destroyed.

Mind you, toxic gas balloons with smiley faces... No! Stop it. My genius mind needs to stop thinking about dastardly plans. Move on!

Now, where is that pestle and mortar?

TARDIS! Locate. Pestle and Mortar! Last used during that Daemon debacle.

TARDIS! No wait! Cancel that search.

I left it in that church which of course was demolished. I shall have to purchase another.

Right, time to set a course for Harrods, Earth.

Fantastic Kitchenware department and I do love their macaroons especially when I find a beard crumb a little later, what a treat!

Record End.

Audio off.

Audio On.

53

Um, TARDIS, delete last line. The one about the macaroons and beards.

One Week Later.

One would expect with a time machine it would be a matter of minutes to find those ingredients. That bloody owl living on a planet obliterated out of all space and time was a tricky one to find, but find it I did! Well done Master; One outward bound poaching ship caught in a little artron energy was enough to bring those pesky fowls back into existence for a crucial few minutes. Shame the energy tore the ship apart, ripping the poachers into time shreds, but it was rather an enjoyable watch. So here we are, one curious right-angled Bamplummian Owl gland ready for the pot.

TARDIS! Did you video that ship exploding for my future entertainment? Good. Log it under Poachers Perrrril!

No, just one 'R'. I was laying on the theatre to amuse myself.

One Day Later.

So TARDIS! Here is my masterpiece!

My finest concoction of pure and unadulterated evil ever! Ten drops and the Doctor's sickeningly righteous DNA will fall apart in the most ignoble way. The tenth drop will be the catalyst whilst the other nine will adhere themselves to his DNA strands like caviar to a blini.

TARDIS. Do we have caviar?

Never mind.

Now onto setting up my most audacious master plan yet.

Audio On.

Record.

Twenty Minutes Later.

And stop Record!

There you are. The best, most ingenious, diabolical, genius, brilliant, evil and rather unpleasant plan ever. Clever Master!

Ten fully detailed plots only a god of my intellect could plan. The Daleks, the Cybermen, and err, the other ones will *all* worship me. Then I shall have them *all* in my grasp and then use them to destroy everything good, everything nice, everything cute and cosy in the universe, Ha-ha-ha! I wish I could pat myself on the back. Must get a 'Pat on the Back' machine one day. Or nip back one day and do it myself.

Better check I haven't missed anything out…

Audio on.

Playback last 20 minutes.

Cough… cough… hurrumm… squeakysqueaky… yumyum… Ta Ta Ta.

Voice warmed up and…

One: *The Death of Queen Arcturus.*

An important part of the universal peace process in 3026 in the Bevadier System – a fixed point in time. I shall leave a bomb ticking in the citadel and a note from the terrorists of Gar for demands. I shall then antagonise the local turtle people to attack the villages of Gar, each wearing the Queen's banners on their shells. Colour blind, the turtles won't see them or know that I had ordered them to paint the symbols on each other's shells. Foolish amphibians will be powerless under my hypnotic influence. The following civil war will leave the Queen perilously close to being assassinated, a little persuasion and a handful of gemstones to the right nutcase and… well, let us just say that she won't be wearing any more ball gowns to impress the local princes. Haha! The Time Lords need this fixed point to have a peaceful outcome so no doubt their lapdog, the Doctor, will be asked to help smooth the antagonism out. He will arrive, sort out the mess and will be treated to a feast. This is where I come in as a Bredierium waiter and deliver a roasted Bucka, glazed and cooked to perfection. The Honey glaze will be his downfall! Ha-ha-ha-ha!

Two: *Jack the Ripper Terrorises New York City in 1978.*

An easy idea, why I never thought of it before is beyond me. So, I start by giving H.G Wells the power of time travel…

Twenty Minutes Later.

Perfect. Next stop, outfits. Off to the charity shops we go TARDIS. Charity shops, thrift shops, op shops, all perfect places to find a diverse range of cloths ranging from the horrific to classy. First stop, that one on Earth KAOH – *Kids Afraid of Horses* or something! There is also that natty little tailor in Shaftsbury Avenue, London for the more exuberant display; wide collar and white suit, Earth flares, large sunglasses and crocodile shoes– I think for the Space Yacht Mystery, plot 5.

Ten Years Later.

TARDIS! A shot of Space Whale Gin.

I deserve this. Can you believe it? Years of sweat and toil to put into practice the most devilish plan ever hatched by anyone in the universe, ever! Master you have surpassed yourself, why thank you Master you are the most handsome and clever being in the known universe...

And beyond?

Yes of course, and beyond.

Gulp!

Mmm, extinct species gins are the in thing in the Crab Nebulae you know, Master.

Indeed and now I believe it is time to work!

TARDIS set a scan for that Doctor buffoon's whereabouts and let us get these plans moving.

I wonder where the imbecile is?

Probably in his lab at UNIT or in an armchair drinking wine with those politicians he so despises. Such a hypocrite!

Not on earth? Alright TARDIS, sweep the Milky Way.

Probably with the Draconians quaffing Papple Juice and talking trivial peace making with...

What? Are you sure? Well alright then, sweep the middle of the Galaxy. Perhaps he is back home licking the Time Lords'... WHAT? I don't believe it! Well try the outer rims of the universe and all of the others galaxies. All of them!

NOW!

Don't panic, Master. The Doctor is around somewhere. Unless those blasted tin cheese graters have vaporised him! Daleks, tsk! Ridiculous blobs of rage have absolutely no sense of flair for death.

TARDIS! That cannot be right. Do an internal clean of the sensors and... oh, you have.

When was he last spotted?

Ogrons and Daleks? I knew it. A battle on the cliffs of Dover? England? Earth? 2045? What happened? Show me!

Tap the matrix... ah, here we are. So the Doctor falls into the crack of a dimension shambling monster and that's it? So he could be anywhere, in another dimension?

ANOTHER DIMENSION!

56

He will never make it back!

What a ******* waste of time!

How could you do this to me, Doctor? Of all the selfish, stupid, idiotic things to do! I have spent 10 years getting this super plan, this mega-plan together and you go and vanish from ALL of time and space?

Sob. Sob. I am not crying. Master do not cry. How dare you Master! I am NOT Crying!

TARDIS erase the last section from the Matrix uploads, otherwise those pompous fools in the citadel will live off that moment on social media for millennia at least I can erase any chance of repeats on those Matric nostalgia shows!

TARDIS! Open up the punch bag with the Doctor's face on it.

OOF! Take that. OOF! And that! OOF! You stuck up Prydonian twit! OOF! I HATE YOU! OOF! I DESPISE YOU! OOF! I WOULD TEAR YOUR BAGGY ONEROUS FACE OFF IF YOU WERE HERE! OOF! Phew.

And breathe.

Calm now.

Breathe.

TARDIS. Please land on the Ogron planet.

Breathe.

Three Minutes Later.

Scanner!

Yes. He will do.

TARDIS. Open doors.

Hello Ogron.

Bye Ogron.

Just a little push.

There we go, slight stumble and off the cliff you go.

Long way down.

Oh. I do love the scream of fear.

And wait a moment, ah, there it is.

What a mess these beasts make.

Too far to hear the back crack but the rocks are beautifully painted.

And breathe.

Better Master?

No Master.

Not really.

Still really very angry.

Maybe I should throw myself off.

Why not?

What is the point now the Doctor has gone? He was MY Nemesis. MINE!

I need to vent. I need to murder more things.

I could kill all of the Daleks and Thals with a virus?

Dull.

What about the Time Lords? I could just shoot them all up! Like a rough petty gangster, go all a bit 'common people' for a change.

No.

I would be lying to myself, where is the style in that? Mm? I would be remembered as a petty murderer as opposed to the Artist of Demise.

TARDIS! Can you hear me? I am sulking! Make me an omelette! And get out the sonic clippers – it's time for a face change.

Oh… what's the point?

I needed to imbibe the Doctor's death this time, I deserve that smugisfaction! I feel denied a moment of perfection and for it to be rudely taken away from me like a rattle from a baby, a gazelle from a tiger, flesh from a disease, makes me feel less of a genius mastermind than usual and more an amateur , a rookie. A schoolchild!

For I am the MASTER. ME! THE MASTER! How dare you TIME!

How dare you snatch away what would have been my greatest ever victory. I bet it was those interfering bags of bones, the Time Lords. I HATE YOU! Do you hear me? You wrinkly pack of old d…

Wait. What is that? I swear that is the sound of, no, yes… noooo… yes it is! But how! Never mind!

TARDIS! Remove us from this place immediately!

And hold that Omelette!

The Doctor is BACK! Hahahahaha!

Ten Deadly Plots Later.

Damn and blast! How does he do it! He has escaped my clasp yet again. A perfect plan 10 years in the making! Damn you Doctor I will erase you from the Universe if it is the last thing I dooooo!

And…

Audio off.

TARDIS! Cigar and armchair.

The smooth creamy Manapa made from the finest coffee fur beetles. Mmm.

It's funny how these things turn out. In my dark mood I randomly push an Ogron off a random cliff unaware that that particular Ogron who is falling to his demise happens to be a Time Lord experiment full of chrono-viruses. The dashing of his brains upon the rocks releases said viruses which triggers a random time portal releasing the very same dimensional shambling monster that swallowed the Doctor's TARDIS out of all existence in the first place!

I do love the way the cosmos throws these – how do those vulgar Earth people say it – curve balls, that's it, into my time streams.

Welcome home, Doctor. Sob.

Oh how very annoying, crying with happiness.

TARDIS. Why is the recorder still on? Useless machine! Erase all moments of weakness from those last lines. Insert maniacal laughter and close recording!

Right, time to think about the Master's next deadly plan. I am already utterly bored.

How about this Master? Frame the Doctor for a crime he didn't commit. Hackneyed.

On… Gallifrey! Genius!

Phwahahaha. And breathe.

TARDIS! Time for dessert. Jellied Ogron brain mousse I think. Very fitting.

A dangerous meal but I am feeling like a gamble! Eaten in the wrong way the acidic content could melt my entire body away! Then no outfits would ever suit me! Hideous!

TARDIS!

Spoon!

Conversion Therapy
Paul Driscoll

Storm was the last of her kind. At least she was so in the minds of the Coopers who loved her unconditionally. If truth be told, up and down the country there were hundreds of other Storms. Every single owner assumed that their dog was the sole survivor of the Canine Cull Act of 2459.

The carriers of a plague of devastating proportions, all dogs on Ravella, the Earth's flagship colony world, had been given a death sentence. The official line, backed up by shedloads of incontestable evidence, was that without such drastic measures the human population would face extinction by the turn of the century.

By way of compensation for their loss, registered dog owner were offered a robodog for rent. Originally designed as security bots to patrol shopping precincts, businesses and government buildings, they were initially a source of much anxiety, particularly with the young. On paper, they made unlikely substitutes for family pets, but after a few design tweaks to enhance their appeal to children, the take-up rate hit the roof.

Charlie Cooper, a first class roboteer who specialised in making artificial limbs and organs, had been keen to comply with the 2459 directive, but his heart broke when his only child, Jenna, begged him not to take Storm away. At first he allowed the family pet a temporary reprieve, confining Storm to the cellar and muzzling her. The next day, he'd come home from work with a robodog in the hope that Jenna would form a new bond. The plan failed spectacularly.

Even when Storm became terribly sick three months later, it was clear that no matter how cute the robot, it would be no substitute.

"But she's sick Jen. What if she's contracted the plague?"

"Dad, she's got flu. That's all."

"Even so, it would a mercy to end her life. It's not like we can take her to a vets for treatment."

"Then treat her here, Dad."

"And how exactly do I do that?"

"Invent a cure. You have to make her better again."

It was a challenge that Charlie found impossible to resist. One night, he took the chocolate Labrador to his private laboratory – the glorified shed, as Mrs

Cooper called it. He made a promise that the next time Jenna saw Storm, the dog would be as good as new.

∗∗∗

Throughout her period of confinement, Storm would sleep during the evenings; not that she had a choice. During the nights or whenever Charlie was out at work, she would need to be on high alert in case the daily trespasser finally decided to attack. Tonight was no different. She woke up at nightfall to find the masked intruder again, messing about with Charlie's equipment and talking to Storm as if they were best buddies.

"Nine weeks, it's taken the fool nine weeks to finally realise that you're ready to be released. I adjusted the formulas, upgraded all the necessary components on day one. I should have factored in the human race's propensity to be side-tracked by inconsequential details. There are bound to be inefficiencies in a species that keeps lesser lifeforms as pets."

The intruder was about to leave again, when he turned to face Storm.

"I suppose it's about time I introduced myself. I mean you ought to at least know the name of your new owner."

Slowly the intruder removed his cowl, revealing the face of a thousand nightmares. As Storm tried to bark, the monstrous creature laughed manically.

"Hush, hush my dear and still your silent fear. I am usually referred to as the Master. And you will obey me. Hush, hush, hush…"

∗∗∗

The next day, Charlie was ready for the grand reveal of the new and improved Storm. He called Mrs Cooper and Jenna to join him on the veranda overlooking his shed. Mrs Cooper chose instead to watch through the kitchen window, preparing herself to pick up the pieces as ever. There was no way she was going to show consent by standing with her husband. She'd been arguing with him all night about the stupidity of his actions, but he'd stubbornly insisted that Jenna would come round to the idea, adding that he had a surprise up his sleeve that would change her mind.

"Are you ready Jen," said Charlie, holding Jenna's hand. "It's time to call Storm, go on…"

Jenna shrugged.

"Here girl… here girl," she said, doubtful of getting any response.

62

With a twinkle in his eye, Charlie fumbled in his coat pocket to press the remote control for the shed doors.

He needn't have bothered. Without warning, the doors exploded. From out of the smoke, a robodog leapt out, petting Jenna and knocking her off her feet.

"That wasn't supposed to happen," said Charlie, sheepishly, as the automated sprinkler system kicked into gear.

A concerned Mrs Cooper rushed out of the house, castigating Charlie.

"It's ok," he replied. "It's ok. Look…"

After the initial excitement, the robodog had rolled onto its belly, yelping expectantly.

"I want Storm. Where's Storm," said Jenna, rushing towards the shed.

"Wait," said Charlie sternly. "It's her, Jen. This is Storm."

"Jenna," said her Mother. "Try the Storm Dance. See if she responds to your moves."

"Storm dance?" said Charlie.

It was a routine Jenna and her mum had spent ages mastering. It was possible that Dad had programed a robot to share Storm's skills and characteristics, but as far as Jenna knew, Dad had never seen them do the dance before – he'd always been too preoccupied with work to notice.

To her astonishment, the robodog performed the dance to perfection.

"Don't you see what this means?" said Charlie, excitedly. "You don't have to hide her anymore. Nobody will be any the wiser. You can even take her on walks."

"Is she in pain?" asked Jenna.

"Does it look like it to you? She's fine inside herself."

"It's not the same, Dad. I mean how can we snuggle up together?"

Charlie bent down and smiled.

"Storm's next trick stays strictly inside the house. Understood? Come on girl…"

Inside the kitchen, Charlie pressed a combination of buttons on Storm's silver back. To Jenna's relief and delight the metal armour and helmet split apart revealing the familiar face of her best friend.

"The metal shell cannot be completely detached, not without killing her – so never try to do this manually, understand?" cautioned Charlie.

Even Mrs Cooper was beginning to warm to the idea now.

"If it goes wrong, can you reverse the process?" she asked.

"Erm, yea – with a bit of care," lied Charlie.

"Okay," she said. "It's just a trial – we're clear on that yes? If it doesn't work for Storm or Jenna then you make her normal again, do you understand?"

63

Despite a thorough and invasive examination, Charlie was unable to detect a fault in either Storm's cybersuit or the internal components that had been connected to her neural pathways. So when several weeks passed with no repeat of Storm's explosive entrance, he put it down to a start-up glitch in the software. The lack of damage to the unit itself was reassuring.

Jenna soon learnt to see the same old loveable dog behind the cyber-shell. As each day passed, the need to open her up decreased. But Storm didn't quite go back to being her old self. She refused to sleep in the new-fangled robodog kennel next to the porch. She even rejected her old home – the wooden doghouse in the cellar that had been kitted out with her favourite cushion and toys. Instead, every night Storm would wait outside Mr Cooper's shed and howl. In the end, the family had to move Storm's bedding into the lab and abandon their attempts to get her to sleep inside the house. Reluctantly, Charlie installed a dog flap and left her to it with a stern "now don't you go exploding on us again. There's some pretty valuable stuff in here."

***

It was the middle of the night and Jenna had snuck out of the house to spend the rest of it with Storm. She'd told herself that somebody had better check up on her to make sure all was okay, but in reality, without her best friend for company, she'd not been sleeping at all well. She had moved her bedroom into the cellar the day they first took Storm into hiding, fearful that someone would come and take her away like a thief in the night – perhaps even her Dad who had been worried sick about defying the authorities and being found out. It seemed to bother him much more than the possibility that Storm might have been carrying the plague.

It was a squeeze getting through the dog flap, but that was about to become the least of Jenna's troubles. She'd come armed with treats in case Storm was awake and made an excited commotion, but once inside the lab, she immediately dropped them all. The last thing Jenna had expected was to be greeted with a threatening snarl, as if she was a total stranger.

"Hey girl. It's me, what's up, eh?"

Storm growled and dug her metal paws into the carpet, ready to pounce.

"I've brought your favourite treat, it's…"

The robotised dog charged at Jenna and forced her back towards the dog flap. With Jenna now pinned against the wall, Storm pressed against her stomach, causing her to bend double.

"Alright, I'll go. I'll go…" Jenna screamed, pushing the dog flap open with her backside. "Stop it, you're hurting me."

"You heard the girl. Back off."

The Master, who had been hidden in the shadows the whole time, was always going to prevent the dog from seriously injuring the girl. But it had been such fun watching her suffer, he'd left it until the last minute to intervene.

Jenna collapsed, winded and confused, as Storm let go and turned to face her father's desk at the far end of the lab. To Jenna's astonishment, a hooded figure was sitting there, dressed in black rags. The stranger was holding up some kind of ornate staff, wagging it at Storm.

"She doesn't understand. She feels no pain," said the Master, enviously.

"Who the hell are you, and what are you doing sat at my father's desk?"

"She would tell you that herself, but thankfully your father has too much self-respect than to debase himself with a talking robot dog."

Storm was confused, feeling a divided loyalty that was hard for her augmented brain to process. A tear trickled from her eye socket, dripping onto her metal snout.

"It's okay my dear," the Master said. "Your master forgives you."

Storm walked over to the desk, her head bowed in submission.

"No, not me you foolish cybermutt. Your master knows you were only trying to protect her, isn't that right Miss Cooper?"

It suddenly struck Jenna that she had no reason to be afraid. This crazy individual was clearly not a professional burglar, and that really only left one suspect.

"Judging from the clearly put-on voice, you're obviously someone I know. And I can only think of one person who'd be trying to steal my Dad's secrets."

"Girl. Let me assure you, nobody ever recognises this face. Follow up visits just aren't my thing."

"Oh give over, Harold, you can drop the silly voice now. The game's up. This ridiculous competition between my father's company and yours has gone way too far."

"But then again. Once seen. Never forgotten," continued the Master, ignoring Jenna's guesswork.

The Master hammered his staff onto the carpeted floor four times, laughing manically as the furniture shook with the resultant vibrations. Such was the force of it that Jenna was knocked off her feet. When she looked up, her

65

Father's filing cabinet, a permanent fixture behind his desk, began to open inwards. "But that's not possible," Jenna muttered to herself. The trio of drawers weren't fake the last time she'd rooted through them.

Storm howled and jumped repeatedly on the spot as if her circuits had developed a fault, but Jenna could barely hear her dog's distressed cries over the disturbing sounds that were now emanating from the cabinet. Jenna held her ears in a vain attempt to block out the synthetic and primal racket. She wondered if a small animal was being tortured inside the cabinet, but in reality she was the one in pain.

The Master turned his back on Jenna to face the cabinet.

"Let there be light," he pronounced, stretching out his staff.

Immediately, several rays of brilliant white light emitted from the cabinet, bathing the entire lab in its revealing glow.

The tortuous experience had now become a full-on sensual assault; the chords of pain, the intense lights, Storm's distressing behaviour, and the huge shadow of the Master that danced around the room as if it had a life of its own, were all conspiring to reduce Jenna to a nervous wreck. She huddled herself into a ball in the corner of the room, unable to move, despite the way out being right beside her.

By contrast, the Master was invigorated as if he was drawing life from the cabinet. The once hunched figure was now stood bolt upright and looked twice as tall as a result. Jenna wasn't sure if it was her fear or imagination getting the better of her, but she could have sworn he was now hovering several inches off the ground.

Head down, he glided towards her.

Storm tried to come to Jenna's aid, but still all she could do was jump on the spot.

"And there was light," pronounced the Master, his voice echoing both around the room and inside Jenna's mind

Theatrically, he took off his hood and raised his head.

"Take a good look, girl. Behold. The face of evil."

***

Hideously deformed after the events on Tersurus, the Master had been battling through the most intense physical pain in a desperate effort to hold back death. He should have been kinder on himself and allowed the ravages of time to take hold, but instead he fought against it with every fibre of his twisted being, spurred on by the arrogant notion that he could find a cure. His best option was to return to his people and plead for a new cycle of regenerations, but he considered the required act of contrition a step too far. The alternative – offering up a gift in exchange for his salvation was equally humiliating. The Time Lords deserved nothing.

The Master would never have survived this long had he not accidentally found a way of using the heart of the TARDIS to top up his life force. Rather foolishly, he had been trying to replace a faulty TARDIS fuel link, despite his befuddled memories, when he made the providential discovery that intense exposure to the time vortex could jump-start his dormant regenerative cells.

As a side-effect, the Master's mind and body would briefly revert back to his old self, just long enough for him to become aware of the person he had lost, both physically and emotionally. He found he could only look into the vortex for a few seconds, but those fleeting moments were lifesaving. They rejuvenated his mind and spirit and gave him access to memories that might be critical for his survival.

Each time the heart of the TARDIS closed again, the Master's body would morph back from his last regeneration (the debonair one with the beard, as he liked to call it),   into the decayed and ghoulish figure that had escaped from Tersurus. At first, such experiences gave him hope that the process could be permanently reversed, but he soon realised that whenever he tried to heal himself, the damage became all the more severe. He was, in effect, having to repeatedly recreate the trauma and the pain of degeneration in order to stay alive.

He was already well past the limits of his pain threshold when he had reached breaking point. Something more drastic was required, a plan of such effrontery that it might change him forever. Pain had always defined him, and now that he was, in one sense, more masterful than ever, he feared that the removal of suffering would render his continued existence pointless. The challenge was to come up with a way of inoculating himself that would allow him to still be a monster.

The irony wasn't lost on the Master that of all the species he had met in his wanderings across the universe, it would be his old friend's precious human pets who would offer him the best source of salvation. He would never understand why the Doctor spent such a disproportionate amount of time protecting and rescuing the Earthlings and their colonies, but now that they were going to be the key to preserving his life, at least all the Doctor's interventions finally seemed worthwhile. When all this was over, he simply had to find the Doctor to tell him the good news.

He could have done with the Doctor right now, he thought. The Doctor knew how to manipulate people into travelling with him in the TARDIS. Looking at Jenna's face, he had a feeling he was going about it in completely the wrong way.

***

"I used to be quite the charmer," said the Master, stroking his beard.

"If you say so," said Jenna.

The Master knocked four times again with his staff. The doors of the filing cabinet slammed shut, in response. "All people see these days is the face of evil."

He flinched in pain. His facial features grew all the more hideous as he fell to the floor in agony.

"Try and remember the first face you saw, not the beast I have been reduced to," he said, through gritted teeth. "I am sorry if my words frightened you. I like to save time."

"What are you?" said Jenna. "A phantom? A science experiment gone wrong?"

Jenna wanted to run and tell her Father, but Storm, now free of whatever had been preventing her from moving, was crouched over the sick man. Tentatively, Jenna joined them, hoping she could still trust her dog's instincts.

"I am what you will become. I've travelled back in time to warn your Father," said the Master.

"Time travel? Well, I've heard it all now. You're sick. Not thinking straight. Maybe my Dad can help you. He's a scientist you know. Specialises in cyber-eugenics."

"I'm banking on it. Your Father made me what I am. If he can't heal me of this curse then nobody can."

Suddenly Storm barked excitedly and ran through the dog flap.

"Now's your chance to find out. That'll be him now," said Jenna.

Typical humans, thought the Master. They never get their timing right, always either hopelessly late or spectacularly early. He wasn't quite sure if Storm's nightly training exercises had been sufficient, but with Cooper at the door, and having already been busted by his daughter, the Master had little choice but to bring forward phase two of the plan.

***

"Show your face, whoever you are," shouted Charlie, approaching the shed cautiously. "And don't try anything silly, now. I'm not afraid to shoot."

Storm bounded towards him, knocking the rifle out of his hand and pinning him down onto the muddy pathway.

"Ouch, you're stronger than you look girl. I knew I should have used a lighter alloy. Not what's all this commotion about Storm, eh?" said Charlie. He opened Storm's suit to comfort her. "Come on, we'd better sort it out before you wake…"

"Dad," said Jenna sheepishly, as she climbed out of the dog flap.

"Jenna? What are you doing here?"

"Dad, we have a visitor."

"I knew it, get back in the house," shouted Charlie, priming the weapon.

"No, no it's not like that. He's in a bad way and he's come to you for help."

"Be that as it may, we can't be too careful. Now, get back to bed and let me deal with this."

But Jenna was having none of it. Defiantly, she crawled back inside the shed.

Charlie shook his head at Storm as he resealed her casing. "Sometimes I wonder if I should have made control suits for the kids too, just so that I could override them when they go rogue. We better go see what she's been up too. One of those stray dogs, I shouldn't wonder."

***

When Jenna returned to the lab, she found the Master lying prostrate beside her Father's desk. He was struggling to breath and mumbling incoherently. The rasping, seedy tone of his voice was unchanged, but with the poor man in such a vulnerable and weak state she no longer interpreted it as sinister and threatening. She wondered if he was as damaged on the inside as he was on the outside. Perhaps his vocal chords had been burnt just like his skin.

Jenna was trying to comfort the Master when her Father opened the shed door and joined them with Storm. His first concern was for the integrity of his equipment.

"What are you playing at – bringing strangers to our door at this time of the night? A stray dog is one thing, but a man? And smuggling him inside my lab, of all places."

"This has nothing to do with me, I only came to see Storm. How was I supposed to know a man would be hiding inside? Dad, forget your bloody equipment for now, I think he's dying."

69

"Good. Saves me a job. How dare he break in here and use my lab as a doss house."

"You don't mean that, Dad. He said he'd come here to find you. Something about you making him the way he is and having the power to fix him. Do you know him?"

Charlie took a closer look at the stranger and instantly recoiled.

"Maybe – before whatever horrific accident befell him, it's impossible to tell without a name. But come on, Jenna. I know you like to give people the benefit of the doubt, but there are limits. I've no idea what's happened to him, but, if you ask me, the only cure is a merciful death."

"One thing he said keeps going round in my head – 'you made him?' He looks like the victim of a terrible chemical accident or an experiment gone wrong. Knowing your work, it could be either."

Suddenly, the Master sat bolt upright, his distended pupils swirling around independently of each other.

"Cyberman," he said. "I am... or rather, I was, a Cyberman. An early prototype, one of the first of our kind."

"I don't have a clue what you are talking about," said Charlie.

"It all started with a family dog. But in days to come, you will use the same technology to create human Cybers. Protecting us from the pain of disease. Keeping us alive artificially. At first you will be hailed as a hero – the saviour of the human race. And then they will rise against you."

"The man is clearly delirious. We need to call for a doctor," said Charlie quickly, looking extremely uncomfortable.

Her father's change of attitude surprised Jenna.

"You've changed your tune, Dad. You saved Storm, brought her back from the brink of death, can't you help him too?"

"A dog doesn't need a doctor," said the Master, not bothering to hide his contempt for the word. "She needs a master to follow. Trust me, if you don't listen to what I'm saying, your precious dog will become like me. Indeed, the process has already started."

The Master opened Storm and pulled back her fur. To Jenna's horror, the skin underneath was full of blisters.

Charlie bit his lip, signalling to Jenna that he wasn't as surprised by the stranger's revelations as he'd been making out.

"Dad, tell me he's wrong..."

"He knows, my dear. He knows..." said the Master. "Your dog is part of a bigger experiment your Father has been working on for years. It will be a great success. But it will turn into a disaster. The flesh will begin to reject the metallic

70

augmentations, an allergic reaction heightened by the fact that those you tried to save were carrying the plague. We feel no physical pain, but we know what's happening, and we are angry. We are angry because of your shoddy workmanship. This is no life. People rebelled, removed the armour and discovered the horror of what we had become."

"We've run thousands of tests, developed a fool-proof suit," protested Charlie. "It cannot happen like that. I don't believe you. In any case, it was only meant to be used on humans in a dire emergency, as a last resort. It was more a theory than a plan."

"A theory that you made a reality the minute you decided to save your family pet. If you want proof, then let me take you to see your future. Better still, help me to perfect the technology. Together, we can ensure that this offshoot of Earth-types doesn't follow the way of every other Cyber-race."

***

The Master took Charlie Cooper and his daughter on an extraordinary whistle-stop tour of their future in his remarkable flying filing cabinet. They charted the history of cyber-conversion, beginning with the founding years on Ravella. Dressed in dummy cyber-suits, they stood with the cyber-crowds outside the Capitol to watch the ceremony to honour Cooper's scientific achievements. The Master told them that these Cybermen, like Storm, could open their suits at any time and could feel every single emotion except pain. But their overriding mood was one of relief – relief that they had been granted a way of surviving post-plague. Despite the successes of the first upgrade programme, there was still sadness, regret and smatterings of protest. There weren't enough suits to go around, which was more than offset by the fact that few could afford them anyway. The majority of the population would spend the rest of their lives in containment.

"Aren't we creating some kind of temporal paradox by being here?" said Charlie.

"Relax. The universe is easily fooled," replied the Master.

As they walked back to the TARDIS, Jenna was distracted by some movement in an adjoining passageway. Fairly certain that she had seen an unconverted young girl rifling through the bins, she went off to investigate.

She followed the child down the passageway. It was a dead end. The child turned and smiled before shooting Jenna in the chest with a tiny handgun, sending shockwaves through the suit. A group of other kids came out of hiding and they dragged Jenna's lifeless body onto the steps of an old warehouse.

71

"More spare parts for you, Drex," said the girl, through the intercom system.

Alerted by Storm, Cooper and the Master arrived just as Drex was about to collect the goods.

"Wait!" shouted Charlie. "That's my daughter."

"What are you going to do about it, rich man? Shoot me with your headlamp?" laughed Drex.

"No need," said the Master. "Show him, Cooper... your face, man – show him your face."

Reluctantly, Charlie removed his helmet.

"You see," said the Master. "We are just like you – here to get the merchandise. I hope for your sake the girl is unharmed."

Charlie removed Jenna's helmet.

"She's still breathing," he said in relief.

"Of course she is – our weapons are designed to damage software and programming. Sorry to have inconvenienced you," replied Drex, glaring at the girl who was still clearly expecting payment.

***

"How come that Drex fella didn't recognise me? I thought I was a national hero," said Charlie, back inside the Master's TARDIS.

"You've been a Cyberman for months. Faces have become privatised, forgotten by all but immediate family and friends."

They stopped off again on Ravella, six months further into its future. The colony world had been turned into a warzone. The Cybermen, now aware of their horrendous physical damage, were revolting. These Cybermen had been fitted with weaponised upgrades to stamp out the last of the unconverted: weapons that they had now turned upon themselves.

The Master showed the Coopers a de-conversion centre where individuals were being freed of their suits.

"It's horrible," said Jenna.

"Yep – but it's weird how none of them are as badly disfigured as you," said Charlie, suspiciously.

"I could have shown you worse cases," replied the Master. "Do you want to see what happens to you next? I've been saving the best until last."

"Well, I..." began Charlie.

There was no point continuing, The TARDIS had already arrived at the next destination, taking the choice out of his hand.

"Isn't this..." said Jenna, looking at the scanner.

"Where I work," confirmed Charlie.

This time, instead of leaving the TARDIS, they watched the unfolding events remotely.

The Cyber-Cooper was arguing with his bosses.

"I am sorry, but I cannot countenance such a step. It would remove what it means to be human."

"Sealing the suits permanently and enhancing the pain suppressor to cover all emotions is necessary. Otherwise we will destroy ourselves."

"Well, I'm done here. We will lose our individuality, our identity and the capacity to love and be loved. You might as way make us all sound the same while you're at it."

Charlie looked on proudly as his future-self stormed out of the room.

"What do you think you do next Mr Cooper?" said the Master.

"I'll probably campaign have the lot of them decommissioned."

"You don't succeed. In a thousand years from now, the Cybermen will be one of the most feared races in the universe. Their technology will be second to none, but they will lack any trace of residual humanity. All emotions will be gone, and so too most of the flesh. There is little left of the human body inside them. Certainly nothing that can be recovered. A terrible irony. If only your emotional tin men had been given the perfect armour in the first place. We would never have suffered such degenerative effects."

"Can we go home now? I don't want to see anymore," said Jenna.

"Why are you doing this? Are you trying to punish me?" said Charlie.

"On the contrary. The Cybermen of the future have the technology that I need to survive. But I don't want to become like them. That's where you come in, Mr Cooper. I want to give you your job back – only one thousand years into the future. I can offer you the chance to work with their scientists in creating a new race of Cybermen – the kind you first imagined them to be."

"Dad, please no…"

"Little girl, do you really want to let your Father live with the knowledge that he is responsible for the extinction of your species? Besides, this could be the only way of saving your precious dog. A whole new, non-allergenic suit awaits."

***

One thousand years later, whole civilisations had been upgraded by the relentless Empire building of the Ravellan Cybermen. At first they targeted the scattered Earth colonies. Not satisfied with such progress, they extended the program to incorporate compatible humanoid lifeforms. Finally, they opened it

73

up to all manageable species' – which basically amounted to any non-telepathic race that was robust enough to survive the process.

Every single species they encountered was pre-classified according to a chilling imperative. The lucky few would be marked for deletion. The rest would be involuntarily assimilated.

The Cyberleader was barking his next order to the 939 missionary fleet. Some six hundred Cyberships had been orbiting around their latest acquisition, the fertile and lush Elemerian Meadowsphere, awaiting further instructions.

"Cybernation of the Elemer system at 99.99%. The Forest World has been acquired. All units retreat and move on. Retreat and move on."

***

The largest ship in the fleet, home to the mission controller, his Cyber-generals and chief scientists, was the first to pick up the order. The senior officers had been gathered in the control room, in readiness to coordinate the new mission imperative.

The Controller addressed them.

"Marching orders 439. Do we have agreement?"

"Agreement sealed," said the others in unison.

The distinctive transparent dome of the controller's helmet began to flash wildly.

Every single Cyberman in the fleet froze as the information was downloaded and interpreted according to their position and status.

"Marching orders delivered," the Controller grated. "Cyberfleet relocating to the Fifth Moon of Wasaria. All units have been notified: the primitive chainmasters, the Wasarians, will be welcomed onto the upgrade program. Failure rate is predicted at less than 1%."

***

"We've landed already? What happened to the wheezing and groaning sound?" said Jenna, apprehensive about coming face to face with the latest model of Cybermen.

"Do you really think that a ship that is able to morph its shape to fit the surroundings would be designed to announce its arrival?" sneered the Master. "That's not how it works. The noise you speak of is merely for effect. It reminds me of an old deluded friend of mine. Those who know the sound, speak of the hope it offers. I like to confound their expectations, unless stealth is required."

"You still haven't explained how you came by this craft, or how you became such an expert at flying it," said Charlie suspiciously.

"It may surprise you to know that you weren't the only Ravellan working on secret scientific projects. All will become clear when you have found a way to remove my pain."

The Master pulled the door lever.

Jenna held her hands over her ears and winced as the door creaked opened.

"Shouldn't that have been silent too?" she said.

"No matter how hard I try, I never can get him out of my mind," muttered the Master, absently. "Come on, Cybermutt! It's time to test out your latest upgrades."

To Jenna and her Father's horror, Storm walked out ahead of them, straight into the heart of Cyber command.

"Latest upgrades?" said Charlie, nervously.

***

The Cyber Controller took a while to process the fact that the door the intruders had just walked through hadn't been there before. The technology behind the trick intrigued him enough to not kill them on the spot.

"Lower your weapons," he ordered his officers.

The Master bowed in deference.

"Controller… High command…"

Charlie and Jenna held each other's hand, fearful that their deranged guide had been in league with these Cybermen all along.

"What magic is this?" barked the controller.

"Ahh, the disguise. You like it? I must confess I never knew she could do doors."

"Explain or you will be deleted."

Storm jumped forward, poised to attack, but this time the effect was far from menacing. She landed, unceremoniously, with her legs split apart on the slippery metallic floor. The Cyber-controller picked her up by the neck and launched her across the room.

"Storm!" shouted Jenna.

"Cybertechnology of the most primitive kind. You have defiled this ship and all who travel in it. You will be deleted," said the Controller.

"Wait. We have come to volunteer for an upgrade," said the Master. "And in exchange I offer you my TARDIS."

The Cybermen, as one, immediately aimed their weapons at the Master.

75

The controller's helmet flashed wildly and, within seconds, the Cybermen were immediately joined by the rest of the ship's Cyber-crew.

"One of you is the Doctor? Explain," demanded the Controller.

"Oh, wouldn't he just love the assumption. As if he's the only Time Lord who matters. I haven't brought the Doctor – not this time," replied the Master. "I've done better than that. Check your records – the human stood beside me is your creator."

"You lie. We walk in eternity. We have no beginning. No end."

"That dog you threw away like a piece of trash? She was the first of your kind."

The Master banged his staff onto the ground, repeating the same four beat pattern Jenna had seen him use in her Father's shed. The TARDIS, disguised as a door, opened. The Cybermen did not hesitate to shoot at it on mass.

"Get down," shouted the Master.

Charlie and Jenna ducked as Storm, suddenly revitalised, started shooting laser bolts out of her eyes, catching the Cyberfleet completely unawares.

One by one they were dispatched, starting with the Controller, leaving only the chief scientist alive.

Storm began to shake violently. They all ducked as, like a deflated balloon, she careered this way and that across the room. Finally, she hit the back wall and exploded.

"No!" screamed Jenna, running over to the smouldering remains. "What have you done?"

Charlie glared at the Master before joining Jenna to comfort her.

The Master walked up to the scientist who, having been disconnected from the controller, and by extension, the entire Cyber-race, was flailing wildly.

"I am the Master and you will obey me."

"I am awaiting new orders," said the scientist, much calmer now.

"Excellent. Join my friend here and make me whole again. With your technology and his expertise, I will be converted. Free me of my pain, but increase my hatred."

"I am awaiting new orders," repeated the scientist, walking disorientated into the conference table. He looked around for the Master, as if he could see multiple copies of the Time Lord.

"What is going on, here?" said Charlie.

"The hypnosis isn't powerful enough. It has affected the creature's vision but no more. I must boost the signal."

The Master stepped into the TARDIS.

"Wait – you can't leave us here," said Charlie, as the door dematerialised.

"I am awaiting new orders," repeated the scientist.

Charlie stood up to face him. The bravado really didn't suit him, thought Jenna.

"Well if that's the case, and if this Master fella is right and I am the reason you exist, then how about you obey me instead? Order the destruction of every Cyberman."

As the Cyberman attempted to process the command, the TARDIS rematerialised, this time in the form of an anachronistic Grandfather clock.

The Master stepped out and attempted to hypnotise the Cyberman again, this time with the added support of countless swinging pendulums in the scientist's broken field of vision.

"You will end my pain. You will upgrade me. This order cannot be countermanded," said the Master.

"We will end your pain. We will upgrade you," the Cyberman replied.

"Mr Cooper, show him how to make a new race of Cybermen. One that feels everything but suffering. Starting with me. Do that, and I will see to it that you and your daughter are returned home."

"But what's to say it won't go wrong again?" said Charlie, burdened by the guilt of what he had created. "Order their destruction, instead. This is abhorrent."

"Success rate 74%. Variables can be resolved by using a test subject first," grated the Cyberman.

The Master looked at Jenna and allowed himself a painful smile as cracks formed across his stretched cheeks.

Charlie shook his head. "No, no, no… I would never…"

"But she could live forever," said the Master.

"Who wants to live forever?" said Jenna. "It's unnatural."

"And what you are now, isn't?"

"And what's that exactly?"

"You don't already know? Perhaps a demonstration is in order."

Typical humans, thought the Master, their propensity for denying their mortality always staggered him. He took out his Tissue Compression Eliminator and, reluctantly, reprogrammed it. "Sorry to do this to you, dear," he muttered, addressing the TCE rather than Jenna. He'd love to be able to miniaturise another human or two, but, for once, he had to show restraint.

The Master pointed the weapon at Jenna, and with a cackling, psychotic laugh, he fired.

Jenna turned a shade green and collapsed, unconscious.

"What have you done to her?" cried Charlie, running to his daughter's side. "What was that thing?"

Jenna's face was filling with blisters, and large clumps of hair were falling from her reddened scalp.

"You really don't want to know. Don't worry, Sadly, I've had to repurpose the weapon. She's not dead, I've just used it to speed up the process."

"Process, what process?"

"The plague. You are honestly telling me you didn't know, either? Your daughter is infected, and it's all down to you. I can reverse the condition back to its current state, but even then, I give her nine months at the most. It was a fundamental flaw in your original design, Cooper. You should have made your dog untouchable."

***

Heavy hearted, but driven by his desire to save Jenna, Charlie had agreed to carry out the operation – on one condition. They would install all the relevant upgrades back in his own time and place. His shed was fully kitted out with the advance cyber technology of the future, and together with his cyber colleague they created the perfect shell for Jenna. The Cyberman shared secrets that would enable Charlie to overcome the deficiencies that caused the breakdown in the original batch.

But the process was now irreversible. After he had sealed Jenna inside the cyber-suit, Charlie knew he would never see her face again.

"You will always be my beautiful little girl. Nothing could ever change that fact," he said, fighting back the tears. He kissed her forehead and turned away as the Cyberman completed the upgrade.

"Wake her. Wake her now," said the Master, impatiently.

Slowly, with a single-note scream, the likes of which even the Master had never heard before, the new-born Cyberman came to life. He liked that noise, it was his version of the sound of hope.

The Cyber-Jenna convulsed.

She was alive again. Alive like never before.

Jenna walked, stiltedly, towards Charlie.

"D… D… Dad?"

"Congratulations," said the Master. "The prototype is a success. The first of a new race of Cybermen."

"I'm carrying the plague too. Let me be the first to join my daughter," said Charlie.

"You will be third in line," said the Cyber-scientist. He grabbed the Master and carried him over his shoulder into the conversion chamber.

"Oh, I don't think this will be necessary, do you?" protested the Master.

"Isn't this what you wanted in the first place?" said Charlie.

The Cyber-scientist carried on regardless, strapping the Master's waist into the chamber.

"This order cannot be countermanded. You will be upgraded."

"Oh, I don't think so," the Master sneered. Before his hands could be tied, he snapped in half one of several wires hanging over his head. He held each end against his temples, forcing the electrical current to run through his degenerate body. He rolled his hands together and grinned at the Cyberman. A charge shot out from his now open hands like a bolt of lightning, striking the Cyberman's chest unit.

The Cyberman stumbled as his mind was scrambled.

Within seconds it was clear.

"I am awaiting new orders," grated the Cyberman.

"Oh if you insist, now kindly release me."

Silently, the Cyberman obliged.

"One last order before I depart. Kill him. Kill him now," demanded the Master, pointing at Charlie.

Before Jenna could defend her Father, the Master struck her with another charge from his electrified hands, completely immobilising her.

"Delete," said the scientist.

The Master watched Charlie's death with delight. There had been little reason to smile in this cursed body, but at least the abnormal regeneration was ending on a high.

"What a perfect Cyberman you are. You have let go of your past and embraced your future. Congratulations on your promotion to Cyber controller. I'm leaving you in charge now."

"Where will you go?"

"To do the same. But for me, Gallifrey awaits."

Just before he departed in his TARDIS, once again disguised as a filing cabinet, the Master threw the Tissue Compression Eliminator onto Cooper's desk.

"I looked after it for you, but you'll be needing this when the creatures you make in this girl's image turn feral. In about a week's time, if memory serves. You will also have to remove all emotions from the units. They must be like you."

"I am awaiting new orders," said Jenna. The words were the same as the scientist's earlier, but they were loaded with emotion. Confusion, loss, vulnerability and need all rolled into one, but no memory of why she felt the way she did, or even of who she was. She would need to learn it all over again.

"Just do what your Father here tells you," said the Master, patting the scientist on the back.

***

"You are allowed to be happy, you know. It's not every day you get to create a whole new race of Cybermen and wipe out another," the Master told himself, annoyed that his joy had been so short-lived. If only the Doctor had been around to witness his latest triumph – that would have given him even more cause to celebrate. In reality, the Master hadn't made history. He had plagiarised it, turning another's story into his own. In his efforts to find a cure, he had come across a version of the silver warriors who could live free of physical pain without losing their independence and emotional integrity. Jealously had driven him to change history and make sure such a race could never exist. Everything that he had told Cooper was a lie. His original design had been perfect.

The Master had ensured that the Ravellan Cybermen would be fitted with emotion suppression chips. By adding the technology of an entirely different race of Cybermen to the Ravellan prototype, he had created the conditions that would make them go rogue and in need of the limiters. He had taken Charlie and Jenna to various points in their people's revised future before deceiving them with the Mondasian fleet, but it wasn't Cyber-Charlie who they had witnessed trying to prevent the Cybermen from removing all emotions. It was Jenna, fighting her conditioning.

Instead of corrupting the Ravellan Cybermen, the Master could have become one of them. For a while he was tempted – it would have saved a grovelling or risk heavy mission on Gallifrey. But despite the preservation of individuality in Cooper's original design, he would have been just one among many. Such anonymity, he simply could not countenance.

The Master's interference in the development of the Cybermen hadn't all been an expression of his jealousy, however. The idea of commanding a whole army of them had been motivation enough to fight on through the pain. Furthermore, he had come out of the experience with some useful supercharged powers. He made a vow that if he achieved the impossible on Gallifrey, one day he would return to the Cybermen. He might even find a way of using them to get the Doctor back onto the right path.

Fallen Angel
Dan Barratt

The wooden-cased grandfather clock went whirling out over the horizon as the dome closed over the Capitol. Out it shot, over vast swathes of crimson grassland and silver leafed forests before rising over the Death Zone and off into the upper atmosphere. From the Capitol could be heard the screech of klaxons, shrieking and wailing into the night sky. On board his TARDIS, a curious black-cloaked figure stabbed excitedly at the central control console, leaping about the room like a deranged insect. Suddenly, the sound of the Capitol's radio defence band burst into the air, crackling its way over the sound of the groaning TARDIS engines.

"…alpha sixty, prime nautilus…"

The Master let out a shriek of excitement. It was the call-sign! They were coming for him. Only moments ago, invigorated by the intense energy of the Eye of Harmony, he had fled the Panopticon. No matter that his plan had not succeeded, he had attacked the very heart of the Time Lord empire. The killing of an outgoing President was one thing, the denigration of their most sanctified temple was another. In their complacency, it had seemed inconceivable to them that such a thing could ever happen. The statement he had made could not have been clearer and, clearly, it had hurt. The very centre of Time Lord power could no longer be considered impregnable. Now, at last, they had no option but to respond.

There was a sharp burst of static.

"Aeolus fourteen umbra… Temporal missiles launched and locked on to renegade time capsule…"

The Master gave another shriek of delight, his ghoulish face bathed in the glow of the rising and falling central control column. "Ladybug, ladybug fly away home, your house is on fire, your children will burn…" he crooned in mawkish delight. The missiles were gaining now. It was just a matter of timing… "Wait…!" he hissed. "Just a moment more…"

"Missiles have found their target… I repeat, they are locked on target. Even if he dematerialises now, he cannot–"

The little craft, now out in the darkest tracts of space, began to shimmer and fade as the nose cone of the missile made contact. Suddenly, there was a vast explosion, a gigantic sphere of blinding light, rings of energy rippling out into the blackness. Reaching their maximum circumference they should have

81

dissipated, but instead, the energy of the explosion began folding back in on itself. On board, the Master, his hands rooted firmly on the controls, was shrieking with delight. Without warning, the ship's doors flew open and, with crazed, lidless eyes, he gazed out at the tidal wave of energy that was racing towards him. Deadened almost completely by the roar of the oncoming implosion, the radio monitor blurted: "…echo sapphire cardinal… Enemy craft is absorbing the temporal missile energy… I repeat, it is *absorbing* the explosion!"

The Master's control room was now a raging furnace. Screaming in agony, the burning monster lifted his hand to his blistered face and then, with all the force he could muster, he plunged it firmly down on the console. The energy now began to swirl, forming a giant whirlpool of fire as it was absorbed into the console's central column. Bursting with excess energy, the craft now disappeared from Gallifreyan space and re-materialised in the upper atmosphere of a little blue-green planet. It bobbed and somersaulted excitedly for some minutes before dropping down and landing with a heavy thump. The doors flew open and the charred body of the Master was thrown to the ground as the craft reconfigured itself to blend into its surroundings.

***

The vicarage door flew open and in burst the reverend in a state of feverish excitement.

"Elizabeth!" he shouted, his face as red as a berry. "Elizabeth!"

"Richard? Is that you?" a voice cried.

Friday was Mrs Potts' baking day and, although it was now late afternoon, the lounge floor was still strewn with mounds of bread, slowly proving under carefully draped white tea-towels. The smell was utterly mouth-watering but Reverend Potts was far too excited to even notice. Clumsily, he began to pick his way across the floor until he found his way barred by a sea of rising dough. His wife's face peered around the door frame, her expression changing to one of horror.

"Wait!" she wailed, flapping her oven-gloved hands in the air. "Don't move!"

The reverend, not the most agile of people, was terribly accident prone. His wife knew he could destroy hours of work in a matter of moments.

"Elizabeth!" he cried, his face full of wonder. "You must come and see! A most incredible thing has happened. Truly! You must come and see!"

The vicarage stood amidst a row of tall narrow houses on the edge of the village green overlooking the church. Elizabeth didn't have time to change out of her house slippers but managed to throw a cardigan over her house-coat before emerging through the little wooden front door framed with pink roses. Her husband was already at the garden gate, urging her to hurry.

"Come Elizabeth, quickly!" Potts called to his wife and, taking her arm, they hurried along the lane that skirted the village green. They failed to notice the twitching net curtains in the windows of several of the cottages as they hurried along. The village old lady network ensured there were always inquisitive eyes watching furtively from every corner, no matter the time of day. The couple had almost reached the village store when Mr Thompson emerged. The little shop bell tinkled merrily as he came out. He lifted a box of rosy red apples from the stall beneath the shop window.

"Reverend, I wonder if I could have a word?"

Reverend Potts did not stop but continued in a daze, a beaming smile painted across his face.

"Mr Thompson, I really am so sorry," Elizabeth apologised, a little embarrassed. "I don't know what's got into him this morning. Really I don't."

"It's these kids you see," Thompson continued. "Really, something needs to be done. The little blighters keep making rude arrangements with my fruit and veg. Look at this!" He pointed to a courgette that had been placed rather suggestively between two perfectly round rosy red apples. "It frightens the old ladies. Really, it won't do!"

It was too late; the reverend was almost halfway across the green.

"Something needs to be done reverend!" Thompson called.

Elizabeth could do nothing more than answer with an embarrassed shrug as he hurried on after her husband.

Reverend Potts finally stopped once he had reached the church lychgate. Elizabeth could see he was trembling as she drew alongside him.

"Richard," she said tenderly, "what is it dear?"

"Come!" he said, his voice filled with excitement. "You'll see!"

They stepped inside the church. The reverend closed the door with a heavy thud which reverberated into the shadows. Elizabeth breathed in the comforting musty air and surveyed the prayer books, piled neatly along the backs of the pews.

"Richard? What is it?" she whispered.

"Look!" he said impatiently, pointing to a bundle of black rags, heaped in the middle of the floor. She stared at it intently.

"See, my love!" her husband exclaimed. "It is a fallen angel!"

"But, how did he get there?" she whispered. The reverend's face was beaming.

"I found him outside, in the churchyard. He was slumped at the foot of the big stone cross by the vestry door. It was lucky I noticed him." Elizabeth looked at him in confused silence. She tried to picture the heavy stone cross in the churchyard but couldn't seem to recall it.

"I dragged him inside and lay him here," he continued. "I couldn't risk anyone seeing him. Who knows what they may have done?"

She felt fearful as he stepped in front of her, his arms outstretched.

"Richard!" she hissed. She felt suddenly, unaccountably afraid. "Richard, he's not an angel! What can you mean? He's a man. A traveller or a vagrant or something. He could be dangerous. We should go to the police."

"I looked across the churchyard and there he was," said the reverend, as if he hadn't heard his wife's concerns. "His body was shimmering with golden light. That's when I knew." He turned to face Elizabeth, his eyes wide open. "He fell from heaven, Elizabeth. He fell into *my* arms! Help me lift him up, will you?"

She forced herself to reach down. The black mass was crisp to the touch; not at all like fabric but dry and brittle like fallen leaves. She recoiled at first and then, grasping at the creature again, found that the surface clung to her skin. Her fingers seemed to tingle with electricity.

"Did you feel it?" she whispered. She could not hold back the nervousness in her voice.

Slowly, the thing began to move. Elizabeth gasped as a single, thin, bony hand began to reach across that little space toward them. Silently it moved, like a tiny white serpent, searching the air around it, bones protruding beneath thin, translucent skin. It fell suddenly to the floor. They could just make out the minute rise and fall of the creature's chest and the faint sounds of shallow breathing. It was as if the thing were gradually coming to life. Elizabeth could feel her heart pounding as the creature began to lift its head. A pool of lurid light, strained through multi-coloured glass, splashed over a face of bare bones poking through hanging patches of rotting flesh. As the horrible apparition tilted its head up into the light, its demonic eyes came blazing out at them like two exploding stars. Elizabeth screamed. Pulling away from her husband, she ran down the central aisle, through the nave towards the front of the church, her slippered feet making dull soft slaps on the hard stone floor.

At the far end of the nave, her husband stood, transfixed. "Angel?" he whispered, kneeling gently before it. The creature opened its mouth, as if trying to speak. "Elizabeth!" called the reverend, "bring some water!"

Nervously, she made her way back up the aisle towards them. She scooped a little water in her cupped hands from the font and quietly knelt beside the creature. Like a cat, the creature lapped at the cool clear liquid. When it had finished, she regarded the bulging, lidless eyes staring up at her.

"We need to get him out of here," she said suddenly and decisively. "Wait here." In a few moments, she had returned to her surprised husband with a small tea trolley she had found in the vestry. "Here, let's get him on to this." The reverend quietly helped her lift the angel onto the contraption and looked at Elizabeth excitedly. "We should probably go through the vestry and around the back of the church," he said, "if we're to stand less chance of being spotted."

Together they wheeled the trolley, bearing its perculiar load, down through the church. The black heap of rags wobbled drunkenly as they went, while one of the wheels squeaked noisily. When they reached the vestry, the creature was again beginning to stir. Elizabeth took a surplice down from one of the clothes pegs. She fixed upon the angel's face. Its once horrifying features now seemed more familiar somehow. She placed a finger to her mouth and made a hushing sound before throwing the billowing white gown over creature. It seemed to cover most of the body. It would have to do.

"Richard, my love, get the door, would you?"

Outside, the light was fading and all seemed thankfully quiet. They were halfway along the usually deserted lane when Mrs Butinsky, a large lady who ran the village Women's Institute group, came cooing along behind them.

"Coo-eee!" she sang, drawing closer. "I say-hay!" Mrs Butinsky was waving a little lace handkerchief in the air as she drew towards them. Elizabeth could see it silhouetted against the pinkish glow of the setting sun. "Ooh-ohh!" she warbled as she joined them. "Whatever have you got there?"

"Oh, hello Mrs Butinsky," beamed Elizabeth, forcing as much enthusiasm into her voice as possible. She glanced furtively at her husband. Mrs Butinsky scooped up her glasses, which were hanging over her large sloping bosom on a chain, and peered more closely at the strange mound on the trolley. Then she looked up at Elizabeth, fixing her in an inquisitorial stare, and smiled.

"Cassocks!" exclaimed the reverend, coming to his senses just in the nick of time. "We're taking them home to be cleaned."

He smiled awkwardly at his wife who simply grinned back in bemused silence. Mrs Butinsky stared at the trolley, her eyes narrowing. The reverend and his wife looked at each other, Elizabeth raising an eyebrow and inclining her head, almost imperceptibly, towards home. Taking his cue, the reverend shoved the trolley off. The force of the jolt was enough to cause the surplice to become dislodged, exposing the top of their visitor's head and causing a thin arm to come lolloping slowly out from under its shroud. The creature murmured softly and, as her husband rushed to replace the cover, Elizabeth, who couldn't be sure if Mrs Butinsky had noticed, tried to divert attention with a little forced laugh. Then, as they scurried away, Mrs Butinsky rushed indoors and immediately made a telephone call.

"Eve dear, Bella here. Emergency meeting! Get the gang together and have them here in half an hour. And Eve, bring the chocolate creams… it's going to be a long night!"

***

The house was in darkness when the Potts reached home. In the gloom, they wrestled with the thin brittle body and carried him upstairs.

"That was close!" Elizabeth hissed. "Do you think she noticed?"

"We'd best put him in the attic room," he said, ignoring her question. "He'll be less likely to be seen up there."

"We're not expecting any visitors are we, Richard?"

"No, but anyway," he added with humility, "he'll be closer to home up there."

It took a moment before Elizabeth realised what her husband was referring to. She smiled and gave a little sigh at the thought of carrying their precious visitor yet further. The narrow attic stairs rose from the opposite end of the landing. Once they had finally reached the little Spartan roof-space, they placed him carefully into the little cot-bed there. Elizabeth found an old blanket in a box beneath the curtain-less window. She unfurled it in the air before drawing it over their guest. It caught and scraped over the creature's dry, black robes but she made the best of it she could. She gazed at its ghoulish face, at its blank, staring eyes. Somehow, its features held no horror for her now. Smiling, she took her husband's hand and, together, they crossed to the window and gazed out at the blackened, star filled sky.

"Who knows where he is from?" she said softly. "Out there, somewhere. You were right Richard: this poor little angel fell into our arms. It's up to us to help him. We're all he has now, his only hope." A tear glistened in the corner of her eye and ran, just like a shooting star, down over her cheek. Over their shoulder, out of sight, the creature smiled just a little and then quietly slept.

***

On the other side of the green, light spilled from a downstairs window and into the flower filled garden of Mrs Butinsky. The little front room was filled to capacity with five rather large old ladies crammed into bulging armchairs. Tea

86

cups had been drained and the fire had become nothing more than a mound of glowing embers. Discussions were coming to a close.

"We're agreed then, ladies," intoned Mrs Butinsky solemnly, the light of the fire throwing an unnatural glow over her face. Mrs Truscott, who had been busily knitting most of the evening, stopped and peered over the top of her half-moon glasses at the chorus of excited ladies. A woman of few words, she coughed loudly. The room fell silent in order to hear her speak for the first time all evening.

"Who is going to tell them?" she asked simply.

There was a murmur of realisation now in the room as they all suddenly realised they had not considered this key aspect of their plan.

"We can draw lots!" exclaimed Mrs Pritchard. This was greeted by a chorus of nervous muttering. Mrs Butinsky smiled.

"There will be no need for that, ladies. I shall tell them." The relief was palpable.

"I say!" cried Mrs Danby excitedly. "How terribly exciting this is! The old gang, back in the saddle! I think this calls for a celebration!"

Mrs Butinsky gave her a knowing wink before disappearing through the open doorway. The room was filled with excitement as Mrs Danby poured perfect measures of amber sherry into tall thin glasses and handed them out. So long they had been retired, so many years they had spent in this sleepy little village, cut off from everywhere, quietly living out their remaining years. Now they were rediscovering some of their younger spirit. Mrs Comlosley and Mrs Pritchard toasted and giggled, Mrs Truscott finally laid her knitting to rest and smiled in all the right places at Mrs Danby's excited chatter. Eventually, the talk died away and they all turned to see Mrs Butinsky silhouetted in the doorway.

Slowly, she strode into the room and, in the half-light, they could see now that she was carrying something: a role of cloth. She placed it down carefully on the coffee table in the centre of the room and then, with some ceremony, pulled at the knotted straps and gently unrolled it. Thus undone, the roll of fabric stretched across almost the entire length of the table. They could see now that it contained a series of pockets, each with something inside. The room was silent, save for the occasional spit and crackle from the fire. Mrs Butinsky gazed at their wide-eyed faces. Mrs Danby licked her lips in anticipation.

"Ladies, make no mistake, what we are about to do is deadly serious. You will each need to be on your guard. Once we embark on this mission, our little collective will no longer be safe. You will each need to protect yourselves."

And then, Mrs Butinsky slid her hand into one of the pockets. Almost as one, the ladies collectively drew breath as she slowly drew from inside a red and silver polished metallic object.

There was a little squeal of excitement as she held up the laser blaster for everyone to see.

***

The attic room was dark and silent when the creature awoke. Awkwardly pulling himself up, he stared across the room at the little window tucked into the eaves. Moonlight spilled through the panes and onto the bare floorboards. In the silence his mind drifted back to his final days on Tersurus. Lying there on that cold, desolate plain, gazing up at the Tersuran moon, wracked with pain and despair, he felt a shadow of the man he had once been. For the first time in his life he was suddenly forced to contemplate his own death. He had taken an enormous risk. The Dalek onslaught had been ferocious and he had been caught in the crossfire. Unable to regenerate, his body nothing more now than a decaying husk, he had only just managed to drag himself away through the slime.

The Dalek fleet long since departed, he had gazed up into the midnight sky. In agony, he waited. He had no idea if the emergency signal from his TARDIS would get through; or, indeed, if anyone would come. And then suddenly, as if in answer to his prayer, he heard a soft singing on the wind and the figure of a man came looming slowly out of the mist. He felt himself being lifted from the ground and carried to the safety of his ship.

When he awoke he found it was the renegade, Goth who had come to him and saved him. By a miracle, he had been snatched from the jaws of death and returned to Gallifrey, his home planet and the very seat of those he had hated. Goth was easy to blackmail: a promise of knowledge, of power. The fool! And so, he was able to slip once again into the shadows, like a spider, lying in wait to pounce upon its victim.

Goth who was once his deliverance now became his servant, a thing to be manipulated and deployed as necessary, to be disposed of as soon as his usefulness had run out. He was simply unimportant. The assassination of the Time Lord President, the Master's most audacious plan, would see the destruction of his own race whilst securing for him the most important prize of all: eternal life! Patiently, in the catacombs beneath the Time Lord Capitol, the Master awaited the arrival of his pawn, the Doctor.

In his desperation to harness the power of the Eye of Harmony to regenerate his failing body, perhaps the Master had gambled too much. That final desperate brawl with the Doctor had proved more than his ravaged physiognomy could manage. Somehow, he had managed to slip away, to escape Gallifrey to end up here, on this miserable world once more. Why here? Why did he somehow always end up here?

The Potts' attic room faded slowly to black once more as the Master drifted into a fitful sleep.

***

The next morning, not unexpectedly, a little deputation arrived at the vicarage. The reverend quickly locked the door to the angel's room before rushing downstairs to greet the two old ladies from the Women's Institute.

"Do come in, Mrs Comlosley, Mrs Pritchard. My wife was just making some tea. Won't you go through?"

He could see they were about to speak but he didn't want to get himself embroiled in lengthy discussions which may force him to tell untruths. Waving his short little arms in the air, he brushed past them, failing to notice a furtive hand gesturing towards the towering wisteria and a flash of pleated skirt diving into the shrubbery. "Alas, I have pressing things to attend to, I'm afraid!" he called from the garden. "Please do enjoy your tea! God bless!" And, with that, he was gone.

"Well!" exclaimed Mrs Pritchard. Her companion had already moved on and was eagerly greeting the reverend's wife in the kitchen. Before long, they were both sitting at the kitchen table, Mrs Potts pouring tea, Mrs Comlosley already skilfully working around to the reason for their visit.

Outside, in the vicarage garden, Mrs Danby had her foot on the wisteria and was trying it for support. Happy that it would hold her burgeoning physique, she started to climb. From across the green, a pair of binoculars glinted in the sunlight through an upstairs window.

"Of course, that's the trouble with being a reverend's wife," continued Mrs Comlosley. "So much to do."

"Well, I don't really think of myself as being any busier than any average housewife," Elizabeth replied. Mrs Pritchard sat, listening intently, stirring her tea round and round and round, adding an occasional murmur of agreement.

Unseen, Mrs Danby had edged higher and higher and was now within sight of the attic room window ledge. She placed her foot on the next branch and felt it bend under her weight. Stretching up, she hauled herself towards the glass.

"We housewives have to support our husbands, don't we?" continued Elizabeth. "But, of course, you wouldn't understand. Sugar, Mrs Comlosley?"

"No, thank you," she answered before ploughing on. Ignoring the barb, she turned to Mrs Pritchard.

"You see how devoted Elizabeth is. No sooner is she washing and ironing for her husband than she's put upon to do the laundry for the entire church choir."

"Mmm," nodded Mrs Pritchard, her teaspoon winding round and round in her cup, making little scraping sounds against the china. Elizabeth's eyes narrowed.

"Take last night," she continued, turning to Elizabeth. "There you were collecting all that washing from the church and, let's face it, it's not really yours to do, is it love? I suppose the reverend doesn't want the village to know he gets you to do it. That's why you collect it all in the dead of night…"

Mrs Danby just managed to raise her eyes above the sill when, unexpectedly, the little gable window flew open. Like the tongue of some terrifying lizard, the Master's arm came flying out and in one powerful movement, Mrs Danby was dragged inside.

Through her binoculars, Mrs Butinsky caught a final glimpse of her friend's ungainly posterior as, with skirts flying through the air, she disappeared inside. With a decisive thump, the little window slammed closed.

"Oh my," cried Mrs Pritchard. She felt suddenly worried for their unseen accomplice and abruptly stopped stirring her tea.

"I, I think it's time you went, ladies!" exclaimed Elizabeth with some agitation. "I really do have so much to do this morning!"

"But, Mrs Potts," said Mrs Comlosley.

"Come along ladies," she sang, ushering them out of the kitchen. "Please, you must not think me rude but I really am very busy."

When they reached the hallway, Elizabeth squeezed past them and opened the front door. Suddenly, there was another noise from upstairs. Elizabeth crossed to the stairs.

"Mrs Potts, is there someone else in the house with you?" asked Mrs Comlosley. Mrs Pritchard gazed out through the open front door and watched Mrs Butinsky's binocular lenses glinting in the sun. Elizabeth laughed distractedly.

"No, no! I think it must be the neighbour's cat. We're looking after him, you know," She was practically shouting now in order to try and distract them from the sounds that were emanating from the attic. An unstoppable Mrs Comlosley, however, was already half way up the stairs.

"Please!" Elizabeth called after her, mounting the first few stairs. Mrs Pritchard leaned in towards her, and took her hand. "I didn't think your neighbour had a cat," she said, a little menacingly.

***

Mrs Butinsky lowered her binoculars and began feeling under the bed for the wooden box. She opened the lid to reveal a large radio. It resembled an old-fashioned art deco wireless, a mass of geometric curves surrounding a central circular dial. She switched on. The dial slowly lit up. There was a high-pitched whine as the tuner fixed on the correct intergalactic frequency followed by a crackle of static. The equipment was old and outdated but it still worked.

"...sub-beam delta shadow zero zero... this is an emergency channel. State your reason for calling..."

Mrs Butinsky lifted the microphone to her lips. "Get me the General. I have an urgent message!"

"Please identify yourself." The voice brimmed with forced politeness.

"This is an open channel. I will do no such thing until I speak with the General."

"Your call is being disconnected. Do have a nice day."

"No! Wait!" There was a silent pause. "Oh alright. Have it your own way. This is retired commander, Themis, formerly of the Celestial Intervention Agency. I have an urgent message regarding the whereabouts of the renegade the High Council is seeking. You will put me through to the General right away!"

***

When Mrs Comlosley reached the landing, she could hear odd sounds of scraping coming from above. Her eyes darted to the little set of narrow stairs at the end of the landing. "Ah!" she exclaimed, and headed off like a heat-seeking missile towards her target. She ignored the protestations of the reverend's wife that assailed her from the top of the main staircase, giving a little sing-song as she went. "Woo-hoo!" she cooed as she reached the little attic room door. She tried the handle but it would not open. She called out: "Hello! Hello in there!" and placed her ear to the wood. Silence. "Hello!" she called again. "Is there someone there?"

Elizabeth had now reached her and began tugging at her sleeve like a child demanding sweets from its parent. "Mrs Comlosley, really," she began but her

91

voice was cut short. Despite her husband having locked the door, it now slowly began to creak open. A narrow sliver of light appeared which widened and widened until, at last, the whole of the little attic room was visible. Mrs Comlosley stepped inside followed by Elizabeth, nervously searching the room with her eyes. Mrs Pritchard remained out of sight at the foot of the narrow stairs. Slowly she reached into her bag, her hand searching out the blaster inside. Suddenly, with a whip-cracking slam, the little door closed. She heard a stifled cry from the reverend's wife. "Damn it!" she muttered quietly before she hurried from the house.

***

Mrs Pritchard sounded crestfallen as she recounted the sorry story to Mrs Butinsky.

"He has Mrs Comlosley in there, and the reverend's wife," she said gravely.

"And Mrs Danby," added Butinsky. Mrs Pritchard gasped. "She went rogue. I saw her climbing up the reverend's wisteria." She studied her friend's nervous face.

"Now come along dear," she said encouragingly. "It's not as if he's escaped. We know exactly where he is and *they* have been informed. We'll have a nice cup of tea and wait until dusk. Dusk is always the best time for mounting surprise raids! By the time we have them cornered, they will be here to collect our visitor and take him back to Gallifrey."

As the afternoon darkened, clouds began to gather, filling the sky with ominous foreboding. There were a few lone dog-walkers on the village green but these had all disappeared by the time the rain came. Mrs Pritchard was sitting in the kitchen looking more nervous than ever when Mrs Butinsky emerged from upstairs.

"Bella! I'm frightened." she cried, meekly.

"Don't worry dear. They're on their way. They'll be here around eight-thirty, our time. Better get our coats on!" she added, with just a little excitement.

"Ought we to be doing this?" asked Mrs Pritchard. "I mean, we are all long since retired from the CIA. We came here to this planet to relax, to enjoy our final years in peace and solitude. There is no possibility of regeneration for any of us now. I should bally-well be at home sipping sherry, enjoying a good jigsaw puzzle! Instead, here I am with you, pulling on gum-boots and heading off to arrest a renegade Time Lord! Good heavens, what are we doing?"

"Having fun!" Mrs Butinsky exclaimed gleefully and she clapped her hands together just to illustrate her point.

When they reached the Vicarage, they rang the bell but there was no answer. They tried the door and it swung gently open. The house was in darkness.

"Come on!" whispered Mrs Butinsky, pulling out the laser blaster from her inside coat pocket. She raised an eyebrow in the direction of Mrs Pritchard and waited for her to do the same. With their blasters held upright and their backs to the wall, they carefully edged their way up the stairs. In a moment of shared nostalgia, they both looked at each other and smiled. Mrs Pritchard seemed to be rediscovering the spirit of her youth. Suddenly, the light was flicked on and they were both confronted by the reverend who had just returned home.

"What the blazes do you think you are doing?" he exclaimed. Mrs Pritchard made a hushing noise and, waving her arms in the air, rushed down to meet him.

"I will not shush. This is my home. I demand an explanation!"

Mrs Pritchard swept the reverend towards the kitchen.

As Mrs Butinsky continued up the stairs, she could hear their voices arguing softly. When she reached the little attic room door there were no sounds coming from inside. All she could hear was the rain pelting down on to the roof slates above. The crack around the door was momentarily illuminated by a pulse of lightening. She listened for the rumble of thunder which followed in its wake a few seconds later. She checked her gun.

"He's got them in there?" whispered the reverend nervously as he and Mrs Pritchard joined her on the stairs.

"Stay there and keep quiet," Mrs Butinsky hissed coldly. And with that, she lifted her leg and gave the door a surprisingly heavy blow with her foot. With a simultaneous flash of lighting the door flew open.

"There he is!" shrieked Mrs Pritchard at the top of her voice and the ladies squeezed through the narrow attic room door followed by a stunned reverend Potts. At the other end of the room, Elizabeth sat bound and gagged on the floor, framed on either side by a similarly constrained Mrs Comlosley and Mrs Danby. Mrs Pritchard was staring at the rain-streaked window, where she could see clearly the disfigured face of the Master, peering inside. She raised her gun but it was too late: in an instant, to a resounding crack of thunder, the creature was gone. She ran to the window which was now clattering in the wind. Flinging it open, she leaned out into the rain and looked down.

With alarming speed, the Master had already reached the ground and was now lurching through the darkened, rain-soaked garden. Mrs Pritchard aimed her blaster again and fired. A lightning bolt of energy tore through the darkness and hit the ground at the creature's feet, sending up a flurry of thick, heavy soil. The Master continued scrabbling through the little garden. Pritchard aimed her gun again but this time there was a cry from Elizabeth who, freed from her bonds, was now at the window beside her.

"Wait! Don't shoot!" she cried and quickly pushed Mrs Pritchard's arm to one-side which sent a second bolt out over the village green. Down below, her husband was shielding his angel with outstretched arms.

"The fool!" Pritchard scowled and she quickly turned and left the room. As Elizabeth watched alone from the attic window, she could see the cowled figure of the Master running now across the lane. She saw him almost collide with a mother walking hand-in-hand with her young son, clutching a shopping bag. He seemed to stumble before lurching onto the green. There was a scream and Elizabeth realised that he was carrying something. She could not see what it was but it seemed to be causing him some difficulty. Then, as the awful scene was ignited by a flash of lightning, she realised, with dread, what it was: he had taken the child! The mother's shopping lay scattered over the ground, bottles and tins rolling away, abandoned now as the poor child's mother ran in the direction of apparition carrying her sobbing child. Elizabeth too cried out but her voice was silenced by an angry rumble of thunder. The ladies began fanning out of the vicarage, blasters poised, gaining steadily on the Master and driving him towards the church. Elizabeth knew that, somehow, it was always going to end there. Looking down, she could see Mrs Pritchard had emerged from her front door and was remonstrating with her husband.

"Please!" the reverend pleaded. "For the love of God…"

"Mrs Pritchard!" Elizabeth called from the window. She saw her face look up, bathed in the light from the open front door, blinking repeatedly as great droplets of rain fell into her eyes. "He has a child!" Either she could not hear or she did not understand. "He is carrying a child!" Elizabeth screamed again but, this time, her voice was swallowed by a roar of thunder. Realising it was no use, she rushed downstairs and out of the house to meet her husband. By the time she had reached him, Mrs Pritchard had left to join the others.

"Richard!" she cried. His wide-eyed look of anguish alarmed her.

"I have to go to him…" he muttered. "Have to. Don't you see?" And, in a moment, he had disappeared into the night.

By the time the Master had reached the lychgate, his pursuers had tightened the net considerably. Beyond lay the church, nestled amongst rows of weatherworn gravestones. He was now virtually surrounded. The little boy squirmed and kicked under his bony arm.

"Shut up, you little brat!" he hissed. The child screamed.

"Put the child down," intoned Mrs Butinsky with calm precision. With blasters raised, they waited. The rain beat down steadily in accompaniment to

94

the sobbing of the poor boy's mother who stood trembling in the arms of Mrs Truscott.

"Put the child down, I shan't ask you again!"

"Hah!" exclaimed the Master and held the little boy aloft. The child screamed, his face caught in frozen terror in a flash of lightning. A peel of thunder tore through the sky and echoed out over the hills.

"Perhaps we can discuss terms?" Mrs Butinsky offered and slowly began to walk forwards.

"Get away!" the Master scowled. "I'll kill him!"

"Oh, I don't think so, do you?" She was quite close to him now. "It wouldn't look very good at your trial would it? But then, what is one more death in the long roll call of deaths for which you have been responsible, hmm?"

The Master fixed her in his icy stare.

"And then, of course, there is the question of probity."

He could not suppress the soft chuckle which now seeped from his mouth.

"Even for someone with your lack of morals, it isn't very courageous of you to hide behind a child, is it? Is that what you would want to be remembered for?" Her voice began to take on a gentle mocking tone. "After all of your high ambitions, after all that we have seen, your final moments to be spent cowering behind an innocent child? Is that what you would have history say?"

She was barely a few paces from him now. He studied her silently, not allowing himself to be drawn by her mocking insults. Somehow, this woman seemed familiar and she sensed that he had noticed it.

"Ah, do I see a recognition at last? Think, Master, think back…"

He tried not to flinch at the sound of his name being spoken but he could not hide his surprise. Now there was no point in hiding it.

"Do I… know you?" he said softly. All about them the rain continued to pour.

"For hundreds of years the Celestial Intervention Agency had been tracking you, watching your every move. It helped us to allow you to think of yourself as a free agent, free to come and go as you pleased, free to dabble in the affairs of others. Your predilection for power and villainy concerned us of course, but our agents kept a close eye on you. When the Time Lords looked to punish the Doctor for his meddling, it suited our purposes for them to banish him here on Earth. It only needed some subtle persuasion on our part. We knew that your feud with the Doctor would keep you here as well and, that way, our job would be made all the easier. True, there were times when you posed a wider threat, but the Doctor fulfilled his role. He managed to rein you back in."

The Master was now utterly rapt.

"You know, despite its name, the CIA rarely chooses to involve *itself* in the affairs of others… we have always preferred other means…"

"You mean you always preferred to get others to do your dirty work for you!" the Master jeered.

"It was our job to intervene whenever the High Council were happy to stand by! As your appetites became a little too gluttonous, you gave us no choice but to intervene directly. As Commander, I was charged with the responsibility of apprehending you and returning you to Gallifrey. It was then that we, shall I say, lost track of you. Our agents reported that you had gone over to the Daleks."

The Master now shrieked and gurgled with delight. "Give you the slip, did I?" he crooned. "You CIA are worse than the Time Lords: hungry for control, for power, and yet cowering in the shadows, you craven hearted, spineless cowards!" He spat as he punched his vitriol out into the air. For a moment, Butinsky almost lost her composure but then managed to regain control.

"I don't mind admitting, you did manage to make things a little difficult for us. I and my colleagues here were instructed to drop the case and abandon all hope of ever tracking you down." There was a note of bitterness in her voice. "I simply couldn't abandon the job, not even in retirement. So, I kept listening, in the vain hope that I may, one day, pick up the trail. Then you led the attack on Tersurus."

The Master was suddenly startled.

"I heard your distress call. It was Goth who responded, wasn't it? Evidently, you had been betrayed by the Daleks?"

"I led them there. I led the assault on the Time Lord outpost. It was my plan! I deserved the glory! We destroyed it utterly, my first blow against the people who I hated most, the ones who had made me an outcast from the very beginning. Betrayal was always the Daleks' way. They meant to kill me. Instead they left me like *this*!" He shrieked this final word into the night sky, his wet and fleshless face upturned in the moonlight.

"So, with Goth as your aid, you took the fight to them," she said, matter-of-factly. "Right to the heart of the Capitol."

Suddenly, an ear-piercing scream filled the air and, tumbling out of the undergrowth in a series of incredible backflips, came the unlikely frame of Mrs Danby. Over and over she flipped, her skirts whipping through the air, on a trajectory aimed straight at the Master. When she was within striking distance, she made a final, powerful leap skyward. Her blaster, nothing more now than a streak of silver and crimson, when careering off into the tall grass. Quite oblivious to the oversight however, Mrs Danby effected a perfect somersault and flew straight into the startled Time Lord with a decisive thwack! Stunned by the blow, the Master released his grip on the child, catapulting the little boy upwards as he went tumbling to the ground. At the same moment, her face contorted in shock, Elizabeth appeared seemingly from nowhere. With her eyes on the prize, the child fell, stunned and silent, into her arms and she scurried away to reunite him with his relieved mother.

Mrs Danby now rose to her feet and, brushing herself down, strode off miraculously, quite as if nothing had happened, to her applauding friends. The Master was now back on his feet. He cooed softly in the moonlight. Suddenly, there was a shout from the direction of the church. The Master turned. His wife gone, it was the reverend who now stood alone, facing the crowd.

"Drop your gun, Mrs Butinsky!" Reverend Potts bellowed. She could see clearly his trembling hands clasping Mrs Danby's mislaid blaster, the silvered surface glinting in the moonlight. "I said drop it!" he screamed, training the ray gun on her. She dropped her gun. "Now the rest of you!" he shouted. They hesitated. "Come on," he chided, "or she gets it!" First one old lady dropped her gun then, taking their cue from each other, they each followed suit.

"This way," he shouted, addressing the Master, "the church will give you sanctuary." Slowly, the Master began to walk towards him. "You fell into my arms and I promised to keep you safe. I will not let you down."

"Bless you, my son," chided the angel. And, in a moment, he had run between the gravestones and into the shadows.

"Angel?" cried the reverend desperately. As he crossed the graveyard in pursuit of his heavenly visitor, he heard a curious sound on the air. When he reached the doorway to the vestry, the angel, and the stone cross where he had been found, had disappeared.

***

When the Time Lord security force arrived, they found themselves being greeted by a room full of old ladies, their spirits as dampened as the clothing they wore. They were huddled now around Mrs Butinsky's roaring hearth, bathed in candlelight, sipping tea and munching on sausage sandwiches. Commander Maxil seemed less than amused to have been summoned halfway across the galaxy for no purpose other than the offer of a cup of tea.

"If you'd just been here a little sooner, you would have seen we had him cornered. He would have been yours for the taking!" said Mrs Butinsky despondently.

The Commander turned and muttered to his subordinate. "We can't go back empty handed! They'll have my guts for garters. I'll be back in the Chancellery Guard!"

"I assume the Time Lords will leave us be," Mrs Butinsky continued. "I mean, there won't be any 'repercussions' will there?"

"What 'repercussions' could there be?" he answered, gruffly. "You're just a lot of retired old ladies. And besides, we don't have any jurisdiction over the CIA, lady. More's the pity."

"Hmm. Well, just so long as we're left in peace," she toyed.

"Just one thing. He *was* actually here, wasn't he? He's wanted pretty badly and I wouldn't want to think this was just some mad old ladies having us on – know what I mean?" He sounded worryingly threatening.

"Really," she exclaimed, with exaggerated offence. "I've never been so insulted!"

"No, well. Just so long as you know – we don't take kindly to people wasting our time. I don't suppose the Master gave you any clue as to his next destination?"

Mrs Butinsky gazed out of the window, her eyes settling upon the little statue of a man standing in her garden, speckled with moss and bathed in soft moonlight. On the windowsill, a tiny moth danced ever closer to the flame of her burning candle.

"None, I'm afraid. None whatsoever…"

Pulling Wings off Flies
Jon Arnold

Somewhere near the middle of infinity[1], two boys sat either side of a board. They had moved on from their childish games of Sepulchasm and five-dimensional chess to the games adults played. Infinity had begun as a training simulator for Time Lords, to give them an understanding of the consequences of meddling in the universe. It involved thinking in five-dimensional terms, each player attempting to impose their idea on a model universe and became the grand sport of the Time Lords. Games between skilled players could last millennia, even, it was rumoured in one extreme case, eons. Legend had it that the game between Malipert the Insolent and Peccant the Arcane will go on until the end of our universe and perhaps even beyond, with both players considered to have been driven light years past the point of madness and into some alternative multiverse of sanity. All this was known to the boys and yet they played, flickering civilisations in and out of being, lighting and snuffing suns and creating and breaking galaxies in their competitive visions of existence. As happened with all such amateur games the initial adrenalin rush of limitless power slowed rapidly as the maintenance of their respective, competing visions became the order of the day. The seconds between moves became minutes, hours, even days.

And then, suddenly, one of the boys cried out in frustration, lashing the board with his hand and sweeping away the carefully arranged pieces of both sides. Cursing, he stormed out of the Infinity Room through the doorway he had just imagined...

***

"Observe."

Glitz obeyed. He had no choice in the matter. The voice was cold, commanding and sharp with the edge of a calm madness.

The Master plucked the crystalline flower from the soil. He twisted it in his fingers, examining it from every angle. He raised the bloom to his nose, and inhaled deeply, the aroma seeming to amuse him. He smiled in that way that only the truly powerful or mad did, a smile of cruel happiness.

The scent reached Glitz's nostrils. It was glorious, the scent of childhood happiness and undiluted joy. Even a soul as mercenary as Glitz's was

---

[1] This is clearly an illogical concept. However, if the Time Lords had even the scantest regard for the rules of logic they would never have conquered the fourth dimension.

99

unavoidably moved. "'Ere, hang about... I know a bloke who could make a trillion grotzits off that perfume."

"Silence." With a single word the Master dismissed Glitz's visions of wealth, women and indolence like dust on the wind. Locking his gaze into Glitz's, he raised the tissue compression eliminator to the flower and pressed the button. Obscenely, parodying the blooming of the flower, the instrument's head opened, glowing green. The flower itself wilted, twisted and eventually shattered into blackened shards.

The Master examined the shrivelled remnants with the same care and attention he'd paid to the plucked flower. With a chuckle he turned his hand upside down and let the flower fall to the earth.

Glitz looked mournfully at the wreckage of his dreams. "Suppose there's another of these about then. Don't suppose you're up for letting me find it?"

The Master's eyes narrowed. "That flower was unique. In the entirety of space and time there are no more like it."

Glitz felt like weeping. The Time Lord clearly had no appreciation of the lifetime of extreme comfort and wealth he'd just destroyed. Sod the intricate structures, the infinite fractal ripples caused by a single ray of light in the right place, Glitz's idea of beauty involved a bank account with a lot of zeroes in it, none of them the first number.

The Master was suddenly alert, narrowing his eyes at a distant sound of approaching hooves. "Come, Glitz. We are done here." He led the short walk back to a nearby boulder. They entered and in short order the boulder quietly vanished from the verdant gorge.

A horse and rider trotted into view. The young woman caught sight of the blackened remains against the greenery, and her thoughts turned bleakly to the futility of existence. The thoughts whirled and developed in her mind for the rest of her journey.

Observing the seemingly insignificant incident on the monitor in the dark console room the Master watched, and laughed.

***

Some years later...

On the night of Insinglis, the freaks came out. The Carnival of Chaos saw the streets of each city in Belarbis lit up with thousands taking to the streets in bizarre and glorious dress: everyone dressed as animals, monsters or angels in costumes or rainbow hues (and plenty which seemed to invent new and impossible colours). Few stayed in, with those that did remaining at home either to protect their senses from being overwhelmed by noise and spectacle or to practice their particular misanthropy, a form encouraged by the Bard Sedessa's Epic of the Broken Flowers. There were rarely any violent incidents: it was seen as a festival of healing and bringing together. It was so encouraging of bringing together that ten months after the festival there was something of a population surge as inhibitions fell away: with healing and coming together, love often followed naturally.

Glitz would much rather be joining in than waiting on a street around half a mile from where the main festivities were happening. He loved a good knees-up – not only the chance for a few of the local intoxicating beverages but with everyone else inebriated there was always the chance to pick a pocket or two. Instead he was hanging about, waiting for the man with the plan (well, he assumed there was a plan) to sort out what he was doing. Most of the people he could see round here were in their autumnal years, if not their winter ones. The celebrations were, shall we say, more gentle in these parts and with the old giffers seemingly all in possession of all their marbles, opportunities for a good, honest crook to amuse themselves were few and far between.

Across the street, an old man dressed up like some kind of hamsteret[2] was caught by a sudden knot of revellers and fell heavily to the ground. Glitz ignored it. What had a good Samaritan ever got for their troubles bar smugness and self-satisfaction? And that wasn't an accepted currency in any bank Glitz knew of.[3] Fortunately for the old man, one of the hindmost revellers felt differently. The boy (a looker, Glitz admitted – he'd have made twenty fortunes if he was ever blessed with trustworthy, handsome features like that) crouched beside the man, checked for potential injury and told his friends to go on. With help, the old man struggled to his feet and asked the boy if he'd help him back to his home. Supporting the heavily limping man, the boy led the way down the street. If Glitz hadn't been such a cynical soul and suspected the lad of pocketing a few grotzits from the old geezer by honest or deceitful means, it would have warmed his heart.

---

[2] A genetic descendent of the Earth hamster, which is far more dangerous than their ancestor. They have currently accounted for the extinction of four hundred and seventy eight species and three colony worlds.

[3] It is in fact a recognized currency on Sobranos 3, but as the civilization was located twelve millennia after Glitz's time and fourteen million light years from his furthest point of galactic travel, he can be excused for not being aware of it.

He was waiting another half an hour before the communications device on his wrist beeped, telling him to return to the TARDIS. Bleeding typical Time Lord, leave you hanging round waiting without giving you a smidgeon of an idea of what was going on and then just tell you to come home like some lost mutt. Not even letting a poor soul with the thirst of someone who'd just spent a week in the middle of the Sahara a chance to sample the local grog. Sighing wearily, Glitz trudged toward the TARDIS, which had incongruously disguised itself as an extra house at the end of a terraced street.

Surprisingly, given the Master's usual fastidious approach to security, the door was open. Glitz raised an eyebrow on this and tugged on his bulletproof vest, just to reassure himself. He'd learned the hard way that it didn't pay to be too careless. Particularly when that first room was so bleeding dark.

He popped his head round the door. "Hello? Anyone home?"

There were footsteps. Leaning heavily on a walking stick, the old man Glitz had seen tumble earlier appeared from the other side of the console. He nodded at Glitz.

"Afraid you're out of luck mate, this ain't the place for strays to wander in." The Master would have a fit if he saw muppets like that wandering about the place.

"So I hear."

"I know you've had a bit of a bash, but you might want to be on your way before the owner of this gaff comes back. Not one for company if you know what I mean." Glitz checked there was no one else about before continuing. "Between you and me, he's a bit of a nasty one, don't want to get mixed up with him. So go on, hop it." Glitz nodded towards the door.

"Bit of a nasty one?" The tone was mocking, a cruel impersonation of Glitz's own words. "Oh my dear Sabalom Glitz, you're as easy to fool as that meddling popinjay." The old man's back straightened, years falling away from him. He shed the costume, revealing the black garb underneath, and a whirl of blurring light removed the wrinkles and straggly beard.

"Erm… I didn't mean a word of it honestly." Glitz's mind was hastily summoning all the charm and tricks which had fooled many an overly good-natured beak (and a fair few bad-natured ones too).

"Silence! It is of no import. We have much work to do before we are done." Gimlet stare there – Glitz didn't fancy his chances and made a mental note to get off at the earliest possible stop.

"But, erm… why the disguise? What's the point?"

If anything the Master's gaze hardened and sharpened. "It is not for the likes of you to question a Time Lord. If I needed you to know what I was doing I would have told you."

"Bet it was something cunning though wasn't it?" You could never go wrong flattering the old ego of these types. Might be imagination, but the Master was edging towards mollified.

"To lesser creatures such as you Glitz, maybe. To me... merely a day's work." He moved toward the console, crisply activating the machine.

With that the house vanished, leaving behind only a twisted, doll like figure behind to show that it had ever been there.

A few streets away, the dead boy's friends met another group of revellers. And one girl from the new group went home with a different partner, and lived an entirely different life to the one she originally had.

***

They continued to whirl through the planet's history, stopping at what seemed to Glitz to be almost random points and changing events in minor ways: a would-be artist never picked up a paintbrush and settled for a middling career in the civil service; a businessman of ruthless intent picked up an extra takeover or two; a festival turned into a riot; the last few members of a peaceful species of animal were wiped out (though the TCE inspired doll version of the last one did grace the Master's trophy cabinet). Glitz often scratched his head as to what the Master was up to. And after about the thirteenth or fourteenth stop he asked what the bleedin' hell was going on, despite the earlier warning.

"Look at me Sabalom Glitz," ordered the Master.

Oops. Curiosity frazzled the feline, didn't it? Glitz didn't want to, not again. Not into those eyes. He didn't know which was more terrifying: the blank, psychotic calm or glitter of madness they held when the mask slipped.

"I held the power of life or death over all creation. For one moment... for one moment a movement of my thumb would have ended creation, all life from the amoeba to the President of the High Council. For that moment Sabalom Glitz... for that one moment I knew the power of God." The glitter was there now. "And in that moment, I knew the truth. The weight of God's power is a fool's desire. The power of destruction... it means nothing. True power is nothing so trivial as life or death, it is shaping the universe to your will."

"Well, it's a lovely story, sure you can get a few grotzits for it on the talk vids."

The sneer in the reply was audible. "You think of nothing but wealth. Wealth is a poor substitute for power, Glitz. Power is the reason I must rid myself of the Doctor. He… he prevents me from imposing my design upon creation. Once I am free of him… I am truly free."

"And how does scragging one flower help you do that? Knocking off some overly good-natured halfwit? What good does that do for a god?"

"You understand nothing do you? Mortals!" Glitz could almost taste the contempt in the last word. "You see nothing of the weave of time."

"Well no. The only weaves I know are the ones the old geezers round my way are fond of having stitched into their bonce." Glitz paused. "Although there is that ancient Earth thing I flogged to six different mugs."

"Pah! I am a Time Lord, Glitz. One of the should-be rulers of the cosmos. We see the big picture, the warp and weft of consequence. And for the most skilled of us…" Glitz could almost see the Master preening. "…we see everything. What was, what is and what could be. And we can take that knowledge and use it to change everything. There is nothing… nothing we could not achieve. And yet the fools and weaklings of the High Council sit on the side-lines, rotting away. In all our history only Morbius had such vision and it was pathetically narrow. He dreamed only of conquest." The Master paused in his rant to catch a breath. "I dream of a universe shaped to my will. My desire. Creation as I might order it. And only the Doctor stands between me and my ultimate goal. No other of my race has the will."

Flatter the ego, as he'd thought. Always works, particularly with nut-jobs.

"So what have I got to do with all this?"

"You Glitz… you have a special role. I cannot be seen to directly interfere. The last, most important act must be yours." Once more the madness glittered. Glitz dreaded to think what he might be forced to do.

***

The young man had had a very bad night. He had told his partner of all his plans, hopes and schemes for the near future – a glorious future. But his partner had rejected it with a look of horror on his face. He had backed away, shaking his head, as if the person he'd once found so physically irresistible was now an object of unutterable horror never to be touched. He'd run out into the night, away from his now former lover. Once the tears had run dry – and yet they still always seemed to be there, willing to burst at a moment's notice – the man ran after him, searching. He screamed the name into the darkness, but could hear nothing, not even the distant sounds of running feet. He set off quickly, randomly, crazedly, heading away from the house, desperate to persuade the one he still loved more than anything else in the world that he was right. He reached the road, just following his head and began running, as if pace could keep up with the head start his ex-partner had, as if emotion could solve every problem and wipe away everything that just happened. He ran and ran, careless of any potential traffic. Ran, as if blind chance would be kind enough to preserve him. Ran…

Bang.

He found himself on the ground, looking up. Where he had just been, a car zoomed by, angrily sounding its horn at the pair of fools in the middle of the road. The man who'd taken him out of the way of the car was fairly short, bearded and strangely dressed… but he had a winning smile. Bit old maybe, but you could still see the traces of the youthful rogue – one of those who'd probably love you and leave you.

"Th… thank you." It seemed inadequate. He hated how his now ragged breathing and the adrenaline of the near miss made him sound so weak.

"No bother mate." The man dragged him up to his feet, dusted him off. "Just take a little more care next time, eh?"

His hands went to his pocket, found the now slightly crumpled packet of cigarettes. He took out the least damaged one, pulled it out… damn, no lighter.

"Hang on fella." The man pulled out a thin rectangle from his pocket and aimed it at him. For a moment the world seemed to hang in the balance. "Here you go." He fired the device and the end of the cigarette lit up. One drag and his lungs were filled with the sweet smoke, helping him to breathe, to get his body under control.

"Now take care of yourself. Don't worry about that fella – plenty more gumblejacks in the ocean, if you know what I'm saying." The man winked, paternally rather than lasciviously. "Head back to the old abode and sleep it off."

He nodded quickly – slightly too quickly with the adrenaline flowing. No need to say anything more. The man was right. He'd been weak. Almost been diverted. Tonight he could recover, tomorrow… tomorrow was a new day. For him and the world.

Glitz watched the young man stride off into the gloom. He wasn't used to doing someone a good turn without a suitably hefty recompense for his altruism. But that was what the Master had asked of him and well, he wasn't sure if a mark seven postidion life preserver saved you from dollhood. Ah well, chalk it down to the fine art of self-preservation.

Glitz walked into a nearby tree. Seconds later the tree noisily vworped out of existence.

***

The Master was busy at the TARDIS console, efficiently working the controls. He didn't so much as acknowledge Glitz's entrance. Well there it is, thought Glitz, not even a nod. Rule one of any job, keep everyone onside, at least while you needed them.

He decided not to push the point, particularly given what the Master might do if he *didn't* need him. Silence didn't come easy to him. Made him sweat, the result of one too many unpleasant interviews with the sort of copper who didn't believe an honest man.

After what seemed like an infinity, the Master began chuckling. Small at first, then rising in a pitch of hysteria. Glitz wasn't sure what was worse: the silence or the sudden amusement at nothing. He wasn't sure which kind of madman he preferred.

"Oh Glitz," said the Master when the laughter had subsided enough for him to get the words out between chuckles. "You have no idea what we've done do you? It's beyond your poor human mind to conceive." This set him off again.

"Well… no." Glitz was careful. He didn't want to spoil the good mood. "It's just well… saving someone's life is a little out of character isn't it?"

The Master had stopped laughing but the eyes still glittered with amusement. "Sabalom Glitz, your tiny brain has entirely missed the point."

"What point?"

"The man you saved… Karidian Wayles. Saving his life was the whole point of our journeys. I told you Glitz; the universe shall bend to my will. And it has. Wayles was a nobody when he originally died. An insignificant insect to history who achieved nothing. But given the right circumstances… the circumstances we have so carefully created… he becomes a giant. The man who changes Cardalia's history from one of peaceful union to a notorious empire."

"So, hang about, I…"

"Pick a name from history, Glitz. A mass murderer. A barbarian king. A paragon of cruelty. That is Wayles. As Earthlings would have it… you are the man who saved Hitler."

Glitz sensed an opportunity. "Surely there's a few quid in it for me then? Pop in on my old mate Wayles and he'll be happy to see me?"

"I show you one of the wonders of the universe, and all you think of is profit?" Glitz wasn't sure whether that was disappointment or disgust. The

106

Master's lip curled. "Very well." He pulled the lever that would effect materialisation. Scant seconds later he looked up.

"Outside those doors is a new world, which never existed. You are the first being to witness it Glitz. A new time. I am almost envious." The Master operated the door control and gestured to him. "Go on."

Nervously Glitz stepped out.

In all honesty he'd been expecting something grander. The Master's TARDIS had materialized in the middle of a great courtyard. It was slightly shabby, none of the grandeur the sort of person who wanted absolute power usually went in for. The statues were more abstract, perhaps being imaginative representations of animals rather than people. No grandiose paeans to personality and reminders of beloved leaders. Ivy climbed the walls, and benches dotted the area in geometrically pleasing patterns. It felt like a place of peace. On one of the benches lay a seemingly abandoned newspaper. Naturally nosy, Glitz went over for a quick shufti, see what he could learn. He picked it up, had a quick read of the headline. His eyes widened. The boss wasn't going to be too pleased...

He re-entered the TARDIS warily.

"Well? What is it?" The Master seemed irked by his return, as if he had interrupted preparations to leave. Which he probably had. Silently, Glitz passed him the newspaper. The Master glanced at it, took it in. His eyes widened and his nostrils flared. He began to read the paper, faster than any human could possibly have done, accelerating and cursing in some liquid tongue it seemed impossible any mortal larynx should have been able to produce. Suddenly he began tearing the paper, furiously ripping it as if to deny what the words told him. Wayles jailed for life for violence and attempting to foment coups. Harmony and order restored, stronger than ever in the wake of attempts to undermine it. As he tore a card fell out, clattered to the floor. The Master glanced at it, ran his fingers through his neatly ordered hair and grimaced. He let out a howl of rage. Glitz took a quick glance at the card, just in case it was worth anything. While the Master was raging, he quickly scooped it up and decided to make a run for it. The prospects for an entrepreneur like himself weren't too good hanging round with an unstable nut-job. He exited quickly, looked round the courtyard and scarpered as quickly as his feet would allow. After all, if this was still a world of peace and prosperity there'd be a few naïve souls around who might be persuaded to part with a few shekels to help a man in need. Behind him, he heard the sound of the Master departing. He'd gotten away, anyway. Just have to keep an eye out, just in case. He glanced down at the card he'd half-hinched. A thick black stripe bisected it diagonally downward from right to left, with mathematical symbols in the top left and top right corners. In the middle a large black seal was surmounted with a golden question mark.

He couldn't be sure, but ten grotzits would get you several thousand that a man who wore question marks on his lapels would use it as a calling card…

In the vortex the Master continued to rage. His nemesis had foiled him once more. But not next time. There would always, always be a next time. After all, he only had to win once…

***

The other boy looked at the destruction and sighed. Slowly, patiently he restored the board to the start of the game. Ordered, harmonious once more.

Until the next game.

The Greater of Two Evils
Mark McManus

The time vortex swirled with shifting, myriad colours. A tiny point of light sped across this vast canvas at unimaginable speed, briefly leaving a comet-like tail which soon disappeared into the iridescent kaleidoscope. Very few vessels in the universe could survive this environment, but the Time Lords of Gallifrey had long since mastered travel through this domain. This TARDIS belonged to an exiled Time Lord known only as the Rani.

Inside the time machine, the Master was pinned against the wall by centrifugal force. He watched, unable to move, as a *Tyrannosaurus rex* grew in size before him. Time spillage from the sabotaged console was accelerating its growth, and it was soon mature and strong enough to stand on its hind legs, despite the powerful energies swirling around the control room. He tore his eyes from the creature to look to his right and check how the Rani was faring. It appeared his fellow Gallifreyan was also held immobile by the temporal forces at play.

The pair had recently forged an alliance on the planet Earth. The Master had hoped that, with the Rani's help, he could finally rid of himself of his greatest enemy: another Time Lord known as the Doctor. He would then harness the Rani's genius at biochemistry to conquer the universe. But somehow, the Doctor had sabotaged the Rani's TARDIS and now they were careering through the vortex. The tumultuous take-off had caused a specimen jar to fall and break, releasing the *T. rex* embryo.

In another few moments, the dinosaur was much taller than a man, standing around twelve feet high. It opened its huge jaw and let out a deep bellow, before swooping down towards the Master. He winced as the creature's hot, fetid breath hit his face and the great lizard's eyes examined him hungrily.

***

The Master strode into his own TARDIS control room and paced around the console. The interior was quite different to that of the Rani's: matt black walls and the hexagonal helm that was more traditional than her smooth, circular touchscreen version.

"Well played, Doctor, well played," the Master purred as he prowled. "Trapping me in an out-of-control TARDIS with a pre-historic predator. I really must think of something particularly unpleasant for you next time we meet."

He looked forward to besting his arch-enemy at their next encounter. But first he would need to escape this current situation. Unfortunately, he wasn't really back in the safety of his own time-ship. In the face of imminent danger from the *T. rex*, the Master's Time Lord training had automatically taken his conscious thought to his 'mind-TARDIS'; a place where his brain could work at lightning speed to engineer a plan to ensure his survival. Of course, the mental landscape didn't need to be a TARDIS, but most of his people instinctively retreated to a projection of their TT capsule because of the symbiotic bond they shared.

This was a discipline the Master had often found difficult, his mind too often clouded by thoughts of vengeance and power. On this occasion, however, he did not need very long to think of a solution…

***

The Master's eyes snapped open, and he was back in the Rani's TARDIS. With difficulty, he moved his hand into his pocket and produced his trusty Tissue Compression Eliminator. It was still set to the highest level – total disintegration. With a supreme effort of will, he raised the weapon with both hands and adopted his well-practised firing stance. He aimed at the enormous dinosaur and the cover of the muzzle opened out. But the expected deadly red beam failed to appear. Aghast, he pressed the trigger again. The *T. rex* sniffed at the black, tubular weapon, and growled.

"Weapons… don't work… in here, you fool!" snarled the Rani, her voice distorted by the raw time spilling around.

"Temporal grace?" he shouted back. "Why… haven't you… de-activated it? I… turned mine off… centuries ago."

"Because… I'm a scientist, not a… homicidal… maniac!" the Rani retorted.

At this, the dinosaur's huge, scaly head swung in her direction, and it roared again, as though recognising the person who had captured and experimented upon it.

***

The Rani slipped into her own mind-TARDIS: a quiet, calmer and intact version of the room in which her physical body stood. Her first priority had to be getting the ship back under control, but there was no way she could reach

110

the console from here. Hands on hips, she studied her mind's recreation of the console. The telepathic circuits were a possibility. This model was advanced enough to have a telepathic field which meant that the pilot could interact with the TARDIS without physically touching the circuit, unlike older models like the one the Master used. But the room was awash with time spillage, and would be very dangerous for her Time Lord mind to project through. Of course! There was a much simpler solution to rectifying the sabotaged velocity regulator…

***

Back in her real TARDIS, the Rani opened her eyes just as the dinosaur opened its mouth to attack her. She found the Stattenheim Control in her pocket. It was a device she had invented to pilot her ship remotely, one she was particularly proud of because it had evoked such envy in the Master and the Doctor. She stabbed the button that cut the engines. The sudden deceleration jolted the *T. rex* off-balance and sent it careering into her shelving unit, smashing it to pieces. The huge dinosaur was on its side, trying get back up.

Free from the g-factor that was trapping her, the Rani wasted no time in running towards the console. She looked over at the Master, who had reacted just as quickly and was also making his way to the ship's controls.

The Rani slapped the Master's hand away as he reached towards one of the console panels and moved round to check their position.

"What are we going to do about your overgrown pet?" asked the Master, nodding towards the struggling dinosaur. "Do you have any more of those tree-mines?"

During their recent adventure on Earth, the Rani had deployed some diabolical land-mines which had rewritten the DNA of their unfortunate victims in an instant – turning them into trees.

"No, I left them all in Redfern Dell. No doubt that meddling Doctor has defused them all by now," she replied bitterly.

"Yes," replied the Master, sharing her distasteful look, "Anything to preserve a few more of his precious humans."

***

Across the unfathomable depths of the universe, and in a completely different epoch of history, the Doctor paused from instructing Peri on the best way to make a cup of tea. He scratched his head absently, as though something

111

important had fleetingly crossed his mind. No, it had gone. He shrugged and continued his lecture.

***

The *T. rex* had recovered its balance and was roaring in frustration again. It was now around fourteen feet tall; not full-grown, but large enough to have to stoop somewhat against the ceiling in the control room. Maddened, it lowered its head and stalked around the console towards the Master, who was forced to retreat back to the entrance.

***

Back in his mind-TARDIS, the Master leaned against his console and considered his options. His weapons were useless in the Rani's ship. He couldn't get to the console. There was nothing to rely on but his wits. But then, he thought with a smile, his wits were the sharpest weapon in his arsenal!

***

As the dinosaur's great head came menacingly towards him, the Master held out a hand and projected his hypnotic powers at the creature. "I am the Master, and you will obey me," he muttered. Of course, the dinosaur wouldn't understand the words, but it helped the Time Lord focus his mesmerism, and the persuasive, silky tone might calm the beast. The Rani gained dominion over her subjects with biological tampering and DNA manipulation. While he admired her skills in that area, the Master enjoyed the simple pleasure of exerting his will over others, breaking through and crushing another being's resistance with only the power of his mind.

This monster had a tiny brain; it was all instinct and aggression – hungry and territorial. It took all of the Master's effort to stop the *T. rex* in its tracks.

***

The Rani watched with grudging admiration as the Master held her experimental creature at bay. The black-clad figure was dwarfed by the great lizard. Eyes closed, his face was a mask of concentration, one hand held before him as though trying to physically hold back the towering creature. The strain on him was clear; he wouldn't be able to hold back the slavering mouth from devouring

112

him for much longer. *That would be one problem taken care of, and then she could easily take care of the Tyrannosaurus.*

***

The Master grunted in surprise; there was more to this simple animal's mind than had first appeared. He found a surprising, unnatural augmentation to its brain. It was like pushing open a door that he expected to be locked. Forcing his consciousness into this unexpected mental nook, it was now much easier to control the dinosaur. There was enough basic intelligence here that he could project a false reality where the *T. rex* perceived the Master as a more dominant specimen. The Master visibly relaxed and opened his eyes. As he turned to look at the Rani, the *T. rex* mirrored his movement and swung round to face her too. The Master smiled.

"I think we need to renegotiate the terms of our agreement," he told her. The Master laughed – a gentle, mirthless chuckle. "With your TARDIS, all your research and experiments, not to mention my new friend here, I don't think I'll need you any more, Rani."

The dinosaur walked, much more calmly now, round the console towards the Rani.

"How dare you?!" she demanded, scandalised by the attempted mutiny.

The dinosaur was almost upon her.

***

Her consciousness in her mind-TARDIS once more, the Rani knew immediately what the Master had stumbled upon in the *Tyrannosaurus rex's* brain. She had been breeding these specimens to be obedient guards for her palace on Miasimia Goria, the planet she ruled. It had suffered a lot of unrest recently, not least because she had been experimenting on the minds of her subjects.

A little alteration to the dinosaur's brain meant they would understand basic commands. She'd even kept the specimens in her control room, rather than the laboratory, so that as they grew their minds would become imprinted with her voice. The augmentation couldn't be fully developed in such a truncated gestation as this *T. rex* had endured, but she had to try...

***

"Stop!" she commanded as the huge creature bore down on her.

113

The dinosaur paused uncertainly.

The Master frowned and concentrated harder.

"Get back!" ordered the Rani.

The creature retreated hesitantly.

The Rani smiled. Her mastery of biochemistry was clearly more than a match for the Master's hypnotic influence.

"Kill," she said quietly.

The dinosaur growled and turned on the other Time Lord.

"No!" the Master hissed through gritted teeth. "You will obey *me*," he insisted, increasing the mental effort he was exerting.

The dinosaur stopped again, and looked back at the Rani.

"KILL!" she shouted imperiously.

The *Tyrannosaurus* continued stalking towards the Master.

***

As the certainty of a grisly death bore down on him once more, the Master projected all his mesmeric power into the tiny brain of the huge predator.

"You can't fight biology with parlour tricks, you posturing nincompoop," gloated the Rani.

Trying to ignore her taunts, the Master whispered, "I am the Master, you will obey me," like a mantra as he concentrated on regaining control.

"Finish him," she said.

The Master felt the small part of the dinosaur's brain that allowed control suddenly rupture as it fought to obey its mistress' orders while he bombarded it with contrary mental instructions.

It bellowed in pain and rage, and then snapped its huge jaws down towards the Master. He dived into a forward roll, and dodged the razer-sharp teeth just in time. As he rose to his feet, he found himself by the corridor that led into the rest of the Rani's TARDIS, and hared away into the bowels of the ship.

***

The Rani was left on the other side of the control room, the enraged *Tyrannosaurus* in the way of her following the Master into another part of her TARDIS. She, too, realised there was no controlling the beast now. She started to slowly edge around the console, but the dinosaur also moved round. It stopped as she did, and when she tried to go the other way around the console, it mirrored her movement and moved to intercept her. It was only a matter of time before it became bored of this cat and mouse game, and went in for the kill.

***

Using her mindscape again, the Rani looked around the virtual, Tyrannosaur-less control room. As in her real TARDIS, the remaining dinosaur embryos slept peacefully in their intact tanks, mounted on plinths. *Such unexplored potential*, she thought. She stroked the side of the nearest container, as though to determine a weakness in the pre-historic hunters. But instead, the gauntlet she was wearing on her left wrist caught her attention.

***

In her real TARDIS, the Rani's eyes narrowed as she moved round the central console again, emptying the last three phials from her gauntlet out onto her palm. She hoped it would be a strong enough dose to knock the dinosaur out. She'd had to use one capsule already on the Doctor's pitiful human sidekick. As the *T. rex* prepared to pounce, she carefully broke the capsules into her palm, and flung the powder full into the creature's huge snout.

She leapt back as the Tyrannosaur reared slightly, swayed, and then pitched forward unconscious, its jaw hitting the floor just short of the plinth around the console.

With a sigh of relief, the Rani set back to her work on the ship's controls.

***

The Master had slowed to a walk when he realised the *Tyrannosaurus rex* wasn't giving chase. He'd already run past a few doors which interrupted the grey, roundel-studded corridors. He carefully opened the next one he came to, hoping to find a weapon to take back into the fray. If he could dispose of the Rani and her vicious pet, he would take this TARDIS and all the Rani's experiments to set about conquering the universe. Alliances, he thought, were only worthwhile until he had a chance to get the upper hand on his ally. He assumed they were usually thinking the same thing.

The lights responded automatically as the door opened, illuminating a cavernous room beyond: the wardrobe room, he thought dismissively. As he cast his eye across the chamber he saw racks of glittery, feminine suits with large shoulder-pads. The Master didn't really see any need to for different outfits; as

115

with his *modus operandi*, he had found his style and was sticking with it. Besides, his ensemble defined elegance. He raised an eyebrow as his gaze swept across a display of revealing male outfits which the Rani dressed her servants in. Just as he turned to leave the room, he noticed another section dedicated to disguises and nodded appreciatively.

The Master wandered further down the corridor and turned a bend. There were no more rooms along here, and the corridor kept curving round until it unexpectedly opened out into the control room again. He smiled grimly. The Rani had reconfigured her TARDIS' interior to lead him back here. He span round to look behind him and saw only a dead-end.

The dinosaur was lying across the floor, apparently unconscious and breathing heavily. The ship was still in flight, the silver rings of the time rotor rotating together steadily. There was no sign of the Rani.

The Master moved as quietly as he could across to the console. The great Tyrannosaur shifted slightly as he crept past, so he stopped. It seemed to settle back down and he continued to the controls. The ship was now under control, and on course back to Miasimia Goria. He moved around the dais, and tried to scan the interior for the Rani's whereabouts. He was studying the readouts so intently, that it was only when he caught a movement in his peripheral vision that he was alerted to danger. He looked up sharply. The *T. rex* was once more on its feet and looking at him hungrily.

***

Once she had programmed the ship to shepherd the Master back to the control room, the Rani had made her way to the second most important room in her TARDIS: the laboratory. Once there, she had dead-locked it behind her to make certain she was safe. *Why did she ever ally herself with this maniac?*

Since they had left the Academy, the Rani had heard many times about the Master colluding with aggressive aliens, only to have the tables turned against him: Axos, the Nestene Consciousness, the Gaderene... The Rani had assumed she could simply use him as others had. She decided there and then that, in the unlikely event she ever needed a Time Lord ally in the future, she would take steps ensure she was in complete control.

For now the Rani would need to deal with both the Master and the dinosaur to regain control of her ship. The *Tyrannosaurus rex* was a fearsome creature, but it wasn't the biggest predator she'd encountered in Earth's Cretaceous period. If she could synthesise a pheromone for the even larger *Spinosaurus*, there might be a way to regain control of her experiment.

The Rani's laboratory was an enormous space, filled with technology and a menagerie of specimens from a thousand different worlds. As she made her way through the equipment, her stomach lurched uncomfortably.

Now what?

The next moment, her feet lifted off the floor, as did some of the equipment around her. *The Master has turned off the gravity!* She floated now, just out of reach of any suitable surface to push off against and propel her towards anything useful.

So, he had taken control of the TARDIS. At least if he deleted the laboratory, the safety protocols would transmat her to safety.

***

Returning to her mind-TARDIS, the Rani ran her hand along the console as she considered her options. She stopped at the panel which housed the telepathic circuits. With a smile, she realised that without the time spillage she could now use the psychic field to access the telepathic circuit and operate the console. Choosing to remain in her mind-TARDIS, the Rani placed her palms onto the panel of the imaginary telepathic circuit in front of her to help focus, reached out with her mind and interfaced with the ship.

In her mind's eye, the TARDIS showed her that the *Tyrannosaurus rex* was awake, and once again menacing the Master in the control room. She thought about simply waiting for the creature to tear him to pieces; but decided she wanted to be rid of both of these destructive beings as soon as possible. With a mental command, she opened the TARDIS doors to the vortex outside. The Master grabbed hold of the console as the time winds tried to rip him out of the ship. Some of her other precious samples were swept outside, but, no matter, she could always go back and collect more dinosaur eggs to experiment on.

The Master clung on, his face a mask of desperation. The huge dinosaur started its inexorable slide towards the door, its mighty claws gouging into the floor as it roared in defiance. For a moment, the Rani thought the creature looked too large to fit through the entrance, but the cosmic forces were enough to tear it into the vortex beyond.

"Close the doors!" the Master screamed. "I can't hold on much longer!"

Seeing events in her mind's eye through her TARDIS' sensors, the Rani watched impassively.

"Rani!"

It was clear the Master couldn't resist for very long. In the end it happened suddenly. One moment the Master was hanging there, his legs flailing around in the air, the next, he was plucked out into the maelstrom of the space/time vortex.

"An ignoble end for a miserable, misanthropic creature," the Rani said to herself, repressing a shudder as the view of the vortex forced into her mind a childhood memory of facing the Untempered Schism. The insane patchwork of colours outside also reminded her of the Doctor's hideous coat. Now she was rid of both of the arrogant fools. She closed the doors and restored gravity to her laboratory with another thought-command, and then returned her consciousness back into her physical body. Straightening her tunic, she composed herself and stepped from the laboratory back into the corridor.

The sound of her heels clicking on the smooth, polished floor echoed around her as the Rani headed for the control room. She thought she heard another sound beneath it, a susurration, and stopped. The corridor was silent, save for the low, powerful hum of the ship's engines. The Time Lady shook her head; having hostiles in her TARDIS had disquieted her. This had always been her sanctum from the universe.

A thought crossed her mind: if any other samples had escaped in the chaos, there could be anything loose aboard. Once she was back on Miasimia Goria, she would need to conduct a full inventory. If a Drashig embryo or a Krynoid pod became active, Rassilon only knew what might happen.

The Rani arrived back in the control room and sighed as she took in the state of the place. Large claw marks scarred the floor where the *Tyrannosaurus rex* had resisted being expelled. She ducked under the console to set about repairing the damage the Doctor had wrought to the navigation system and the velocity regulator. As she checked the Zeus plugs, she thought she heard a sound again, and paused. The control room seemed to be getting darker. Standing up, she checked the read-outs. The power levels were normal. The room was still getting darker, though.

There was that sound again. She cocked her head to one side. *Was it the engines?*

The noise was getting louder. A repeating, staccato sound. Hhh... hhh... hhh.

It almost sounded like...

"Heh, heh, heh."

The Master's laugh.

"Where are you?" she demanded haughtily.

The Master laughed delightedly.

"Oh my, dear Rani, you *have* been naive," the smug, familiar voice boomed all around her.

"How did you get back in my TARDIS?" she asked, circling the console warily.

"I never left your TARDIS," came the disembodied reply. "I'm still here, in control of her."

"How can you be? I'm at the console." The Rani checked under the panels. *Where was the pesky stowaway?*

"He-he-he, I'm at the console. The *real* console, that is."

No. It couldn't be. The Rani started operating the controls on the console at random. Nothing. Even the scanner screen wouldn't activate. She slammed a fist on the surface.

She was still in her mind-TARDIS.

***

The Master allowed himself another little chuckle. A black glove lay on the console, and he was holding onto the telepathic control of the Rani's TARDIS with one bare hand. With the other, he manipulated the console to steer the ship back to Earth. It was always difficult, flying an unfamiliar capsule, but he seemed to be on the right course. Behind him, a huge *Tyrannosaurus rex* skeleton lay across the floor, taking up much of the control room.

Seconds from being consumed by the dinosaur, the Master had hatched a new plan in his mind-TARDIS: Time-spillage had caused the *T. rex* embryo to mature too quickly, so he created a more controlled burst of temporal energy from the console to age the creature to death. He had kept on going until it was a skeleton; the decomposing corpse would have smelt so bad he might have had to use his respiratory bypass.

He suspected the Rani might try to access the telepathic controls remotely, so used the circuit on the console to project his powers of mesmerism across the network and create a false reality to fool and trap the Rani. He had been particularly proud of the images he had created of his own apparent exit from the TARDIS.

Unfortunately, he couldn't hold the Rani in his psychic trap for long, and certainly not without maintaining constant physical contact with the telepathic circuit.

"We'll be landing soon, Rani," he told her. "For just long enough for me to disembark, and then I'll send your TARDIS on its way. By the time you get out of your predicament and back to the control room, I'll be long gone. Just in case there are any hard feelings, you understand?"

"You'll pay for this you treacherous cretin!" came the reply from the Rani's mind.

The Master left her with a chortle, and withdrew his hand from the controls. As he retrieved his glove, the time rotor came to stop. Pausing only to pat the enormous skull of the vanquished *Tyrannosaurus*, he opened the doors and stepped out into the darkness. He had considered taking one of the other *Tyrannosaurus* embryos with him, but the beast would require constant concentration to control.

The Master turned to watch the Rani's TARDIS dematerialise with a rasping, scraping sound. He congratulated himself on walking away from his latest temporary alliance with what he considered a victory. *Now to retrieve his own TARDIS.* He had no desire to see any more of this dismal century in northern England, where he had left his craft.

It was dark, and the Master immediately noticed how humid it was. *Of course, he must have landed back in the Rani's bathhouse.* Carefully making his way forward, his eyes quickly adjusted to the dim light, and he realised he was actually outdoors. He could feel warm wind on his face and rock underfoot. Now that the sound of the departing TARDIS had faded, he could also hear animal noises.

Soon, the Master's surroundings became brighter as the sun rose, illuminating his surroundings. He found himself on a rocky ledge, a huge valley opening out before him. The Time Lord groaned and fell to his knees as he saw a herd of *Stegosauruses* drinking from a lake, while *Pterodactyls* wheeled in the sky above him. In the distance, a volcano belched smoke and rumbled ominously, causing some *Diplodocuses* to stop grazing and break into a run.

An Alien Aspect
Richard Gurl

The searing flash cut through the bay like a god swinging a mighty blade, lighting the sky like doomsday. The sea boiled, the sand burned, and in the air a large vortex appeared from nowhere. Its insides swirled like paint down a drain. Out of the maw of kaleidoscopic colours came forth a black pod. If anyone saw this, they would surely have compared it to an animal coughing out a morsel of food. But the only beings here were fish, and they had perished in the heat, their bodies dotted on the water. The otherworldly object had the charred bodies of two creatures wrapped around it. The remains exuded an unearthly smell, one which would deter any predators. As the waves lapped around the man-sized capsule, the vortex vanished with a crackle of electricity. Night didn't return immediately though, as the charged air still gave out an otherworldly glow. Thirty minutes later, normality resumed, and the sea was again bathed in moonlight.

The object's arrival had attracted attention, and as the dark returned, five jeeps and five small trucks drove along the shoreline towards it. The atmospheric disturbance had made its presence known for miles, and the nearby radar and tracking station had momentarily registered the pod. In minutes, heavily armed soldiers were on the scene, prepared for any surprises. After determining any dangers, the object was loaded onto the back of the leading truck under the watchful eyes of two men with beeping equipment. Swiftly and efficiently they worked, barking instructions to each other to remain vigilant.

These electrical storms had occurred a handful of times of late, interrupting a quiet of 20 years where alien intrusions hadn't been recorded. But this was the first time that the regular vortex visitations had produced something of an extra-terrestrial origin.

***

Professor Quilter was one of UNIT's scientific advisors. The unassuming man ran a hand through his greying hair as he looked upon the alien coffin. That's what he had called it, for even though no scan could penetrate the smooth design, he was certain there was a body inside. The round symbols on the lid were indicative of planets, and underneath was an inscription and several ideograms that could not be translated.

Quilter's lean frame showed signs of agitation. He was a worrier, and a workaholic. Not having slept for a day, he was also in need of coffee. The man next to him peered through the window at the coffin, his surly manner in need of some urgent answers. He was the type of man that was used to getting them, certainly from his subordinates. Kellen walked over to the opposite window.

"Those things – you're sure they pose no threat?" Kellen's tone conveyed a need for confirmation. He turned to Quilter, and the Professor answered with the utmost certainty.

"Dead, Captain. Burnt to a cinder, or very nearly. Whatever they were, the journey killed them, if they hadn't died before then."

"Holding onto that thing for dear life. But were they protecting it, or trying to stop it?"

"That, we'll probably never know. And there's no real need for the guards, Captain. If anything has managed to survive, it won't escape the lab. A rampaging elephant couldn't crack this glass."

Kellen raised an eyebrow. The bodies had been prised off the coffin and were being subjected to tests. The smell that they gave off wasn't as pungent now, but anyone in the vicinity wore protective suits with gasmasks.

"I'll leave two men with you. Briggs and Hollander can come with me. I'm trusting you on this, Professor. Until the expert arrives from Sweden, you're the best we have."

"I'll forgive the insult, as I know you mean well." He cracked a weary smile at the tattooed soldier. "Doctor Karlsson is a good man. I look forward to his arrival."

"If you two can't crack this, then all hope is lost." Kellen may have been a gorilla, but he was likeable enough under the gruff exterior, and usually right about such things. "You carry on, Professor. This facility is on high alert. We may be playing it cool, but we haven't seen an ET in years. This situation isn't to be treated lightly."

"And lightly it isn't."

Kellen's assurances were allayed, albeit only slightly. He nodded his goodbye and swaggered away.

***

Quilter had been here for seven months. Highly respected, he had been headhunted by UNIT, and was unaware of their full history. He knew that he was brought in to assist with strange cases, which these scorched bodies were, but his feet remained firmly on the ground. After all, the terror wreaked by the last alien encounter had reinforced the view that not every visitor to this world brought with them warm greetings. The memory of that time still burned in the minds of those that had survived, and the orbiting robot defences were a testament to that.

The Komadeen took less than a week to wipe out huge numbers of human life. The resulting losses had forced the governments of the world to create new organisations to defend the planet, and UNIT was one such body. The United Nations Intelligence Taskforce handled the majority of the problems for England and the surrounding nations, and they were the best in the world. Of course, the Americans thought this of themselves, but their friendship was strong. Since the destruction of the White House, and when UNIT stepped in to save the day, the relationship became stronger still. America was indebted to them.

Gratitude was what helped build the orbiting defences. The decimated population of the planet could now breathe a collected sigh of relief, knowing that any attack from outside the globe could be repelled. But the recent electrical storms were something else. The last one had left something here, but it didn't seem to be a threat. And luckily, it wasn't a Komadeen vanguard ship arriving from *within* the atmosphere.

Quilter knew the risks for working for UNIT. There were some strict regulations, but they were there for good reason. His life's work was science, and he had sometimes made reckless decisions in his passionate quest for knowledge, but those wild days were mostly behind him now. Considering all this, the UNIT bosses were glad to have his expertise on hand.

His mind wandered to those tasked with building weapons in preparation for anything that could come through the wormhole, should it reappear. Immediate decisions were made for such a contingency, even if the dangers were unforeseen. With this in mind, a contingent of American soldiers would soon be here to help. These alliances were important in times such as these. His mind returned to the coffin as he finished his coffee.

The detailed analyses didn't offer anything new. The coffin had a blackened surface, and underneath, gloss could clearly be seen in small patches. This is where the symbols were visible. Transferring it to this facility, not more than three miles from the point where the object had emerged into this world, had been the logical option. But the equipment here wasn't really of much use. Quilter cursed to himself as this once again overtook his thoughts. The computers were showing that whatever this thing was, it was impervious to any scan. It was obviously constructed of something not known on Earth. Frustrated and inwardly excited at the same time, Quilter also found himself at a loss. This wasn't the first time. Yes, he was determined and intelligent, but not being able to progress ate at him; an annoying worry born out of a dangerous curiosity. The machines and equipment weren't exactly old, and were quite capable of examining and assessing anything else, but now, they seemed redundant. He would, however, persevere.

Strangely, the coffin did register when it had first appeared out of the wormhole, hence why it had been found. But whatever the reason for the brief radar appearance, it had seemingly now rectified itself. Perhaps the entry into this atmosphere had caused a temporary fault to occur in the object's wiring, if indeed, it had any kind of wiring.

The professor called out to a colleague. "Benson, have there been any changes since the last test?"

"No sir. Not at all." Benson sniffed, pushed his glasses back up his fat nose and shifted his short body uneasily. "We've been running tests for four hours. I don't think we're going to have any success."

"I agree. What about the bodies?" They both turned to face the other lab. The small team in there were busying themselves with the burnt carcasses.

"They've had *some* success. More than us. It's all very frustrating." With that, Benson waddled back to his work. Quilter stepped closer to the thick glass.

"I won't let you beat me", he whispered.

***

All that coffee to keep him awake over the last working day had also prevented Quilter from having a successful night's sleep. Having only had only two hours' worth, he was eager to examine the coffin yet again, but now from a different angle. It could have been the caffeine that was still in his system, or maybe it was adrenaline tinged with frustration, but he was determined not to let the damned thing get the better of him. Last night was strange. In his short sleep, Quilter thought that it was calling to him. This thing was taking over every thought, waking or otherwise.

He was walking to the lab that contained the bodies when Brook met him in the corridor. Brook was in charge of the alien inspection team, and the red rings around his eyes proved it.

"Professor Quilter, just the man. These things… they're most definitely dead, with no signs of any activity, cellular or otherwise. The tests show them to be hundreds of years old."

"Are they the same species?"

124

"They appear to be. One has fallen apart, but the other one had a stronger shell, as well as longer appendages. It looks to be the more mature of the two. We're lucky that they're dead. They're not Komadeen, but they're just as ugly. Not something to be met down a dark alley, or anywhere else, to be honest. I say that despite my professional interest. Oh, the reports have been sent to your computer."

"Thank you, Brook."

They both headed back the way they came, Brook to continue his examination of the bodies and Quilter to read the report. When that was done, he could crack on with the coffin. *The coffin.* Whatever was in there would be a prize worth examining, that's for sure.

He keyed in his computer's security code and touched an onscreen menu. The report from Professor Benson and his team appeared, and as he read it, he sank into his leather chair. The very same chair that he had often slept in when he was too tired to make it to his quarters, a block away. He wasn't presently tired, though. Maybe soon, when the lack of sleep would finally catch up with him. For now, he was buzzing. The prospects of solving the mystery of the coffin had given him an objective for today. High hopes indeed, but he was ever the optimist.

"Fascinating… tough malleable shells… but what were you doing? What *are* you?" He digested the information and spun in the chair to face the lab where the remains were. Then he moved slightly as if to face the alien capsule. "We'll get to the bottom of…"

He stood up, only to have to steady himself on the edge of the desk. There was a slight feeling of disorientation, and his office blurred around him. He gave himself a moment, allowing the feeling to pass. Everyone was too busy to notice him, which was just as well, as he didn't want anyone fussing over his lack of sleep, or his reliance on coffee. Especially Benson. He meant well, but he was in no position to offer health tips. Whatever had caused this swiftly passed, and he made an empty promise to himself to get checked out later. As he left the small office, he couldn't remember what he was just thinking of. Normally, this would worry him, but the thought quickly passed. He had a job to do…

At the outer door to the lab, Quilter punched in a code. He seemed oblivious to the questions directed at him by his colleagues in white coats. He moved to the area where the decontamination suits were stored, and carried on to the next door. Tapping his code into another security pad, he heard his name shouted as he went through the door without wearing a yellow suit. An alarm blared, and he paid no notice to the panic that he was causing around him. Technicians stopped in bewilderment as a red glow was thrown onto their work area. People ran as protocols were instigated, and the scientist in the lab with him ran to the door.

"Professor! What are you *doing?*" But there was no answer. The yellow suit exited the laboratory, and proceeded to watch with the others as Professor Quilter had apparently lost all good sense.

He stood before the coffin, totally helpless against the force that compelled him to disregard all safety procedures. Somewhere in his mind he was aware of what he was doing, but he was powerless to stop himself.

"Obey…" he said to himself, and he placed his right hand on the symbol on the upright pod, secured upright in an anti-gravity stand. He took a step back as a lid opened, the crack and hiss of the movement forcing off the burnt debris around the edge. The lid opened swiftly to the left on several hidden hinges, as Quilter's use of the word *coffin* now appeared to be validated. The body of a man lay inside, his arms crossed. There was a gasp as everyone outside the lab watched. There was another as the man came alive, his skin still pallid under the reddish glow of the lights.

It was now that some sense of control was returning to Quilter, as he stepped back at what was before him. The man in the black outfit was laughing at him, his arms now free from his chest, fingers flexing. No one entered the lab to help him, as the doors had been locked and sealed. *No one wanted to.*

"What the hell?" Quilter said, as the man, still laughing, looked down at him. Blue eyes glinted with mischief as the figure suddenly stopped and fixed him a stare. As Quilter looked on, transfixed, the face of the man – his pure black goatee, his swept-back hair – dissolved away. In his place were a few steps leading to darkness. The scientist walked in, overtaken by sheer curiosity, a vestige of obedience, or both.

As he stepped down, gravity seemed out of kilter. And yet, he wasn't falling. Lights came on, and he saw that the few short steps had led to a long walkway. Not only that, but before him was a large room, humming with the sound of subdued power. Quilter was astonished: at the black walls with pale circular indentations, at the hexagonal console at the centre of the room, and at the overriding fact that this place was *inside* a coffin! His breath was well and truly taken away. Bigger on the inside! He looked back whence he came, at the steps leading to the outside. *Those first few steps… the inside re-aligning itself to compensate for the fact that the casket was upright – ingenious!* The weird sensation he had experienced on entry had an explanation. He continued to marvel at what was around him, and as he slowly stepped onto the main floor near what must be the control centre, he halted. The place was the size of a cathedral, and then some. Columns of white marble were snaked by cables and ducting that went to the ceiling, wherever it was. Peculiar antique furniture was scattered about the place, and the vastness couldn't be determined because of the lack of light. Glass cabinets held large samples of precious stones, and a workbench was adorned with various tools, all of which looked unfamiliar. The whole place was a mix of very old and very new, but yet it seemed to match. Beside the dead console, with its tall, central glass column and the many surrounding switches, lights and buttons, was a large gold box. Next to that was another coffin. This one was horizontal, but apart from being in pristine condition, it was identical to the exterior of this vast room; black and shiny, and no doubt occupied.

***

Outside in the lab, there was panic. Technicians and assistants were being escorted from the complex. One of the witnesses to Quilter's entry into the coffin was sobbing because no one could do anything. The penalty for attempted entry *into* a lab during an alarm was severe. Not that anyone could gain access, but these rules had to be enforced. Containment was the word, and it was a much better word than *death,* especially if you didn't obey the rules.

The woman, Doctor Tobin, had to be prised away from the area. "Ian! Iaaaaan! *He went inside the pod!*" she screamed, before she was sedated. As she was carried out, Captain Kellen came running in.

"What the devil's going on? Somebody mentioned a ghost! And Quilter... went *inside the thing?*" The two soldiers that had remained behind earlier hurried up to Kellen, fresh from ensuring the labs were empty.

"Walked right into the damn thing, sir," said Turner.

"It's true, sir," added Tate. "In a trance. Everyone saw it happen." Kellen looked at his men, sure that they did their best, and wished that he had left more soldiers here.

"Everyone's out?" asked Kellen, double-checking that the evacuation procedures had been adhered to.

"Sir," said Tate, as Turner nodded in agreement.

"Tate, stay on the doors with the others. Turner and I are going to break in!" Turner gave the Captain a look.

"It's alright, son – we won't get shot, as we're exempt from those rules! *Now go, Tate! Hop to it, lad!*"

As Private Tate ran outside, the thought of breaking into the lab tickled Turner. A chance to let off some steam.

***

During the commotion, a nearby room was producing a surprise, but this was nastier than a vanishing professor. Across the corridor from the coffin, one of the creatures, burnt beyond belief, was repairing itself at a cellular level. Fire-damaged DNA was undergoing a resurrection that would see it reborn like an alien phoenix rising from a near-ash state. Its mate was dead and had crumbled away with no hope of a new life, and this would add to its anger. In a short space of time, UNIT would encounter another threat. One that was not only angry, but in pain from an accelerated rebirth. And ready to strike...

***

Quilter couldn't hear any of the outside noise. He knew by now that he must be in a vessel, but he had no idea what type. One thing he *did* know was that he had come across the scientific discovery of the century. He'd have to make his way back up the steps and out into the world soon, just to let his colleagues know that he was okay. Now though, he had to see what was in *this* coffin.

He took a deep breath, knelt, and gingerly placed his right hand on the symbols that adorned the alien sarcophagus. He now knew what to do, but not what to expect. What or who would he find inside?

As the familiar, but smoother, movement of the lid took place, he found himself looking at the face of a different man. Unlike before, this one was real flesh and blood, and was taller. Older looking, but with thinning blonde hair, a short greying beard and... *cold blue eyes!* Yes, Quilter found himself like a rabbit in headlights as the eyes bore into him. Unable to turn away, he heard a well-spoken voice seep into his mind, his will once again under someone else's control.

"I am the Master... and you will obey me!"

***

The UNIT pulse rifles were effective weapons, but the glass was still holding. Firing at the glass door for over a minute was doing no damage whatsoever. Even aiming at the same point was just proving how well-designed the structure was.

"Exactly how many people *have* broken through these, Captain?" enquired Turner, after Kellen gave the signal to cease firing.

"None. The punishment regarding breaking it only really refers to the old-style glass, which we've improved upon. But we don't mention that. It keeps people in check."

Turner smiled.

"I won't say a word."

Before they could raise their rifles to fire again, several loud bangs came from behind them. As they turned, the revived alien threw itself against a window and stuck there, its long limbs smashing the walls with all its might. The screeching adding to the terror.

Turner went white, and Kellen shouted an order.

"TURNER – RESUME FIRE! OUR MAN'S IN THERE!" The creature was also attempting to break through. Four long tentacles were thumping against one spot, whilst its body was now twice the original size. It looked like a scaly bean bag, with movement underneath the surface resembling the shifting of beans, except this thing was full of bile and hate. There was no discernible face, but a protuberance shot out and revealed a hissing mouth full of razor-sharp teeth, before withdrawing back into the moving mass.

Turner stopped firing and cast a horrified look at the ruckus in the lab behind him. Kellen screamed an order to focus, and the attack on the glass resumed. Small cracks *did* start to appear, but not in the window *they* were attacking…

***

"You call yourself the Master? What of?" asked Quilter of the man in the coffin.

"Everyone I meet," chuckled the man, before coughing. He was evidently weak and in a bad way.

"That's quite… egotistical," Quilter replied.

"It has been said."

Quilter's initial fear had dissipated somewhat, although there was an underlying sense of unease… of menace. The hypnosis made him obey, but he would still have helped. The professor wasn't one to turn his back on anyone. He tried to laugh at the Master's reply.

The Master coughed again, interrupting the feeble noise that came from Quilter's throat.

"You say this is Earth, Professor? Of all the places…!"

"You don't appear to be the best pilot, what with being in a coffin, and all. This… *ship*," said Quilter, looking around, "this ship looks in need of attention."

129

The interior wasn't in a bad way, but there was an aura of need about it. The Master knew what he meant, as Quilter continued.

"Which leads to the all-important question – why a coffin? In both instances."

"I have a flair for the theatrical, as you saw from the old telepathic projection. Apologies. The interactive image of me was generated by the TARDIS telepathic circuits. Sometimes it's enough to scare most people off."

There was another cough, longer this time. Quilter's mind was racing with questions – this man had changed his appearance, but how? What was a TARDIS? Why had he crashed to Earth? What was the connection to the things in the lab? *The things in the lab!*

"There were two creatures wrapped around the coffin," he said, sure that they should be mentioned. At this, the Master's expression changed. He attempted to sit up and did so with Quilter's help.

"The Zimoxi. Still alive?"

"Both dead, but only one is intact. Although, it's nearly been burnt to nothing."

"That doesn't guarantee death. Help me out of this."

Quilter did so, and the lights dimmed briefly. Somewhere deep within the ship, a bell tolled.

"I'm going to hazard a guess and say they're not friendly," Quilter said, trying humour in a nervous situation.

"My dear fellow, you have nothing to fear from me, so long as you obey my commands. Which you will. *Those* things, however, are of a different breed, and very *unfriendly*."

Quilter supported the Master, but quickly released him out of shock. The Master's hands and face had started to brighten.

He fell to the floor, as his body glowed a bright yellow-orange, before being consumed by a brilliant glare.

***

Outside, there was a flurry of activity between two groups of uniforms. The dark green of the UNIT troops had been joined by the dark brown of the Americans, of which there were only a few. A last-minute mission had detained the others. The white and yellow-garbed scientists had been driven to safety, and ten men were now running toward Kellen. What they saw upon turning a corner in the corridor froze them in their tracks.

At the end of the corridor stood two soldiers, both firing to their left. There was nothing unexpected about that. But opposite, and through the glass windows on the right, they saw a terrifying creature the size of a car. Four long appendages were trying their best to destroy the wall, but had so far only produced a foot-long crack. The beast could be heard squealing over the sound of the gunfire. The insides of the lab had been obliterated, and the red lights were contributing to its foul mood. Those, and the accompanying sounds, made it look like a monster on a ghost train ride. But this horror was most definitely real.

Kellen and Turner stopped firing as the men reached them. The captain saw that with the returning Tate were Briggs, Hollander, and seven Americans. *About damn time* thought Kellen, and was pleased to see their pulse rifles at the ready.

The American in charge, Sergeant Dalton, gave an order to fire at the previous target. With this much firepower, entry would soon be achieved, unless they were stopped in their tracks by the Zimoxi. As it had just reached full-size, it was more than a match for the weakened glass, and the lengthening crack suddenly gave way. With a howl of victory, it shattered the whole of the wall.

Orders were barked in the chaos, and six men turned and began an attack on the brute. Dalton got off a few rounds before he lost his footing on the floor due to all the broken glass. He fell, badly cutting his left arm. Before he could fire again, a thick limb snaked through the air and wrapped itself around his legs. Picking him up in the confined space, it viciously swiped him about, knocking over several of his comrades. Five men fell and never got up.

It was then that the glass finally succumbed to the pulse rifles. With a crash, the lab wall was breached and the soldiers hurried through. It then hit Kellen that the coffin lid was closed. With the creature very nearly upon them, death seemed inevitable.

***

Inside the TARDIS, the Master was face-down on the floor. Seconds before, he had been screaming, but now he was completely still. Quilter was frightened by what had just happened, but hearing his name he steadied his nerve to kneel beside the prostrate figure.

"Don't worry, Professor Quilter. This happens…" The voice was different. It sounded younger, not as deep, and quite smooth. They both stood. Quilter then gasped, taking a step back.

The Master had changed.

"Regeneration. But I feel *different*. More so than I have previously. Maybe it has something to do with a faulty TARDIS. I was dying before, but the Zero Casket didn't do much for me. All very intriguing…"

The Master was now a leaner man with dark brown hair, and had the look of someone in his 40s. He was slightly grey at the temples, with a distinctive thin nose and brown eyes. Completely different.

"I can see that this is rather a lot to take in…"

"You can say that again!" exclaimed Quilter, stepping forward to study his features. The Master was amused.

"Most of the time it's pot luck. Time Lord lottery. If we're dying, we regenerate."

"Time Lord? Regeneration… You're right, this *is* a lot. You mean to say that you can change your whole body? Remarkable! And… a *Zero Casket*? That's what it is? *What is that?*"

The Master ran a hand over his own face as he talked, getting used to the new contours.

"I came here in a state of near-death. Kept alive in a faulty casket. Like the rest of the ship, which is missing some of the interior, one part of which is an actual Zero *Room*." He reached into a pocket and pulled out his laser screwdriver. A quick scan provided him with an answer. "Yes, as I thought. And I couldn't use this inside the casket, before you ask. Being inside also enhanced my telepathic abilities, which is why I had you break into the lab. But I must have latched onto you when I was asleep, as I can't recall any conscious decision to do so."

The Master pocketed the device, and carried on talking. He began to pace, and as he did the sound of a bell resounded again.

"Oh, this can't be good…" said the Master. Quilter had by now forgotten the sense of unease that had earlier hung over him. A lot had happened. But this new Master gave off a totally different feeling. His thoughts were punctuated by another scream.

The Master's fists were clenched and his face was morphing again. Through gritted teeth he said "*Unstable.*" This time though, there was no lightshow. Instead of energy erupting from within, his features rapidly changed in a soft haze. It was if an old film was being played where the lead character was being replaced. He'd stopped screaming, but he had managed to stagger to the TARDIS console and held on.

As Quilter looked on helpless, the Master's appearance transformed – from his young self to a swarthy man with a beard, then to a bald man. Then *another* Master with a beard – the same as the projection from earlier – and there was even a woman. Then stabilisation resumed as the new, younger face looked back at him once more.

"Like I said…not good," he whispered, before collapsing for a second time.

**

It was mayhem in the laboratory. Twenty feet from where the door once stood, a small group of men were fighting for their lives; surrounded by broken bodies, shattered glass, and splattered blood, and with ammunition quickly running out. Shouts and screams pervaded the air, and four scaly alien limbs thrashed wildly.

All the guns were now trained on one part of the Zimoxi, an area that now resembled an eye. At first it looked to be the creature's one weak spot, until the eye disappeared into the body and re-emerged protected by a hard, translucent eyelid. The dark-red football-sized organ that had suddenly grown on the top of the body now reassessed its enemies.

There was good news, though. Full-sized, but not fully-developed, the organism started to feel the force of the weapons. Its shell, tough as it was, was beginning to crack. One or two scale-like covers now fell amongst the glass fragments.

The men were backed into a corner. Privates Turner and Tate tried to draw the creature away as Kellen placed a hand on the casket's symbols. The lid didn't open. Cursing, Kellen tried again, but was knocked off his feet by a tentacle. So too was Tate, then Turner, and both their fates were abruptly sealed. Kellen would mourn them later. Now he was angry, like the Zimoxi.

Another limb smashed the Master's TARDIS off its stand, and it fell onto its back. With the last of his pulse rifle blasts, Kellen swore at the creature. As he did, the lid opened, and Quilter emerged with the Master. Kellen noticed that the stranger was holding what he presumed to be a weapon of some kind. The Master stumbled, but he continued walking.

Kellen watched in amazement as the object in the man in black's right hand glowed brightly and the power intensified. With the man now in the firing line, Kellen ordered his soldiers to stand down.

The Master's hands shook, and he directed the weapon, now at full power, towards the Zimoxi. The creature stopped its movements, its limbs frozen in the air. The eye blinked with the colour of rage, and a shrill scream filled the building.

As they all looked on, the Zimoxi diminished in size. In no time at all it had gone from a rampaging monstrosity to a motionless toy-like figure on the floor. Dead.

"Tissue Compression Eliminator," said the Master as he put the black torch-like weapon away. "Trust me when I say that it's the best way to stop a Zimoxi. If you have the opportunity, that is."

"So that's what it is," muttered Kellen, walking over to the lifeless body. He raised a leg and brought a boot down onto the alien, at last causing damage. "That's for my men."

Everyone caught their breath. Kellen was grateful for this man's help. Whoever he was, he had emerged just in the nick of time. Quilter then received a glare from Kellen. "No need for guards, eh?"

***

The place was a complete mess. It would take a while before a rebuild could take place, strengthened glass included. The bodies had been stretchered away, and Doctor Karlsson had finally arrived from Sweden. After the shock had subsided, he was briefed on events, and had joined Quilter and the Master in the infirmary. The Time Lord was being assessed, and was very weak and feverish.

"The UNIT uniform," he enquired, as he felt his two hearts beating furiously.

"Ah, it's old. The men have had it for about… oh, twenty years now," said Karlsson.

"I haven't seen this variation before. I've neglected to ask what year this is," said the Master, looking at himself in a hand-held mirror, his hands still shaking.

"Year? Why, it's 1996," said the Swede. The Master put the mirror down and gave a puzzled look.

"Where's the Doctor?"

"Are you quite alright, old chap? You're—"

"*The* Doctor. Your scientific advisor." The name had caught Karlsson's attention. The old man sat down on the bed next to him.

"You knew the Doctor?" asked Karlsson, with a look of surprise.

"*Knew?*" intoned the Master. "He's… *dead?*"

Karlsson nodded. "He gave his life saving us. The Komadeen… he beat them, but at a cost. We've kept a lid on his loss since then. It does morale good if folk think he's still around. Plus it could deter any invasion."

"And his TARDIS? Dead too, I presume?"

"We don't know. When he died, the Doctor's TARDIS dematerialised, never to be seen again."

Quilter listened with interest. Karlsson was privileged to have knowledge of the Doctor, and would be sure to tell Quilter and Kellen what he knew when

134

he had the chance, off the record. A recommendation for clearance to the information would be filed for him and for Kellen, in light of recent events, even if they were already fully qualified to hear it now. After all, rules are rules, especially for UNIT.

"I pitted wits against him. He was greatly respected," the Master reflected. "It finally makes sense. I knew the Doctor, but not *your* Doctor." He stopped shaking. "I've crossed realities. Something I've done before, but under better circumstances. From my universe to this one! The TARDIS and I caught a plague after passing through a quasar. She malfunctioned, and the spatial infection caused her engine to create a vortex incursion. That would explain the recent activity – something that'll be rectified when she's back to full power. The infection was – *is* – killing me. I can feel my insides burning. And regenerating in this universe has compounded things. I feel ill... and *strange*. By that I mean... *nice*. Normally, I would describe that as sickening."

The two scientists exchanged puzzled looks. This universe had obviously never had a Master. Quilter wished he could fully understand what the Master's jargon meant, but he grasped the basics. He was in trouble. A point proven when his regenerations once again started to randomly take hold.

***

Quilter and Kellen supported the Master as Karlsson shook his hand. They were in a makeshift lab on the other side of the building.

"I'm sorry to see you go."

"Dying forces this on me. Staying would also mean my demise, and I have no regenerations left. I do have the one task that needs accomplishing that will ensure my survival, but it isn't without its risks. However, I wish that I could remain. Being this universe's saviour appeals, but that would mean filling some big shoes. It would, in part, be an atonement for all my sins." He laughed weakly. "Perhaps dropping the name 'Master' would have been a step too far. Although Doctor Magister has a nice ironic ring, don't you think? The name was lost on them, but they all smiled regardless.

"Are you ready?" Quilter asked.

"I am."

Karlsson nodded to the Time Lord. The three men entered the TARDIS, again hanging on the anti-gravity stand.

Quilter was trying to lift his share of the Master's weight, but the stronger Kellen was doing most of the work. As they came onto the walkway, the few short steps were accompanied by the strange feeling of dimensional adjustment.

Lights revealed the glory, although not all, of the wonder that was the TARDIS interior. They stopped, and Kellen swore in astonishment at the large console room. Karlsson was momentarily dumbstruck, despite having heard of transcendental dimensions.

It was bigger than a room needed to be, but that was Time Lords for you. Show-offs. Of course, not all Time Lord incarnations were braggarts, and the Master had indeed used smaller rooms in the past, but this one was as grandiose as they came.

Because the ship wasn't at full power, and because the room was so big, the light didn't penetrate every corner. Even so, there was plenty to admire. Boarding the TARDIS for the second time afforded Quilter to notice steel beams around the edge of the room, dark wooden panelling on one far wall, and framed paintings of alien landscapes in the semi-darkness. When the Master's health improved, so too would his TARDIS. The Doctor wasn't the only Time Lord with a symbiotic connection to his ship.

Ahead, the casket was ready for the Master once more.

"It's in there. As soon as you've unlocked it, you go." He was weakening by the minute.

Quilter took a key from the Master, placing it into an ornate lock. A mechanism clicked, and the lid unlocked. He took a large glass jar out of the gold box, in which nothing but liquid was visible. Kellen placed it next to the Master, and smiled.

"Think of it as a necessity," said the Master. "Goodbye."

The outer door of the ship – the lid – secured itself with a deadlock as they exited the craft. They were now free of the hypnotic commands that the Master had planted in the last minutes before entering the TARDIS. It was an essential safeguard, as Quilter, Kellen, and Karlsson wouldn't be receptive to what he had planned.

As they watched, the TARDIS dematerialised, groaning away into the ether.

***

Inside the casket, the Master spoke, but not to himself.

"The only way to cure myself is to have you within me. You'll cleanse me of the infection, and change this new incarnation, but you'll also imbue me with a new life-force. I'll live on, but I'll soon need a *new* body…"

Whatever was in the stasis jar could hear, and it knew its task. There would be a merging, a stabilisation… a continuation.

Stealing the creature that was in the jar was an incredibly risky move, especially as it was a newborn hybrid queen of two very unpredictable, regenerative species. The Zimoxi were dying, despite their resilience, and had produced a new lifeform. The original Deathworm Morphant had been ingested by the female Zimoxi, and then rebirthed. The Master had stolen it away in an attempt to prolong his existence, experimenting on lesser beings first, of course. But he never got that chance. He was immediately given chase, trying to shake off the Zimoxi by passing through a quasar, which created new problems.

The new offspring was obviously smaller than its secondary female parent, but no less dangerous. Both the queen's DNA and the Deathworm's psychic abilities had been enhanced, to deadly effect. A new creature was born, its destiny different from the norm, although one still full of dark purpose

The Master removed the lid, and moved the jar over his prone body. The watery form that was the Deathworm Morphant slid out of the glass and down the Master's gagging throat, its serpentine tail wriggling as it went.

As the jar smashed onto the floor, the Master convulsed, before his body settled. Then he opened his yellow eyes as an evil laugh took him over.

The console room lit up fully, and the time rotor started to move.

Skaro, and fate, beckoned.

Plaything
Tim Gambrell

Falling, yet not falling.

Travelling, without a sense of control.

Existing here…
    …there…
…and also…
…in all points…

at once.

The vestiges of Bruce, the human whom the Master had absorbed when he appropriated his current body, planted an image in his mind of a crumb and a vacuum cleaner. He scoffed internally; limited human perception – he had not been *hoovered* up. Yes, once over the threshold the TARDIS' link to the Eye of Harmony had indeed sucked him in, but now he was in limbo. His full-length Time Lord gown rested still and grandiosely around him; only the howling in his ears and the confusion before his eyes revealed the fact that he was not stationary. The singularity conduit that linked the Doctor's TARDIS with the actual Eye of Harmony could do a variety of things with him. It may hold him indefinitely, it may carry him to the black hole, or it may spit him out into the time vortex, like an indigestible pip. Whatever happened, prominent in his thinking was the knowledge that he had to settle himself into a trance-like state or risk being driven mad by the maelstrom surrounding him; he had to reach a psychic null point, where he could split his consciousness so that he could maintain his bodily equilibrium whilst simultaneously extending mental feelers to seek help, should anyone be travelling in his vicinity. It was the only chance for him to secure survival beyond a reliance on random chance.

The Master's snarling, demonic face gradually eased into the sardonic laughter of a total maniac. The game was afoot again, a new chapter had been opened, and he would relish the challenge.

He closed his eyes and attempted the meditative refrain, taught to him eons ago now. The pressure was building in his head, and he was aware that time was short…

WHUMPH!

The singularity conduit had ejected him into the time vortex. It was an environment he was familiar with, having traversed it for much of his lives thus far, although he was usually protected from its violence within a TARDIS. Without that, entering the vortex was like being smacked by a tennis racquet on all sides and at all points at once, physically and mentally. The Master flailed and hurtled over and over. His stolen human body too weak to cope with the stresses. It screamed, and he screamed inside it. The flesh peeled away from its feeble skeleton, layer by layer as the time winds flayed him mercilessly. For a fleeting moment all that remained was a shimmering snake, its eyes the epitome of scorn and hatred, then slowly, as the serpentine mouth lisped its way around the mantra, the body reconfigured itself into the taut, muscular features and square jaw line of the sneering Los Angeles paramedic.

He was now naked – any control he could exert over the flesh wouldn't extend to ephemeral fabrics such as clothing. This annoyed him, he'd grown fond of that gown. But such fripperies could be replaced. He tucked himself into a foetal ball and reached out mentally for anyone or anything nearby that could assist him.

An eternity passed in mere fleeting moments.

His breathing steadied. Awareness bled in from his surroundings; he was side-on against a cold, hard surface, still rolled up in a ball. He was somewhere, at least, although his centre of gravity was unclear. Slowly he opened his eyes; his fulsome lips parted stickily and he took a deep shuddering breath.

"For goodness sake put some clothes on, man."

The disciplinarian voice came from nearby, but before he could orientate himself and ascertain anything specific he found himself flattened, smothered under a pile of heavy cloth. He scowled. Try to make a fool of him, would they? No. Not this Master. He lay still a moment before throwing the material to one side and springing to his feet, poised like a cat (now those were fun times!)

A humanoid female was staring at him from a short distance away. She wore a pin-stripe suit and a wry smile. She gestured to the floor with a flick of her eyes, and the Master looked down at the pile of cloth from under which he'd emerged; it was his Time Lord gown.

"I took it from your memory. Seems you rather regretted losing it; the fact was preying heavily on your unconscious thoughts. Vain?"

140

With animalistic fervour, he swept up the gown and wrapped himself in it. When he swished open the front again he noticed that underneath he was once again fully dressed in his regalia. He smiled, flexed and postured. Yes, there was still a lot of pussy cat in the mix, despite his serpentine tendencies. The female spoke again, interrupting his musings.

"I have just rescued you from limbo, and a life little better than undeath. I was expecting a modicum of gratitude, instead I appear to have re-energised a posturing peacock."

The Master stopped and smiled at her. "I'm sorry," his adoptive North Atlantic drawl emerged as a husky whisper. "Thank you," he noted her business suit, "whoever you are."

"I am an Eternal, Time Lord. I have no name. You know of our kind, I'm sure?"

He nodded, careful not to display any shock at her knowing his species. "I do. You are psychic leeches, dullards lacking imagination, trawling the timelines for diversions; forever bored, forever complaining."

"Unless we appropriate an ephemeral to keep us amused, to give us purpose."

"Like I said, psychic leeches."

"So, what have you got for me, *peacock*?"

"I am the Master."

"I know. I have read your immediate subconscious, you very naughty man, you. It was thrilling, if brief."

"I will not be used."

The female laughed. "We will see who gets bored first."

The Master pulled out his shades and smiled.

***

The Master opened his serpentine eyes. His right arm was cramping, crooked under his chin as he lay back on the *chaise longue* with a silk shift artfully draped across his torso. The Eternal stood at her easel a short distance away.

"Don't move!" she barked.

The Master smiled at his own impropriety. "How did I get like this?"

"Darling, you fell asleep. I decided to paint you to pass the time."

"Stripped and fashioned in this way?"

"In all your pre-Raphaelite glory. You're a bit too tanned for the period, though, so I'm giving you a porcelain complexion and heroic curls."

He couldn't help it – the Master burst into laughter, which ended abruptly as the *chaise longue* disappeared from beneath him, and he clattered to the floor – or what passed for a floor in the void. He was fully clothed again, and alone. Ignoring his aching behind, he stood and looked around.

"Hey," he called, "You still here?"

There was a sulky pause.

"Always," came the eventual reply – seemingly from everywhere at once.

"Where?" he said, gazing around him in an attempt to locate the voice.

"Everywhere. All around you."

The Master rolled his eyes and grinned slyly. "How… disconcerting."

"You require a physical focal point?"

"No."

"A body against which to aim your callousness and snarky venom?"

"I am beyond such two-dimensional needs."

"Good. Let me in."

"No."

"I wish to inhabit you."

"I *said* no."

"I will wait. Your guard will drop. And I will strike."

"Try me."

"This, THIS is living!" The Eternal laughed jubilantly.

"*This?*" he spat, "this isn't living. It's a discussion around a contrary viewpoint. Will you tell me when my five minutes is up?"

"I do not understand."

The Master frowned briefly. "Oblique human cultural reference, inherited from Bruce," he said, chiding himself. "I need to watch out for such nonsense bleeding in to my psyche."

***

The Master skulked like a caged animal. He was not physically restricted in his void environment, but he had mapped out a zone within which he would alternately prowl and sit. *So I won't get lost within myself*, he told himself.

"I hear you." The sweet, dismembered voice of the Eternal possessed the very air around him.

"Get lost – ha!"

"I will. Within your mind."

"You won't."

"I will,' the playfulness dribbled into his ear like treacle, making him shiver. He paused in his prowling.

"Quit it."

"Never."

"You will exhaust me and then I will be garbage, of no further use to you. The longer I can withstand you, the longer I continue to live." He was aware of molecular excitation around his face, like a faint breeze – enough to brush his nasal hairs.

'The aura surrounding you is quite fascinating," the Eternal said. "So angry, so confident, so... wicked. It promises much to entertain me within."

The Master sat himself down, lotus-like, in perfect meditative state. "Try."

There was a pause. Nothing happened.

The dismembered, sing-song voice took on an edge. "Knock knock. Nobody home?"

There was another pause, then a sharp electric shock arced through the seated Master, forcing his limbs to extend with a sudden ferocity and causing his back to arch. He screamed in agony, then lay, slightly smoking and breathing heavily.

"Oops." There was the slightest guilty giggle. "Too much? Difficult to judge I'm afraid. Only I do so hate bad manners."

The Master waited for his cramped leg muscles to stop spasming. Then, without comment, he very calmly began to pace once again.

"Careful. Every third step will be electrified."

The Master began to skip instead. The atmosphere around him seemed to smile.

"You're funny. But you see, every which way I win."

"La la la..." His tuneless non-singing was terrible.

***

Later.

"Open up to me," she said. He smiled, remaining calm. "Pleeeeease?"

"I am not your toy."

"I will turn the screw again."

"Turn it. I will give you nothing."

She snapped. "Your life is nothing to me. You understand? NOTHING!"

"Then kill me."

Nothing happened, once again, for some time and yet no time.

***

143

The crowd roared as the Master, stripped naked to the waist, reached out a hand and gripped the throat of his quivering opponent. He squeezed tightly, causing more blood to drip from his scuffed knuckles; the crowd sighed in awe. His opponent's eye's bulged, his pathetic dribbling mouth forming voiceless shapes as his foppish, bobbed hair clung to his clammy, glistening forehead. With a crack the neck broke and the Master hurled the lifeless body from him, spinning round immediately to face the next comer, should there be one.

The rabid howling of the audience abruptly cut off, replaced by the Eternal's hollow laughter. The Master relaxed and took a bow.

"I'm glad you're enjoying yourself," he called. "I'm having a great time, too, personally. Any more weeds and deadwood you wanna throw at me?"

"You've hurt yourself," said the dismembered voice. The Master frowned as he looked at his knuckles, then shook off the excess blood and wrapped his fist in the damp towel next to the spit bucket that appeared at his feet.

"The Ogron was a tough contender. This human body is in fine form, but that mindless ape took it to its extreme. I'm lucky, I guess, that you sent me that wall flower to follow up. Neck so brittle he was barely worth the effort."

"That was you."

"What?" The Master frowned, his snake eyes flashing. It sounded to him like the Eternal was smiling.

"That. Was. You. That... *wall flower*, as you poetically put it."

"Explain."

"You didn't recognise him?"

There was now a green porcelain bathroom suite and a sandalwood wardrobe next to him – not that the Master was fussed by such things in any way. He splashed his face with cold water and towelled down his sweaty torso. He was not surprised to find his baroque clothing within the wardrobe; he dressed himself while he considered the Eternal's words.

"Consul Luvic," he said after a while, trying to make it look like he hadn't wasted too much energy searching for the name. "From Traken."

"And what happened on Traken?"

"Oh please, enough of this TEDIUM!"

"Careful, there's a crack developing in your veneer."

The Master beetled his brows. "Get to the point."

"But then *veneer* is pretty much all there is to you, these days, isn't it?"

"Games. Just games."

"Of course. Amusement to make my existence worth suffering. You know that, my special little man."

144

"Fine. Alternative time lines. As an Eternal you exist outside of time, outside of A to B causality, am I right?"

"Very good, yes."

"So you plucked Consul Luvic from an alternate time line."

The voice trilled a giddy giggle. "Tremas became Keeper, and in your decaying state you bonded with Luvic instead as the most suitable male alternative."

"A foppish weed? I must have been desperate."

"Time was, indeed, short, yes. He had a surprisingly keen mind. You found that you were stuck; little more than a sub-persona floundering against the flitting distractions and deep-seated eccentricities of an unfocussed yet brilliant mind. You could do little with him or his body. Certainly he would be no match for the Doctor – in any of his possible incarnations. How embarrassing for you."

"At least it wasn't the child, Nyssa."

"I brought your unpossessed possession here to put him – and you – out of your mutual miseries."

"Life was wasted on him."

"Would you like to see the alternate timeline where you became Consul Katura instead? What a bitch – although there was little life left in those crusty old bones. You had a very fetching clutch-bag to carry your tissue compression eliminator in. Would have gone rather nicely with what you're wearing now, actually."

The Master, as always, ignored her attempts to get a rise out of him by wafting a hand and changing the subject.

"What I don't understand is, if you have access to all times and all possibilities, how the hell do you lot get so *bored?*"

"Because it is an effort. And after what to you would be an eternity, the effort gets draining; the end never seems to justify the means anymore – unless it is done to taunt or provoke a lesser individual. Only then does the entertainment quotient ramp up sufficiently to make it seem worthwhile."

"Ha! So, what it comes down to is: you're lazy." The Master threw back his head and laughed.

"Live for an eternity yourself, and then judge me," came the starchy reply.

The Master wiped a tear from his eye and sighed. "Sometimes it feels like I already have." He lay down on the void floor.

This time the voice became a sly whisper in his ear. It gave him goose bumps. "Psst. They were all you."

His eyes flicked to either side but he was still physically alone. "All of them that I fought?"

"In your assumed vernacular – uh huh."

"Even the thin bald guy?"

"Even the Ogron. Without the ability to fully regenerate, as your co-opted bodies have decayed, sometimes you've had to make desperate choices to stay alive. Gnuh, I believe her name was. She was one such choice. Quite a looker for her species, I'm told."

There was the briefest of pauses as he licked his teeth. "Fantasy."

"Shame she already smelled like a corpse to begin with, eh?"

The Master growled, despite himself.

"You're weakening."

"No. Self-control. I have ultimate self-control. Your attempts to enrage me are pathetic."

"You're very good, you know?"

"I know."

"One of my best."

"*The* best, I'm sure."

"I could almost admire you, except…"

"Except…?"

"…I think I love you."

***

Silence fell like a brick wall around them. Suddenly the immensity of the void felt like the tiniest of spaces, the most intimate of rooms; nowhere to turn, nowhere to go to escape. It had been said. It could never be *un*said. Now, more than at any other point, the Master was afraid.

"Did you–?"

"Yes," he snapped, then softened. "I heard you."

"What do you say?"

"What can I say? You have to let me go."

"I can't. I am nothing without you now."

"I know. But that's not my fault."

"If you leave, it'll destroy me."

'If I stay, it'll destroy *me* – eventually."

"Catch 22."

"Yeah."

"And I love you."

146

"I know."

"Love me back."

"I can't."

The Eternal's voice, when she finally spoke, was little more than a cracked whisper. "I know."

***

The velvet *chaise longue* had returned. The Master's portrait hung above it. He was reclined, attended to by a single slave girl, dressed according to his desires. She dangled a bunch of grapes tentatively above his mouth; he extended his tongue teasingly, guiding the bottom grape to where his glistening lips could pluck at it. With a *ping* it left the bunch, which jiggled and bounced in the slave girl's grip. The Master smiled at her and she giggled playfully, licking her own lips and toying the bunch around her décolletage. The Master's large, hot hand caressed her naked thigh.

"You are mine, after all," he said.

"I… I am yours to command, Master," the Eternal stuttered in reply.

"You know what I want."

"Yes," she said, gazing into his eyes. Tears welled at the bottom of hers.

"I am The Master, and you will obey me."

WHUMPH!

There it was – freedom, at last!

Almost…

***

The maelstrom of confusion that was the time vortex surrounded him once more, assaulting his senses. He'd played a long, careful game with the Eternal and it had paid off – except, of course, that he was still in trouble. The Master focussed his mind again, reaching out for any escape routes nearby, any charitable temporal wayfarers with whom he could mentally thumb a lift. He was alarmed to find something enormous looming nearby, virtually on top of him; he flailed wildly, certain that whatever it was would cut him down. But nothing ensued. He settled his breathing, returned to his mantra and found psychic inner peace. Calm brought clarity; he became assured that the 'something enormous' he'd detected was not moving. He built a crude picture

147

of whatever it was, guided by his mental sonar. The Master swam to it – a vessel of some kind, and him a mere barnacle against its vastness; he clung to its exterior and made his way along its flank until he found a viable entry point.

Inside. Protected from the vortex. Safe at last? He would have to see on that front. The Master opened his eyes and sank to a crouch on the metal latticework floor as the airlock door closed behind him; the area re-pressurised with a hiss. Distant screaking revealed to him the presence of the *Pterodactyl*-like Vortisaurs outside; the vessel shifted very slightly, like a boat bobbing on a swell in the tide, as the wings of the passing beasts caused undulations in the vortex. If he'd still been out there he'd have been their prey for sure. Something else for him to be relieved about.

So, this ship…

He crept about for a while, peering around corners, opening doors silently, backing off cautiously when sensors illuminated new areas. After a time this got boring and his natural confidence and gregariousness took over; either the ship was unmanned or its crew members were asleep – or just lazy. He began to march brazenly around, announcing his presence with florid gestures and elucidatory expletives, his gown billowing behind him as he stomped through the plush surroundings, looking very much at home. He was aboard some kind of luxury star-liner as far as he could tell; the interior décor was designed artistically, not functionally, clearly with humanoid decadence and comfort in mind. And it was huge. Deck after deck, zone after zone, all pristine, all temperate, all empty of life.

Maybe, he thought, *the vessel had run out of fuel, or it had completed whatever programmed course had been laid in and then been left discarded in the vortex?* He needed to find the bridge. He needed to know if this ship could get him away from there – otherwise all he'd done was to swap prisons again. And his patience had already worn thin. As far as the Master could tell, he'd just spent possibly hundreds of years of his life trapped by an Eternal, resisting mental absorption. But at least there his extrovert nature had someone to talk to, to interact with. Here there was nothing, no one, just himself. For days. That was not a situation which this particular Master enjoyed.

Inevitably, after a while, he snapped.

The Master staggered from the room, breathing heavily and looking very satisfied. He slammed the door behind him, but it rebounded off the frame and swung back open revealing the carnage within. Tapestries torn, paintings ripped, sculptures and *objets d'arte* twisted, broken and smashed. That had made him feel so much better. He grabbed his gown from a nearby side-light, where he'd previously hung it.

As he stalked away from the room, looking for one of the integrated gourmet food dispensers to satisfy his other hunger, he thought he could detect a distant crowing, as of a bird. He paused. Was this madness setting in?

Cawwkk!

No, there it was – definitely this time. A light came on at the furthest end of the corridor. He'd clearly made someone – or something – sit up and take notice through his violent venting. He headed off towards the light.

***

After a while he stopped, convinced either the ship was making a fool of him, or that he was somehow still the plaything of the Eternal.

"Is this still you?" he yelled at the ceiling. "Yeah?'" His voice echoed away into the distance.

With a bleep a concealed door opened nearby, in an alcove between some artwork. There was a brief pause, then a rustle followed by the sudden stench of advanced decay. Masking his mouth and nose with his gown lapel, the Master approached the doorway. Inside was a machine with eight corpses attached, each in their own alcove. The dead figures were all gaudily clad in pinkish gowns, rigid enough to hold their remains upright even after death. Sickened, yet intrigued, the Master examined the nearest one: its wispy, grey hair clinging to the perimeter of its skull through what remained of the desiccated flesh around its head, a head that had sunk below an apparatus that had clearly adorned it in life and covered the exposed cranial braincase.

So, he thought, *these creatures had expanded their brain capacity beyond their natural evolution. They'd ended up here, in a luxury vessel, until they'd somehow died*. Yet again he found himself coming to the same conclusion: life was wasted on the living.

Cawwkk!

There it was again, the cry! He dashed back into the corridor and caught sight of a brief movement in his peripheral vision, a flash of shadow. He immediately set off in pursuit. The lights came on faster and faster as he ran, following the speck of movement that was always disappearing around the bend as he turned each corner. On and on he chased, determined not to let this wisp of – whatever it was, hope, variance – get away. It felt like he'd run for miles when, all of a sudden, a door slid open in front of him at the end of the corridor and he burst onto the flight deck: a dead end. He looked around in desperation, but the bird – he was certain it was a bird – was nowhere to be seen. There were no other entrances or exits.

Enraged, the Master slammed his fist through a nearby console. Live current arced through his frame, setting his nerve ends aflame, but he was so pent up with frustration by this point that he rode out the pain, gritting his teeth against it and using it to vent his anger in a twisted display of self-harming. The current eventually fading away, he pulled his fist free and stood, panting, as his gown sizzled slightly.

Now somewhat calmer, the Master paid more attention to his immediate surroundings and realised precisely where he was. His lust to escape came to the fore; very quickly he grasped the purpose of each console, and the flight controls danced and twinkled beneath his dextrous fingers while he examined the dials and readouts. Everything appeared to be operating correctly, as far as he could tell, it was just that the vessel had been brought to a stop. An itching at the back of his mind kept distracting him, though; something here was not right. Then he realised – according to the readings the vessel hadn't stopped, it had merely *paused*, as if it had been taken out of time at a precise moment. He looked around for a possible reason and his eyes fixed on a large egg-like pod resting on a podium opposite. Could this be an escape capsule? It was certainly some sort of transport vessel, the controls were obvious.

"You can't escape that way."

The Master spun around and scanned the room. Still alone. He bared his teeth; he loathed being toyed with. He turned back to the capsule controls.

There was a fluttering of feathers in his peripheral vision once again, and the sound of wings flapping. He turned to find a crow hovering at head-height immediately behind him. Automatically he backed away in surprise. A figure slowly emerged beneath the crow, as if he'd been concealed behind the very air molecules themselves; the snarling features exuded pure darkness and evil and the Master felt sick to the very pit of his stomach. The crow settled itself to become the figure's hair, and his voice, when he spoke, was like the grinding of the bedrock of the universe.

"Welcome, Time Lord."

"The Guardian of Darkness in Time. I like your taste in gowns." The figure nodded his head slightly in acknowledgment of the facile comment. The Master put his shades on again, and continued, endeavouring to force back the natural fear that any being felt when faced with the Black Guardian. "I seem to be making a habit of bumping into eternal beings," he said. "The sooner I get out of here the better."

"This Kastron vessel is held here in the vortex on borrowed time, milliseconds before it is due to explode in hyperspace."

"Long enough for me to use this pod?"

150

"Nothing here can be altered."

The Master smiled archly, thinking about the room he had trashed earlier and the console he'd just punched through.

"Yes," continued the Guardian, "your wanton destruction has been accounted for."

"What about the food I've eaten, the air I've breathed?"

"I do not wish to harm you, unnecessarily. You may have those. But how about this?" The Guardian waved a hand and the Master saw his TARDIS revealed by a spotlight, in the far corner. He removed his shades and smiled.

"I owe you my thanks," he said, and tried to move towards his craft. He wasn't surprised to find he was held rigid. He sucked his teeth; that's how the Guardians worked after all, manipulating beings into a corner where their only option for survival is to do the Guardian's bidding, to become their tool. The Master sighed. "And it feels like I've only just got away from being one Eternal's performing monkey."

"I saw," said the Guardian. "She regrets, of course, but it is unlikely that she will find you again. They are such dull beings, easy to manipulate by anyone with a basic level of skill and patience."

The Master nodded in mock appreciation. "Damned by faint praise. You do me *such* an honour."

"So...?"

"So?"

"I will return to you your TARDIS, your freedom, but in payment you must act as my agent, and do my bidding. Those are my terms. Do you accept?"

A brief pause. "I often wondered if this day would come."

"What is your answer, worm? My patience is short and this vessel will return to hyperspace and explode at any moment. Remain on board and evaporate with it, should you wish." The crow stretched its wings in preparation, as the Guardian began to fade away beneath it. The Master panicked.

"Wait!" he yelled, in earnest. "I agree. I will be your agent."

The Guardian solidified once more and sneered at his gutless tool. The Master felt a burning in his right palm and, looking down, found his TARDIS key there in his hand.

"What is your bidding?" he asked.

"You will know, when the time comes," said the Guardian.

The Master looked into the Guardian's eyes, orbs of pure black, revealing nothing at all. He shook his head, smiled a confident, determined smile, flipped the key in his hand and walked past the Guardian to his TARDIS. He paused, briefly, to caress the vehicle. Then, before the key could turn in the door the Guardian spoke again.

"Remember, Time Lord, when the moment comes, you will know my bidding."

The Master nodded thoughtfully and entered his TARDIS.

***

The Guardian watched as the TARDIS dematerialised, the Master's insane laughter clearly audible above the wheezing, trumpeting engines. He nodded to himself.

"Cooo," said the dove, sitting where the crow had previously been. With a flash of brilliant light, the Black Guardian became White.

"Thank you, Time Lord," said the stern but kindly old voice.

And with his duplicity complete, the Guardian of Light in Time faded away.

In hyperspace the Kastron star-ship exploded.

Parental Controls
Daniel Wealands

At first, there is nothing but a noise. Something like an electric hum, almost an audible vibration, resonating inside my head. It seems to shock me into a state of semi awareness, like half waking from a dream, though what dream I don't know exactly. Everything is blank, but not a flat blank, like an empty canvas, no... more like an empty bucket that was full until recently, the contents still fresh on the floor but rapidly seeping through the cracks. I cling to the suds that remain, hoping to jog something.

A title? No, more than a title, a name.

Master? More definitive?

The Master.

Yes!

"I am The Master!" The words breaking forth in a sleek and velvety tone from my mouth, breaking some of the cell doors down in my memories.

Yes! I am The Master. I am a Time lord, my past begins to return to me, Gallifrey, lofty ambitions, plans and schemes, more thwarted than achieved, and another name too, always there, always buzzing like an insect.

Doctor.

My rival, my opposite number, yes it's all coming back now.

Actually, no, no it isn't. I remember nothing recent. Where am I? And where ever this is, how did I come to be here?

As all this is swirling round my head, mingled with that ever present hum in the back of my brain, my vision, so far non-existent, begins to brighten and return. As I begin to focus on my surroundings, I realise I must be delusional, or hallucinating, for it looks like I'm in the control room of the Doctor's TARDIS!

"Finally awake then?" comes a sharp voice from behind me. "I was starting to wonder if you were ever going to come to."

I whirl around to face the voice, which belongs to a young man who is casually leaning up against the central console staring down at me, arms folded across his chest.

"You've been lying there for hours doing nothing, I was about to give up hope on you quite frankly."

"And who might you be?" I enquire as I get to my feet, "And how is it we are here?" As I speak I check my pockets for my Tissue Compression Eliminator, hoping I can simply dispose of this pest and get onto more pressing matters.

"I'm Adi, I'm here because you're here," comes the bored response, "and if you're looking for that little device of yours, it's long gone. Sorry to disappoint you."

For a moment I am lost for words, I simply stand and stare at him as he casually looks me up and down as though inspecting a horse he is about to purchase.

"Well, I must say, you don't live up to all the hype at all so far. I don't see what all the fuss was about really. He really talked you up to be something... something..."

"Prodigious? Breath-taking? Striking?" I offer.

"No, dangerous I think he said, but quite frankly you seem oily at best."

I raise myself up to my full height and square my shoulders without realising I'm doing it.

"You'd do well to choose your words carefully, for I am..."

"Yes the Master, I know." interrupts Adi, distractedly picking at lint on his sweater. "I'm afraid it doesn't do anything for me."

"I'm sorry," I say, when I have regained my composure, "but who exactly are you? I don't remember you being one of *his* lackeys. Usually they tended to be more... feminine and prone to inane questions... unless this is just a prelude to some hidden well of stupidity?" I add with just a twist of venom.

My barbs seem to have no impact on him, either he is very slow witted, genuinely unimpressed or incredibly good at hiding the overwhelming enormity of having had his character crushed before his eyes. I decide to stoke my ego and believe the last to be true.

"No, you're right, I'm not one of his companions, or assistants, or whatever term he's using these days." Suddenly my opinion of this Adi fellow improved. "I'm here because of you, without you there is no me here and vice versa as it were, or so I've been led to believe anyway. He was waffling on quite a bit and dropping more names than I cared to listen to, something about symbiosis and integration and possibly involved someone called Steve Jobs? I may have stopped listening at some point." He sighs and gives a disinterested wave of his fingers. "Look, never mind all that, what are we doing?"

"Doing?" I ask. "I'm not sure I follow."

"Well he said that once you came round you'd likely be plotting something, and I was to supervise you."

In my head a flurry of obscenities attempt to form, to express my anger and disgust that the Doctor had felt me so predictable. I must be too enraged as none seem to fully form before flitting off to make space for the next foul barrage of possibilities.

A moment passes in silence between us.

"Supervise?" I eventually repeat.

"Yes."

"In what sense exactly?"

"What?"

"In what sense are you to supervise me? I mean, if I were plotting some nefarious scheme to thwart The Doctor and sabotage his ship for example..."

"Must you always speak like that?"

"Excuse me?!"

"All that panto villain speak, is it really necessary? Who are you trying to impress, there's only me here and quite frankly you'd be wasting your time if it was all for my benefit."

While I was doubtless cut by this, I couldn't help but appreciate the sting that it had caused. It was rare to find someone quite as acidic in their manner as me. I found, against my better judgement, that Adi was definitely growing on me. With a little moulding he could make quite the companion.

Damn! Did I really just think that? Companion? ME?! In future I shall use the word minion, or perhaps henchman? Can't be seen to be slipping in these things.

"Just answer the question, if I were to try and either destroy or steal this ship would you be compelled to try and stop me?"

Adi sighed and leaned against the console.

"Firstly, I seriously doubt you'd have the prowess to steal this thing, which, quite frankly seems a ludicrous idea anyway. I mean it's hardly a conspicuous way to evade capture is it? Pretty sure the owner will have some sort of tracker and immobiliser set up too. And secondly, why would you even consider destroying it? You do realise if you do that we'd both go up with it, right? Or did you happen to have a spare escape craft stashed somewhere about your person and furthermore do you even know where we are? We could be circling a black hole or a super nova and you want to blow up the only thing keeping us safe and alive."

I stand for a moment, mouth agape.

He sighs again and shakes his head. I try very hard to mask my sheepishness with a thin sneer. I get the impression that Adi isn't buying it for a second.

"Ok," I eventually blurt out, "what would you suggest I do when presented with such a unique opportunity – unlimited access to my arch rival's entire base of operations?" I fully expected him to be clueless about what we should do and prepared to enjoy a small measure of gloating.

"Surely the first step should be to try and figure out why we are both here in the first place, don't you think?" he replies with an arched eyebrow.

Damn. He really is insufferable.

I don't respond at all, I simply turn to stare at a console screen in front of me, idly twiddling some dial or other in mock interest while I try and wrack my mind for slivers of what led me here.

"I remember something. Something big, physically big I mean, some huge hulking monstrosity, towering over me." I pause as flashes of sensations and sounds begin to break forth from behind sealed doors in my mind. "And fire, raging fires all around me. No, us. Not just me, I'm not alone. He is here too, with one of those humans he's so fond of." The rooms of my mind all seem to empty at once in a torrent of images, feelings, sensations and voices, all vying for supremacy, all wanting to be seen, heard and experienced. I gasp as the flood washes over me. Adi says nothing but simply smiles that thin knowing smile again.

"I remember."

"Go on then," he urges.

"I was on the tomb world of Lagann, I was going to summon back one of the Old Gods as the locals called them. In truth, they were celestial architects, world builders, long since gone from this dimension, forced out because of the actions of one of their own, Tamarog the Defiler, who treated all that they created as playthings and viewed himself as a god. Fearing what he was capable of, and worried that others may develop the same notions, the architects created a rift and cast Tamarog into it, sealing him away from the universe before finishing their works and moving on themselves to dimensions new. I intended to release this creature, harness its power and use it to enslave the cosmos and make it bow to my will."

"I'm guessing it didn't quite work out that way though did it," chuckles Adi.

"No, it didn't," I sneer back. "The beast had grown feral over millennia in the rift. It was a mindless force of devastation, nothing could control it, not even me."

"And that's when he arrived?"

I stop for a moment, lost in a memory.

"Yes."

"And he saved the day and returned you here."

156

"Not quite, no." I pause, not sure I really want the truth of the matter to be spoken, to do so would make it real again. For now it was just a memory, a phantom in my mind that could almost be made to be imaginings of a psyche pushed too far. If I say nothing, I can push it back, ignore it, refuse to believe it. But it demands to be spoken, to be acknowledged.

"I saved him."

Adi's smile broadens.

"Go on," he urges.

"He had arrived all noble and virtuous as usual, his pet fawning over his every imposing and honourable word. I'd already realised the beast was a monstrosity and was about to simply flee and let it do as it wished, until it killed the companion."

Adi seemed to be in genuine shock at this revelation, almost as if the notion didn't fully compute in his mind. He does that odd looking head tilt that dogs do when you ask them a question sometimes.

"I don't think I've seen Him look quite so lost before, like a child separated from its family in a crowded place, scared and confused. He just stood there, looking at the red smear on the ground that was only moments ago a friend. I didn't even think, I simply acted. I knew the creature made to do the same to him and I acted. I boarded my own time capsule and flew it directly at Tamarog, while setting it to a temporal self-destruct, dooming it to be forever trapped in an ever blossoming super nova with my craft, and I assumed, me with it. I remember leaping from the ship at the last moment, vainly hoping to make it clear of the temporal implosion field, fully expecting not to."

"You did this for a man you keep trying to kill?" Adi scoffed.

"Yes," I respond, barely aware that I am responding. Lost in that infinitesimal moment as the heat of the blast flares up my back and I see him, eyes locked on me, not in disgust, or disapproval, but in a look I've not seen since we were Time Tots, respect, love even.

I smile, only for a fraction of a second, remembering that look. I expect a tear to fall and give me away entirely, but non come, thankfully.

I cough theatrically and try to regain my composure.

"And then I awoke here, with you," I eventually sigh dejectedly, with as must dismay as I can muster. "Anything between those two moments is a blank to me. I can only surmise that he saved me somehow and you are the scrappy new replacement for the red smear." Oh that was cruel, I think to myself as I say it – I'm trying too hard to cover my feelings now.

Adi seems to be completely oblivious by my barbs though.

"So," he begins, slowly and deliberately. "Having had your life seemingly plucked from the jaws of certain death, your first thought to repay this kindness was to either steal or destroy the home and ship of the man who saved you?"

"Oh spack off!" I blurt out in a rage. Because of my fragile frame of mind he had finally hit a nerve and made me lose my composure.

Hang on...

Spack off?

That's not what I was meant to say.

"Ssss... Ssspp... Spack. Oh what the frock?!" I spat, my tongue and vocal chords completely ignoring the messages from my brain. "What the duck is going on?! Why can't I swear? I'll bet that bar-steward is behind this isn't he?!"

Livid is an understatement for my state of mind, but somehow it was the most articulate I could be without the use of a great many four letter words that paced in my mind like angry caged lions.

"Ah, you noticed then," Adi chipped in, still sporting that ever widening shot eating grin.

Shot... sssho...

Son of a birtch, I can't even think the words!

"I think, perhaps, it's time I come clean about a few things to you," he cooed, clearly relishing the moment. "You see, you were half right when you surmised he saved you. He tried so very hard to reach you in time."

Tried?

Unfortunately the blast had already done its damage and your body was, well, shall we say well done or extra crispy?" He gave a small laugh at this. His mood seemed to be shifting more and more as he went on, become less genial, more maniacal.

More like me.

"He realised there was no hope for that cremated carcass but refused to let that be the end of it."

I felt a great void open up in the pit of my stomach, or more precisely, I didn't feel it. To be clear, I experienced the sensation of the world falling away from me, but only in my mind. All the usual accompanying physical signs, such as a tumbling gut or weak knees, were strangely absent. My body was as impervious to these emotional responses as my mouth was to the urge to issue forth torrents of vulgarities.

"I don't like where this conversation is going Adi. What did he do to me?"

"He downloaded you."

"HE WHAT?!"

"Yes, he poured the entirety of your consciousness into the memory banks of the TARDIS and gave you this shiny new cybernetic body to shuffle about in then left me here to get you, shall we say, settled in?"

"And who in the bliddy heel are you exactly?" I exclaim, trying very hard to blurt out at least some minor cursives and still failing.

"I told you, I'm Adi, or to use my full title I'm the Automated Device Installer."

***

The sudden reality of it all comes sweeping over me in a torrent. All the strings of thought pull together, bunching into a sinewy cord and form something not unlike a noose.

"You're a flocking desktop install wizard!" I manage to whisper.

"I suppose you could call me that, yes."

"And the swearing?"

"He engaged the parental controls before bringing you online. You may have also noticed that you're not quite so hell bent on domination and destruction now either. I've been filtering you while we've been having this conversation, you may have noticed me taking on some of your less attractive qualities during this process."

"Well that explains me getting all choked up over things then."

"Exactly, without some of those more insidious qualities, your softer side has begun to emerge."

"Oh, well how trucking delightful," I sneer.

"Yes, clearly your cynicism, snark and sarcasm evaded the purge," Adi despairs.

"Where is he now?" I demand "I have a few choice words for him, and it may take a while for me to describe them all fully."

"With the High Council. They are very upset with him for saving even part of you after what you did. It took all the might of the C.I.A to finally put out that super nova time loop you unleashed, not to mention covering up the whole resurrection of Tamarog the Defiler and the destruction of Lagann." He tutted at me like some patronising teacher. "They want you wiped off the hard drive completely. He is arguing for your survival."

There were so many things running through my mind.

Could I even call it my mind anymore?

Am I still me or just a shadow?

159

Will I be allowed to continue to exist, and if I do will he ever let me hear the end of it?

Oh God! Am I permanently tethered to his ship now?!

All these mixed thoughts and emotions boil and foam in my head, desperate to escape into the world in a cry, a shout, a phrase to sum it all up.

Eventually it spills out in a single sentence.

"Well this is a total Fluster cluck."

Splinter of Eternity
Iain McLaughlin

All things considered, time travel was pretty damn weird, Andrea Hansen thought to herself. There was no doubt that it was absolutely brilliant, but yep, time travel was pretty damn weird. In the last week she had seen both Elvis Presley and Mozart perform – though not together, obviously.

That would have been just *too* weird.

Despite the dips into history and the countless adventures Andrea – Andy to her friends – had experienced, the odd thing was that every Monday morning she found herself back in the little University canteen making bacon rolls for hungover students.

This particular Monday had been particularly trying all day. For once the stress had been nothing to do with travelling in time. Instead, the pressure had all related to the opening of a new exhibit in the Egyptian section of the University's museum. While she was fascinated by the exhibit, she was more interested in the stress it was causing two of her closest friends. Ibrahim Hadmani, the museum's curator, had spent months jumping through hoops, schmoozing and charming countless dignitaries in order to secure the artefacts in the new exhibition… and all while getting married and bouncing back and forward in time with Andy and her closest friend, Erimem – or the Pharaoh Erimemushinteperem if she was to be given her full title.

Maybe the weirdest thing of all – even weirder than Andy's girlfriend being a pirate captain in the late Seventeenth Century – was that her best friend was an uncrowned Pharaoh from Egypt in 1450BC… who now worked and studied at a University in 2019 London. She also had a house that was a universe of its own. Yep, Andy had to admit that was pretty weird, too.

In fact, since Andy had met Erimem, weird had become the norm.

On cue, Erimem looked into the canteen. "Are you finished?" she asked.

Andy looked around the canteen. The food that could be stored was in the fridge or the freezer and anything that couldn't be stored had been picked up for a local charity to pass to those who needed it. The tables and worktops were clean and the day's takings had been secured. "Looks like it," she answered. "How did today go? Did your visitors give you the sign off?"

"Sign off?" Erimem's brow creased for a moment before understanding appeared in her face. "They have finally agreed to allow us to open tomorrow," she said. "Life was much easier when I could simply command people to do as I wanted. Sometimes I miss those days."

"I could call you 'Your Highness' if it helps," Andy offered, casually wandering across the canteen to her friend.

"Would you?" Erimem asked just a little too brightly. "Really?"

The friends laughed and Andy pulled the door open. She turned off the lights and they both went outside into the corridor, where Andy promptly locked up. "Fancy a drink in the Pint Pot?" she asked.

"Only if we can also have chips," Erimem answered. "I deserve chips today."

"You're chips mad, you are," Andy said fondly. "Yes, we can have chips… if you let me have a quick shufti at the new exhibition."

"I know what a shufti is," Erimem said, thoroughly pleased with herself, "and yes you can see the exhibition."

"Cool beans." Andy was about to continue when a horrific wail screamed through the air. "The alarm!"

"The exhibition?" Erimem asked.

She didn't wait for an answer and Andy had no choice but to run after her friend.

***

They reached the entrance to the Egyptian exhibition a few seconds before Ibrahim. A warning light flashed above the doors.

"There's somebody inside," Ibrahim said, keying his passcode into his phone where an app transmitted to the lock. As soon as they heard a sharp click they all hurried inside. There was countless millions of pounds in priceless artefacts inside the room, including Erimem's own jewel-encrusted gold death-mask. For that reason the museum's security systems were state of the art.

How the hell could anyone have got inside?

The Egyptian exhibition was a long room with two rows of glass cases in the middle of the floor and other artefacts in cases along the walls. Two more, smaller, rooms led off the side.

It was only as they rushed into the room that Andy realised they could be running into trouble. "What if they're armed?" she asked.

"Oh," Ibrahim said. "I hadn't thought of that."

"Then we will deal with them in other ways," Erimem answered.

"Care to share?" Andy asked. "If you've got a plan I'm up for hearing it."

"Did I say I had a plan?" Erimem asked quietly. "I don't remember saying I had a plan. Why does everyone think I've always got a plan?"

162

"Oh, crud."

The three friends spread out, carefully moving along the aisles, staying in sight of each other. At first Ibrahim assumed there had been a malfunction in the security system because it looked like nobody else was in the room.

Then they saw the intruder.

One man, slim with neatly cropped dark hair, was kneeling by a case containing one of the lesser artefacts in the entire presentation. He didn't look up as they approached.

"If you leave now, you can live," he said calmly. "That is your only warning." His velvet-smooth voice seeped malice.

"Those are brave words for a man alone against a greater enemy," Erimem answered.

"Only greater in number," the voice replied calmly. "And you have ignored your warning." He turned and pointed a little black device that looked like… well, Andy chose not to think what it looked like or how much Ann Summer would charge for it. He aimed it at Erimem and it flashed red.

As soon as she had seen the device in the man's hand Erimem had dived to the side. It saved her life. A corner of the case just behind where she'd been standing shattered. The intruder turned his weapon towards Ibrahim. An expression of malign glee appeared on his face as his fingers moved to operate the weapon…

He grunted as something small and solid smashed into the side of his face. He reeled and dropped the weapon, which slid away under a case out of reach.

Erimem pulled back her arm to hurl another priceless piece of carved Egyptian stone at the intruder, but the man lurched away. He pressed a button on a small box and all of the lights went out, dropping the exhibition into near darkness, lit only by the light from the corridor. A few seconds later the overhead lights flickered back into life.

There was no sign of the intruder.

"Where the hell's he gone?" Andy muttered.

Ibrahim craned his head, peering into the furthest reaches of the room. "I don't see where he could be hiding," Ibrahim said. "I know this room inside out. I don't know where he went to."

"Neither do I," Erimem admitted. She was still clearly on edge.

"He's gone." The smooth, educated voice came from behind them. "And I can't say I'm sorry to see him go."

A handsome man of around forty was standing at the back of the exhibit leaning on the doorframe. He flipped his floppy hair out of his eyes.

"Really?" Erimem said. She was eyeing this newcomer with the same mistrust she'd shown the intruder. "Why is that?"

A boyish grin crept onto the man's face. "Because he's the most dangerous sociopath this planet's ever seen and he has absolutely no qualms about killing. He would see everyone on this planet dead to get what he wanted. You're lucky to still be alive."

"It wasn't luck," Erimem said testily. "It was years of training."

Ibrahim picked up the ancient piece of carved stone Erimem had thrown at the would-be thief. "And an absolutely priceless artefact – which is still in one piece, by the way."

"And so are you," Erimem added.

Ibrahim nodded vigorously. "Which is obviously far more important."

Their attention had returned to the newcomer at the door. He had wavy, dark hair and a bit of a posh voice. He was handsome if men were your thing, Andy thought, but most of all he just seemed charming. It was an old school word but it suited him. His clothing was similarly old school, comprising dark trousers, a purple waistcoat over a black shirt and a kind of dark frock coat that sort of shimmered in the light. She guessed that he was maybe closer to thirty-five than forty but in good shape.

"And who are you?" Erimem asked.

"Me?" The newcomer ran a hand through his unruly hair and just beamed. "I'm the Doctor. Pleased to meet you."

"The Doctor?" Ibrahim sounded cynical. "What kind of name is that?"

The Doctor's smile didn't shift. "That's a question I get asked rather a lot."

"And do you have an answer?" Ibrahim asked.

"Not a good one," the Doctor admitted, "at least not one I could explain without making you think I should be carted off to the nearest funny farm."

"Try us," Andy challenged. "We're quite open-minded."

"Very well," this Doctor fellow answered, "I occasionally work for a slightly secretive military intelligence unit which looks into what we should call... the *extraordinary*?" He seemed surprised that no-one was startled by his revelation. "Such as aliens?" he added, sounding almost hopeful. "From other planets?"

"What about time travellers?" Andy asked bluntly.

The Doctor seemed even more bemused before a broad grin spread across his face again. "Well, yes, we'd investigate those, too." His eyes flicked around the room. "You don't happen to have any about here, do you?"

Ibrahim avoided any uncomfortable questions by indicating towards the glass case containing the coffins of two young princes. "Everything in here is from other times," he said, "including our two honoured guests. They came a long way to be here."

"Point taken," the Doctor answered. He looked at the case the intruder had been trying to break into. "Our would-be thief has come quite a way, too, and so has what he was after."

"Which is?" Erimem asked.

"Can I show you?" the Doctor asked. He didn't wait for an answer before making a bee-line for the glass case in question. He beamed an encouraging smile as he passed his hosts. "This," he said, pointing to a long, thin shard of what looked like obsidian, "is what he was after."

Erimem looked far from impressed. "We had had many such things in Egypt. They was common in our palaces."

"I know." The Doctor looked at her with interest. It seemed to Andy that somehow he had recognised that she didn't belong in this time. "But you talk about Ancient Egypt with quite an authority."

"Do I?" She lifted her chin in defiance.

"The University prides itself on its remarkable depth of teaching," Ibrahim interrupted. "Erimem is an extraordinary student."

"I'm sure she is," the Doctor agreed genially. "Although Erimem is quite an unusual name, isn't it?"

"It's traditional," Ibrahim answered evenly.

Erimem looked at Ibrahim fondly, reminding Andy that Ibrahim was actually a distant, many times over, great nephew to Erimem. "It has been in our family for a long time," she said.

"It has," Ibrahim agreed.

"Splendid," the Doctor clapped his hands together. "Now if you'll just let me take this shard to my organisation for safekeeping everything will be absolutely fine and we can all get home in time for... well, whatever's on telly tonight."

Erimem stepped between the Doctor and the case. "Why does this other man want the shard?"

The Doctor gave a most disarming smile. "Well, that's a long and unlikely story."

"We're used to those," Andy said. "Try us."

"You won't believe me," the Doctor said.

Andy shrugged. "You'd be surprised what we might believe."

That seemed to tickle the Doctor. "All right," he said. "This shard is a fragment of something extraordinary, something that has existed since the birth of the Omniverse."

"The Omni-what-now?" Ibrahim asked blankly.

Andy scowled at him. "The Omniverse is this universe and all the other parallel universes and other dimensions. It's the collective name for absolutely everything ever. If you read comics you'd know that."

"Okay," Ibrahim shrugged. "I'll read more comics."

"I read *The Beano*," the Doctor offered. "Anyway, as I was saying, the shard is part of an object from the birth of everything. The name that follows it seems to be 'the Eternity'. Rather ostentatious but there's nothing much I can do about it. Fragments of the Eternity exist in every reality in the Omniverse. Nobody really quite understands what it is or how it was created. Nobody knows why it's splintered across every universe but it *is* a source of extraordinary power. Again, no-one knows its limits but in the wrong hands it could be incredibly dangerous."

"And the man who tried to steal it is the wrong hands?" Andy asked.

"About as wrong as they could be," the Doctor confirmed. "The wrongest of the wrong. There's not a wrongier pair of wrong hands anywhere in space and time. Except maybe the Jahubi people from Tetratraxi. They developed their equivalent of mobile phones and became so obsessed with using them that their hands evolved getting bigger and bigger. Not one of them can get their hands through the sleeves of a good sweater." He became aware that three sets of eyes were just staring at him. "Anyway, back to our unwelcome guest, he's a villain who calls himself the Master."

Andy's eyebrows lifted. "Sounds kinky."

"What?" the Doctor looked bemused. "Oh, no, nothing like that. Well, not in that regeneration anyway. He's a vicious, amoral megalomaniac obsessed with power."

"He's Donald Trump?" asked Andy.

The Doctor shook his head. "Oh, no, he's from a completely different planet altogether."

"Donald Trump or the Master?"

"Both," the Doctor answered, "although one is considerably more intelligent than the other. Or perhaps I should say one is considerably less intelligent than the other." He sniffed. "Than *any* other, really."

"So, this Master is an alien?" Erimem asked. She was obviously keen to get the conversation back on course.

The Doctor seemed to understand the real reasoning behind Erimem's question. "Oh, yes. But don't be alarmed – so am I. Two hearts, respiratory bypass system, lots of other good things."

"Right," said Ibrahim in a flat voice. "Two hearts."

The Doctor looked delighted by the response from Erimem's group. "Interesting. Apart from a bit of sarcasm none of you are particularly bothered by the idea of me being an alien or by the concept of infinite universes. You're all remarkably open-minded or…"

"Or…?" asked Erimem.

"Or you really have got some experience with aliens?" the Doctor said. "I hope they were friendly."

Andy wasn't ready to admit to this stranger that they had all travelled to distant times and worlds. She certainly wasn't ready to tell him that Ibrahim had recently returned from his honeymoon in the far future. "Aliens? Don't be silly."

"It's not silly," the Doctor protested. "Lots of aliens are friendly. We don't all have pointed teeth, green skin, wear dustbins and want to shout you to death."

"We know," Ibrahim said irritably.

"Ibrahim!" Andy knew how much Ibrahim hated being talked down to, but sometimes…

The museum's curator looked embarrassed by his gaff. "Oh, sorry."

"So, you've met aliens?" the Doctor said thoughtfully. "That makes all of this much easier."

Erimem scrutinised the Doctor carefully. "And you are an alien, helping a semi-secret military organisation investigate other aliens across every universe?"

"Not quite," the Doctor corrected her. "Infinity's rather large. The unit I work with tend to stick to *this* universe. To this planet, actually. Can you imagine never seeing another alien sky?"

The three friends glanced at each other. It was a small, involuntary reaction but the Doctor pounced on it.

"Hah! So you've all been to other planets as well. This makes life much easier. You have a broader range of experience than most."

"Meaning what?" demanded Erimem. There was no hiding her distrust of this newcomer.

"Meaning," the Doctor aimed his answer directly at Erimem, "that you might understand how important it is that I get something as dangerous as this out of temptation's way and taken somewhere safe. It could destroy *everything*."

"What exactly is it?" asked Erimem, "other than ancient and powerful."

"And rocking the whole omniverse," Andy added.

The Doctor looked vaguely irritated at having to explain further. "As I already said, nobody is quite sure, which is worrying enough in itself. Research done by my people, who are very boring but very clever, suggests it might be

167

some kind of anchor existing in every universe at the same time and possessing the properties which allow it to exist in those different universes." He looked around his audience. "I don't know how widely you understand quantum theory but the physical rules of each universe are different. Sometimes the differences are minimal, sometimes they're huge. For example, gravity may not exist in one universe or another may not have had the sudden expansion following the Big Bang... there's no limit. It's infinite. And this object manages to exist in all of those realities, with different, often contradictory properties..."

That sounded like the most impossible thing Andy had ever heard – which was saying something. "Is that possible?"

The Doctor gave a wry smile. "No, but that doesn't mean it can't happen. I assume you've seen the impossible before."

"Most days," Ibrahim admitted.

"And twice on a Tuesday," Andy added. The cat was out of the bag so why deny it?

Erimem was more interested in the potential danger. "The shard has the potential to destroy everything in every universe. That is why it needs to hidden away."

"Exactly," the Doctor agreed.

"And you are the person to hide it?" Erimem went on.

The Doctor shuffled, looking slightly embarrassed. "Well, if it's me or that scoundrel we chased away, I'd pick me every time."

"I am sure you would," Erimem answered.

The Doctor was scrutinizing Erimem. Her face seemed to have struck a chord with him. "You know, you're very familiar. Have we met before?"

Andy didn't like the idea of anyone knowing where Erimem had come from. The fewer people who knew, the safer her friend was. "This is hardly the time to try to throw her a line."

"Throw her a what?" The Doctor seemed thoroughly confused before realization slowly dawned. "Oh no, it's just that her face is very familiar," he said. "I'm sure I've seen her before."

"She's just got that sort of face," Andy said blandly.

Erimem glanced at her friend. "Have you just insulted me?"

"Only a bit."

The Doctor ignored the byplay. "No," he said, "I've seen her before. It'll come to me... in time perhaps."

Erimem was clearly not in the mood for word games. "Very clever, Doctor."

"Pharaohs are unforgettable." The Doctor gave a slight bow. "I'd be intrigued to know how you wound up here."

"It's a long story," Erimem answered.

"I imagine it is. I'm sure you have time. Lots of time."

Andy could see Erimem straightening her back and flexing her hands. She was getting ready to act if she had to. "You are a very clever man."

"I keep telling people that," the Doctor agreed wistfully, "but nobody listens. Now, about the shard…"

Ibrahim interrupted, "Which is a historical Egyptian artefact."

"And quite possibly the beginning of the end of everything, ever," added the Doctor. "Which is why I want to get it to safety."

Erimem still showed no sign of trusting this newcomer. "How do we know you can protect it?"

"Ah, well, that's a good question," the Doctor conceded.

"Do you have a good answer?"

Erimem was blunter. "And why are you and this Master the only alternatives for custody of this dangerous weapon?"

The Doctor seemed to be thinking of something else entirely before he snapped back into the room. "Pardon? Oh, right. We're not the *only* alternatives. And that's the problem, really. As more races develop the technology to identify this shard for what it is, more are going to come for it. Most of them won't be as friendly as me." He shrugged sadly. "The Master is only the beginning, I'm afraid."

Erimem gave the Doctor's response some thought. "Where would you take it?"

"Well, it would rather defeat the point of hiding it if I told you wouldn't it?"

"*We* could hide the shard," Erimem said, still stood between the Doctor and the display case. "If it is as dangerous as you say."

The Doctor took a deep breath and made an obvious effort to be reasonable. "There is nowhere in the universe you could hide it."

A swift look passed between Erimem and her friends, which the Doctor noted.

"And what does that look mean?" he asked.

Erimem ignored the question. "Why should we trust you?"

The Doctor put his hands in his pockets and wandered around the exhibit. "Because I have a winning smile, I once danced a half decent tango with Louise Brookes and I make a spectacular shepherd's pie. I'm also quite experienced at this sort of thing. That's why my unit let me deal with it my way."

"And if we do not choose to let you do things your way?" Erimem pressed.

"We're civilized people," he smiled genially. "We'll work something out."

An odd beeping sound echoed through the exhibit.

"What the hell's that?" Andy asked Ibrahim.

The Doctor pulled a black box about twice the size of a mobile phone from inside his pocket. He looked at the box's screen, complained and smacked the heel of his hand against it twice. It bleeped again in a slightly different tone. "Oh, that's interesting," he said.

"What is?" demanded Andy.

The Doctor looked up, his face a picture of forced innocence. "Oh, nothing."

Erimem didn't entertain the evasion for a moment. "You ask us to trust you but you do not answer my friend's question."

The Doctor looked sheepish, caught in a very poor attempt at a deception. "That's fair." He held up the box. "According to my little friend here, the Master is cutting across from another universe... this universe here." He pointed to a line of text on the bottom of the screen.

"How?" asked Andy.

The Doctor hummed absently as he read the details running across the screen. "I don't know the mechanism he's using but the physics would take about four years to explain and by my reckoning we have around thirty seconds because he's opening a portal back to this universe about thirty metres..." he waved an arm around his head a few times before pointing at a side door-arch, "...that way."

That was Erimem's call to arms. She reached into a broken case and grabbed two *khopesh*, her favoured Egyptian fighting daggers. "Arm yourselves. He is willing to kill us. We must be willing to defend ourselves."

Andy and Ibrahim both reached in and plucked swords from the display.

The Doctor's hand came down on Ibrahim's "No. You can't kill him."

Ibrahim shook his hand free. "Why? Is he immortal?"

"No. He's..." the Doctor hummed, "...we were at the academy at the same time. I know him well. I want to stop him but I don't want to kill him. Do you understand?"

"No," Erimem said flatly. She glared hard at the Doctor. "If he is as dangerous as you say we should be willing to do whatever we need to do to defeat him."

The Doctor met her stare face on. "Not if it means killing him. Not if you can help it."

Erimem didn't answer the Doctor directly. She turned to her friends. "Defend yourselves. Kill only if we must."

The Doctor gave a grateful nod. "Thank you."

170

Erimem fixed her eyes on this newcomer. "I do not kill if there is an alternative, Doctor, but if my life or my friend's life is in danger I will not hesitate." She turned back to her friends. "And neither should you."

Ibrahim interrupted. He was staring at the doorway the Doctor had indicated. "Where the hell is he?"

They waited a few seconds, scanning the doorway, waiting for some sign of movement.

They waited.

There was nothing. No sign of...

"There!" Ibrahim pointed to the side of the door. He was right. The Master was slipping in at the side.

"No," Andy shouted. "Over there."

She was right, too. The Master was also sneaking in on the other side of the wide doorway.

"And over there," said Erimem pointing past the doorway into the room beyond where the Master was also moving towards the doorway... several times over. "He can't be in all these places at one time." She snorted. "Forget I said that. Time travel monkey-bananas stuff."

"He's projecting," the Doctor called. "Only one of him is real."

"Which one?" Erimem asked.

"That will be the one who tries to kill you," the Doctor answered.

"Oh, that's heartening," Ibrahim grumbled.

Andy swung her sword to hold back the nearest Master. He ignored it and ghosted straight through Andy. "Oh, that's horrible," she gasped, "right through me. It's just *not nice*."

Erimem attacked the nearest Master. "I have this one." Her *khopesh* slid through the Master without resistance and she roared in frustration. "He has no honour."

Another Master had stepped in front of Andy. "I'll stop this one."

Erimem called across. "Leave him, Andy. He is not real." She hurried towards her friend. "None of them are real. He wishes us to run away from what we are supposed to be guarding." She moved Andy a step back from the door.

"Okay," said Andy, "so where... *bloody hell*..."

Erimem's *khopesh* cut through the air and dug into the Master's hand.

He yelled in pain and dropped the weapon he had been carrying. "Get away from me."

Erimem's blades caught the light as she approached the Master. Andy and Ibrahim also closed, their swords raised. "I do not think so," Erimem said

171

coldly. "You should control your hair. The others are all neat. Only your hair became untidy."

"Listen to me," the Master said in a warm, calm voice. It sounded reassuring and reliable, as comforting as a lullaby. "Nothing has happened here tonight. You will return to your homes and remember nothing of tonight. I am the Master and you will obey me."

Erimem looked at him. "You are the Master," she said, "and we will obey you."

"That's better." The Master's shoulders rose as he regained control of the situation.

"When heaven freezes over," Erimem added in a sour voice.

"In your dreams," Andy added, before glancing at her friend, "and it's when *hell* freezes over."

"Is it?" Erimem looked disappointed. "I will get the hang of these phrases. I will."

"A solid eight out of ten for effort," Andy offered in consolation.

The Master was looking at the three who were aiming blades at him. "Why didn't the hypnosis work?"

"Hypnosis?" Andy shrugged. "Beats me."

"Your primitive brain should have given in easily."

Erimem bristled. "This *primitive brain* is telling me to break your arm, so be very careful."

The Master took a step backwards. He clearly took Erimem's threat – and the threat from the swords held by Andy and Ibrahim – very seriously. He continued backing away.

"So, that's how you got here, eh?" Andy said. "Nifty."

The Master had backed away towards a shimmering spiral of silver and blue which crackled aggressively with dangerous-looking energy.

The Master kept backing away. "It's how I escape back to my own…"

"Escape?" said a rich but fatigued voice from the vortex. "I don't think so."

A man of around sixty stepped from the spiral of energy. His greying hair was swept back. His eyes burned with intelligence and a general sense of weariness. He gave the impression of a careworn eagle.

The Master looked at the newcomer with loathing. "Doctor!"

"I just can't trust you an inch, can I?" the newly arrived man said. "I offer you the chance to take part in experiments to save the universe and all you can do is try to take it over."

"Not just this universe," the Master snapped. "*Every* universe."

"Typical," the newcomer replied.

172

Two soldiers followed through the portal and quickly fastened a sort of electronic handcuffs around the Master's wrists.

The newcomer looked at Erimem's party, who all still held blades ready to attack. "If you don't mind I'll put him back in his cell. Bread and water for a week or two might put him back on his leash."

"Can you ensure he never troubles our universe again?" Erimem demanded.

"I'll do my best." The newcomer nodded for the soldiers to take the Master back through the portal.

"Thank you," Erimem said. She looked at the older man thoughtfully. "The Master called you something… may we know your name?"

"People usually call me the Doctor," came the reply.

"Really?" Andy looked at the man suspiciously. "We have somebody here going by that name."

"Do you?" the older man who called himself 'the Doctor' didn't seem at all surprised. "Where is he?"

Andy looked around. There was no sign of their Doctor. "I don't know."

The older Doctor looked slightly disappointed. "Probably best that I don't meet him anyway. It never ends well. He'll only be jealous. Anyway, goodbye."

He stepped back into the roiling vortex and was whisked out of existence. A few seconds later, the portal also disappeared, leaving three friends to look at each other in a mixture of bewilderment and relief.

"So where is the Doctor?" Andy asked. "Our Doctor, I mean."

The answer was obvious. "The shard!" Erimem yelped.

They ran back to the glass case containing the shard everyone so desperately wanted. The Doctor was kneeling by the case, running some kind of cutting device along the glass.

"No, Doctor," Erimem said. She made no attempt to hide her anger. "You will not take it. We did not give you permission."

The Doctor didn't look up. "I thought you were busy with the Master."

"We were," Erimem replied, "but he was taken away."

"By you apparently," added Ibrahim.

"The Earth-2 you," Andy clarified, "or whatever they call the world that other Doctor came from."

"Ah. The Doctor. I might have known he'd spoil things."

Erimem shook her head. "I do not understand."

The Doctor stood slowly, his back still turned and his head bowed. "Oh, this is just not going to work, is it? I tried," he said almost to himself. "I *really tried*."

"What are you talking about?" demanded Erimem.

173

A vicious edge crept into the reply. "He's always so nice and friendly and chatty. Underneath it all he knows you're no better than chimpanzees who've been slightly housetrained but he *still* treats you like you're something more than that. He's the same in almost every universe. Doesn't he just get tired of being so relentlessly *good* all the time?"

He looked up…

For the first time Andy noticed that he had a beard. Where in the name of all that's hipster had his goatee come from? She would have sworn that he didn't have a beard before. She was sure of it. At least she thought she was…

"You are not the Doctor, are you?" Erimem said.

"Very good." The reply was condescending. "You're the suspicious one. Let's see if you can guess who I am."

"The Master?" Erimem asked. "From this universe?"

"Almost."

Andy completed the puzzle. "From a different universe."

"That's more like it," the Master said with a patronizing superiority. "Good chimpanzee. Have a banana."

Andy snorted. "Different universe, same scuzzy beard."

Ibrahim shook his head in confusion. "Why didn't we see that before?"

"The other one mentioned hypnosis," Erimem said. "Did you hypnotize us?"

That charming smile returned, although there was a definite edge of malice behind it now. "A low level suggestion to foster trust," he said "The best I could do with three of you. It didn't work with one of you, though. On some level one of you knew I wasn't the Doctor." He aimed that at Erimem. "Which is very interesting… but not interesting enough to make me stay for a chat. So I'll take the shard and be on my way."

Erimem lifted her *khopesh* in a clear threat. "No, you will not."

The Master produced a small stubby weapon from his pocket. "A bit of advice, don't bring a knife to a Tissue Compression Eliminator fight."

"Is that funny in your universe?" Andy asked.

The Master shrugged. "No, but this is."

He pushed the glass case holding the shard. The glass toppled and smashed on the floor.

"I really should kill the three of you," he said, retrieving the shard, "but it's more fun to let you know you were taken in and just to know that I beat you. That will really hurt. Especially *you*, Pharaoh. Don't think I didn't spot your Death Mask back there as soon as I arrived. I still don't know how you got here. I still don't care. You ruled the world but you still lost to *me*." His smile became maliciously cold. "Think on that."

174

He turned and ran towards the far door. Andy and Ibrahim started to chase after him but Erimem held out a hand to stop them. "No. Do not chase him."

"Why?" demanded Andy.

"He's getting away," Ibrahim protested. "With our exhibit."

"I know," Erimem said calmly. She waited until the Master had almost reached the door before calling out, "One thing, Master."

The Master stopped in the doorway and turned impatiently. "Yes? What is it? I do have other universes to humiliate."

"You like to finish with a funny line, don't you?" Erimem said, slowly walking towards the Master.

"I think it adds a certain something."

"I understand," Erimem nodded. "We did something similar in my palace. If we were there now I would say… *don't let the door hit you on the way out.*"

There was a *click* and the metal safety doors slid hard into place, catching the Master between them, crushing his leg. The sound of a major bone shattering filled the room. The Master screamed in pain but still managed to pull his way through the doorway letting the doors clang shut.

"He's still alive." Erimem sounded disappointed.

Andy scooped up two fallen objects from the floor. "He dropped the shard, though. And his gun."

Erimem held up her mobile phone. "Ibrahim and I both have an app to control the doors." She thumbed in a code and the doors slid open.

"I wondered how you got the doors to close," Andy grinned. "Aren't you a clever Pharaoh?"

"Don't tell anybody she's got that app," Ibrahim added. "I'm not supposed to share it."

They hurried through the doorway. A short distance into the corridor they found a pool of crimson on the floor.

"Ooh, blood." Andy winced. "I'm not good with blood."

Twenty metres along the corridor, another portal between dimensions was forming. It didn't look exactly the same as the one they had seen a few minutes earlier, but it was similar enough to be recognisable.

The Doctor – no, the Master – was pulling himself along the wall towards the portal. His right leg dragged behind him, useless and trailing blood along the floor.

"Stop where you are," Erimem called.

The Master looked back over his shoulder and increased his pace. "I don't think so." He had almost reached the portal.

Erimem lifted the Master's own weapon. "I will fire if you do not stop."

The Master glanced back. "Would you kill an injured foe?" he asked. "You talked of honour, Pharaoh. Is it honourable to fire on an injured man who is trying to escape the field of battle?" He shook his head. "You won't fire. Your ancestors would curse you if you did."

"Invoking my family was a mistake. I am not a savage. I do not need to shoot at *you*."

Erimem fired.

The vortex screamed. It lost cohesion, beginning to collapse and spiral in on itself. Branches of energy spat out before being dragged back into the rift. They lashed out, flailing like the limbs of an injured beast. One impaled the Master through the stomach. As the energy recoiled it ripped him back into the vortex. It churned and spat for a few seconds before abruptly disappearing.

Andy stared at the empty space. "What happened?"

"I do not know," Erimem admitted. "I thought the device might shrink the portal trapping him here but I was wrong."

Andy looked ahead suspiciously. "Do you think he's dead?"

Erimem shook her head. "I don't know. He was cunning but that storm between worlds was violent. It may have simply taken him from this place."

"It's gone from here, anyway," Ibrahim said with relief.

"So have both Masters," Andy added, "and I won't miss them."

Erimem held up the shard which had caused so much trouble. "But this must also go."

"Where?" asked Ibrahim. "It won't be safe anywhere in the world."

"Or the universe," Andy added. "Actually, that's a thought isn't it?"

***

"So," Ibrahim sniffed, the most powerful artefact in the universe... you're using it as a door-stop?"

"Yes," Erimem nodded.

"Seriously?"

"It doesn't look right anywhere else," Erimem said defensively. She looked down at the piece of black stone which held open a door leading from the main living space of her villa out onto the terrace and the wide meadow beyond which ran down to a river. The villa, the grounds beyond, the river and all the animals there, including a friendly herd of Woolly Mammoths were all artificial creations in an equally artificial universe existing outside of any natural aspect of creation.

"Okay," Andy agreed. "Your house, your rules."

"*My* universe," Erimem corrected. "And no-one can track the shard to my universe."

Andy nudged her friend. "Don't show off."

"Why not? I'm Pharaoh and I have Woolly Mammoths."

Ibrahim had gone to retrieve a duplicate of the shard and was gazing at it with glee. "Hey, when you said the machine here could make an exact copy I didn't expect it to be so…"

"Exact?" Andy offered.

"Exactly!"

Andy tapped the duplicate. "But this one doesn't have the magic juju."

"That's a relief," Ibrahim said. "Okay, we better get this back and then phone the police about vandals breaking in."

"It's too bad he turned out to be a villain," Andy said sadly. "He did have style. Despite the beard."

"Come on," Ibrahim said. "Back to the Uni."

"Ibrahim is right," Erimem agreed, leading the way to the doorway back to the real universe. "Do we have time to pick up chips before we summon the police?"

The Devil You Know
Daniel Tessier

It was a cold, still midnight in October, and Olive Hawthorne woke with a start.

She sat up in bed, her nightdress damp with cold sweat. She was normally a sound sleeper, ever since her youth, but the last few nights had been uneasy and restless. She stepped out of bed uneasily, a little shaky on her feet. She wasn't as young as she once was, and it took her a little longer to get her bearings these days.

Slipping into her dressing gown, she walked through her bungalow to her tiny kitchen, and poured herself a glass of cold water. She unlocked the back door, stepped outside and sat, a little uncomfortably, on her doorstep. She looked up at the clear sky, the Moon shining brightly down upon on her. The stars were out. It helped her feel at ease.

She sipped her water, tired but wide awake. In her younger days, she would have been preparing for ritual celebration. Tomorrow was All Hallows Eve, or as it was once known, Samhain. It was the witches' New Year, and a harvest festival, and she would have marked the occasion with her coven. In recent years, though, she'd grown out of such things. She still kept her faith close to her, but spells and rune casting weren't everyday pursuits of hers anymore. In any case, Samhain had been almost forgotten around these parts, replaced by the Americanised version of Hallowe'en that encouraged children to dress up and run riot. Miss Hawthorne found it all rather tiresome now.

She placed her glass down and gazed up at the stars. The Pleiades shone down from Taurus, its presence a reminder that tonight was the eve of the dead, a time to remember the spirits of those lost. Miss Hawthorne settled into nostalgia, and began to drift away.

A sudden screech jolted her to awareness. She looked up again at the sky and caught the briefest glimpse of a winged figure darting through the night, silhouetted against the Moon. Surely far too large to so suddenly vanish from view.

She shook her head and rose to her feet. She must have nodded off, and caught sight of a bat when its screech woke her. The half-wake mind plays all sorts of tricks, after all. She almost made herself believe it, but Miss Hawthorne had always had unerring instincts when it came to the occult, and she could not shake the feeling that something was stirring this evening. There was a presence in Devil's End, and she knew squarely where the blame lay.

***

The following morning, Miss Hawthorne marched herself down to St. Michael's, known to all the locals simply as 'the church', as fast as her ageing legs could carry her. She was determined to have it out with the new vicar, who had replaced the previous incumbent after his retirement a few weeks previously.

She stormed through the churchyard, pausing for a moment by an ornate gravestone, upon which a grotesque statue perched. She had passed it a hundred times before, but this time it unsettled her somehow. Steeling herself, she rapped on the church door.

The door creaked open, the heavy oak weighing down on the ancient hinges. In the doorway stood a middle-aged man in a long black robe and dog collar. His hair and beard were greying, and he wore a determined expression.

"Reverend Masters," she said, "just the man I was coming to see."

"Good morning," replied the vicar. "Miss Hawthorne, isn't it? To what do I owe the pleasure?"

"I was hoping to speak with you about the events on Devil's Hump," said the witch.

"Ah," said Masters, smiling placatingly. "I wondered if you might. Are you concerned with the planned opening of the Hump?"

"Indeed, Reverend, indeed I am. I prefer to keep myself to myself these days, but I do have very grave concerns."

"I understand. Some of your fellow villagers had, ah, warned me that you may object should the Hump be opened again. You have quite the reputation in Devil's End."

Miss Hawthorne felt a little swell of pride at this.

"It's true, I did involve myself in the occult arts in my younger days, and I was there when the Hump was opened before. It led to disaster then and will do so again."

"Most of the people of this village would consider you something of a crank," said Masters. "Then again, they may well say the same of me. I've read up on the events all those years ago. Are you truly convinced that what happened that night wasn't simply hysteria? A few villagers who let their superstitious beliefs get out of hand?"

"I am absolutely certain, and I fear it will happen again. Last night I cast the runes for the first time in years, and they warned of terrible misfortune to come. Terrible portents have plagued the village in the last few days. Sudden deaths

180

with no warning or ill health, stillborn livestock. People have reported seeing horrific things in the night. It's all a warning of what's to come."

"Indeed," nodded the vicar. "That's precisely why I am here."

"Really?" responded Miss Hawthorne, surprised.

"Indeed. When I learned that archaeologists planned to try to reopen the Hump, I put myself forward as the replacement for the former holder of this post. There could be deadly consequences if it is opened again."

"I had thought you might take some convincing."

"Not at all. I have studied the dark arts for many years."

"It is not right for a man of the cloth to be dabbling in these dark forces," insisted Miss Hawthorne.

"I disagree. The best way to defend against such things is with knowledge. I believe I am singularly qualified. I have dedicated my career to studying the occult. However," added the priest in a diplomatic tone, "I would greatly value your expert input on the matter."

Miss Hawthorne softened a little at the flattery as he continued.

"It's just that I'm not sure what you expect me to do. I doubt very much the archaeologists will be swayed by my opinion, let alone the film crew."

"Film crew?" responded Miss Hawthorne.

"Oh yes. BBC4, I understand. Eager to capture the great event for national broadcast."

"Reverend, if we could just try to explain to them the danger they are placing themselves in, surely they will listen."

"I'm not so sure they will," said Masters, closing the church door behind him, "but I suppose it's worth a try."

He led Miss Hawthorne through the churchyard and towards the vicarage, where a beaten-up old Honda sat. He opened the passenger door for her in a show of manners, but the witch paused before getting in, looking over her shoulder.

"Is something the matter?" asked Masters.

"I'm not certain," replied Miss Hawthorne. "I could have sworn something was following us."

***

The Devil's Hump was a barrow mound that rose from a field about a mile out of Devil's End. In itself it was unremarkable, but its historical significance made it a prime location for archaeological interest. For the last few years, however, it had lain untouched, the clay and soil hastily repaired over the site of the last

181

attempt to open it.

"It's All Hallows Eve 1999, and the burial mound of Devil's Hump is finally due to be opened... How does that sound, Jan?"

"It'll do perfectly fine, Steve," said the reporter, fixing his tie and admiring his dark reddish hair and trim beard in a make-up mirror. He turned to the young blond presenter and asked him, "How do I look?"

"Handsome as ever," replied the presenter, "although I don't see why you care. You're not the one who's in front of the camera."

He smiled.

"I always like to look my best."

"You'll look a sight better than those archaeologists," said Steve, tilting his head in the direction of the scruffy mob who were preparing to open the mound. "I thought Tony Robinson was heading that part?"

"He's come down with a sudden illness," said Jan.

"Him too? That's, what, six people now? And all different things?"

"Mmm. Most interesting, don't you think?"

Steve looked at the reporter, who stared back inscrutably.

"You creep me out sometimes, you know that?"

"Good," smiled the reporter.

Steve scrabbled through some notes as a battered car drove up to the site, pulling up next to the coach that had carried the crew in with a noisy struggle on the soft ground. To his dismay, a man in clergy's robes and an older woman in decidedly hippyish get-up climbed out of the car.

"Oh god, what now?"

"We need to speak to someone in charge," said the vicar in a strident tone.

"I'm presenting this dig," said Steve, "and I'm not disturbing the specialists unless there's a bloody good reason."

"What about the threat of the dark forces of the netherworld?" said the woman. "Is that a good enough reason?"

"Please, Miss Hawthorne," said the vicar, "let's not get overexcited. My name is Reverend Masters, I am the vicar for the parish and I must insist that the dig be halted, at least until we've spoken to someone in authority."

"And why's that?" sighed the presenter.

"The last time the Devil's Hump was opened, there were horrendous consequences. People turned to violence, it escalated to utter madness."

"The army had to be called in," added Miss Hawthorne.

"I know," said Steve, "there's all sort of weird stuff linked to this place. That's why we're here. It's history and it makes for good television. People love a bit of hysteria and murder from a bunch of yokels."

182

"Please," said Masters, "don't dismiss it simply as hysteria. It wasn't merely the army who were sent in to take control, it was a group called UNIT, tasked with protecting the world from unknown forces. Surely that tells you that there is something more to this?"

"I know all about UNIT," said Steve, who had presented an exposé on them a few years before. "They've been all but disbanded after that shambles at the Hong Kong handover. And that was only the latest in a long history of catastrophic blunders. You think their involvement means we should take this rubbish seriously?" He shook his head, his patience running out. He called over to the throng of techies and support staff. "Um, security please?"

"Please, you have to listen to us!" insisted Miss Hawthorne. "There is great evil here!"

"Sure there is, love," said the presenter as two burly men in black uniforms strode up. "You can explain it all to these nice gentlemen here." He gestured vaguely at the two guards, but the heavyset pair were rooted to the spot, staring at something in the sky behind him. "What now?" he sighed.

Jan calmly pointed to the skyline.

"I do believe we have bigger problems than a couple of interfering locals," he observed.

Steve, Masters and Miss Hawthorne looked, as one, in the direction of Jan's pointed finger. In the sky, approaching them with alarming speed, were four winged figures. As they came closer, it became clear that they were hewn from stone. Their grey, pocked visages were bestial and hideous. The creature at the front of the group was particularly monstrous, its face locked in a rictus sneer.

"By the Goddess," said Miss Hawthorne, "that's the statue from the churchyard!"

"They're all from the churchyard," said Masters. "It looks like we were followed after all."

"Bloody hell!" gasped the TV presenter, taking shelter behind the two terrified security guards.

The winged terrors descended on the crowd of archaeologists and televisual types, screeching and flapping their wings. The assembled people screamed and gasped in horror, running in all directions.

"Everyone," said Masters, "onto the coach!"

***

Steve led the panicked rush onto the vehicle, followed by all and sundry clambering aboard in panic as the creatures harassed them. In a few minutes,

183

the terrified people were crammed aboard, save a few who had made it to their own cars. The coach began to drive away, but the flying beasts launched an attack upon it. Their stone claws dug into the frame with an agonising screech of metal as they did their utmost to turn the vehicle over. Windows smashed inwards as clawed hands reached in to assail the passengers.

"We have to do something," said Miss Hawthorne, a new resolve coming over her. It had been a long time since she had cast a spell, but she had studied the arts for years and it wasn't something easily forgotten. Taking a deep breath, she put herself into a place of calm resolve, and began to chant.

"Wise One of the Waning Moon, Goddess of the Starry Night, I call on you! May the energies be reversed...
From darkness, light!
From bane, good!
From death, birth!
Begone, fiends! Avaunt!"

The creatures relented in their attack upon the bus, turning their attention to the witch. They flew in her direction as the coach accelerated away towards the village, churning up mud as it went.

"AVAUNT!" yelled Miss Hawthorne.

The monsters seemed momentarily stunned, and then collapsed to the ground, reverting to inanimate statues. They landed in the muck with heavy, dull splats, embedding themselves in the soil.

Miss Hawthorne stood there, astonished at the efficacy of her incantation.

Masters and Jan the reporter, the only people to have remained behind to witness her triumph, sounded equally impressed.

"Miss Hawthorne," said Masters, beaming, "that was remarkable!"

"Indeed it was," said Jan, turning to them. "My name is Jan Markazi," he continued. "I've also studied the history of the Devil's Hump. The horrors committed here go back for centuries. I am as dedicated as you are to containing this evil, believe me. That's why I'm here."

"Then you'll help us keep the barrow closed?" said Miss Hawthorne.

"The Hump is already partly opened," said Markazi. "It was never correctly sealed after the last attempt. Our best course of action is to open it completely, enter, and find out exactly what is waiting for us inside. Only then can we hope to deal with it, fully and finally."

"But that's the last thing we should do!" objected Miss Hawthorne.

"I agree with Mr. Markazi," said Masters.

Miss Hawthorne looked at him in surprise.

"Surely you can't seriously be suggesting that we actually open the Hump?"

"Miss Hawthorne, we can't hope to contain whatever is in there without understanding it first. The barrow is already compromised, it has been since that breach all those years ago and now it's only become worse. You saw those things! The forces of darkness are already manifesting. The genie is out and we can't just put a cork back in the bottle. We have to go all the way with this."

Miss Hawthorne still felt unsure, but Masters gently took hold of her shoulders and looked her in the eye.

"Trust me, Miss Hawthorne. Please."

"Very well, Reverend. If you're sure this is the only way."

***

Miss Hawthorne sat at the side of the barrow, holding her pentacle amulet in her hand tightly in case of any further visitations. Masters and Markazi dug earnestly at the barrow, breaking through the thick clay and compacted soil.

"We need to work quickly before the crews come back," said Markazi. "A few goblins might scare them off for a while, but they'll be back before long."

The wall broke through fully, muck collapsing down into the darkness. Markazi pulled a pen torch from the pocket of his overcoat. The torch illuminated a sloping run that led deep into the barrow.

"Miss Hawthorne!" called Masters. "We're through. Will you accompany us?"

"Of course I'll accompany you," replied the witch, pushing past the two men. "I'm the senior figure here. You'll need me should anything happen."

Miss Hawthorne held her pentacle ahead as Markazi shone his torch into the darkness. They walked cautiously onwards, down into an expansive cavern.

Miss Hawthorne jumped as oily torches on the walls suddenly burst to life, their flames flickering, illuminating the cavern and the human bones that were piled up on stone slabs along the cavern walls.

"Who lit those torches?" asked Masters.

"I should think they're magic," said Miss Hawthorne. "What concerns me more is that we're standing in a crypt."

"Druids and cultists have been sacrificing people here for centuries," pointed out Markazi, "where did you think they put the bodies?"

"Every time the barrow has been opened, chaos and horror has followed," added Masters, ominously.

Miss Hawthorne spotted something on the floor of the cavern, off-centre and covered in dust. She leant down and swept the surface clean. It was a stubby, roughly conical object about a foot long, in a dark grey material that felt metallic to the touch.

185

"What on Earth is this?" she wondered aloud.

"Nothing from Earth," said Markazi. "That is a spacecraft."

"Oh, really," scoffed Masters.

"Angels and spirits and the dark arts don't bother you," said Markazi, "but spaceships are too much? You disappoint me, Reverend."

"It does seem a little far-fetched," said Miss Hawthorne. "Isn't it a little small for a spaceship?"

"Why do you think UNIT was set up all those years ago? You're not the only one who's capable of research, Mr. Masters."

"Never mind that," dismissed the vicar, "look here." He lifted a torch off the wall and held it towards the floor beneath his feet, illuminating a large pentagram in blood-red paint.

"Excellent," said Markazi. "We're definitely in the right place. Now, traditionally a blood sacrifice was required to summon the dark forces, but with the psychic energy already brewing around here, I think this shall suffice." He removed a pen knife from his coat pocket, nicking his thumb, and squeezed a large blob of blood onto the pentagram with a flourish.

The ground rumbled.

"What in the name of the Goddess are you doing?" gasped Miss Hawthorne.

"Are you quite mad?" snapped Masters. "We need to approach this with care and control, not by throwing blood around and disturbing who knows what!"

"Too late now," smiled Markazi.

The ground rumbled again, and a tiny glint on the floor began to grow. In moments, it resolved into a tiny, humanoid figure. In a few moments more, a monstrous figure stood before them. Seven feet tall, with bulging muscles and long, hairy arms ending in vicious talons. Its legs were furred and ended in cloven hooves. Its face was twisted into a fanged snarl, its eyes blazed with fire and its head was crowned with gnarled, curved horns.

Miss Hawthorne gasped. It was the Horned King, the Beast of Abaddon, the Fallen One. She was staring up at the very Devil himself.

"Who has summoned me?!" boomed the voice of the monster, in a deafening roar.

"Miss Hawthorne, we have to subdue this beast," declared Masters. "Please, with me!"

Masters began to chant, deep, sonorous strings of words in Latin, Greek and Aramaic. In spite of her fear, Miss Hawthorne joined in the chant – the words of her faith, calling on the spirits of Samhain to protect her.

As Masters continued to chant, the devil was visibly weakening. The creature's ungulate legs buckled, its clawed fingers clutching at its horned skull.

186

It looked at the vicar with red, slitted eyes – a look of pain and fury on its face.

"Cease this!" it snarled. "I will listen to your demands."

"I have no demands," stated Masters. "I wish only for you to stand down!"

Markazi stepped towards the vicar.

"Oh, I'm sure we can come up with something a little more ambitious," he said.

Miss Hawthorne gasped as the journalist pulled a pistol from the confines of his coat. Without so much as blinking, Markazi shot Masters, the bullet puncturing the vicar's chest. The shot rang out deafeningly, echoing around the cavern.

Masters slumped to the ground. Miss Hawthorne rushed over to him, but she was too late. She felt the life leave him. His spirit had left his body.

"Why?" she demanded. "What possible reason do you have to kill this man?"

"That insignificant little man would have wasted this incredible opportunity," replied Markazi. "I shall take full advantage of it." He began to chant, repeating the arcane words that Masters had used to subdue the monster. A smile spread across his bearded face.

"Mal lettil ah dah Yram…" he intoned.

It had little effect. The devil stood straight upon his cloven hooves once again, looking down malevolently at the man who would try to control him.

"I do not submit to you," boomed the creature.

"Azal, last of the Dæmons, heed my words!"

"You know my name," said the monster, "and the name of my kind?" The growl had taken on a questioning tone.

"I do," stated Markazi. "I know your kind of old. The great travellers of Dæmos. You came to this world thousands of years ago, to begin a long trial of mankind."

"Who are you?" cried Miss Hawthorne, horrified at the man who stood tall in front of the very devil himself.

"I am the Master," he exclaimed, holding his hands wide. "You may better know me as Professor Emil Keller, or perhaps as Ke Le. I've had a few aliases over the last twenty years or so."

"You are not from this world," stated Azal. It was not a question.

"So good of you to notice," replied the Master. "I am far above these pitiful primates, as are you, great Azal. I demand that I have the right to your great power, not these primitives."

Miss Hawthorne looked between the Dæmon and the man who demanded his obedience, desperation and power lust on his face, and she couldn't decide who looked the more thoroughly evil.

187

"No," boomed the Dæmon.

"What?" cried the Master.

"The Earth creature may have been primitive, but he had spent many months preparing for my summoning. His power was evident. Yours is not."

"His power?! You think the terrors that awoke you from your sleep came from him, that white-hearted fool? This is what summoned you!"

The Master reached into his greatcoat once more, pulling out a pale earthenware flask, mottled and distorted with age.

Azal tilted its head slightly as it looked at the trinket.

"A bottle?"

"You think you're old, Dæmon? You have no conception of the powers that existed in this universe before you came along."

Miss Hawthorne, in spite of her fear, had to know what he had. The bottle looked harmless, but she could feel the power emanating from within it.

"What is it?" she asked. "What do you intend to do?"

"When I escaped from China, I spent many months travelling across Asia, looking for a way off this benighted planet. In the Middle East, I uncovered this – the flask of Hastur."

The name struck fear into Miss Hawthorne's heart.

"The Unspeakable One!" she gasped. It was a monstrous evil that even she had never suspected could really exist.

"Worshipped as Yama, Fenric, and any number of things over the millennia. I had hoped to use its power, but it proved just as stubborn as you, Dæmon. I managed to contain it back in its prison, after a gruelling series of games that taxed even my intellect. Even so, the power of Hastur attracts all manner of, shall we say, unusual activity. Just the sort of thing to evoke strong negative emotions in a village full of humans."

The Dæmon knelt down, bringing its bestial visage terrifyingly close to the Master's. The creature's hot breath warmed his face, and he grimaced slightly.

"I defy you, little man," snarled the Dæmon in a low rumble.

The Master sighed.

"Well," he said, "don't say I didn't give you a chance."

He dropped the bottle onto the stone floor, where it smashed into a dozen pieces. Thick, oily fumes escaped from the debris, sickly green in colour, twisting as if alive while moving through the air. The gas steered towards the lifeless body of the Reverend Masters, slithering into his nostrils.

The body jerked upright, stiffly rising to its feet.

Masters opened his eyes. They shone with the same toxic green hue as the fumes that now animated his body.

"Free…" hissed the Unspeakable One, through dead lips.

"Yes, well, you're not going to have much time to enjoy it," apologised the Master. He pointed up at the towering form of Azal. "This gentleman considers himself to have complete power over mankind. I imagine you might have something to say about that."

The animated body of Masters looked up at the Dæmon with undisguised hatred and contempt.

"It is I who wields power over this world," it hissed.

"I'll leave it to you to sort out the details," said the Master. He stooped down to the miniature spacecraft that still sat on the crypt floor. Reaching once again into his capacious coat, he removed a small, black circular device, which he attached to the ship. "Miss Hawthorne, this handy device will reduce the weight of the ship enough to allow us to move it, but I will require another pair of hands. Unless you want to stay here while these two slug it out, I suggest you lend me a hand."

The living cadaver opened its arms wide, and unleashed a series of electrical bolts that arced towards the Dæmon, who staggered backwards, before retaliating with a vicious swipe of its claws. The body of Masters was thrown into the cavern wall, but creakily returned to its feet.

"You are truly evil," said Miss Hawthorne, "but these devils are worse!" She ran over to help the Master.

The cavern was illuminated in flickering blue as the Dæmon unleashed its own torrent of lightning bolts at the animate cadaver. Miss Hawthorne flinched as the body writhed, but it still stood, flesh smoking and hissing.

"Out of the barrow with me, now!" commanded the Master, and he and Miss Hawthorne heaved the tiny ship. It was like trying to carry a boulder upstairs, but between them they hefted the object up the slope and out of the Hump. They dumped it onto the damp grass. Miss Hawthorne collapsed onto the ground, exhausted.

"Now what do we do?" she asked.

"We?" said the Master, with a cruel laugh. "We don't do anything." He pulled a slim cylindrical device from his pockets and pointed it at the ship. "You may want to move out of the way as I provide this vessel with the energy it needs to resume its full size. It's all the same to me."

A beam of white fire shot from the end of the device and hit the ship, which began to vibrate alarmingly. Miss Hawthorne gasped and stepped back, as the ship began to increase in size rapidly. In moments, it was the same rough size and shape as the Hump, but stood proudly above the ground.

There was a rumble from the ground beneath. With an earth-shattering

189

crunch, the barrow erupted. Azal pushed its way out from the crumbling earth, while around him, crystals of ice and frost spread across the grass, rapidly approaching Miss Hawthorne and the Master. The Dæmon grew, increasing in size in the same way as the ship, but it did not stop until it was towering over them both.

The now mangled body of the Reverend Masters floated up into the sky, bringing the phantom face-to-face with the Dæmon. The sickly green glow that emanated from the body spread outward, tendrils of energy interacting with the stone gargoyles and grotesques that lay strewn on the ground. The petrified creatures began to move again, reanimated by the dark power of the being.

"Goodbye, Miss Hawthorne," said the Master, wrenching open a hatchway in the side of the alien craft. "Thank you so much for your help in this matter. Do enjoy the Earth… what's left of it."

He slammed the hatch shut behind him. Miss Hawthorne could only watch as the ship lifted into the air and, without warning, accelerated into the sky and out of site. A barrage of air hit her and forced her to the ground, as the ice encroached upon her. She looked helplessly up at the two nightmares as they battled each other, the Dæmon throwing bolts of lightning at the gargoyles that swarmed around it, while the possessed body of Masters attacked with its own noxious energies. The sky began to darken as black clouds formed overhead, while from the very earth itself a haze of fire began to rise.

The last thing Miss Hawthorne saw before the combination of heat, cold and fear overtook her was the two monstrosities making their way towards the village of Devil's End, as all Hell truly broke loose.

One Night in Wartime
Stephen Hatcher

Cautiously he opened one eye and took in his situation. A cell – that was nothing new, nothing that he hadn't become far too used to over the years. But this time was different; something didn't feel right. Oh, that was interesting. It occurred to him that he had no idea how he came to be here. There appeared to be quite a gap in his memory. Now, what was the last thing he remembered? He thought for a moment. Ah yes, of course; the castle on the island – Trenchard. And then *he* came to visit, to check that he was comfortable. *Him*, as patronising and annoying as ever. And the girl, Miss Grant, she was there too. It was starting to come back to him now. He remembered their visit, but then nothing. How had he come to be here? He was clearly still a prisoner, but of whom?

He tried to sit up, but found he had been strapped to some sort of bunk. All he could do for now was move his head and look around. A plain cell, metal door shut; to the right of it a locking panel with one blinking red light; an upright control console of some sort, with a number of buttons; and two bunks – two. And the other one was also occupied – he wasn't alone. Seeing who was strapped unconscious to the other bunk, he remembered more. He remembered who his captors were and why he was here. He chuckled to himself. Of course, that was it. It was her, UNIT operative and *His* companion, Miss Josephine Grant. Patience now, patience. They would be coming to see him soon enough.

She stirred – the girl was waking up.

"Miss Grant, hello. Wake up please. Hello, Miss Grant. Can you hear me?"

He saw her eyes open and took quiet pleasure in the look of alarm she gave him.

"You, the Master! I might have known it." He watched her pull against her bonds and then give up, in the realisation that she too was helpless. She turned angrily towards him, "now just you untie me and let me go."

"But Miss Grant, as you can see, I am in precisely the same predicament that you are."

"Don't give me that. What are you up to?"

"I can assure you, Miss Grant, I..."

At that moment he was cut short as he heard the sound of bolts pulling back and the door opened. There was no mistaking the familiar shape that glided into the cell: the metallic skirt with those bumps, the purpose of which he had never

191

fathomed; the dome with the flashing lights, just in case anyone wasn't quite sure when the creature was speaking and the eye stalk – what a curiously impractical means of seeing that was; the two arms – the weapon and the sucker; and then there was the faint whiff of ozone that seemed to accompany these creatures wherever they went. It was a truly ridiculous creature, but for all that the Master was in no doubt as to just how deadly it was. The Dalek stopped at the console, extended its sucker arm and manipulated one of the controls. With a faint whir, the two bunks swivelled into a vertical position. The Master felt the bonds tighten around him, holding him more firmly in place. The Dalek approached him and spoke. "You are known to us. Why have the Time Lords sent you here?"

"The Time Lords? If you truly know who I am – and why would you not know? – then you will also know that no one sends me anywhere, least of all the Time Lords."

"Then why are you here?"

"I came of my own free will, in friendship, to propose an alliance – and to present you with a gift."

"A gift? What gift?"

"This girl of course." He nodded towards Jo Grant, who stifled a cry. "The girl, Miss Josephine Grant, companion of your greatest enemy."

At this, the Dalek became visibly agitated. "The Doctor? The Doctor's companion. You lie. Where is the Doctor? Why are you here? Answer! Answer!"

The Dalek extended its sucker arm and placed it on the Master's head. He convulsed as he felt an overwhelming pain seize his every nerve, but he resisted the urge to scream.

"Answer! Answer!"

The girl cried out, "Stop, stop. You're hurting him."

"I am telling the truth. This is the Doctor's companion, consult your data banks," spat the Master through gritted teeth.

The Dalek paused as if in consideration. It retracted the sucker arm and moved back to the control console. The Master slumped briefly in relief, then he straightened up again and watched the Dalek operate a switch. A screen lit up and a succession of human faces began scrolling down, finally coming to rest on the face of the girl in the cell – Jo Grant.

The Dalek returned to confront the Master, who looked it defiantly in the eye stalk. "Now will you believe me? Cut me down from here so that we can talk".

"The girl has no value to the Daleks. Why have the Time Lords sent you here?"

"I keep telling you, no one has sent me."

Once again the Dalek applied the sucker to the Master's head and once again the pain was all-encompassing. When it was over, the Master took a moment to regain his composure, then spoke, quietly and coldly. "No one sent me. I am here to propose an alliance. As for the girl, take her or don't. Do as you like with her, I really don't care."

"Why you…" exploded Jo Grant furiously. "Just you wait until the Doctor gets here. He'll…"

"Silence!" The Dalek turned towards her. She fell silent, meeting its cold gaze.

"The Daleks have no use for you. You will be exterminated."

Without further warning, the creature fired. Jo Grant didn't have time to cry out or to flinch before her lifeless corpse fell to the floor.

The Master watched her die, without reacting. "Very well, you didn't need the girl. You have made your point. Now perhaps you can release me and we can discuss our common interests and our future collaboration".

The Dalek turned back to him and uttered one word. The Master froze in horror, "No, I…" The Dalek fired and the Master slumped dead in his bonds.

***

Cardinal Karlan turned from the screen to his fellow Time Lord. "It would seem you were right, Larello. This one has all the cunning and ruthlessness required, but his arrogance leads him into carelessness and over-confidence. He won't do for what we need. Switch it off, let's try another one."

Larello flicked a switch and the Dalek and the two corpses in the cell faded away, as if they had never been there.

***

Nyssa awoke with a start and took in her surroundings. Not another cell! How had she got here? She remembered landing on Deva Loka, feeling unwell and returning to her bed. And now this. Well, clearly this wasn't the TARDIS, so it was probably safe to assume that someone had brought her here.

"Hello, my dear. I was wondering if I should wake you, but I see there is no need."

She froze at the sound of that voice. It was a voice that she had once loved more than any other, but it was different now. All the warmth it once held had

193

been drained and replaced with cynicism and cold-hearted evil. She turned to see that once-loved face; a face that had been stolen by her father's murderer.

"The Master. Where have you brought me to?"

The Master chuckled quietly and walked over to her. Behind him, she could see an incongruous wooden wardrobe. It was doubtless his TARDIS and almost certainly, he had brought her here in it, but why?

"There will be time for that later. For now, we must prepare ourselves to meet our hosts."

He walked over to a panel by the door. Pressing a switch, he spoke into a grill. "Daleks, listen to me. This is the Master speaking. Come in now, I need to speak to you".

There was no reply, but almost immediately came the sound of bolts being drawn back, and the door opened. Although she had never seen one before, Nyssa recognized the creature that entered from a thousand childhood tales, not to mention those that the Doctor had told. The dread that the Dalek inspired in her was very real.

It spoke. "Your offer is refused. The Daleks have no need of renegade Time Lords."

"But I have brought you the girl, the Doctor's friend, as a token of my good will."

"The girl may be of some use. You however, have no value to the Daleks."

Nyssa became aware that the Master was edging towards her.

The Dalek turned to face her. "The girl will be interrogated. She may have useful knowledge."

"But I brought her to you. Together, you and I; the Master and the Daleks; we can defeat the Time Lords."

Nyssa said nothing, her eyes fixed upon the Dalek.

"The Daleks will defeat the Time Lords. You will be ext…"

The Master didn't give the Dalek time to fire; he threw himself behind Nyssa, pushing her towards the Dalek. At the same instant the Dalek fired, hitting her at point blank. She took the full blast and fell dead to the floor. Before the Dalek could recover its balance, the Master ran to his TARDIS. He pulled open the door as the Dalek prepared to fire again. Then, Dalek and Master both froze, caught in a lifeless tableau.

**

"This one is worse than the last. He has all the over-confidence and arrogance of the others, but with none of their courage or determination."

Karlan nodded and Larello flicked the switch. The occupants of the cell vanished again. Karlan sighed, "That's four of them now. None of them have what we need and the situation is becoming urgent. Let's look at the next one".

Larello turned a dial on the control console and the two Time Lords watched the screen intently as another projection took shape.

***

In the cell, the single shape of a man came into being. Tall, with slicked-back dark hair, the man was wearing a long leather coat and dark glasses. He looked up melodramatically. When he spoke, it was in a pronounced American accent. "Well now, what have we here?" At that moment, two fingers fell from his left hand to the floor. The Master shuffled uncomfortably, gave an embarrassed grin and kicked them deftly into the corner of the cell as if nothing had happened.

***

"No, no. This one just won't do at all. For one thing, he's falling to bits." Karlan was becoming more and more frustrated. "Just look at him. Turn him off; this sort of pantomime is the last thing we need."

"But Cardinal, don't you think we ought at least to have a look at him; to be certain? After all, he is the last one."

"No, we haven't got the time. Despite the victories that the Doctor has won, we are losing the Time War. At the rate things are deteriorating, the Daleks will soon be upon us. The Doctor has been successful, precisely because of who he is; a maverick – unpredictable and uncontrollable. The High Council, in spite of their reservations – and there were many – have decided that we need another such maverick operative. Someone who can, along with the Doctor, win us the war, but someone even more unpredictable, more ruthless; someone less governed by that moral code that has on occasions held the Doctor back."

Larello looked uncertain. "But, the Master? He's never been a friend of Gallifrey. Can we really place our hopes in him?"

"The Master may be our only hope. Clearly, those of his incarnations that we have already seen will be of no use to us, but we must continue to explore all options in order to decide which of his regenerative forms is the one that can win us the war."

"But Cardinal, you speak of exploring all options, but we've done that now. We've seen them all. Our options have run out."

195

Karlan paused before answering. "That's not quite true Larello."

Larello gave a quizzical look.

"Press the switch and you will see."

Hesitatingly, Larello obeyed the command and both Time Lords watched the screen. The figure that materialised seated on the bunk appeared older than those that had come before. He was shorter in stature, with short, grey hair. His cold blue eyes stared unblinking ahead. He remained frozen, immobile.

Larello looked to his superior in horror. "But that's impossible."

"No, not impossible, although certainly a most unusual step; and one only to be taken in the most extreme of circumstances. The High Council have called up a new incarnation of the Master from the Matrix; a composite version of all his previous selves. This one is a last resort, designed in case all the previous versions proved unusable – as now they have."

Larello shook his head, "But that's incredibly dangerous. The Matrix doesn't exist to create new Time Lords."

"Which is why we needed to be certain, why we needed to be absolutely sure that none of the others would suit our purposes. Now, I won't ask you to do it, the responsibility must be mine. Stand aside Larello."

Hesitatingly, Larello ceded his position at the control panel and stepped slowly back. Karlan took his place and flicked the switch. He turned to Larello with a grim look. "There, it is done. I just hope it will be worth it."

The figure in the cell remained immobile, showing no sign at all of any change in his condition. Then as Karlan and Larello watched on with trepidation, the cold blue eyes blinked slowly. A humourless smile spread across the malevolent features. Then the head moved and he began to look around the cell. Rising to his feet, he went to explore his surroundings, examining every inch in great detail – the bunks, the door, the instrument console. Then to Larello and Karlan's consternation, the new-born Master turned to face them directly. It was as if he could see them as clearly as they could see him, although they knew that this was impossible. Then he spoke. The voice was quiet and cultured, soft and enticing. Every syllable dripped honey, but there was no missing the underlying menace.

"Oh hello, there. Are you watching carefully? I hope you can see. Well, I appear to be your prisoner – for now. Now, isn't that amusing."

The look of astonishment that Larello gave Karlan was met with one of alarm. Neither spoke. As they continued to watch, they could see the door to the cell sliding open. The Master had his back to the Dalek that had just entered. In one movement, he retrieved a blaster from inside his clothing and without turning, fired on the Dalek, destroying it completely. The remains of the creature shimmered and disappeared.

The whole time, the Master's gaze had not left the two Time Lords." Well now, that was interesting wasn't it?" he said. "Did you find it interesting? I do hope so. Have I passed your little test?"

"Quick! Turn him off. This is all wrong."

From Karlan's tone, Larello knew that the situation was serious. He reached for the controls and flicked the switch to turn off the projection. His sigh of relief was cut short. Karlan was still staring in alarm at the screen. Nothing had changed.

The Master chuckled quietly. "I'm afraid that won't have any effect upon me. I'm not quite like those projections you've been experimenting upon. I'm afraid this is very much the real me. Yes, me! Just imagine! The Master, returned to live again. I must thank the High Council for that. Will you pass on my thanks? Oh no, of course, how silly of me, you're not going to be able to, are you?"

Larello's attention was drawn back to the control panel, where a single red light was flashing furiously. "Cardinal Karlan, we need to get out of here. Now!"

The two Time Lords dived for the door. Karlan pressed the key pad, but nothing happened – the door remained resolutely closed.

"Goodbye then gentlemen, must dash."

The Master's voice was the last thing Karlan and Larello would ever hear. They had barely enough time to share a look of fearful realisation before the room was engulfed in a ball of fire. The intensity of the inferno ensured there would be nothing left of them to regenerate.

The Master spoke to himself as he turned and walked over towards the console, "Yes gentlemen, goodbye. I'm afraid you won't be able to take my message to the High Council. Still, never mind, I'll be able to tell them directly, soon enough. Yes, I'll tell them. I'll tell them that I'll fight in their Time War, as and when I want to; under my terms. I will not be prodded and poked and experimented upon. If they want my services, they need to be very clear about that. They need to understand that I am the Master and they will obey me."

With a final chuckle, he opened a hitherto unseen door in the side of the console and walked into his TARDIS. With a loud wheezing noise, the console disappeared.

The Patient
Tim Gambrell

Everyone looked on for days as the battle raged in the skies above. Around the distant twinkling stars, within the blackness of space, shapes danced and flashed. Colours blossomed and bloomed, straining at the edges of perception; shockwaves heaved and rucked in all directions. It was a free show for everyone, but Costan felt an ache in the very marrow of his young bones: this didn't bode well for the human colony settled there on Keefney 4. First there were the visions, the flashes of another life – a life that was almost the same as theirs but different: greyness, choking filth and oppressive technology. Waves of tall buildings, endless seas of land vehicles, it all washed through Costan's peripheral vision – yet it was nowhere to be seen when he turned his head. But something was up; he coughed up a grey gobbet of sputum – it smelled of petrochemicals.

And then, quite simply one night, the sky was wiped clean before their very eyes; the battle vanished. Watching this happen, Costan felt his world shrink, as if possibilities had suddenly ceased and boundaries had been erected around them. He frantically scoured the firmament for more signs. As dawn painted the sky its more familiar lilac hue, Costan noticed a single point of darkness remaining above. He watched as, in silence, the dark point grew larger and larger. Something was coming their way; something big. When it was larger than his splayed hand, Costan suddenly feared and ran. He ran and ran all the way to his home, screaming in terror as something innate told him that they were all in danger. At the door, he turned to check behind him, and that was when the ship impacted.

The crash was tremendous in all respects. The noise was deafening; searing heat and blinding light exploded from the impact and washed over the land. Costan's teeth melted mid-scream, and his eyeballs crystallised and cracked in their sockets. The parched flesh then charred on the remains of his skeleton before slowly reducing to dust on the deadly breeze. By the time he would have hit the ground, nothing of him remained.

Silence; utter, deafening silence.

For an eternity.

Or a moment.

Time no longer mattered.

And then, from somewhere – nowhere, and yet everywhere – there was a speculative click and a notional whirr. Then a hypothetical hum. The planet shuddered as if someone had just walked over its grave and, quite suddenly, time reversed and life found itself dragged back into existence. Structures rebuilt themselves, the dead reformed as they had been in life; Costan found himself screaming in his doorway and looking at the crashed spacecraft which had suddenly appeared between his family home and the village. The scream died on his lips. A few startled la-la birds flap-waddled away to peck at the perimeter hedge. Costan breathed heavily for a few moments then turned and walked into his home.

He hadn't slept, and the time for such things had passed, so Costan went straight to his room, freshened up at the wash pan in the corner and changed into clean overalls. He watched the dust motes as they danced on the sunbeams streaming through the gaps in his raffia blinds – as usual. His mother would claim it was time for him to give the room a clean, no doubt. Feeling as revived as he was likely to get, Costan wandered back through into the living space where his mother, father and sister were now seated, eating their daily *dahlee* fruit. Costan stretched and flexed and popped three small fruits in his mouth with practiced ease; the smaller ones were always the sweetest – although you had to watch out for the pips.

"You off to the fields?" his father called, as Costan headed towards the door. He mumbled something affirmative through his bulging mouthful and spat a pip into his hand, before signifying an explosion and waving a cheery goodbye.

***

The temperate westerly breeze tenderly caressed Costan's face as he strode along the crop-lined pathways towards the village. On a normal day he'd be heading there to receive his daily work allocation from the Ruling Committee. But today was different; today there was something huge and hot and broken obstructing him. He approached the wreckage with wonder.

Costan's eyes may have feasted as he advanced, but his nose rebelled; the stench was atrocious, and it left a metallic aftertaste on his tongue. The very *essence* of the crashed space craft was fundamentally wrong, anathema to the way they had chosen to live on Keefney 4. He shuddered. But despite the discomfort the crash site induced, Costan knew there might be injured people inside and that he needed to be true to himself and help any survivors if he could. He took pride in being a good citizen – a helpful person.

Sporadic crop fires littered the perimeter of the crash site, but Costan nimbly made his way through these to one of the enormous rents in the flank of the metal leviathan. Inside was a mess of twisted metal, melting plastic and sparking wires, but the bloody carnage Costan had feared was singularly lacking. Perhaps, he thought – he hoped – the vehicle had been unoccupied when it crashed? After clambering through the wreckage for some time he finally stumbled across a sole occupant: a formally attired man apparently in the latter half of middle age. The man was lying, crumpled and bloodied next to the crushed remains of what appeared to be a vessel or possibly a dispenser of some kind. Whatever it was, thick fluid oozed from cracks in its outer casing and pooled on the floor beneath. The smell was sickening, like cream left out for days under the hot sun.

Costan heaved and retched as he scrambled over the metal debris. The closer he got to the recumbent figure the more dizzying the stench became, causing him to lose his footing and yelp as his fingertips caught on some fizzing wire ends. He snatched his hand away immediately and his foot slipped through an unbalanced floor plate. Costan yelped again and swore at his own clumsiness. He pulled himself upright, and the flooring clanged back into position. He spat to try to stop himself from throwing up and heard the figure stir. The man opened his bleary eyes and locked them on to Costan momentarily. Costan was amazed that, after what must have been a terrible ordeal, the man was still alive.

"H–help me…" the figure croaked, bubbles of bloodied saliva forming at the corners of his mouth. "Ta…"

"It's okay," said Costan, "don't thank me yet. But I'll make you better, I promise, then you can thank me. Come, I'll take you to my home – it's not far."

The figure swallowed, then coughed. Moving the dispenser's plunger arm off the man, Costan bent and scooped him up into his arms. The figure gave a little grunt as he did so and held a hand to Costan's shoulder – an autonomic gesture of dependence.

He saw no one as he staggered out of the crash site. If anyone else was taking an interest then they were obviously taking it from afar. No doubt there would be a meeting of the ruling committee this morning. He would tell them of the man he'd saved if they came asking. Perhaps. Something itched at the back of Costan's mind, something that told him this patient was special and needed to be kept secret. He walked home, only occasionally pausing to adjust his load.

Costan wiped around the stranger's nose and chin, and tucked him in to his bed. He would sleep on the floor until the man was better. His mother looked on from the doorway, concern etched on to her heavily lined face.

"Have you not been working today, Stanny?"

201

"I must tend to this man, Mother. He is injured. It is important to me."

"I see. You are a kind lad. But there is also our family to feed and clothe. The first of the harvests will be due about now, I'm sure."

"Father is out there. He earns more than I can."

"Your father is getting old, Stan."

"Where is Zilla? Send her to the fields."

His mother did not answer, she just walked silently away. Costan didn't see, he remained focussed only on his patient, lying deathly still and breathing shallowly.

***

"Son?"

Costan jerked in the chair as he sat beside his bed and once again wiped fresh blood from his patient's face. The voice was his father's.

"Father, come and see. I've saved a good man from the wreckage."

He stood and stepped away from the bedside to allow his father to take the seat. He watched as his father approached, staring down at the patient.

"You know he's a good man?"

"I…" The patient shifted slightly in the bed, as if spasming briefly. "Shh, shh," said Costan soothingly. "Was there a meeting in the village today, Father? About the crash?"

"We are not to go near it. The committee have decreed the area is no longer part of the settlement."

"Will it be guarded?"

"Such questions, Costan. It is harvest time, everyone is needed to work in the fields – including you. You can leave your patient tomorrow and return to the rosters. Mother will check on him while you're gone."

"But Mother is always so busy, Father. I dare not take the risk. He needs constant attention."

"Costan, I have said, and you will obey. Your mother will look after him during the day and you can tend to him in the evenings – if the committee allow him to stay."

"If? No, Father, no. We cannot tell them."

"Son, we have to. It is our duty as members of this society."

"No. They will take him away, or he will become a spectacle. He needs peace and quiet and gentle care."

The patient's eyes suddenly flicked open. Costan saw his father back away out of the chair, holding the patient in his gaze the whole time.

202

"What is it, Father?"

"Costan, who is this?" His father's voice was etched with fear.

"I do not know that yet, Father. Does it matter? He is sick and needs help."

Costan watched as the two men stared at each other.

"The eyes," mumbled his father, "they are… evil. He must go."

Costan dashed forward, intercepting his father as the older man reached out his hands to grab the patient.

"No, Father!"

Surprised by his own strength, Costan had already forced his father from the room and wedged the door shut before he realised precisely what he'd done.

"Thank you," croaked the figure in the bed.

Costan wasn't sure if this was followed by a weak cough or a light chuckle, but by the time he returned to his seat of vigil the patient was once again unresponsive.

***

The following morning, Costan was awoken by the sound of weeping from outside his door. Checking first that the patient was comfortable, he unbarred the door and crept through into the living space. There he found his mother and sister in tears. They rushed to Costan as soon as he appeared.

"Oh my son, what happened with your father last night? He has disappeared. What are we to do?"

"Disappeared?"

"I have not seen him since I went to bed. Zilla has been to the village, no one has seen him."

"What could have happened?"

"You fought, didn't you? You have never fought before. Why has that changed, Stanny?"

"Father wanted to hurt the stranger."

"I do not like this. I am wishing you had never brought that injured man home with you."

"And I do not understand this intolerance."

Costan turned to go.

"May I see him, the stranger?"

The question caught Costan unawares and his immediate impulse was to scream "no!" He realised as he mouthed the word how proprietorial he was being and nodded his assent instead, holding out his arm in a 'help yourself' gesture to the bedroom door. He watched his mother enter before heading to the food box, where only scraps remained.

***

Costan heard a wooden tapping, somewhere in the distance – which was odd since he was working in the open fields. Except – was he working? Why were the crops so tall? Or why was he so small? And it was dark. No. It was the crops, closing in around him, blocking out the sunlight; the heavy yellowing leaves pressed on his shoulders, pushing him down…

Costan jerked awake in the chair. Zilla was there in front of him, a hand on his shoulder. "You are needed in the fields, Stan," she said gently. "Leave your patient; we have no food now."

The rest was a blur. Somehow Costan had lost control; he'd virtually hurled his sister from the room and once again jammed the door shut before returning to sit beside the patient in his bed.

The patient smiled up at him. Yes, he had cold eyes, but he'd been in a battle and such things were bound to take a psychological toll on people. The patient's face and head were looking much improved now; the bleeding had stopped and the cuts and grazes were healing over nicely. His steel-grey hair was thicker and quite striking after a thorough brushing. He pushed himself up the pillow slightly and smiled again at Costan.

"Thank you Costan," he said, his voice low and oily but exuding authority. Costan could tell this was someone of senior rank, someone important. This would bring glory to his family, he was sure.

"You still need to rest."

"I just want to drink some water without choking, or you spilling it."

Costan smiled with embarrassment at his own lack of skill. "Sorry."

"It's a small inconvenience considering what you've done for me, boy, think nothing of it."

"What is your name, stranger?"

The patient smiled but didn't answer directly. "Would you like to know what I was doing on that spaceship?"

"I assume you were in charge?" The patient laughed long and hard at this.

"There was a war. There *is* a war. There will be a war. There always has been a war and there never was a war, and never will there ever not be a war." The patient grew in stature as he spoke, and as he grew more rigid so his voice became a mere expectorate of loathing.

Costan didn't even pretend to understand, but he looked upon the patient with caring, considerate eyes, and the patient told Costan wild tales of incredible peoples, inconceivable weapons and mind-blowing battles.

"What you witnessed in the stars above your planet for those days was a battle that for us lasted mere seconds – an encounter, a scuffle, nothing more. But would you believe that when we entered your star system you were a strong, technologically advanced human colony, covering four viable planetoids?"

Costan thought about his visions during the battle, the things he could almost not see in his peripheral sight. The grime he had coughed up. He nodded.

"One blast of alternative time and the whole of this sector was rewritten instantly. You became a small rural colony, turning your back on technology. Such power. Ha! We are like gods…" The patient's eyes glinted manically as he stared out into the distance.

***

Costan woke late the next day, feeling very weak. He dragged himself from his makeshift bed on the floor, but only as far as the chair which separated him from his patient; he couldn't have slept well – although he neither recalled having a bad night, nor indeed going to bed in the first place. He sat, burying his face in his hands and trying to gather himself together. His quickened heartbeat throbbed in his ears, along with the laboured rasps of his breathing.

Costan remembered he wasn't alone; the presence of the patient helped him focus. Despite his clattering and panting, the figure in the bed remained peacefully slumbering. The regular rise and fall of the blanket against the sunlit backdrop behind belied deep, powerful breaths. Costan felt proud, vindicated. The mercy he had shown, the care he had given, would pay off. And not just for him, but for his whole family. He must tell the others. But, of course, there were none of the usual sounds of morning life.

Confusion again. Why was no one else up and about? Mother always rose early to air the house, feed the la-la birds, open the water valves. Around the edges of his bedroom door no light shone. With an effort, he stood and left his room. No one was in the living space; the shutters were closed and the rest of the house still sat in darkness. He called out. No one answered. He checked the food box; empty. And, goodness, how his body ached. What was going on?

Leaving the shutters closed, Costan wandered to the front door and threw it open. Intense sunlight hit him like a focussed beam. Costan staggered, momentarily, as if the sunlight had substance, before masking his eyes from the glare and stepping out. It hadn't occurred to him that he was still wearing only a vest and bed shorts. He noted some kerfuffle towards the village so he set off to see what was going on. As he approached he saw that there was a guarded cordon around the wrecked spaceship.

"What's happened, fellow?" he asked a guard as he approached.

"Name?" asked the guard.

"Costan."

"The Overseers have ordered the wreckage out of bounds."

"That happened days ago. I didn't think they could spare anyone to guard it? My father said–"

"It needs to be guarded while it is made safe."

"Safe?"

"Safe. There is some… equipment held by the Overseers that registers danger to health. Fallout."

"What is 'fallout'? Has something dangerous fallen out of the wreckage?"

"Perhaps. Go home Costan, there will be a curfew and your family will be told when you can return to work."

"I don't know where my family are. We have no food."

"I will see if some can be sent to you. Now return home."

Costan turned, breathing with exertion after the exchange and started dragging his legs homeward. If there was indeed danger in the crashed space ship, he was glad he'd not been back near it for a few days. But right now he needed to go back to bed, that much was clear.

***

A noise caused Costan to stir. He woke stiffly and found himself on the bench seat in the living space – he hadn't even made it to bed. Had he been that tired when he got home? He couldn't remember again. Ignoring the screaming pain in his back, he pulled himself into a sitting position. A figure was moving around across the other side of the room, rushing about and fussing energetically. It was the patient, now dressed in his original smart clothing again. Costan swelled with pride; he had helped the patient recover from his injuries, and now the man was well enough to live an active life once again. The patient turned, alerted by Costan's laboured grunts.

"Ah, you've awoken. How are you feeling?"

"Terrible," Costan replied. "My whole body throbs, I'm freezing cold, my head is buzzing, and I feel sick." His throat was like sandpaper too, but this was obvious from the sound of his voice.

206

The patient showed no concern, grabbing a small collection of items into a cloth bag and moving instead to a tall clock against the far wall.

Costan frowned through his pain. *That hadn't been there before.* "What's… where did that come from?" he managed to mutter, before collapsing back onto the bench and rolling on to the rough floor, coughing. He saw the patient's fine black shoed feet approach across the room towards him. One of these feet reached out and nudged his shoulder, forcing him onto his back. He looked up at the face of his patient: a twisted, scowling face with eyes full of scorn.

"That clock is my TARDIS. That'll mean nothing to you, of course, but I want this to: I am The Master, and you have obeyed me."

Costan had thought he was already cold, but at these words – and the hatred evident in the patient's eyes – a chill ran through Costan's spine; he'd only wanted to help a sick man, how had it all come to this?

"I assume you do realise that you're dying? I'd wager you have little time left, but I doubt the knowledge will help you at all." The patient started to wander further and Costan followed him with his eyes as best he was able. "But just so you know, every evening since you first brought me back here you have done my bidding under hypnosis. You were such a willing dupe, I almost didn't need to bother. You've been going back to the wreckage for me, systematically searching it for this," he gestured to the clock, "so I can escape. Which is what I'm about to do. You see there's a war on, and I need to win."

The patient turned to leave, then, seemingly with a second thought, he turned back to Costan. "Oh, and the reason you're dying is that you deactivated the engine shielding to enter the section of wreckage where the TARDIS was found. But don't worry yourself unnecessarily, the resultant fallout will actually kill everyone in your pitiful rustic colony. I think your Overseers have now realised, but of course in eschewing technology at large they can provide no protection to anyone. All they can do is register that it's happening and then sit and wait for the eventuality. Pathetic." He popped a small tablet in his mouth and swallowed. "But you can die happy in the knowledge that I have taken precautionary medication myself, though, so all your tender care to revive me won't have been in vain."

"You've, you've killed us all…?" Costan croaked.

The patient raised his eyebrows, opened his palms and squatted down next to Costan. "This may not be the best time for pedantry, my friend, but actually I *saved* you all in the first place. You see, I activated a time reversal engine – just at the point at which we crashed, as it turned out. It covered a localised area only, because it had been damaged. The planet was devastated, of course, but

207

then everything hereabouts was brought back again. Now, wasn't that generous of me?"

***

Costan was woken by a sharp rick to his neck. He hissed involuntarily, too weak to do anything else. He must have passed out. The scowling patient had a grip on his hair and had forced his head back.

"You hear me? I haven't killed everyone, *you* have." The patient's face was jubilant; he gave an evil chuckle as he dropped Costan's head.

Costan didn't feel his head hit the ground; his sight was blurring and his breathing was becoming more and more laboured. He knew he didn't have long left. But he had to know where his family were.

"My... fam... family." His voice was little more than a hoarse whisper. The patient performed an overdramatic expression of forgetfulness and skipped three paces to one of the wall cabinets. He opened the double doors and Costan could just make out a row of dolls standing on the shelf. Zilla's? He couldn't recall seeing them before. "I don't..." he mumbled.

The patient grabbed the dolls and brought them to Costan, taking great pleasure in forcing each one into his face. Costan's face crumpled as he recognised close up the shrunken remains of his father, mother and sister.

"Seems they had a bit more about them than you. Didn't trust me; your lovely mother even tried to kill me. Naturally I had to dispose of them if I was going to see my plan through. But if that's everything I think it's time for me to go. Thank you for your kind assistance, Costan, it really has been appreciated." With a twisted smile he turned, crossed the room and disappeared through the door at the front of the tall clock. There was a brief pause before a trumpeting, wheezing noise filled the room and the clock slowly vanished before his eyes.

Costan lay on his back, shivering feverishly, holding the shrunken remains of his family to his chest, and waited for death to take him.

Quod Periit, Periit
Simon A Brett

The black wooden front door closed with a decisive thud as the last bodyguards entered the building, muffling the sounds of multiple camera shutters snapping and blinking in the street outside. The man known to the world as Harold Saxon breathed in deeply, bouncing on the knuckles of his feet and relishing the change from paving slab to soft carpet underfoot.

He felt a gentle squeeze to his left hand and was reminded of the female stood at his side. Her pearlescent face and large pale blue eyes creased into a smile of sorts; china-white, expensive teeth framed by thin red lips and shoulders hunched, drawing her slight frame into a shape he imagined some human beings might term as 'cute'. He smiled, feigning an appreciation that would appear appropriate for the species he was currently mimicking.

"We did it, Harold. We're finally here!" she said, light in tone and clawing for a positive response from her husband.

He turned to her, pursing his lips into a tight grin. For a moment his eyes flickered to the array of suited men surrounding them. He threw a casual wink to those looking.

"Lucy, Lucy," he offered, softly, "have you *really* found a cause for impatience? Yes, I did get us here and yes, I would have been here sooner had the journey not been *so* worth it … but," he said, a singular digit in the air and pulling his wife toward him, "if I'm not mistaken, I've still achieved success in record time. Commoner to Prime Minister in less than 18 months flat!"

Saxon checked himself. Had he really sunk so low as to celebrate a feat so below his heritage? A goal so miraculous for any homo sapiens, yet pedestrian for a Time Lord of his talents.

"Darling, you're *so* clever," Lucy Saxon responded, screwing up her face and body once again, all the while swinging her shoulders back and forth, almost as if she were dancing to an 80's pop record no-one else could hear. "We make quite the team!"

He resisted the temptation to question her considerable underestimation of his intelligence and to pat her on the head. Instead, he placed a hand gently on her cheek before bringing his head beside hers, slipping his fingers under her hair and out of sight before pinching hard onto her earlobe. She breathed in sharply.

"Unlike you, Lucy…" he whispered, "I've *always* known my place."

209

He placed a kiss delicately on her cheek.

With the glint of tears shining in her eyes, Lucy stepped away from her husband and looked to the only other female in the hallway – her personal assistant, who nodded and signalled toward the staircase ahead of them. Clutching the side of her head, Lucy followed the woman up the stairs and away from the gaggle of officials below, leaving a singular broken diamanté earring on the carpet.

Harold stood silent for a few seconds, then turning from side to side he passed his eyes up and down the length of hallway before reaching into the inside pocket of his suit jacket. He withdrew two objects: one, a cube, the other small and cylindrical.

"I don't know about you, but I expected something a bit more Willy Wonka." He proclaimed. "A bit more Wizard of Oz. Instead it's all a bit … Antiques Roadshow."

The audible gasps of suited men filled the room as Harold Saxon, the brand new Prime Minister of the United Kingdom stepped away from them decisively and began to make his way down the corridor, towards the centre of the house. He threw an object over his shoulder, which landed squarely in the middle of the group.

"Rubik's cube. First to complete three sides gets to be Chancellor," he called. "Any more than three is probably pushing it," he added, under his breath.

Out of the crowd, one man, broad of shoulder and belly stepped away from the mounting squall of bickering politicians that was now coalescing into a scrum. His dark blue loose fitting designer suit hung on his frame like a number of large mozzarella cheeses might settle in a potato sack. Whispered barbs about their latest leader bounced between the politicians as the children's puzzle clattered in frenzied hands. Henry Somerton, meanwhile, was happy to leave his contemporaries to bicker. This was an excellent opportunity to cosy up to Saxon and dig for potentially priceless information. He surreptitiously licked his hand before taming his hair with wet fingers.

The new Prime Minister was currently performing the Electric Slide between the framed pictures on either side of the corridor ahead. Mr. Saxon, it seemed, had started to redecorate.

Reaching the first of the portraits, Henry stifled a snigger as he decoded the scrawl of black marker now adorning the right honourable gentleman displayed before him. Round glasses and a pointy beard disordered the man's features whilst a speech balloon erupted from his mouth containing simply the word, 'AMATEUR'.

As Henry followed Saxon's progress, he was greeted by further defacements.

210

'SPINELESS'. 'TRAITOR'. 'PUPPET'. 'BOOOORING'. Varied negative exclamations erupted from the mouths of previous Prime Ministers now wearing scribbled hats, spectacles, facial hair, fangs, wings and at times the most grotesque of disfigurements a set of kitchen knives might muster. Henry slowed as he approached one particular picture. He closed his eyes tightly for a second before nervously opening them. He was relieved to find that a female participant of the gallery had been largely untouched, save the caption, 'HELLO SEXY' encased within a heart-shaped bubble. Henry gave a brief sigh and was about to continue when he noticed that the words 'still disappointing' had been written neatly in the corner.

Henry had all but caught up with Saxon when he heard the faint, tinny sound of music. Getting closer, he was able to decipher the tones of a pop record from the 1990's: 2 Unlimited's 'No Limits' emanated from a small mobile device in the Prime Minister's left hand; the other busy bringing the artistic spree to a close as he attacked the final picture.

He span theatrically towards Henry and froze. His hand swiped at the phone, bringing silence to the corridor, save for the echoing hubbub from the hallway. The Prime Minister's foot continued to tap out the song's rhythm as if possessed.

"Amazing lyrics, don't you think?" Asked Saxon.

Henry Somerton nodded enthusiastically.

"So what do you think of my first home improvements?" Continued the Prime Minister, bringing his nose close to Henry's, his eyes wide and staring under a pointed and corrugated brow. His foot continued to play out a rhythm, loudly.

"I… I… I…" stumbled Henry, his jowls shaking uncontrollably.

"That's the trouble with us politicians, Somerton," interrupted Saxon, breathing hard into the sweating man's face, "always thinking about ourselves."

As his superior turned away, Henry allowed the air trapped in his lungs to escape. He rallied, wiping a handkerchief across his forehead before venturing for a conversation:

"I like it. I have to say that I was somewhat amused by your comments. Wonderfully satirical."

"Satirical? I was merely speaking the truth! As for the facial augmentations, well, I was just undoing decades of touch-up work. You really think that those are the true faces of your leaders?"

"I… I… I…" muttered Henry.

"Mind you, your country's been run by creatures in disguise on more than one occasion and you people didn't even notice. Even voted for them … but

211

who am I to complain?" Saxon laughed, now stepping from foot to foot in order to keep the beat. "It's almost as if this country offers itself up for subservience. As if it's built into its DNA. My God, you've placed your lives in the hands of the deadliest of monsters time and time again. Who am I to let down a captive audience?"

"If you're talking about that terrorist nonsense and the refit at number 10 then ..." offered Henry.

"Refit? You mean the rebuild? Don't mince your words, Somerton!"

Saxon brought himself close to the man once again.

"I'm just lucky that I was here in time to influence some of the improvements. Although..."

Harold Saxon's eyes turned away from Henry long enough to allow the man a step backwards. He had become transfixed with a section of wall ahead of them. His feet became still.

"What's this?" asked Saxon, now looking uncharacteristically concerned.

"What's what, Harold?"

"It's sir to you. This door."

"A door... sir?"

Saxon gestured towards a blank area of wall ahead of him. Henry had been on the cusp of surmising that the power of office had quite literally bent his leader's mind, when Saxon's fingers touched the surface and, inexplicably, there was no longer textured wallpaper but instead, a door. A very nice, big friendly door made of rosewood and carved ornately with an array of roses and swords to its fringes. From that moment on Henry's memory told him that the door had always been there. His brain stopped checking itself for malfunction and returned to his usual *modus operandi* of turning every situation into an opportunity.

"It's a very fine door, sir. Quite old, I believe. Do you like it? I can find a few more for you?"

"What's it doing here, Somerton?"

"A... A... well, a broom cupboard I expect. Somewhere the old cleaning women keep their bits and pieces, you know. Mops and stuff. Nothing for us to worry about. Nice door, though, nonetheless."

Saxon looked infuriated.

"This. Wasn't. On. The PLANS," he said through gritted teeth.

"Well, I... well, I wouldn't know, sir, I..."

"Oh shut up, Somerton," hissed Saxon. He pulled at the door handle, but it did not give. Like a child losing interest in a toy, he allowed the marker pen to drop to the floor. He reached inside his jacket and retrieved another cylindrical object. This time, metal glimmered under the electric light. Saxon extended his arm toward the handle and a focused beam of golden laser light hit its target. In moments, distorted and smoking metal dropped to the floor.

"Shall we?" said Saxon, simply. He pushed lightly at the door, which swung open without complaint. He beckoned Henry toward the opening.

"Mr. Saxon, I…"

"Oh, seriously, Somerton, do you *honestly* think that this is a broom cupboard? Quit the blathering and get yourself in there."

Harold Saxon lifted one leg, placing a foot squarely upon the man's ample backside. With one swift push, Henry fell forward through the door. After checking the falling politician's progress, Saxon stepped inside himself, pulling the door back into its frame.

A junior minister nursing a number of minor injuries and carrying a completed Rubik's cube had just viewed a man affectionately known as 'Horny' Henry within journalistic circles being bundled into what looked like a broom cupboard by the new Prime Minister, Harold Saxon. He turned around, closing his eyes tightly having been fully warned by his peers that some things were best left unwitnessed within politics. Curiosity getting the better of him, he turned back again. The blank wall that had always been there looked back at him, blankly. In turn, the minister's mind returned the blank look and shrugged. Never a door. Just a wall. And logic would suggest that if there had never been a door then his party leader had most certainly never forced one of his ministers into a cupboard that was never there for whatever activity that obviously didn't exist. "Ridiculous," he thought, shaking his head as he returned to trying to find Harold Saxon in order to show him what a clever boy he'd been.

***

Henry Somerton had tumbled a generous number of steps down a long, winding stone staircase. By the time Harold Saxon reached him, he was already sat upright and happily taking a swig of alcohol from a hip flask. Despite looking decisively dishevelled, his hair sprouting in all directions as if powered by static and his trousers torn at the knees, Henry exhibited a carefree resilience unlike any other Earthling Saxon had experienced.

"I bet you're glad of all those fancy dinners paid on expenses now, aren't you? Plenty of meat on your bones to cushion the fall," laughed Saxon, who beckoned for the man to share his drink with him. Henry handed the bottle over reluctantly only for Saxon to take a sniff of the contents, recoil in disgust and throw it back at him.

"Well, I must say," said Henry, desperately trying to limit spillage while details of the excellent vintage of his chosen tipple tailed off under his breath.

The Prime Minister motioned for Henry to continue down the stairs ahead of him, prodding at his shoulder with the laser device. The relationship with his leader seemed to have taken a particularly dramatic left turn, scuppering the progress he had hoped to cultivate that day.

"*Semper Fidelis,*" Henry said, his mouth smiling, while his eyes said something altogether different.

"*In veritas dolor,*" replied Saxon, jabbing his device acutely between Henry's ribs.

Eventually they reached the bottom of the staircase, which terminated into nothing but an arched opening in the surrounding wall, filled with a substantial oak door. Saxon motioned for Henry to try the handle and as the cast iron ring turned in his hands, it creaked open without disagreement, filling the staircase with intense yellow sunlight.

A glorious blue, cloudless sky greeted Henry and as he stepped out onto the soft ground he shielded his eyes from a beaming sun that gave everything he saw a vivacity and clarity. It took his breath away. The word 'idyllic' immediately appeared in his head, but it seemed insubstantial compared to the view he was trying to comprehend. Somewhere in his photographic memory was a phrase in Latin far more appropriate to the grandeur of things. As his mouth readied itself for the words, Saxon threw him a disapproving look and he remained silent.

They were standing atop a singular hill which looked down onto countless meadows, pastures and fields that softly undulated in gentle curves, sweeping into the distance as far as he could see. Each held the kind of intense green, brown or golden yellow ochre he had only seen on cornflake packets or sweetcorn tins. Trees lined each intersection, abundant in deep viridian leaves and white blossom, while the steady trill of birdsong tickled at his ears in the breeze.

In the space of a few stairs, they appeared to have travelled some distance – that much was sure. This was a very different place, but he was still in England; every fibre of his being told him that. But to his mind it felt like the Home Counties cranked up to ten and filtered of all industry, pollution and … people. This country was as unspoiled as his illegitimate daughter's bottom: the sceptred isle that every red blooded Briton might sense existed under all of the dog shit and chewing gum.

Henry released a small yelp as Harold Saxon placed a hand upon his shoulder. He turned to see him standing in the doorway of a stone tower reaching upwards into the sky. As he looked up, it appeared to fade into nothing after the first twenty feet or so.

"Just look at the dimensions on that," joked Saxon, looking about him. "We ain't in Kansas anymore, Toto!"

"I don't know what to say. I mean, I... I..."

"Don't break a spleen, Somerton. Where do you think you are? How do you feel?"

"Why do you ask?"

"Just curious."

"This *is* England. This must be somewhere in, I don't know, Hampshire or possibly Bucks. But not anywhere I've been, which is surprising," Henry chortled. "But as far as how do I feel? Well, I feel bloody marvellous. Despite falling down all those ruddy steps, but still. *Perfer et obdura; dolor hic tibi proderit olim.*"

Harold Saxon shook his head at the relentless Latin and stooped low, picking a singular blade of grass with his fingertips. For a moment he studied it between forefinger and thumb before placing it into his mouth. He clasped Henry's wrist aggressively, forcing him to open his hand.

Saxon made a range of faces as he sucked and chewed before finally spitting the piece of grass, still in one piece and undamaged, into the centre of Henry's hand.

Henry would have taken issue with the frankly disgusting behaviour of the Prime Minister had his attention not been so easily supplanted by the blade of grass that now sat straight and perfectly intact in the palm of his hand. More curiously, it slowly turned upwards, seating itself vertically; its tip pointing straight up towards the sky; a pulsing blue dot of energy at its base. Before he had a chance to study it fully, Saxon knocked it from his hand. Both men watched as the blade floated to the ground before slowly returning to the exact spot where Saxon had picked it from its root.

As the Prime Minister set off down the hill, Henry found himself bounding to keep up with the outwardly younger and fitter man. He yearned for his bicycle which would have made short work of the downward incline, however, strangely he did not find himself getting out breath. Energy seemed to exude from the ground beneath him and it bled upwards into his leg muscles. He took each step with a lightness that he had not known since his running days at Eaton.

Saxon and Somerton strode briskly until a singular plume of white smoke rising upwards ahead of them became apparent.

They eased their pace as the terrain flattened out for a time before beginning to dip steeply once again. Within moments they found themselves looking downward into a large, almost spherical well carved out of the land. It was green and lush with not a patch of naked rock to be seen. A small circular stone cottage had been built at its flattened centre with a chimney that, unhindered from any sign of breeze, sent the column of smoke vertically into the air.

After a careful climb down to the base, they reached the cottage's wooden entrance; a door of sorts created out of a number of misshapen strips of bark. Saxon held his laser device at the ready and turned to Henry, smiling broadly.

"I think that I'll let you knock."

"Oh, I wouldn't hear of it, in fact…"

Henry felt the pressure of a metal object pressing into his ribcage once again.

"Shall I do the honours?" he said, at least two octaves higher than before.

Henry rapped three times against the wood. The door rattled under the strain, beginning a vibration that appeared to travel through the remainder of the cottage and downwards into the earth beneath their feet. Both men took a number of steps away from the building with Saxon continuing to keep his weapon trained upon the doorway.

The cottage flickered like a dying hologram, becoming more and more pixelated by the second, before finally disappearing altogether. In its stead, hovering a metre from the floor, was a neon blue, glowing round ball measuring approximately 10 foot in diameter. The sphere seemed to be constructed entirely of relentlessly mobile tight, curly hair that rotated in swirls and coagulated like oil on water.

"Twenty-first century English mode initiated," came an echoey voice. "I am the backup. Choose your restoration point well." The speech was clear, loud, effeminate, possibly American by descent and somewhat threatening around the mid-range.

"I'm sorry?" offered Henry before being shushed into silence by Saxon.

"I am the backup. Choose your restoration point well."

"That's sort of what I thought you said. Do go on," said Henry before being struck hard around the head from behind.

"Quiet, you simpering lickspittle!" said Saxon, sharply. "It's talking to me."

"Two voices?" returned the voice, this time slightly lighter and more human in tone. "That's unexpected. Hang on, where the hell are you?"

Both men were taken by surprise as the ball rotated, revealing an outwardly human face nestled within the curls.

"Ah, there you are. I am the backup. Do choose wisely," said the giant mouth. It smiled a wide grin, by way of the intimidating vision of two glossed lips and a set of teeth so uniform and impressive that Henry found himself momentarily calculating the cost of dental treatment. Two large wide eyes, with pupils like plasma balls blinked, innocently.

"The backup, you say?" ventured Saxon, now circling the floating head. It slowly turned, monitoring his movement. "That would suggest the recording of historical information in case of data loss."

"This is a facility for date-marked restorative modular chronoscaping in the event of system collapse. Do choose wisely."

"Choose *what* wisely, exactly?" asked Henry. He flinched, awaiting the next blow.

"Well, what do *you* think, Somerton, Henry Somerton? The man who hides his intelligence and dare I say it, *desperate* yearning for power in a hermetically sealed shell of clandestine buffoonery? Pick a year."

"I... I... I..." said a suddenly prone Henry.

"Roman numeric coding recognised. I, I, I. Third age binder definition. Please hold on to something permanent," said the head.

Static filled the air and all about the two men, a shimmer of sparkling silver washed over the landscape. In a matter of seconds, fields were replaced with forests of trees, manmade lakes and clutches of small houses. Roads erupted from the earth, creating veins between the settlements. To the west, a small town formed and in moments smoke began to erupt from tall chimneys extending up from brown and grey factories.

"Ohhhh, clever," said Saxon. "But nothing I've not seen before countless times. Tell me. Your programmer. Their name?"

"Geoffrey."

"Geoffrey? Just Geoffrey?"

"Geoffrey of Monmouth. Galfridus Monemutensis. Galfridus Arturus..."

"Oh, ARTURUS! Arteries of Gallifrey," said Saxon, suddenly showing some ease with the knowledge. "Of COURSE! Damn Time Lords. Even when they're all supposed to be dead they still manage to get everywhere."

Henry threw his hands up, head shaking.

"You know I used to share a gym with the useless, sentimental old fool back on my home planet," continued Saxon to everyone but no-one. "Makes sense. Started a lifetime's work of dramatising the history of every planet then stopped for no reason when he got to Earth. Loved your pathetic world, not unlike another loser I know. Wrote great stories too, but a few too many happy endings for my liking."

Henry, having decided that he knew nothing of the obscure university lodges of which Saxon was speaking, placed a finger in the air before saying, "hang on... you can return the land... this land... England... to a previous state?

217

Before the war. Before the industrial revolution. Before we joined the… hang on, all of this in front of us is just a whatchamacallit, isn't it?"

Saxon looked almost impressed with Henry's dissemination of the onslaught of technology way beyond his monkey brain. There was obviously far more going on in his head than flannel and clumsy ambition. "Just a simulation? A thumbnail? Here, yes. Until you find the 'apply' button, I imagine. Then it's bang goes M1, hello donkey wagons."

"On confirmation, all current data will be overwritten and returned to its previous state," confirmed the head.

Henry's legs gave way and he sat down onto the grass for a moment, scratching at his tidal quiff and sending a shockwave through his straw-like hair. Then he stopped, his face an all new expression of determination and purpose. It was like the backup system on his computer. The one he kept having to ensure didn't mirror his photograph folder.

"I mean, sir, if this is true then imagine the votes we'd get. Imagine the *power*," he offered, suddenly welling up at the prospect. "I mean, can we tell it a specific year responding to the Gregorian calendar? Even just, well, 2004 for instance. That wasn't a bad year."

"Of course," said the head. "Geoffrey programmed me for every civilisational format and eventuality. The collapse of capitalism, the rise of the feline oligarchy, the last great flatulence and so on. All available in Esperanto, Euro Mandarin, Third Grape or even Last Equestrian Low Brow. But now I'm showing off. Your request is a simple one. Transition would correspond to the closest backup point. Observe."

There was another wave of energy and the men looked about as the town grew into a city, forests disappeared to be replaced by housing estates, the roads expanded and spread, varicose across the land while the sky grew dimmer, punctuated by aircraft and contrails.

Henry did a little dance, punching the air like a boxer. He looked very pleased with himself.

"Okay, you were both talking all things Galfridian," he said, "and to my understanding Geoffrey of Monmouth was the chap who documented the whole King Arthur thing. So let's see King Arthur."

"As I say," interjected Saxon, "he did write a good story and you people do have such a sickly habit of appropriating immigrants, then making out that they were always English to begin with. Arthur won't be saving you today or any other day."

And with that, he kicked at the grass at his feet. It wrinkled up into a flap of turf, revealing circuitry sprouting from the earth beneath. He stood up straight

218

and pointed his laser device towards it.

"No, wait! What are you doing?" Shouted Henry.

"What do you think I'm doing? I'm shutting it down," said Saxon, without emotion.

"But… but… but… it's miraculous! We have a chance to go back – to go back before our mistakes. Back before the wrong choices!" pleaded Somerton.

"Back before I got into power, you mean?" offered Saxon, chuckling to himself. "Oh, Sommerton, Sommerton, I can read you like a dreadful autobiography. You have no idea what I have planned for this place. For the whole planet. You could always begin pleading with me if you like, Henry. That always goes down well."

"Oh good," said Henry, somewhat relieved and devoid of self-respect. "So we can talk about this? I mean it's a great idea isn't it – being able to go back before the '70s and all that. Very, very popular with voters, don't you think?"

"Ah, yes, the voters. Thing is, I'm very much a future man. As in, *I'm the future, man*. My choice. Not yours, and certainly not theirs. I've reduced whole planets to rubble before now, so to me this is nothing more than flicking a…"

"Apply!" shouted Henry to the head. "Apply now before he can…"

A beam of golden light shot at the ground.

***

And then there was nothing but a cream wall of textured wallpaper. Henry was sat on the carpet being studied by a number of black suited politicians, mumbling under their breath to one another. To his left, Harold Saxon discussed a completed Rubik's cube with a young junior minister before turning his back on him and taking to the stairs.

In front of Henry was a blank wall, staring back at him, blankly. No sign of a door, but then, there had never been one. And there had never been a staircase, or a door, or a cottage, or a floating head with a cosmic afro. There would never, he thought, broken-hearted, ever be an England as perfect as the one he'd witnessed. But then that thought was also lost.

The new chancellor turned to him, offering him a hand up.

'Too many whiskeys, Horny Henry?' he said, cheekily.

***

Henry Somerton removed the padlock and lifted his electric bicycle from the rack. For a moment he pondered the maverick nature of the new Prime

Minister. The public loved a wildcard. Someone who said what they thought, plainly and was rather dashing with it. He ran his fingers through his hair, sending it into an all new sculpture of thick follicles and made a mental note to be more like that man in future – once, of course Harold Saxon was no longer, actually, 'the future'. People just liked Saxon because he seemed to be 'good' and say 'good things'. He told the people what they wanted to hear. That, in itself, might be a useful tactic in future.

"*Fere libenter homines id quod violent credunt,*" he muttered to himself.

Though image was nothing without policy. Without a cause. And he was very good at making them up on the spot. In fact there seemed to be one particular idea sitting at the forefront of his mind, though he couldn't quite figure out where it had come from.

He wheeled his bicycle towards a pedestrian crossing. A white van was resting, stationary and illegally riding over the black and white striped causeway. It rolled to and fro, its engine revving with impatience for the red light to change to green up ahead.

He tapped on the window of the van. The driver turned and looked at him, blankly.

"I say, old man," he shouted at the window, "how does the idea of putting things in reverse sound to you?"

Cheese, Beans, and Toast
Sami Kelsh

"Stupid! Bloody! Machine!"

The Master kicked the vessel's stupid central column hard enough to leave his toes stinging for a solid minute. The twiddly thing was refusing to reset itself and take off again. It was always the bloody twiddly thing.

Of course, it was entirely within the Master's technical knowledge to rebuild a new twiddly thing, but he would need spare parts, which meant venturing out into whatever miserable backwater of a planet he found himself stranded upon. Also, his coffee had been disappointingly watery that morning, and since he had used up the last of the Garafraxan milk-bread two days earlier, he'd been forced to settle for two slices of toasted Hovis. Granted, Best Before February 1951 was a fine vintage for toast, but Garafraxan milk-bread was *divine*.

It was not the worst day the Master had ever had, but it was by no means pleasant.

Giving his hair a dramatic fluff and his pockets a quick check for essentials – keys, psychic paper, cinnamon chewing gum, the broken twiddly thing, laser screwdriver, the usual – he scanned the scene that lay before him as the door hummed open. Perhaps, he thought, as the machine re-cloaked itself behind him, this planet had their own version of milk-bread. Stepping out into what seemed to be an impenetrable cloud of deep-blue dust, he found himself surrounded by what looked to be an ostentatiously dark vault of sorts, surrounded by an intricate network of laser sensors. The planet might at least be interesting, he decided.

"Psst," he could just about hear from somewhere behind him. "Psst, hey idiot!"

"Who, me?"

The Master raised an eyebrow. In the dark. Force of habit, he supposed.

"How the hell did you get in here?" whispered the voice. "This is *my* heist!"

"A heist, you say?"

A young woman emerged from the darkness, deftly dodging and weaving her way past the sensors. He could see her clearly now, clad in practical, dark clothing, perfect for slipping in and out unnoticed.

"Oh, don't play stupid," she protested. "You wouldn't be here if you weren't after the diamond."

She gestured behind him, at a dramatically lit glass display case containing what was, in the Master's expert estimation, a rather unremarkable bit of sparkle. If this was what passed for a heist-worthy diamond in this time and place, it was scarcely going to be sophisticated.

"I hate to disappoint you, my dear," the phrase slipped out of him, almost without thinking. There was something about this cheerful, doe-eyed criminal, something almost impossibly reminiscent of an old adversary; or, if he were being perfectly honest with himself, a dear old friend, from many lifetimes ago. "But... I couldn't care less about something as pedestrian as a boring old diamond. I came here by mistake."

"Sure," she smiled, with tight-lipped incredulity. "I haven't the foggiest why else you'd be in here dressed like a jewel thief, but since you *are* here, you may as well make yourself useful, because I'm certainly not leaving here without that diamond."

"Useful?" All things considered, he thought, a jewel thief would make a good assistant in his quest to scout for parts, for which he hardly intended to pay.

"You need to follow my lead," she told him, "unless you want to get us both killed."

"Hmm, dying's overrated I suppose," he replied. "I'll pass. Lead the way."

***

What he eventually managed to learn from the thief, as they seamlessly manoeuvred past various alarmed features, wriggled their way through some air vents, and scaled their way down the dark side of the building, was that the diamond was highly sought after in the sorts of circles where people paid obscene amounts of money for such things – though what a person would do with a stolen diamond was beyond him. Bragging rights? Blackmail? Grinding it into dust to stir into very expensive, glittering cocktails? Keeping it locked in a pretty cabinet to look at and feel smug about oneself? His companion, it turned out, had little interest in where it landed. All that mattered to her was how much she could fetch for it.

"That kind of money plants a lot of trees," she explained.

This was not a sentence the Master was expecting to hear.

"Trees make paper, paper prints more money?" he ventured, as the lift whooshed them to the ninety-sixth floor of her surprisingly modest building.

She shook her head softly. "Maybe it's a roundabout way to repair a dying planet, but when your skills are in picking locks and getting past security, you play to your strengths… All right, all right, fine," she continued, beaming, "it's also ever so much more fun, isn't it?"

The Master smiled. He was right to like this one, he thought.

For a highly-skilled jewel thief, the woman's flat was smallish, dark, and unassumingly ordinary: he supposed, of course, that a lavish display of treasure-stealing prowess might draw more attention to a person than one might prefer. On the other hand, the Master had rarely been one to shy away from a good ostentatious display. Ostentatious displays were fun.

The thief shuffled him off to the powder room to clean up the minor scrape or two he had suffered in squeezing through what had turned out to be a slightly too-small window, and left him to it. He let the icy water pool in his cupped hands, then buried his face in it. It was not a splash as such; rather, it was more akin to a carefully controlled drowning. He wrung a damp hand over his dripping face, and stared into the mirror. This face was now more weather beaten than when he first tried it on, after all that it had seen and done and been subjected to, but it had never looked so free. He felt, cautiously, hopeful.

The thief had already poured two small enamel mugs full of dark, rich coffee.

"Right, looks like it's beans on toast, cheese on toast, or… cheesy beans on toast," she shouted from the kitchen, staring into the fridge.

"What kind of question is that?" he asked her, taking this as an invitation either to a very late dinner, or a very early breakfast.

"You're quite right!" she replied, hauling a few essentials from the cupboard. "As if it could be anything but cheesy beans on toast. Only the very best for my new assistant!"

"Oh please," scoffed the Master. "Assistant? Moi?"

"So tell me," she said, ignoring his protestations as she set a messy plate of food before him, "how does a person find themselves in the third most heavily guarded room in the country, unscathed, by mistake?"

The Master chuckled. "My dear, that would be telling."

"Well then, tell me."

He considered whether it was worth telling the (likely unbelievable) truth, or a carefully crafted, more plausible lie. Perhaps, he thought, it was easiest to be vague. He downed his coffee in one, relishing the lightly acidic burn as it went down.

"I've been living through some interesting times," he said, scooping a generous blob of syrupy beans and rapidly-congealing cheese onto his fork. "Personal things, political things, some emotions… a bit of a bad—"

"Breakup?" she suggested, mouth full of beans.

The Master considered the word a moment, and actually:

223

"You could say that," he shrugged. "No. Maybe. I don't know. I hope not."

"Sounds complicated." She topped up his coffee without asking. It was deep and thick with the fine sediment that had bubbled their way through the filter and settled at the bottom of the carafe. Perfectly adequate, he thought.

"Oh, it's complicated," he confirmed, shovelling a teetering heap of carbs into his mouth. "Last time I saw him, I think it was the first time in a long time I was sure he might have wanted to make it work. I still don't know whether or not I did."

"Sounds like you're better off without him."

"I'm not so sure," he said. It was not as though this longing was something one could simply make a conscious decision to be rid of; rather, it sat inside his heart, like a beloved song always playing over in the next room, just a little too quiet to make out the words.

"Trust me," she assured him.

Despite himself, he did.

"So, you'd like to help me fix my… transport," he told her, swiping the last corner of toast around the plate, absorbing the last of the sticky tomato sauce that had pooled there.

"Sounds fun," she agreed. "What do you need?"

He detailed the list of supplies he needed to repair the twiddly thing in the simplest terms he could manage, in the hope that he would not overwhelm her inferior intellect with the sort of top-tier advanced engineering gubbins they were dealing with.

"You know you can get most of this at any old hardware store," she said, puzzled. "What do you need me for?"

"Do most hardware stores carry…?" He paused, reaching deep into his pocket, in search of the broken twiddly thing. "Would you believe me if I told you I could travel through space and time… if I hadn't broken down where you found me?"

She seemed to be examining his face very carefully then, maintaining eye contact as she funnelled down the last of her coffee, setting the mug down with a heavy clang.

"Now that you mention it, I did rather think you looked a bit like you could have come from space," she concluded, "but I didn't think it was polite to say."

The Master shrugged. "Now," he said, setting the broken part on the table, "what about this?"

The woman nodded, scrutinising the heavily cracked orange stone. "Oh I see," she said. "Well, there's only one place I know of where you can get something like that, but it's beyond high security. Nobody gets in there.

Nobody knows what's in there. But I reckon it's your best bet. I hear they deal with the things from space we're not supposed to know about. But I suppose you're going to tell me you know all about those things, do you?"

"My dear," he smiled, "I do."

"And I do love a challenge."

***

"I assume your acting skills are up to scratch," said the jewel thief, arranging her hair into a neat ponytail. The Master rolled his eyes. "Yes, yes, I know you're very good at being dramatic, but that isn't the same thing as *acting*."

"I once bluffed my way into becoming Prime Minister," he told her, fastening his lab coat.

"Really?" she asked. "I don't remember voting for you."

"Prime Minister of a different planet," he clarified.

It had not escaped his notice that she had very carefully made sure to take the diamond with her every time she left the room – not least because he may have been thinking of discreetly pocketing the thing as soon as he knew she was not looking. She was good.

"Oh yeah," she giggled. "Space alien. Have you got that, what was it you called it–"

"Psychic paper?" he suggested.

"That's the one," she agreed. "That ought to get us through the door, but then…"

The guard let them into the facility with scarcely a batted eyelash, accepting without question that they were a pair of visiting researchers. Now all they had to do was find a new orange twiddly component, easier said than done, especially since it might not even be there.

The facility, for all its secrecy and security, seemed largely to be comprised of dull, grey offices, with the occasional laboratory thrown in for fun. It seemed unlikely to the Master that something anywhere near as important as his missing component would be housed anywhere so boring. There had to be more to this place, he thought: a secret door, perhaps, or:

"Obviously, anything we're after is going to be in at least the third level of the basement," the thief whispered to him, as they waited for the lift. "This is fun. Maybe you should stick around for a while once you've got your twiddly thing. You make a pretty good assistant."

The Master scowled. "For the last time, I'm not your–"

225

"Fiddlesticks," she said. "Basement Level Four access needs thumbprint identification."

"Easy," replied the Master, scrutinising the lift's control panel. "We just find the thumb of someone with access, and… lightly borrow it."

The thief blinked. "Or I can just bypass it?"

"Fine," he sighed. "I *guess* we can try it your way first."

"You said you had a screwdriver," she said, examining the mechanism. "Can I borrow it?"

"A laser screwdriver," he clarified. "Two slightly different things, but an important distinction, I think you'll find."

"Does it screw screws into things that need screwing in?"

"It emits a lethal laser blast," said the Master, producing the weapon from his clever lab coat disguise's pocket-protected pocket.

"Not much of a screwdriver then, is it?" The thief took the screwdriver from him, handling it in a far more cavalier manner than the Master would have liked.

"It's technologically far superior," he insisted.

"Not if you're trying to drive screws, it isn't."

The Master sighed. "I mean, I guess it drives screws too, if you're going to be boring about it."

She smiled. "I am!"

As the lift activated, sending them gliding smoothly downward, the Master found himself torn between relief that his companion had been able to manipulate the security system so skilfully, and disappointed that there was no need to laser anyone. Perhaps later, he thought. Indeed, perhaps there were worse ways to spend his time than to stick around on this planet for a little while: it had snacks, and stealing expensive things from inferior fools was, it turned out, fun. Perhaps it was time for the Master to find a new, superior best friend. As the lift dinged, cheerfully signalling their arrival, the Master affected his best casual Don't Be Suspicious Face.

The doors swooshed open onto a dramatically-lit and seemingly endless corridor of extremely well-locked cabinets. The Master felt his shoulders fall in near-pantomime dejection. Assuming this shady, highest-security secret government facility's archive housed a twiddly thing at all, it would take hours, if not days to

"Found it!"

The thief stood, several cabinets down, proudly brandishing what was unambiguously the very twiddly thing the Master had been hoping to find. The Master (somewhat slack-jawed, despite himself) snatched the stone from her, shoving it securely in his pocket.

226

"H," he began, "how."

"Filed under T for Twiddly."

The Master wondered what other objects of use may be hidden within this archive: weapons of unimaginable power, long-lost rarities, maybe even the crusty end-piece of a loaf of Garafraxan milk-bread. Allowing themselves a few moments to examine the archive revealed, however: fake, fake, probably from a pound shop in the Brassican system, fake, literally a set of hair tongs, and then...

"Ooooooooooooooooooooh," gasped the thief.

The Master examined the item, housed in an ostentatious glass case.

"It looks like a golf ball," he said.

"I thought it was a myth," she whispered, almost reverently.

"Pretty sure it's a golf ball," replied the Master.

"Well, I like it, so it's mine now," she smiled, pocketing the innocuous item. "This little *golf ball*, as you call it, has the power to send out a blast so powerful it can incinerate an entire city."

The Master's eyes widened. That sounded like an excellent souvenir indeed.

"You wouldn't," he said.

"Oh, absolutely I wouldn't," she agreed, her smile radiant with joy. "But just imagine the chaos when they find it's gone missing."

"Uhh, are you guys supposed to be in here?" asked the security guard at the door.

The thief gave him the most withering squint of derision the Master had ever seen.

"Yeah," she scoffed.

"Oh, okay," replied the guard. "Hey, are you guys coming to the staff summer picnic next week? I'm bringing my famous corn-salad again."

"I was going to make a pineapple upside-down cake," replied the Master, as he and his new friend made their way swiftly toward the lift.

"Hope he's not going to be too disappointed when it turns out there's no cake after all," she smiled to him, as the lift delivered them smoothly back to the ground floor.

"I think he's going to have bigger things to worry about."

***

Performing the necessary repairs were easy enough – at least for someone possessed of such superior intellect and technical skill as the Master – and the

227

thief kindly kept a steady supply of cheesy beans on toast coming as they worked.

"Suppose you'll be off back to your home planet now," she said.

"Noooooope," replied the Master. "It's not exactly… we have a *history*."

"The breakup?" she asked.

"Among other things," he shrugged, finishing his third and final plate of toast. "Now, my machine's still stuck in the vault where you found me – at least, I hope it is. I don't suppose you fancy helping me… break back in?"

"I'll leave that to you," she grinned. "Well, that and the fact that a little bird may have just called in an anonymous tip that someone matching your approximate description had stolen the diamond, so you might have an interesting time getting back to your space… thing."

The Master was almost too impressed to be shocked.

"Oof, you are vicious," he said.

"Takes any possible suspicion off of me, and you'll be in space, if you make it that far, so what's it to you?" she reasoned. "I spotted an opportunity – a vulnerability, if you will, and I'd be remiss if I didn't take advantage."

"Of course," he grudgingly agreed. "I might go so far as to say you're almost as good as me."

She giggled. "Almost? Oh, I'm going to miss you. You're so *funny*."

The Master laughed: quietly at first, but building, shaking, tears welling in his eyes, fear that if he was not careful, his sides may indeed split. Of course she had, he thought; indeed, it stood to reason that he was the easiest opportunity for her to keep any suspicion from falling anywhere near her, and once he escaped into the wilderness of time and space, the mystery would remain unsolved forever.

"You are absolutely, audaciously, brilliant," he said, dabbing at the tears forming at the corners of his eyes with his overlong jumper sleeves. "For an inferior human person, obviously."

"Yes, I suppose I am," she agreed. "I hope you won't be too cross with me."

"Obviously I'm cross," he assured her. "Normally, I prefer to do the betraying myself."

"But I took your mind off of your bad breakup, didn't I?"

"You know what?" he replied, his grin growing, "You did. Thank you."

"Well then. Off you go, my little friend. Be gay, do crimes! And don't you go getting yourself caught, or I'll be ever so disappointed in you."

"My dear," he smiled, "I wouldn't dream of it."

And he didn't.

Auntie Mary
Kara Dennison

"Oh my God, suck it up. You're bringing home a C, not getting arrested for a double homicide."

Matilda glared at the envelope in her hand. "Same thing in my household."

"Dad would throw me a party if I brought home a C."

"Yes, I know. You've told me about a dozen times." Matilda shoved the envelope in her shoulder bag, not looking at Bryan. She couldn't. He didn't understand. He wouldn't care. "Now I've gotta listen to the whole thing. Why can't I be more like my sister? Why can't I apply myself? I'm such a bright girl, what's the problem?"

"Then don't go home."

"Right. Um. I do sort of have to."

Bryan shook his head. "Not right away, right? You got some time, right? Or do they have you on like a 4 pm curfew, too?"

"No…"

"Then come on." Bryan peeled off at the next intersection, going left. "There's a bunch of us going to Salvo's tonight."

"But Salvo's sucks."

Bryan grinned. "We're not going for the pizza. Come on, trust me. You'll love it."

Matilda cast a quick glance down the road in the direction of her house. The report card seemed to grow suddenly heavier in her bag. "Fine. But just for a little while. And it'd better be worth it. I'm still not over finding that earwig in my calzone."

"Like I said. Trust me. You're gonna have the best time ever."

***

Salvo's was in a strip mall toward the middle of town, close enough to downtown that it was objectively trashy, but close enough to uptown that people still vehemently called it a "hole-in-the-wall." Sandwiched between a comic book store, with sun-faded anime posters in the display windows, and a comedy club that hadn't changed its sign since October, it leaked a smell of grease out onto the sidewalk before the door even cracked open.

The front of the shop was a tiny hallway with an open kitchen on the right and a bench on the left. The bench was full of old plastic cushions; the kitchen was full of old uprooted Brooklynites.

"In the back," a greying man said upon seeing the two. He was covering a pizza with what Matilda hoped were chopped olives. "She's not here yet, but some of the other kids are."

"Thanks." Bryan gave a quick wave, nodding for Matilda to follow him into the dining area.

"And don't spill no more damn Coke on the rug! You know how much it costs to get them things shampooed?"

Bryan snorted. "Just push a table over it like usual," he muttered.

The dining area was only slightly nicer, with stained glass lamps hanging claustrophobically low over each table. The back wall was made up primarily of a pair of large wooden shutters, which led to what was allegedly the "fancy" private room. Loud conversation leaked through as Bryan pushed them open.

"Sup, guys?"

"Hey!" A girl with jagged-cut black and blonde hair smiled up at Bryan, but the smile dropped. "Oh. I didn't know it was Nerd Night at Salvo's."

Matilda bristled at the chuckles, but Bryan put himself between her and the girl. "Lay off, Trish. She's had a bad day."

"Oh, poor baby. Got a B in English?"

Matilda lowered her head. "A C in math."

The rest of the gathered kids burst into laughter. Matilda pulled away, but Bryan grabbed her by the arm.

"Hey, look. Ignore them."

"I didn't know it was gonna be… you know." She looked away. "I don't belong here, okay?"

"Look, just stick around for a few minutes. They'll be nice. I promise. Right, guys?"

A boy, squeezed into the corner of the room-sized booth, tipped his head back. "Yeah. Sure. We'll hold up our pinkies and wear our spats."

Matilda jerked her hand out of Bryan's. "No. Sorry. I do have to leave." She turned to dash out through the doors.

Running face-first into a well-dressed woman.

"Oh my, isn't this a surprise? *Seven* little ducklings in my duck pond. And nobody thought to tell me?"

Matilda backed up slowly. The woman, though she was slim-built and not particularly tall, was blocking her way out of the room – mostly with arms akimbo and pure presence.

230

"Sorry," Bryan piped up. "That's on me. She was having a bad day, and I thought she might like to hang out. That's okay, right?"

"Weeeeee–llllllll…" The woman sashayed into the room, slowly circling Matilda like a lioness eyeing a gazelle. "I don't *know*. What do the rest of you think?"

"Boo!" Trish heckled, and the other kids – save for Bryan and Matilda herself – took up the cry. Matilda was more shocked than anything else, but Bryan looked angry. The woman turned her head toward the shouting students, then looked back at Matilda, eyebrow arched.

"Oh, my-my-my. They don't much like you." The woman's voice lilted with a soft Scottish accent while cutting with an unexpected steely edge. It was alluring but unsettling, like being hypnotized with a swinging steak knife. Matilda felt somehow both calm and terrified.

"I was just leaving," she muttered under her breath.

The woman smiled shark-like and put a hand on Matilda's shoulder. Matilda took her in: dark Victorian skirt and jacket, little hat pinned just so, umbrella handle looped over one wrist, bits of jewellery that wouldn't be out of place at a rave. "Oh, I shouldn't think so. Not until we've had a chat. Can't just have you running off into the night, you know." She leaned in close. "Tell me, you darling little…" Her eyes darted over Matilda's face, "… mammal. What is it that's got you so sad tonight that you've come here?"

"I got a…" Her voice dropped off.

The woman cupped a manicured hand around one ear. "Can't hear you, what?"

"… I got a bad grade on my report card."

The kids around her broke into guffaws – all except Bryan. The woman arched an eyebrow, gave the gallery a cold look, and–

CRACK!

Everyone fell silent.

"That's better." The woman brought her umbrella down to her side again. Matilda could see tiny cracks in the wall where she'd hit it. What was that thing *made* of? Or – potentially worse – what was *this woman* made of?

"I know acting uneducated makes you all feel quite *tough*." Now the woman had left Matilda's side. She was sauntering toward the gathered crowd, using her umbrella as a walking stick, her voice more a lecturer's than anything. "And frankly, if you *are* stupid, there's not much you can do. But I'll tell you this one time, and one time only: Auntie Mary has no need for anyone too tough to be intelligent."

231

Matilda glanced over her shoulder at the woman's back. The others looked cowed, embarrassed… some even nervous.

"Moreover, Auntie Mary has no time for anyone caught up in being jealous of someone else's intelligence."

Trish blew out a flabbergasted laugh. "Jealous!? We're not–"

"Oh, of *course* you are, you little animal, of *course* you are." Auntie Mary – if that was even her real name – turned back to Matilda. "I know from experience. It hurts to be left behind by someone cleverer. Feels like a fresh slap every time you see them."

Matilda lowered her eyes, staring at the stained carpet.

"But enough of that!" Suddenly, the woman's voice was bright, almost exuberant. "Who's done their homework?"

"Like our *real* homework?" asked a boy to Trish's left.

Auntie Mary rolled her eyes, her head giving a tiny shake of annoyance. "The things I asked you for last time. Who's got them?"

The kids looked at each other nervous.

"Coooome oooon!" She slapped the back of one hand in the palm of the other, accentuating her words. *"Lab*oratory grown ruby, *blow*torch, *hand*held laser cutter. Anyone?" She paused, hands in the air. "Really? No one? Is this what I feed you for?"

"Those… aren't exactly things we can get around here," Bryan muttered.

"Well, not with *that* attitude, certainly." Auntie Mary turned back to Matilda. "You. Anything in the bag?"

Tentatively, Matilda opened her shoulder bag and withdrew a small lighter. "Just this."

The kids gasped. "You *smoke?*" one of them spat out incredulously.

"I'm… trying to get my mom to quit. I keep stealing hers so she can't light her cigarettes."

"It'll do." Auntie Mary snatched the lighter out of Matilda's hair. "Hairspray. Anyone?"

Trish reached into her bag and retrieved a can.

"Not bad." Auntie Mary stared at the two items thoughtfully, then turned a disappointed gaze on the group. "I'd rather have a proper blowtorch, but I wouldn't get far if I couldn't improvise." She placed them on the table. "Ruby and laser cutter in two days. One more try. If I don't get those, I move on."

"Do we still get our pizza?"

"Sorry, what?" Auntie Mary's head whipped around, looking for the source of the voice. "Do you get your what?"

232

It was the boy who'd mocked Matilda just before she'd come in. Under Auntie Mary's gimlet gaze, he was trying to become one with the cushions. "No, nah, nothing, I just…"

The sharky smile. "Of *course* you get your pizza." She turned to Bryan. "You. Friend-bringer. Put in the order. And some ice cream for your new recruit." She dug some crumpled bills out from under a leather… something… strapped to her wrist.

***

Matilda's stomach was full. The pizza and ice cream were terrible, but the conversation had seasoned it to the point that she didn't care. Stories of stars and planets seen up close, of adventures on impossible worlds, of cities burning bright in the night.

"Thank you, by the way."

"What was that?" Auntie Mary looked up from the device on her wrist. They were outside Salvo's now, the owner closing up as the rest of the kids scattered off toward home.

Matilda smiled awkwardly. "For the ice cream. And for not running me out when everyone laughed at me."

Auntie Mary cracked what might have been a half-smile. Or a smirk. Or a wince. It was hard to tell – every expression was so sharp, even her grins seemed filled with menace from certain angles. "Always did love an underdog. Besides…" She put a finger under Matilda's chin, lifting her head a bit and regarding her as though appraising a work of art. "I get the feeling there's more to you than swotty grades." The grin cut wider like a wound. "I do look forward to finding out what it is."

"Walk you home?"

Bryan's voice shook Matilda back to herself. "Y–Yeah. I'm coming." She clutched her bag closer to her. "Thanks… Auntie Mary."

"Come on, she's gotta run. She gets annoyed if you hold her up." Bryan tugged on Matilda's sleeve and led her back toward their block.

"Why do you all call her that?"

"What?"

"Auntie Mary? Is that her name?"

Bryan shrugged. "She's never actually introduced herself. We just started calling her that cos of the Mary Poppins look. You know. And I guess she liked it because she's running with it."

"Mm. And she's from Scotland?"

"Is she? I thought she was from England?"

Matilda shook her head. "Scottish. I think. I wonder what she's doing all the way over here." She rubbed her chin where Auntie Mary's finger had been. "And why she's decided to hang out with a bunch of punk kids."

"She liked you, though. Like a lot." Bryan elbowed Matilda gently. "She usually doesn't give any of us as much alone time as she did you."

"She was telling me how to tell my parents about the C."

"You feel better?"

Matilda shrugged. "Yeah. Yeah, I think so. I'm still nervous, but she talked me through it. I think I might be okay."

"So, you coming back next time?"

"Yeah. I might."

The two parted ways at the next corner, and Matilda shuffled home, report card in hand, ready to face the worst.

The worst was, unfortunately, what she faced.

As her mother began the passive-aggressive queries about mood and health, Matilda remembered the kids at Salvo's, laughing at the idea that this could even happen. As her father ran down the list of reasons this shouldn't have happened – she was in a good home, she wasn't like Those Kids, they treated her well – she thought of Auntie Mary, defending her fear to the rest of the kids. As she picked at the chicken and vegetables her mother had reheated from the hipster grocery up the road, not wanting to tell them she was full on bad pizza and what was likely bargain bin ice cream, she visualized the strange woman's stories in her mind. Cities in the stars, burning to ash in the darkness of space.

She wanted to see it. She wanted to see the glitter of the stars, smell the warm smoke. She wanted to be there. Or anywhere. Anywhere but at this dinner table.

Matilda excused herself upstairs.

Shower. Pyjamas. Brush teeth. Wash face. Try to comb her hair into something that wouldn't turn into a rat's nest overnight. It wasn't even very late, but she wanted to sleep. No… not to sleep. To curl up. To not think. Not even about Auntie Mary's stories. Because she had the feeling that if she did, she'd start crying for want of seeing it all for herself.

Laser cutter.

Laboratory-grown ruby.

Matilda sat up in bed. Dad had those. Both of those.

She slipped across the hall to her father's upstairs workroom.

***

234

"Now!" Auntie Mary slammed the wooden sliding doors open, a dancer making her big entrance. "Let's see which of you darling little cephalopods was listening last time. Who's got Auntie Mary's homework done?"

The room was silent.

The grin that split her face began to turn downward, inverting into a look of disgust. "Nobody? Really? Not a single one of you managed to find those two simple little things for me?"

The kids looked at each other awkwardly. One raised her voice. "Um… the stuff you want… we can't exactly get our hands on–"

"Hors d'oeuvres say what?"

"… w–what?"

Auntie Mary lifted her chin, regarding the room. "You know. I like to think I've been fairly kind to all of you. I feed you. I give you an escape from your humdrum lives. I… *regale* you with tales of my life. I haven't even gotten around to killing any of you. I'd say those are all positives. And what do I get in return? *Can't.*" She spoke in a wheedling falsetto. "Oh, Auntie Maaaaary, I *cahn't*. Oh, Auntie Maaaaary, it's too *difficult.*"

"It is, though," grumbled another of the kids.

In the blink of an eye, Auntie Mary's umbrella was across his throat, and he was nose-to-nose with her. "If you're going to be snide with me, little one, at least do me the respect of speaking up."

"I–"

Clack. Clack.

The sound made Auntie Mary shift her attention from the boy to the table. Placed neatly in the centre was a cylindrical chunk of ruby and a handheld laser cutter. And standing next to the table was Matilda, breathless from her mad dash to Salvo's.

"What's this, then?"

Matilda motioned to the table. "Ruby. Laser cutter. Like you wanted."

Auntie Mary left her victim behind, hooking her umbrella over one arm to free up her hands. She examined the chunk of ruby. "Not very elegant, but it'll do under the circumstances." She flicked her eyes up to Matilda. "Your fellow students have been telling me they can't get these. How did you manage, then?"

"My… dad's an engineer."

"Mmmmm." It was a quiet, interested sound. A cat spotting a bird in the back garden. "Any more things he has lying around that he doesn't know about?"

Matilda blinked. "Uh… probably?"

"Oh, my." Auntie Mary pocketed the two items, then snaked an arm around Matilda's shoulders warmly. "My dear, we may have to have a little rummage later."

The pizza came. The breadsticks came. The stories rolled out. And Matilda couldn't help but noticed that Auntie Mary's eyes kept roaming over to her as she spoke. To read the woman's body language, the stories of war and friendship and anger and love and hate were for everyone. But to look at those eyes – they were for Matilda alone.

When the group cleared, it wasn't Bryan who caught her sleeve to stop her.

"You. Miranda."

"M–Matilda."

Auntie Mary shrugged. "Tomayto, tomahto. You and I need to have a little chitchat."

Matilda glanced at the dispersing crowd. "I... should really get home, though. My parents are already upset with me."

"Well, if they're *already* upset with you, what's a few minutes more? Do they have an angry meter?"

"Nnn..."

Auntie Mary nodded toward the door. Her smile was faint, but not necessarily gentle. "Come back in. Just a private chat. You and your Auntie Missy."

"Missy?"

"Come along! Spit-spot!"

Matilda followed the woman back into Salvo's. The greasy men behind the counter seemed not to pay either of them any mind as they went back into the back room. The table had been cleared, but the limited clientele ensured that the 'party room' hadn't been taken up again.

"I couldn't help but notice you didn't touch a bite of anything."

"Yeah... ah... mm. Not to be ungrateful, but..." Matilda scratched her cheek awkwardly. "Too greasy."

"Can't blame you there," the woman said breezily, tugging on the top corner of the booth cushion. It folded down like a car seat opening into a trunk, revealing a chrome-lined, blue-lit compartment. Matilda blinked in surprise as the woman tapped a button inside the compartment and a full tea – pot, cups, and stacks loaded with sandwiches and sweets – rolled down a conveyor belt and into view.

"You..." Matilda watched as the woman began laying the table with the fancy set. "You just called yourself Missy."

"Yes, well, it's my name." Missy pursed her lips, looking at the ceiling. "For now, at any rate. But I do rather like it. Got a bit of swish to it."

236

The pot was steaming, giving off a strong, smoky smell. "What is all this?"

"Russian Caravan." Missy set a teacup and saucer in front of Matilda and poured. "You know how it gets its name?"

"No…"

"Well, there was this caravan, you see. In Russia." She poured out a cup for herself. "They were delivering a shipment of tea and the leaves got wet. Useless that way. They had to be dried out somehow."

"Yeah?" Matilda took a sip of the tea. It was dark and strong and smoky.

Missy put down the teapot and began shovelling sugar cubes into her cup. "So I set the caravan on fire."

Matilda spat the tea back out into her cup.

"You can really taste the Russians, can't you?" Missy sipped at her tea casually.

"Why? Why would you *do* that?"

Missy shrugged. "Boredom. Pretty lights. Delicious tea."

"I… I should go." The cup clanked into its saucer, and Matilda began searching around for her backpack.

"Oh, Millicent, really. You wouldn't have come back if you weren't a little interested in what I'm doing. It's a bit late to be put off by collateral damage."

Matilda winced away from Missy. "I… I just liked your stories. That's all."

"Ahh." Missy's eyebrows lifted. Her smile was almost serene. "You liked my stories. The stories of cities aflame. Of civilizations destroyed. Of hungry monsters. Of the deaths of gods."

"I thought they were *just* stories."

"Did you really."

Matilda drew in a calming breath.

"Do you know… I saw you in me?" continued Missy with that appraising look again. "I saw that light in your eye. That desire to make things happen. To watch things burn." She took a sandwich from the stacks. "That lighter was nothing to do with your mother's nasty habit, was it? If your mother even *has* a nasty habit."

"Why do you think you know so much about me?"

Missy examined the sandwich held delicately between her manicured fingers. "You're a bored little girl. That's the only reason clever people get bad marks. Boredom. If perfection is constant it goes unnoticed. That bad mark… that was your Russian caravan, wasn't it?"

Matilda pressed her lips together. Her neck muscles tensed.

"Oh, you won't admit to it. I know." A bite of sandwich. "Go on, eat. There's no people in the sandwiches. But I can't vouch for the cream puffs."

"You've had this exact same conversation with all the others, haven't you?"

Missy looked up, her face the picture of innocence.

"You must have," Matilda pressed.

"Now, what makes you say that?"

"Makes sense, doesn't it? You want us to bring you things. That means you're doing something and you need help. You're buying us food. That means you want us to like you. And now you're treating me like the special one." She stared down at the smoky smelling tea in her cup. "Who's to say you hadn't already given that pretty speech to the rest of them before I got here?"

Missy made a low sound in her throat; it took Matilda a moment to realize it was a snicker. She looked up to see the woman's lip curling with amusement.

"Oh, you really are a good one, aren't you?"

"So I'm right?"

"No, you're not right." Missy pouted, a little-girl expression. "Oh, in many cases you *would* be. Your logic is sound. But no, I came here looking for grunts, and grunts are what I got. I never expected to find someone like you." She nudged the stacks a little closer to Matilda. "Usually I'm not on the hunt for a… what is it… 'companion'? But perhaps I could make an exception." She grinned, wrinkling her nose. "Just this once."

Matilda stared at the stacks.

"Oh, go on. It'll be fun. Just a little quality time with the girls. What do you say?"

Slowly, thoughtfully, Matilda took a cream puff.

***

"Tillie?"

Matilda grumbled as she shoved her notebooks into her shoulder bag. "I wish you'd stop calling me that."

Matilda's mom smiled placatingly from the bedroom doorway. "Sorry. Force of habit. Ma*til*da." She said it as though Matilda had asked to be called "Your Majesty."

"I have to go. I'll be late for study group."

"Honey, I know we were harsh on you for that C, but you've bounced back amazingly. You don't have to go to all this trouble."

Matilda snapped her bag shut. "I'm doing it for *me,* Mom. I *want* to. I… *enjoy* it."

"Okay. All right." The hands went up. Her mom always acted like this around her… like she was addressing a kitten that fancied itself a lion. "I just came to

238

ask if you want to come with your father and me to the exhibit at the college this weekend. We're picking up tickets tonight."

"What kind of exhibit?"

"Etruscan jewellery. The exhibit's been touring and this is its last stop before it goes to D.C. to stay."

Matilda shrugged. "Pass." She slid past her mom and hustled down the stairs.

"Hm. Your loss."

***

Missy still had her pizza socials on occasion: free food, story time, and ego boosts for all. But Matilda had taken to meeting with her for a few hours on the weekend since then. Salvo's was allegedly closed on Saturday and Sunday, but there was a side entrance behind the model kits at the comic shop (she was *sure* the door had never been there before). Surprisingly, it led straight into the party room via a secret panel in one of the walls.

And in there, Missy and Matilda worked.

Today, Missy was already working away at a small piece of machinery, about the size of the thing she wore on her wrist. An elegantly decorated cake sat next to her workspace on the table, along with a pot of tea.

"Any Russians in this one?" Matilda asked with a smirk.

"Cheeky. Get your goggles on."

Matilda pulled a pair of safety goggles out of her bag and strapped them on, followed by a pair of gloves. "Why don't you wear any?"

"Not as squishy as you. I can take a few zaps to the face if it comes to it." Missy appeared to be soldering some oddly shaped gears to a series of miniscule axels. "Have we done our homework?"

"Mm." Matilda pulled out her notebook and flipped it open to the most recently filled page. "I wasn't sure about the third one, but I did my best."

Missy slid the notebook over with her free hand, tilting her head slightly to glance at it. "Forgot to carry the *e* is why. Do it over."

"Oh." Matilda pulled out her pencil and began scribbling away. "Where did you learn circular math? I've never heard of it before."

"Obligatory at the Academy. You'll need it for what we're doing next week." Missy looked up, giving a tiny laugh. "And here I always said I'd never use it in real life. Heh."

"So what are you making?"

"Ooh, I can't tell you just yet. It'll spoil the surprise."

Matilda grinned. "It's for me?"

"Not if you don't finish your circular maths, it isn't. Chop-chop."

The two worked side by side in silence. Matilda smiled to herself. There was something comfortable about it. Missy never talked much about where she'd come from – only where she'd been – but she felt a mental connection between them. Something surprisingly warm, from someone she'd initially been quite terrified of. But she wasn't sure what she'd do without their study sessions now. She felt more confident. She was doing even better in school than she had before. And she had a friend. Like a *real* friend. Not just a walk-home-from-school friend.

"Right, that's long enough. Let's have a look." Missy slid the notebook out from under Matilda's hand. "Mmm… mmmmmmm… handwriting's a bit sloppy, but it'll do. You're a quick little learner, aren't you?"

Her hands now free, Matilda busied herself leaning over and cutting slices of cake for the two of them. "I try."

"Mm, well, you're doing a damn sight more than trying. You're flawless to ten decimal places, and I only really need seven at most." She picked up her project, dusting it off gently with one manicured hand. "I do believe, Madeline, this is for you. Stick out your non-dominant hand, if you would."

Matilda put out her right hand. Missy strapped the device to it, tightening the strap carefully. "There… you have… your *very* own… vortex manipulator."

"Vortex what now?"

"It's a little… ah… time and space bracelet. Lets you hop about."

Matilda snickered. "No."

"Granted, I could have simply keyed mine to your DNA, but I'm going to need you moving independently when we get down to business. Consider it a reward for all your hard study."

Matilda stared at her wrist. "I could see the stars with this? Go through time?"

"Well, not *yet.*" Missy undid the strap and took back the vortex manipulator. "It's a very short range one at the moment. You could get to class before the bell, but you won't be visiting any Aztecs. And it stays with me."

"Then what good is it?"

Missy's eyes widened ever so slightly. "Don't look a gift horse in the mouth, Melisandre." Her tone was clipped. "You'll have it when you need it." She stowed the vortex manipulator away. "More cake? It's orange this time."

"Sure." Matilda sat down glumly, cutting herself a slice twice as big as she'd normally take. The inside was five layers, each a slightly different shade of orange, creating an elegant gradient divided by buttercream. "What did you mean, by the way? About getting down to business?"

"Oh, now. *That* would be *telling.*" Missy tapped a finger to the side of her nose. "Just be patient a little longer. I rather think you'll like it."

***

"A little longer" ended up being that weekend. Much to Matilda's own surprise. Her phone went off with a jangly MIDI rendition of *Bang Bang* she knew for a fact she'd never downloaded, rousing her sharply from a lie-in. She grappled one-handed for the phone, squinting at the screen.

Salvo's in half an hour, darlings–

Followed by repeated kiss and umbrella emoji. And an octopus, for some reason.

Darlings? It was early. And Missy did have those nails, after all. Likely a slip. Matilda pulled on jeans and a tank top, dumped everything she thought she might even remotely need into a shoulder bag, and sped out the front door before her mother could ask where she was off to.

The Salvo's parking lot was mostly empty of cars, but it was notably full of people, all gathered around the door, all dressed in black and carrying backpacks that looked made for rough camping. And there was something, she wasn't sure what, slightly off-putting about the sight of them. She approached hesitantly. A few heads turned.

"M–Matilda?"

Matilda stepped back. "Bryan? You guys are…" She'd expected from what Missy said that the rest would be present, but she hadn't expected them to look so… ready. Coordinated. She looked around again, and realized what had put her off.

All of them had impeccable, soldier-like posture. The sort that was usually whipped into people.

"What the hell?" A familiar voice… the girl with the streaked hair. Trish. Despite her new-found good posture, she hadn't lost her sneer. "I thought she was gone."

"What do you mean, you thought I was gone?" Matilda glanced at Bryan. He shrugged helplessly.

"Well, obviously. Auntie Mary didn't invite you to the training sessions. So we figured she'd. You know. Dropped you." Trish was looking askance, as though Matilda were an unpleasant mess on the ground.

"Training sessions?"

241

"Oh, goodness, look at all the punctual little amoebae. It makes a girl's hearts flutter." Missy stepped out from behind a nearby van, twirling her umbrella. "Everyone's looking very trim and prepared. Good, good."

Matilda watched in open-mouthed surprise as the other students fell into line immediately at the sight of Missy. Missy, on the other hand, seemed to be expecting it. She tossed a quiet nod to Matilda, then approached the... well... the troops.

"Checklists out, all of you."

As one, the students whipped out folded pieces of paper, each with a row of check marks printed neatly beside lines of scribble. Matilda felt herself panic. She'd received no such list.

Missy caught Matilda's eye, then gave a slight shake of the head and a gentle eye roll before turning back to the line of students. Matilda could almost hear the voice in her head. *Not you, silly.*

"Very gooood, very goooood..." Missy sauntered down the line, reading the lists casually. "Mmmmm..." She stopped in front of one scrawny boy. "All right, Tim?"

The boy coughed. "T–Tom."

Missy waved a hand impatiently. "Got your switchblade this time, Tim?"

"Yes, ma'am."

"Not a retractable comb?" Her hands were on her hips, her voice mockingly scolding.

Tom swallowed. "Of course not."

Missy stuck out a hand. "Let's see."

Hesitantly, Tom reached into his bag and withdrew what looked like a folded switchblade. Missy flapped her hand for it, finally snatching it away from him. She clicked the button, revealing what looked for perhaps a moment like a shiny silver blade.

Then the tinfoil fell off, revealing a plastic comb.

"Really."

Tom laughed a nervous – terrified? – laugh. "I–I can't get a blade! You know that! My parents won't even let us have sharp scissors in the house!"

"Ohhhh dear-dear-dear." Missy pulled what looked like a heavily tricked-out cell phone from her pocket. "That *is* a shame. After all the discussions we've had."

"But everyone else has them, right? Right?" He looked to his left and right, but his fellow students were staring straight ahead. "I mean, what's one less switchblade gonna matter?"

242

Missy shook her head, a bit like a disappointed mother, and extended the phone toward him. "You're going to have to do better than that, I'm afraid."

"I—"

A beam of blue light shot out from the phone and hit Tom – who exploded into blue light and bits of ash. The students either side of the new gap in the line stumbled aside. Matilda choked back a scream.

"Anyone else have any last-minute replacements they'd like to run by me?" She twiddled the device between her fingers, pursing her lips.

"No, ma'am," came the hushed reply from the line.

"Good. Now, I suggest you all take a few minutes to limber up. Stretch or give each other back rubs or whatever it is you do." She turned to Matilda, putting an arm around her and leading her a few feet away.

"You've been training them," Matilda whispered.

Missy glanced over her shoulder. "Not terribly well, it seems. You think they'd have been more attentive if I gave them some cake?"

"And you… killed one."

"Well, it happens, doesn't it?" Before Matilda could respond, Missy whipped the new vortex manipulator out of a pocket. "Arm out."

Obediently, Matilda offered her left wrist. Missy began buckling the device on securely.

"Um. Excuse me?" It was Trish.

Missy didn't take her eyes from her work. "Not now, sweetheart, Mummy's busy."

"Why is *she* here?"

Matilda felt her shoulders tense.

Missy lifted her head slowly, her hands dropping to her sides. It was a graceful movement, like a time lapse of a lily moving. A very cross lily. "I beg your pardon?"

"I mean…" Trish shifted uncomfortably. "Like, I thought she wasn't part of this. I thought she just came to the pizza nights because you felt bad for her."

"Now when did I ever say that?"

Trish shrugged. "I don't know, I just… feel like she's gonna screw things up for us."

"Well, that's a shame. I suggest you get over that feeling before things kick off." Missy put a hand on Matilda's shoulder. "This young lady is second in command on this endeavour. Anything she says, you accept as though it came from me."

"What?" Trish's posture became aggressive. "Hell no! You think I'm gonna take orders from her? You think I'm stupid!?"

243

Matilda could barely trace Missy's movement, but it took her only a second to end up behind Trish, one arm wrapped tightly around her shoulders, Missy's made-up cheek against hers as though they were whispering secrets.

"As a matter of fact," Missy said in a stage whisper, "I do. That is why *she* is there and *you* are here. And should you have any further problems with that, I recommend you look at the device on her wrist. There's a little button just on the left that works... oh... *much* like my little trinket of a moment before. And I am giving her full license to use it as recklessly as she chooses."

"G–Ggghhhh..." Trish's only reply was a strangled sound of confusion.

Missy smiled over at Matilda. "Tell you what. Why don't you give it a little test fire? You know, just to make sure it's working." She pointed with an exaggerated motion at the girl still in her grip.

Matilda stared down at the device on her wrist. A hush had fallen over the little group. She raised her wrist...

Then jerked it away, firing at a discarded fast food cup. It sizzled into blue, then into nothing.

Missy let Trish go, pouting. "Oh, that's no fun. You get a much better spark off a live one." Trish scrambled back into line, casting Matilda a look somewhere between angry and cowed.

"Right, well. We're already behind schedule, so if anyone has any other issues, feel free to raise them now." Missy had pulled the device from her pocket again and was inspecting it casually. "Anyone? Yes, no, maybe so?"

Silence.

"Lovely! Then you've all got one hour for a loo break." She glanced at Matilda, a trace of bemusement on her face. "That's not too short, is it?"

"That's... uh, that should be fine."

"Off you trot, then!"

The students scattered, more than a few side-eyes tossed at Matilda.

***

"So I'm guessing Auntie Mary's told you the plan?"

Bryan was leaning against the wall of the parking garage, taking practice aims at a sign with what looked like a cross between a Super Soaker and a vacuum cleaner attachment. Well. More like practice *poses*. There was no way all the crouching and over-the-shoulder aiming would be any real help anywhere.

"I, um..." Matilda wasn't sure how to answer. She'd already been given power of life or death over the whole group of them; admitting she had no clue what was going on might not be the best idea at this stage.

244

"I mean, that's probably a dumb question, right? You're her right hand, after all." Bryan laughed, pausing his poses for a moment to regard her. "Not bad for the newbie."

Matilda couldn't help smiling a little. She rubbed her hand over the vortex manipulator thoughtfully. "Yeah. Yeah, I guess so."

Bryan grinned. "And… I notice you still haven't told me what you know. She's trained you well. Whatever it is, I'm looking forward to it."

"Heh. Yeah. It's… gonna really be something."

Matilda looked down to the street from her vantage point. Missy was having words with a handful of the students, occasionally walking quite close to one as if she were about to steal a kiss. Matilda was beginning to learn what that meant. But the murderous little device hadn't come back out yet. Not that she'd seen, anyway.

Her phone blipped out the unfamiliar ringtone again. "One second."

Round the back for briefing. And a snowboarder emoji. For some reason.

"Summons from the boss?" Bryan asked cheerfully.

Matilda laughed and tucked her phone away. "Heh. Yep. I guess the fun is starting." She dashed off, taking the winding stairs down. There was an elevator, but she was tense… and something about the winding descent that calmed her. Gave her time to get her head in order.

Missy was leaning against the building, finishing off what looked to be the last of an ice cream cone. "All ready?" She didn't look up.

"I… uh… don't actually know what we're doing."

"Oh. Of course. Silly me." Missy popped the last bite of cone into her mouth and dusted off her hands. "How are you for robbing a museum?"

"W–What??"

Missy raised an eyebrow. "Not your style?"

"No, I just… I didn't know that's what… that's how we were…" Matilda fell silent. All things considered, she shouldn't have been surprised. And now… after being given so much credit and power?

"No, I'm fine. Let's do it. Let's rob a museum." Matilda punched her fist into an open palm nervously.

Missy grinned, cat-like. "Good. I thought you'd be game. Your bit's going to be very easy, actually. We're going in two stages. For the first stage, I'll need you to cry and be very scared. Think you can manage that?"

"That, uh, sounds doable. And for the second stage?"

"Oh, you're my helper for that! Once the first stage is done, you stick by me and just do as I say."

"Sure… uh, how will I know when the first stage is done?"

Missy pursed her lips coyly. "Mm, you'll know."

Matilda couldn't help but think back on Missy's prim little expression an hour later, when one of her classmates had a gun pressed to her temple.

She shot a terrified look over at Missy, who was in a similar position. But contrary to Matilda's frozen shock and horror, Missy was wailing catastrophically, struggling against her "captor" with all the believability of a director's girlfriend in a cameo. The whole ridiculous scene was playing out in the museum's lobby, with the guests chased out by Missy's spare "troops" and a few police officers trying to decide whether to go for mediation or a clear shot.

"Oh, please, don't shoot them! Just give them what they want!" Missy shot a pointed look in Matilda's direction; but she couldn't move. If it had been Bryan doing the play-acting, she might have been a little more secure. But it was Trish. And after the incident in the parking lot earlier that day, the barrel of her gun was being ground a little *too* enthusiastically into Matilda's temple.

"Cut it out," Matilda hissed.

Trish smirked under her balaclava. "I was told to make it believable. I was never told *how* believable. Still feeling tough, teacher's pet?"

Matilda whimpered, squinting against tears. Then, suddenly, she felt herself dropped to the floor.

"Ugh, too *soon, too soon!*" Missy's voice echoed off the lobby's high ceiling. "Would another minute have killed you?"

Matilda struggled to her feet, taking stock of her surroundings. The police officers were all on the floor; behind each stood a student with a taser. One took off his mask – Bryan. "Sorry, it's just… you guys were looking really freaked out. I thought maybe it was going too far."

"God, you're so soft-hearted. Never mind, never mind. Squad B, barricade the doors. Squad A, with me. You, too, Marina."

Matilda watched as the students split off into groups without a moment's hesitation. Bryan was Squad B, apparently; Trish, with all the luck Matilda was beginning to expect from this operation, was one of a grand total of two people in Squad A. And following close behind her.

"What is this all about?" Matilda hissed to Missy, trying to get away from her unexpected shadow.

"Clearing the vicinity so we have full access. Obviously."

"Sure, but what about security cameras?"

"Already took 'em down," came a voice from Missy's other side.

Missy nodded to him. "He already took 'em down."

246

Matilda looked around at her fellow students, baffled. Somewhere in the last few weeks, she'd turned the whole group of them into high-end operatives. Well – she thought back to the casualty in the parking lot – most of them. She wasn't sure whether to be impressed or terrified.

Missy led them to the Special Exhibits room. The entire building had been cleared, but there was still a lock in place. The student who had disabled the CCTV went to work decoding the lock.

"Is this… a thing you do?" Matilda whispered to Missy.

"What, having fun and stealing things? Gosh, yes. As much as possible."

"No, I mean… the training up."

Missy frowned thoughtfully. "Mm. Sometimes. I usually end up integrating robotics or mind control somewhere along the way, but this has worked out really nicely, I think. And a lot less pre-gaming." The frown melted into a crinkle-nosed grin.

Matilda felt herself shiver internally.

The door gave way, and Missy led her little group in. "Here we are! Final stop!"

Matilda looked around the small room. Pedestals and cases showcased ancient bracelets and necklaces and other ornaments.

"Etruscan jewellery…"

"Oh, you're a fan?" Missy looked over her shoulder.

"No, I…" Matilda shook her head. "I just remember my parents asked if I wanted to come."

"And here you are!" Missy popped a gadget out of one of her pockets and headed for a glass case toward the centre of the room. "Right, I'm going to work on this. Just need a few little favours from the rest of you. Computer boy, could you lock us in?"

"Sure thing." The boy from before began tinkering with the locks from the inside.

"Good, good." Missy worked quietly away at cutting a circle in the glass. To Matilda, it looked almost like the scenes in the old cartoons of people breaking into houses via windows – right down to the eager grin on Missy's face. "And, erm. Melbourne. Kill the other one."

Matilda froze. "What?!"

"Just zap her. The police coming up to the front door will handle the others."

Trish whipped out her gun. "Like hell she's taking me down!"

Missy rolled her eyes. "Oh, *do* stop complaining. You were told this was dangerous."

"Yeah, but if I'm going down, it's not gonna be because of *her.*"

247

"Well, okay, good." Matilda held her hands in the air. "Because I don't *want* to."

"Could you two please finish this up? I'm going to need my helper for some calculations in a moment and we *cannot* have spares here when that starts."

Matilda stared down at her vortex manipulator on her shaking wrist. Trish still had a gun levelled at her. "Do it, I dare you."

"Listen to her," Missy said flatly, growing ever more impatient. "Give her what she wants."

"I can't just kill someone!"

Missy looked up from her work, her expression dark. "You can't just kill someone who's spoken badly of you ever day since you first joined us? Who mocks you at every turn? Who takes *pleasure* in terrifying you? I am giving you a gift! *Use it!*"

At Missy's words, Trish pulled the trigger, her face contorted in anger.

But no bullet struck Matilda.

A blue force field shook around her, eventually settling. Trish dropped her gun, her look of anger now one of terror.

"You... you really would have shot me?" Matilda stared at Trish in disbelief. "God, I knew you didn't like me, but... *really?*"

"I–I'm sorry, I just freaked out." Trish laughed nervously. She looked over at Missy. "Auntie Mary, tell her! I just freaked out!"

Missy glanced at Trish coldly, then returned to the glass case.

"Come on, I know you. You'd never hurt anyone else. You couldn't. I saw you in the parking lot. You–"

Matilda raised the vortex manipulator and pressed the button.

"Ugh, finally." Missy returned from her work on the case, holding a large bracelet across her palm as though showing it off to a customer. She stepped through the ashes that only moments ago had been Trish, shaking them off her boot. "And we're good to go!"

"That's... all you came for?" Matilda stared at the bracelet. "What's special about it?"

Missy shrugged, wrapping it around her wrist and fastening it. "It's pretty and I like it." She glanced out a nearby window. "Ah, the news trucks are here. Excellent. You. Computer boy. Detonate the museum in 60 seconds."

"Yes, ma'am."

"And we..." Missy grabbed Matilda's vortex manipulator, punching a few buttons. "Are out."

***

248

"Please tell me what just happened."

Missy admired her new bracelet in the pink light of an alien sunrise. "I just got some pretty new bling. You just got revenge on a bully. Your local news got a very interesting story."

"And… you sacrificed a dozen teenagers."

"Yes, well, I can't *always* have a cast of thousands."

"Except me."

"I told you, Matilda. There's more to you. I thought this might be an opportunity to shake you out of your comfort zone a bit." She nodded to the vortex manipulator. "And now you can see the universe. It'll work properly, you know."

Matilda stared down. "It's just as well. I can't go home now. I'm a murderer."

"First one's always the toughest. You get used to it." That wound-like grin again. "Anyway, I must be off."

"Wait, what?"

"Other things to do, dear. We had our fun. I have another date."

"But I thought we… you taught me all that stuff."

Missy nodded. "Yes. Of course. So you'd be able to navigate. And calculate tips."

"Not…"

"Oh, dear. No. No, we were never…" Missy gave a strained smile. "Oh, I remember now why I don't do companions. This is really very awkward. Must be *so* much easier when they just get themselves killed."

Before Matilda could protest, Missy had vanished, leaving her to watch her first off-world sunrise alone.

But not her last.

The Diamond of the Gods
Nathan Mullins

"Hello," came her sultry voice. "My name is Missy, but don't let that stop you calling me the most evil bitch on the planet. I suppose you're wondering what it is you're doing here and why you've been selected?"

Her subjects all nattered on to themselves and nodded, waiting for an answer. They were seated in what could easily be mistaken for a Gallifreyan equivalent of the Oval Office.

"You're all going to serve me in my plans," she continued, "because, well, there's nothing waiting for you out here." With a wide sweep of her hand, she drew their attention to the outside world – presented here in a holographic image above the table. "How must it feel to be unloved and unappreciated," she mused. "You must all feel so lonely."

Many objected, shouting and name calling, but Missy stood for none of it. "You will be silent!" she ordered. And they were – they had little choice. She held her laser screwdriver in her hand and pointed it at each and every one of them. "I'm a master of time," she said, "just as you are. I can imagine this is why you fear being controlled by me, because you know that protocol forbids us to interfere in the affairs of others. Well… guess what?" she bellowed. "NOT ANYMORE!"

***

In a flash, the assembled Time Lords had found themselves forcibly strapped into their chairs. The chairs descended through an opening in the floor, taking them deep down into the planet. Once they had reached its heart, they were hoisted onto a conveyor belt that transported them into Missy's TARDIS. The Time Lords were forced to duck their heads as they passed through the doors. It was quite a squeeze but once through, they fell sideways onto the console room floor, where Missy stood standing over them.

"I always knew I'd have men falling at my feet," she quipped, before reaching for the lever to pilot the TARDIS and set the ship in motion. "Say goodbye to Gallifrey boys, for you'll never step foot there again!"

Pinned down on their associates, many were unable to look up as the ship began to dematerialise. Eager to get away from Gallifreyan soil, Missy held on with glee as the TARDIS engines roared into life. When they were clear, Missy skipped about the console room in her long dress and twirled around in front of a mirror. "I'm quite a babe," she chirped. In the corner, she saw her newly recruited servants squirm and try to sit upright on their chairs, only it was no use. "Oh, you needn't stand, nor sit actually…" she noted. "But you could tell me if these new high heeled boots match my sexy Mistress attire?" She turned about and waited for her prisoners to speak, but neither said a word. "Flatterers," she moped. "There is one man who'd say so, I'm quite sure, but he's otherwise engaged, fighting the Daleks in some galaxy somewhere, as I recall rightly." She looked away to tap in the coordinates for their next destination, ignoring the fidgeting Time Lords who made several attempts to break free, before realising there was no escape.

***

"Pipe down back there!" instructed Missy, as once again her detainees made an effort to get to their feet. This time, one of them collided into her with such force that the chair knocked her unconscious. She slumped down in a heap beside the console. With time to spare, others got to their feet and made a last desperate attempt to free themselves from their bonds. One after the other, they grappled with the ropes keeping their fellow Time Lords from escaping, tugging at them without knowing what they were doing, as they stood back to back, or rather chair to chair, until their bonds came loose, releasing them.

"Yes," cheered one, quietly so as not to disturb Missy. "Good job!"

"Am I…" said another, reluctantly.

"Free? Yes…" replied the other. "Now get moving, quickly! We've got to turn this ship around!"

They gathered over the console but couldn't make head nor tail of it. As Time Lords, piloting one of their own time capsules should have been easy. But Missy's TARDIS was quite unlike any ordinary means of transportation. It had almost been entirely altered, so that only she could pilot it. Scratching their heads, umming and ahhing over how exactly they would operate Missy's ship, the only conclusion they came to was to make Missy take them back. They got together the rope she'd used to tie them up and did the same to her, hoisting her up onto a chair and waited for her to come round.

The engines began to wheeze and grind, as was standard for a type forty time capsule. It signalled that they had reached their destination, wherever that may be. They exchanged looks of trepidation.

"Where are we?" asked Weaver, a Time Lord in distinguished robes.

"Check the scanner!" blurted Saber, a young Time Lord, with flowing blonde hair that spilt out from her gold headdress down her armoured chest unit.

Weaver flicked a switch and the scanner revealed that they were on the planet Adamentem.

"We're a long way from home," Saber concluded. "What's she brought us out here for?" She glanced down at Missy who was now stirring and reaching for her screwdriver.

Weaver took it from her before she got a chance to use it. "Don't think about it," he said.

"Ooh, what a commanding presence you have!" she told him, before attempting to get to her feet. She quickly realised she was unable to, and that the roles had been reversed, that she was now a prisoner of the Time Lords, although that would quickly be resolved. She leant back in her chair. "It all looks as though it's going your way, doesn't it?" she mused. "You have me right where you want me. But the TARDIS is not under your control." She said it with such authority. It was like any power the Time Lords thought they possessed was nothing compared to the might of Missy. "But these ropes aren't well tied and I'm sorry…" she said, staring at Weaver, "but the way you're holding my laser screwdriver is all wrong." In that moment, she used all her strength to free herself from the ropes that bound her to the chair and took back control. She jumped up and reached for Weaver, who she threw across the room. Missy's screwdriver was found by Saber. It had fallen from Weaver's hand. But she didn't know how to use it. So she held it out in front of her and pointed it at Missy. It was the best she could do.

"Stop right there!" ordered Saber, screwdriver raised, finger about to press the big red button.

Missy took no notice, walking towards her like a child daring their parent to snap. Saber tried the dial, but the screwdriver didn't fire. "Come on, you're a Lady Time Lord like me," moaned Missy. "Us girls have *got* to stick together, or… perhaps you think you're better looking than me, in which case…" she reached forward and took the screwdriver from her. "Isomorphic controls," she remarked. "It only works for me!" Saber didn't know how that worked or whether it really did. Instinct kicked in and Saber remembered her training the Academy had taught her. She, like Missy, was no ordinary Time Lord. Like the Doctor, even.

In certain situations, when it wasn't known what her fate would be or in what direction her destiny would lie, Saber knew that she had it within her to fight, and she would if she thought there was a chance, that perhaps Missy had mistaken her for being easily beaten and not brave enough to stand her ground.

Missy never saw it coming, until she found herself being hurled over Saber in a move that had her in complete awe. It all went into slow motion for a minute, as Missy fell in a heap and shook her head before looking back. Then the speed of time seemed to return to normal, as Saber laughed at what she had done.

"Don't underestimate me," she told Missy. "I can hold my own. I'm not afraid of you, or anyone that stands in my way."

Missy stood up, brushing herself down, and undoing the knot holding her hair up. "Well, I'd never expected to have as much fun as this," she chuckled. "It's a pity that the male had no desire to be humiliated, quite like yourself, and that your associates," she went on, looking at the other Time Lords as they bowed before her in fear, "have no intention of standing with you in your futile attempts to stop me from achieving my aims." She was striding towards her now with such purpose and fury. "You really have picked the wrong bitch for a cat fight!"

Adamentem, a planet in the Pretiositas nebula 10,000 light years from Gallifrey.

Lennon's face was covered in dirt and dried blood from a battle that had waged for six years, in a war that had been going for twelve, serving with the Angodomani's against a species called the Hanthatron. Both sides had showed little sign of slowing down in their brutal attacks on each other. As the war raged on, the people on either side of the conflict were dispersed and displaced. Battles continued across the planet in small clusters, with small gains on either side making little difference to the overall picture.

Lennon was of the Angodomani strike-force, and had recently been made a general. He had been on his way back from another victory, when in a fit of over-confidence he commanded his men to carry out an opportunist attack on some more unsuspecting enemies. But the art of taking the enemy by surprise, despite his notoriety as a fighter, was not something Lennon knew much about. His background was in farming, so prior to the war the only time he had ever wielded something as sharp as a sword was when it came to harvesting his crop. Unlike the blades of wheat and grass, the enemy was far from being a sitting target. This was one attack too many, and his men had scattered.

He ran through a jungle, the sound of gunfire getting nearer and explosions sending dirt and debris over exotic plant life and vegetation. He ducked for cover when a missile zoomed overhead and careered into a shack. There was a loud boom and only planks of wood and scraps of metal remained in its place.

He got up and started moving again when he was attacked and pushed to the ground.

Lennon looked around and saw one of the Hanthatron – six wavy arms, seven heads, fourteen eyes – planting twelve feet forward, about to end his life. He jumped onto his feet, pulling his sword from his scabbard and swung the slim, silver weapon down on top of the creature, slicing through its thick armour plating. He cut right through its soft centre and it staggered sideways before collapsing. He heard the sound of another Hanthatron approaching nearby and started to run. He was breathless, doing his best to keep at a steady pace, but he could hear the creature behind him charging. It was hard to outrun these things, but he had to give the impression of being fit. If they thought he was fitter than them, they wouldn't mess with him any longer.

He'd been running for so long. More than anything, Lennon hoped that at the end of the war, the running and the fighting would be rewarded with a lot less chaos and, he hoped, some sitting down. The Hanthatron behind him was gaining on him. They didn't seem to tire but if they recognised that their target was speedier and more agile, they would drift away and hunt elsewhere. Often, however, the only option was to hide and hope for the best. The relentless bombings had littered the landscape with craters which made running difficult, but hiding easier.

Lennon leaped into the nearest crater and landed on a broken tree stump. The outline of a door had been carved into the wood, a remnant of happier times when children could play here, he assumed. "I could really have done with a real door, right now," he said aloud. As if answering his prayers, to his astonishment the stump clicked and the outline of the door solidified. Tentatively he pushed it open and stepped inside.

"Who the hell are you?" yelled Missy, looking past the console at the stranger. "Chop, chop," she sputtered, clapping her hands, telling him to get a move on. "And close that door!" she went on, before rushing over to meet him.

When he'd closed the doors, he turned back but was now face to face with Missy. "Err, hi," he said, back straight, taking a step backwards.

"Hello," she said, placing both hands behind his waist as she pulled him towards her. "Give us a kiss." He ducked below her arms and escaped her clutches. He backed up a bit, knocking into the console, and then noticed the Time Lords she'd taken hostage dangling from the ceiling, ropes binding their hands and legs as they hung against the console motionless.

"You're not…"

Missy raised an eyebrow. "Go on, say it!"

255

Lennon gulped. "You're not the Doctor?" Missy laughed and pursed her lips together, grinning like a Cheshire Cat. "I am Missy," she informed him. "The other chap, I'm afraid, is unavailable." Lennon gulped again and shook his head.

"No, no… just you hear things, don't you, about a hero who travels in a shape shifting time machine saving people, going well out of the way to stop evil and, well, frankly… we could do with a person like that – we're fighting a war here that just goes on and on."

Missy was intrigued. "I can do everything he can," she exclaimed, "and probably be of much more use to you," she winked, slowly unzipping her dress.

Lennon wasn't so sure and tried his best to change the subject, moving around the console room nervously.

"These men and women you have as prisoners here," he mumbled, stumbling around the central column. "What part do they play in your adventures?"

She gazed upon them and frowned. "I point and laugh at them when they're naughty," she chuckled. "And they have been so very naughty," she whispered, getting a leg up on the console.

"Look, I don't know what's going on here," uttered Lennon, "but if you say you can help us, then don't delay! This war has been going on for way too long. If there's anything at all you can do to bring it under control, then please, by all means, put your leg down and show me the real you."

Missy chuckled at the prospect of showing her true colours. "And what's in it for me?" she hissed, glaring at Lennon wide eyed and bushy tailed.

"Oh, believe me," he said, smiling. "The reward is very satisfying."

Missy put her leg down and looked around the central column, peeping at Lennon. "Then tell me," she said, sternly. "Satisfy my curiosity. Don't keep me in suspense!"

Lennon began to nod and laugh at the situation he found himself in. "At the very heart of this planet is a jewel quite unlike anything you've ever seen before. It holds this planet together. Its powers are endless. It's what we're fighting for and why this war will last forever, because whoever stakes their claim will have a share worth more than the universe, and power beyond all imagination."

Missy's eyes widened to their full extent. She licked her lips – almost choosing to flirt with Lennon as he stood opposite quivering in his boots. Confronting Missy was like being faced with an impossible dilemma – to flirt back and risk everything or to oppose her entirely and have yet another villain to face, adding to the stupid life forms who sought to destroy his own kind for something so tiny but more powerful than the sun.

"I accept," she replied, taking Lennon's hand and shaking it firmly.

256

Harriet was 47. Next month was her birthday, but after all she'd endured on Adamentem, she feared she wouldn't make it to 48. She'd been one of the few to have been targeted more than once, with the Hanthatron sensing a 'can-do attitude' and a fighting spirit. They knew that she wasn't going down without sending them a message first. In her heart, she was never going to be beaten, so there was no point trying to take her life from her, as her enemies often found out. But the war was beginning to take its toll. She and her warriors were exhausted, many holding out for a miracle, if only to get them through what she considered unnecessary violence.

Harriet's good friend, Lennon, had yet to come back from his latest mission. She feared the worst – she always did. They were close-knit, best of friends, with the right chemistry between them for something more to develop.

It didn't look good – shells were falling from the sky, one after the other, until a thunderous boom shook Harriet off her feet. She landed face down in the mud beside her comrades. She wiped the sludge from her face and looked up at to see Lennon accompanied by a woman.

"Harriet my sweetheart, are you alright?" Lennon ran to help her up. He gave her his hand and she hauled herself upright.

"Fine," she said, looking the woman up and down.

"I think she's gone cross-eyed!" remarked Missy.

Harriet gave her the evil eye and brushed herself down. She was caked in mud.

"Who's your shining friend?" she asked, looking over at Lennon.

"I found her," he answered, "in a ship near to here. She's a Time Lord…"

Missy elbowed him in the stomach. "Time Lady, please… I'm terribly old fashioned… and do I look like a man? Stuffy old civilisation, the Time Lords. They don't like change!"

Lennon rubbed the pain but nodded apologetically. Smoke filled the area and they were forced to retreat, deeper into the jungle. They shared the company of up to twelve men and women who were part of Harriet's unit. She had taken Lennon's place on account of being his second in command. As they trudged through the undergrowth, something snagged on Harriet's foot and she tripped and fell, injuring her ankle.

"Ouch!" she cried, bringing the platoon to a standstill.

"This friend of yours," put in Missy, standing with Lennon. "Bit useless, isn't she, for a Sergeant Major?"

Harriet had overheard and looked up at Missy. "Bitch!" she muttered. She was given a hand by another member of her unit and they hurried on back to base.

***

"Were you always heading to this place?" asked the chief of the Angodomani Security Council, in a live feed to Adamentem. The screen crackled and squiggly lines ran across the faces of those quizzing Missy.

"Yes," she said, stroking her chin.

"Why did you come to Adamentem? What was here that intrigued you?"

Missy thought about this one. The only thing she wished to get her hands on was the jewel at the heart of the planet, but she also realised that was the very point of the war being fought, and it would be ill advised to spill her plans.

"I thought I could help. This war has gone on long enough, don't you think?"

The Security Council chief pressed the palms of his hands together as he spoke with Missy.

"What do you hope to gain?"

Missy shrugged and looked around her at the men and women present. "The satisfaction that I did all I could to end the fighting here on Adamentem, since all other lifeforms have run away, terrified. But I'm not like them. I'm Missy. Other lifeforms tend to fear me!"

Lennon wondered whether such a testimony was enough to appease the Security Council.

"We would like to extend our warmest welcome to you," said the chief, leaning forward into the lens and proffering a hand. His hand came through the other end of the monitor screen and Missy shook it reluctantly.

"What have I signed up to?" she joked, catching the eye of Harriet as she stood behind her, arms folded.

"I'd like to wish you all the luck in the defeat of the Hanthatron," added the Chief. "And when they are wiped off the surface of Adamentem, your orders are to bring us the jewel at the heart of the world. Do that, and half of it will be yours."

A knowing grin appeared on her moody face. The screen switched off and she spun around to face Lennon. "Well then, that settles it," she grinned.

"The Chief is reasonable enough. To grant you half of the treasure we came here for is not to be taken lightly. It's why we are fighting this war, lest we forget."

Missy understood well enough. "But you promised me all of it."

258

Harriet shot Lennon a horrible expression of disgust as her jaw dropped at such an accusation.

"Yes, I did," he responded, turning to face Harriet disdainfully. "I made the remark tactically as a General," he whispered to her quietly, with Missy out of earshot. "Don't worry. The jewel will be ours. First the war must be won."

***

The base was surrounded by a wall with watch towers in its four corners. There was now a much greater number of people than before, all from other military units fighting the same war against the Hanthatron. Many took turns to secure the base while their colleagues regained their strength. Some were tasked with monitoring the airwaves while the Hanthatron communicated with reinforcements. Sometimes the Hanthatron let slip when they were ready to advance, and Lennon and his men would ambush them and buy Harriet and her squaddies some time. Their base was used to produce munitions and as a treatment centre for the injured. Supplies would be delivered there once every week by a transport ship from their home world – Beta-Major, if it wasn't shot down in the process.

The Hanthatron army had set up camp on an island, cut off by the waters on Adamentem. The current sometimes made it difficult for any Angodomani to cross, but the Hanthatron were quite capable of getting from one island to another, using their upper body strength to reach forward as the waves crashed about them, and propel themselves across, showing they were not easily perturbed. High walls had been erected around the camp to hide what was so heavily guarded inside – the ship that had first brought them to Adamentem, and inside it their leader. The Hanthatron's level of ruthlessness gave the Angodomani a run for their money.

It was down to careful planning that Lennon's strike force always seemed to have the upper hand. And Harriet was glad to make use of Lennon's knowledge of the planet, from previous expeditions to the surface to the use of Hanthatron technology. Over the years, he had brought back weapons he'd killed for in order to make use of them himself. Lennon was a killing machine and Missy liked him even more for it. She knew, however, that she had competition from Harriet and reckoned that yet another cat fight was on the cards. She hoped so, anyway – it would be a chance to break the girl and force her to obey her commands.

The Hanthatron were moving. Elsewhere, their own strike force had slaughtered many of the Angodomani. They drove small groups back, many of

259

whom had run out of bullets, but they alone could not stop them. Their many arms reached out and stole their weapons from them, their eyes surveying their surroundings at each and every angle, with each turn of their seven heads. They bore their bloodstained teeth from all the ripping of Angodomani flesh and bone. Their leader – the Hanthaking – was known for getting his hands dirty. He led his troops into battle the second war was declared, tearing down the opposition in his bloodthirsty conquest. They had arrived on the planet to stake their claim for the jewel at its heart, just as the Angodomani had, both fully aware that the only way to settle this was the survival of the fittest, and in comparing their own physiognomy to the Hanthatron's, such a task might prove difficult. The Hanthatron could run faster with their feet – that much was obvious, but they would often trip up in the process and make easy targets. The Hanthaking, however, saw his opponents as puny bipeds with a hunger for victory.

When war was declared, the Angodomani did not back down but threw themselves into chaos. Word got round the galaxy that a great war raged. Other aliens knew of Adamentem's riches but kept well away from the danger. The biggest threats in the known universe came to observe the conflict, but none would intervene. Neither the Daleks, Cybermen, Zygons nor Ice Warriors stood a chance. But on a planet some 10,000 light years away, a civilisation spoke of doing something to end the bloodshed.

***

Gallifrey: At the Outbreak of War.

Gallifrey High Command initially called for the Doctor, for fear of another Time War spreading throughout the universe, but he had gone off the radar again. So Missy was summoned at the request of the High Council. Upon her arrival, Missy was invited to a senate meeting to discuss exactly how she might be deployed. Whatever they came up with was vetoed by Rassilon.

"No Time Lord can interfere," he roared, "whatever may be at stake."

"With respect Lord President, I disagree," said the General. "Remember how the Time War played out… how we needed the Doctors? The scenario we face now is of that same magnitude. You may disagree about the use of this renegade Time Lord, but without the Doctor what is the alternative? The protocol is that such a measure should be put to a vote and the High Council has spoken."

260

Missy enjoyed seeing Rassilon put in his place. Angered by the response, he decided he would have no part to play in proceedings, and took off in a flurry. The debate continued in his absence.

"Well, I'm flattered to be considered your second choice, go-to renegade I must say," said Missy. "But next time, ask me first, eh?"

"We are grateful to you for your commitment to serving us," said a Time Lord. Her name was Saber, once a great warrior now resigned to her position as a noble Time Lady. "It would come at too great a cost and affect us all dearly, were you not involved. None of us want events to spiral out of control. None of us want a repeat of the Time War. Not even Rassilon himself. The Planet's core is the fabled *Diamond of the Gods*, said to have been hidden away in the old times. Myth has it that the jewel was once held in the possession of a creature who controlled the universe, but then imparted his gift of free will unto the stars and gave the diamond up for the planet."

Missy listened carefully. It was one hell of a story and if she was a betting woman she'd put money on the Doctor being the legendary hero of Adamentem. She simply had to get involved now. "So if there is such a rich history attached to this planet, why are we doing nothing to save it?" With that, she raised a device she had been holding tight within her pocket and zapped the Time Lord controls that surrounded her.

"What are you doing?" snarled Weaver, seated at the head of the table.

"Taking control!" exclaimed Missy, preparing to reconvene the meeting.

***

On the surface of Adamentem, Missy had given Lennon notice that she had had an idea. "Alright, let's hear it?" he said, waiting with baited breath to denounce it should it breach regulations.

"I wish to speak with the Hanthatron personally," she offered. "Being a Time Lady, I have certain influence. I can try to bring this conflict to a peaceful end."

Lennon wasn't sure how capable she was of having any effect on the situation, nor in fact the enemy. "Don't you think we've tried before?" he fretted. "They just don't want a peaceful solution."

Missy took a seat on the table all the other soldiers were sitting at. They stopped eating and looked up at her. "You can't be sure of that," she said, as she grabbed at a man's soup bowl and downed it in one. "Sorry," she said, returning him the empty bowl. "You're their enemies," she explained. "They have their orders to kill you. But me… I'm a stranger in town who could make them see why all this is a waste of their time. I'm your bargaining chip!"

Lennon let out a sigh of empathy. "Okay, maybe," he agreed.

"Good, now… these Hanthatron nuts, do they have a leader?"

Harriet shared Lennon's perspective on the situation as he took a back seat and left her to make the decision. "The Hanthaking, but he's a real brute. He will stop at nothing to get what he wants, and as we all came here for the same thing, it would seem that making any sort of deal is firmly out of the question."

Missy didn't like the prospect of reasoning with a psychopath unable to make any sort of neutral judgments. "Right, but what if I could convince him?"

Harriet was intrigued. "Go on," she said, leaning forward, interested to learn more.

"Oh, no, I refuse to give my methods of bargaining for a solution to someone like you, Harriet," was the response. Missy so hated the woman who came between her and Lennon. The gooseberry. The pickle. "I'm sorry, but you'll just have to trust me."

"Go!" said Lennon. "But on your own head be it."

Missy understood, stood up straight, walked over to where Lennon was sitting and placed an arm around his shoulder, squeezing him attentively. "It may all be for the greater good," she beamed, before going off into the night.

Harriet turned to watch her go. There were daggers in her eyes.

***

Missy could hear the heavy footsteps of the Hanthatron as she ran through the dark. It was difficult to see as it was pitch black. She lit up the path ahead with her laser screwdriver. In the distance, far away, the heavy bombardment of the planet continued. The repeated thump of shells coming into contact with the ground, and then shockwave after shockwave, which she could feel through her high heels. Looking around, she sensed that she was not alone. Then something prodded her in the back. She turned about and something shiny took up her vision. She rubbed her eyes as they adjusted to what now stood before her. A voice filled her ears.

"You are not an Angodomani."

Missy bit her lip and shook her head. "Nope, not this one," she croaked.

"Who are you?" it demanded, all seven heads staring at her in complete astonishment.

"A friend, I assure you. My name is Missy and I would like to speak to the Hanthaking, if you don't mind?" The creature breathed like that of a wild animal.

262

"As you wish."

It nudged Missy forward with its long arms and she staggered backwards before turning and walking in the direction it dictated. It was a long and arduous walk, crossing various streams along the route, not to mention the odd live minefield. The unpredictable and often tempestuous weather hadn't helped. Eventually they caught sight of the Hanthaking's lair. Much to Missy's disgust, the journey wasn't quite over.

The 'lair' was a spaceship situated on an island cut off by marshlands. When they finally arrived, Missy was dishevelled and wet through. But she was more irritated by the gentle pitter-patter of rain against the Hanthatron's metal armour. It became the focus of her indignation towards the creature for remaining unscathed by the harsh environment.

When Missy came face to face with the Hanthaking, his seven heads showed multiple expressions of shock and wonderment.

"Who is this female?"

"I come in peace," proclaimed Missy. "The fighting must stop, for it is not merely a waste of life but of munitions too. I know what you came here for, but I'm here to tell you that you were wrong."

The Hanthaking leant off his throne and gazed down at Missy as she stood before him. "Wrong? WRONG? I do not believe so. Explain!" His tone was that of an untameable dictator keen to get his own way.

"The jewel you thought existed does not. It is a myth that you believed because you wanted it so badly. You want to be king of all time and space but do you have any idea how ridiculous that sounds?"

The King stood up and walked down the steps, descending to Missy's height. "You insult my intelligence! You think me a fool, is that it?"

Missy turned her back on him as she paced up and down.

"Not so much a fool but a dreamer," she confessed. "You think just because you're this species' leader, you are entitled to more than what you deserve. It's what led you to this place, like the legend of King Arthur and the sword he pulled from the stone. You came to claim what you see as your destiny, but will your warriors forgive you for the lives lost in your cause? Or will they choose to rise up against you? I know it would be my first priority."

The King strode towards Missy and brushed her aside so that she fell to the floor.

"Do not question my authority!" he threatened. "You are a liar, I have proof that the diamond exists."

Missy wiped the blood from her lip and ran a hand through her hair. "What possible proof?"

263

The King called on its servants. "Bring the sacred scroll."

They promptly returned and presented the scroll to Missy. She unravelled the document to reveal a map of how to find the treasure – a complex network of tunnels all converged to a central point on the map. But instead of an x to mark the spot, there was a series of cave drawings depicting a familiar figure armed with a red handled umbrella burying the jewel at the centre of the planet. It was her arch nemesis, the Doctor. Missy rolled her eyes in frustration.

"So you see," said the King, "I now have no reason to trust you in the slightest." He turned to his guards. "Lock her up!"

One of the guards took the map, while another led her away. But the King of the Hanthatron had no idea who he was dealing with. With her photographic memory, Missy could recall precisely where the tunnel on the map could be accessed from, once she had escaped from the Hanthatron's lair.

***

Missy was fairly sure this was the same creature who had picked her up before. "Tell me," she began, as the creature yanked her forward and propelled her down the ship's corridor. "How much do you know about what's going on here?"

The eyes flickered and gazed back at her, the noses on its faces twitching. "We came here to fight and to die," it answered, "but our fate rests with our leader."

Missy pulled a face and strode up to the monstrosity, planting a hand on its chest. "You poor wee dear. Do you choose only to obey the orders you're given or do you ever think for yourself?"

The mouths curled into a gormless expression. "All warriors would do well to follow their leader, come what may."

Missy tutted to herself, expressing her concerns. "Your leader doesn't give a damn if your species is weakened by this war, so long as he gets his grubby mitts on his precious treasure. After all, that's what he came here for, and I expect he won't leave until he has it, but if you come with me, we can find it before he does and we can be masters of the universe!"

The creature grunted and raised its weapon. "You are a treacherous human female," it snarled. "Treachery is punishable by…"

Missy produced a small bottle of perfume and sprayed first herself and then the creature. It sank to its knees and dropped dead, leaving Missy with a good chance to get clear.

"I'm not human," she said, taking in the aroma. "Far from it!"

She ran at full pelt down one end of the corridor and then down the ramp of the ship, but soon she felt the presence of the Hanthatron close behind her. They had found their fallen comrade and issued an immediate search of the area. They found nothing.

***

"The Time Lady is resourceful," said the Hanthaking, regrettably. "She must be re-captured. Our plans must advance. Seek out the tunnel to the ancient treasure. Find and destroy Missy and all those who oppose us!"

The warriors who stood before their King bowed their heads in obedience.

***

Missy came to a halt in the marshlands. She was cold, wet and miles away from the TARDIS. She took from her pocket her laser screwdriver and held down a switch. The Time Lords who were still hanging from ropes aboard the TARDIS dropped to the floor.

Missy's voice filled the console room as she spoke directly to her prisoners. "I do hope I haven't neglected you for too long," she announced, as the Time Lords picked themselves up and breathed an intense sigh of relief. "But I'm afraid that you are now required to fulfil the task I brought you here for."

Missy tapped another button on the screwdriver and a strange noise filled their heads. They tried to fight it but it was no use. "You will all obey my commands," she said, making her intentions known. "You will meet me at the planet's core. Follow the instructions and the map that I'm sending to you collectively." Missy closed her eyes. As she did so, so did the Time Lords. "Concentrate," she uttered. "We must make the link. As Time Lords, it is within our power." Their minds joined, she conjured an image of the map from her memory. The image solidified in the minds of the Time Lords and, suddenly, they understood their purpose.

***

A huge grin appeared on Missy's face as she ran on through the jungle. She knew how to find the treasure and was on her way there, when she suddenly ran into Lennon who was out on patrol.

"Missy?" he said, somewhat disbelievingly. "I thought we'd never see you again!"

265

Missy was flustered, but hid it well as she hinted at her relative success. "I did what I said I would," she lied, much to Lennon's shock.

"You…"

She nodded. "Yes, I did," she grinned, before Lennon took her in his arms and squeezed her tight. Her feet left the ground as he spun her around.

"You're remarkable," he cheered, leading her back to base. Missy clung on, nowhere near as thrilled as he was. When he broke the news to his colleagues at the camp, Missy's name became the talk of all the platoon, a hero in the eyes of their chief and by all who waited for their return.

Missy was delighted. These primitives were proving to be far easier to manipulate than she had imagined. She had barely needed to use her mind altering powers to bend them to her will, and Lennon's idealism and desperation made him the perfect puppet. It was extraordinary to her that the camp was so quick to believe not only in peace and reconciliation, but that their enemy also wanted the same, despite years of enmity.

"We will meet with the Hanthatron in the morning," said Lennon. "I trust it has been agreed that it is we who will be leaving with the treasure?"

Missy reassured him that he was right.

"Good," continued Lennon, "and assuming intelligence has been shared, are we any closer to finding an access point to this world's core – the place where we might extract the treasure when we find it?"

Missy touched his temples and an image entered his mind.

"But… but… how did you do that?" he said, as she lowered her hands and gazed back at him.

"It's a gift we Time Lords possess."

***

The next day, the Angodomani strike force, under Missy's orders, moved out of camp, armaments in hand and raring to go. Lennon, who was now no more than Missy's puppet, had few thoughts that were his own. His men knew nothing of this, and followed him, blindly like he was some great leader who was going to do great things. Harriet had her own concerns but didn't make them known. She knew that if she did, Missy would have something to say about it, and she didn't fancy her chances going up against the camp witch. She steered clear of Missy as best she could, and succeeded in doing just that.

After the bombs had stopped falling the night before, the Angodomani's were convinced that the message Missy had given them of peace between them and their enemies, was finally coming into play. There was to be no more fighting. Not now that they all believed Missy had negotiated a peace. She had firmly established herself as the head of the camp and the smartest person on the planet. Lennon, more than anyone, out of his desire to please his Mistress, was looking forward to shaking the Hanthaking by his multiple hands, and getting to know his newly acquainted allies. The Hanthatron, meanwhile, were looking forward to a bloodbath and a day of reckoning.

Missy led the way as she guided her newly recruited slaves, save for Harriet, through the jungle. The men and women in what was once Lennon's platoon, marched forward unaware of the fact they were under Missy's mysterious powers. She silenced them when she heard a crunch sound from up ahead. The Hanthatrons that were out on patrol hadn't seen them. Seven heads and they still missed the obvious. Missy and her lackeys crouched low behind a bush, in a hope of remaining concealed. It did just the trick and they stayed hidden until the Hanthatron had roamed on. They were catching up with her, and in part this was *her* doing. It wasn't merely her scent the Hanthatron were picking up, but a signal they were following. A signal sent out by Missy's screwdriver, calling them to her. She just had to evade their capture a little while longer, at least until they arrived where they needed to be.

"Come on," urged Missy, "keep up!" They crossed a large stream that separated the island, along the same path Missy had taken whilst escaping the Hanthatron. There was a tense moment of uncertainty as they managed to get across, each soaking wet with only small cuts and bruises.

"Tell me," said Harriet, taking Missy aside, "if we're now allied to our foes, why do we still keep a low profile for fear of being discovered?"

Missy, it seemed, had an answer for everything and responded in a tone of voice that told Harriet she needn't fear. "Because it's common sense. We need to save all our discussions with our new allies for the Hanthaking, or else we're inviting trouble. Now, let's keep moving, eh folks?"

Harriet felt it only right to question Missy's actions. She was quite willing to put her trust in her so long as she was genuine, but up to now, she had her reservations, and cracks were beginning to show.

"Forgive me," said Harriet, "but that sounds like an evasion."

Missy took no notice.

***

The walk they embarked on took them further into the depths of the jungle, until Missy cried "stop!" Ahead of them was a dark tunnel that neither of them had come across before.

"Have we arrived?" asked Lennon, turning to face Missy.

"We have," she concluded, just as the Hanthaking and his warriors surrounded them from all sides.

"Ahh, your highness," greeted Lennon, "I…" The creatures raised their blasters. Lennon would have died were it not for the sacrificial intervention of a comrade who shoved him aside, taking the hit himself.

"Traitor!" screamed Harriet, taking her gun from her holster and firing at Missy, who was scuttling down the tunnel. She managed to escape in time as those she had lured into her trap perished at the hands of the Hanthatron.

Lennon took cover along with several of his men as they fought back, laser bolts piercing the armour plating of the Hanthatron warriors. The Hanthaking jumped out from behind Lennon and his officers and ordered that they surrender. Harriet was just as quick thinking as Missy was, although no matter how many times she dodged a bullet, she saw no possibility of escape. Not this time. The Hanthatron outnumbered their platoon. And then she was hit. A bolt of intense energy knocked her for six. She was thrown off her feet. Her screams alerted Lennon to her but there was nothing he could do.

"NO!!!" he yelled, at the top of his lungs, rushing over to help her, but the Hanthatron were closing in from all sides. "Know that I loved you," uttered Harriet, whose breathing was slowing as her heart was pounding. Lennon squeezed her hand gently as she closed her eyes and a tear rolled down her cheek.

"Stand!" bellowed the Hanthatron that had butchered Harriet. Lennon, who was crouching beside his friend's body, straightened up and turned to face the creature. "You will surrender!" it demanded, but Lennon refused outright.

"You've taken from me my only love. I can see no end in sight. My people are dead, just as the Adamentians before us were wiped from this very planet by your own hands. And we've been used, all of us, in one woman's selfish plan. I welcome death. Because I failed. I endangered the lives of everyone who followed me here. And for what? A diamond, a weapon that I'll never know existed for real. And neither, I suspect, will you."

In one last act of hopeless defiance he raised his gun, knowing he was about to become the last of his people to fall.

***

The cave to the centre of Adamentem took Missy days to reach. It wasn't well lit and she often stumbled despite having her laser screwdriver to light her way. Some distance behind her, the Hanthatron were on the offensive. Still giddy from the defeat of their enemies, they had but one pest left to destroy – one last victory was all they required before they gained control of space and time. When the tunnel opened up into a full sized chamber, Missy was forced to shield her eyes from the powerful glow of the gemstone. Surrounding it was a barrier – a defence system – an electric current running between each poll in which encompassed it.

"This is going to be tricky," she mumbled. She tried to disarm the security protocols but nothing came of her struggles. There was no way of gaining access to the jewel.

"I do hope I've not come all this way for nothing."

She stepped back and wondered if a blast from her laser screwdriver would bring the cave down around her. A roar from the Hanthatron army startled her. "Stay calm," she told herself and held a hand up to her chest, feeling the quickening beats of her hearts. If she crossed the polls, she'd be dead. The electric shock would kill her. She couldn't squeeze under them as the barrier, along with the current, rose and fell repeatedly, making any attempt to transpose herself from one side to the other difficult.

Missy raised her laser screwdriver. She kissed it softly before aiming at the jewel's defences. She closed her eyes and made a wish. "Here goes nothing," she said aloud, though it was intended as a mere thought. She stubbed her finger against a switch and a bolt of power struck the poll she had aimed at.

The Hanthatron entered the chamber as a fireball imploded before their eyes. Missy was blown off her feet, rocks tumbling down upon her against a wall at the furthest edge of the chamber. The Hanthatron bore the brunt of the blast as debris hit them hard, knocking them off their feet. They were thrown some way back inside the tunnel. As they tried to crawl to safety, unable to avoid the ensuing rock fall, most of them could see their deaths coming. There was a 'boom' as a section of the passage leading from the chamber to the cave collapsed. A crushing noise reverberated around the cavern, and the sound of the injured ceased.

Missy had survived. She kicked away the rocks that had fallen on her, reached out with both arms and finally heaved herself up. Her heels had been broken and her dress torn to bits. She looked around, shaken by what had happened, and noticed the security system had been deactivated.

"Yes!" she triumphed.

Approaching the diamond, she could see that the rocks which had once surrounded it had come loose, and the spotlight over it flickered until the power died. Missy seized the moment and reached for the jewel. As she did so, the ground began to crumble. Cracks suddenly appeared from out of nowhere. Missy held the diamond tight.

"If I can't have you, no-one can," she muttered.

She could feel herself falling. Her legs turned to jelly. The ground was descending into chaos. She thought she was about to die one final, ignominious death, and then a familiar wheezing and groaning sound filled her ears, echoing around the chamber. She fell to her knees looking around for her salvation.

***

A light flashed before Missy's eyes, blinding her as the TARDIS arrived in the same position in which she herself was now standing in, completely enveloping her as she was transported aboard, still clutching the jewel.

"Oh well done!" she announced, clapping her Time Lord 'friends' who stood at the controls. They were only obeying her orders. Missy unclenched her fist as she peered closely at her treasure.

"My pretty," she croaked.

At that moment, three strands of light shot out from the stone into the eyes of the Time Lords present.

"What was that?" screeched Missy.

The Time Lords rubbed their eyes. They had control over their own minds again. "We've been given back our freedom," declared Weaver. "As you must give back what you took from Adamentem."

"Why must I?" protested Missy. "I sacrificed everything to get my hands on this, including the survivors of two great warrior races. Would you let them die for nothing? At least like this, they died in battle. A death worthy of a warrior."

"The diamond liberated us so that we might see you for what you are. It knows that you will use it for wicked crimes against all other lifeforms, the very reason it was protected at the planet's core all this time, with little indication of where it was buried and how to find it."

Missy held the diamond in the palm of her hand. It pulsated with life. It seemed to expand and then deflate, somewhat like an organ.

"And we as Time Lords will stop you." They each closed their eyes.

"Concentrate," said Weaver. "We must be one." Missy knew what action they were taking. She staggered back as she felt their minds ganging up on hers as she stood there unprepared for the mental game the Time Lords were playing.

"NO!" she screamed, as she dropped to the floor, the jewel escaping her clutches as it rolled down the ramp of the ship and back out the doors. Her mind was too weak from the trauma she had been through.

When the Time Lords opened their eyes, Missy was out cold.

"What are we going to do with her?" asked Saber.

"Take her back to Gallifrey," answered Weaver, his associates nodding in agreement. "She must stand trial for her crimes. Genocide, abandonment, felony, betrayal, sacrifice – the list is endless."

Saber was joined by Weaver and the others as they piloted the TARDIS home.

***

Swirling strands of light emanated from the diamond as it returned itself to the planet's core. Power was soon restored. It couldn't bring the dead back into existence, but Adamentem would go on – its name a reminder of the races that had perished in their plight and their greed for power. The war was over, both sides had lost, and Missy was imprisoned on Gallifrey.

She wept as she stood in the dock, answering to the list of offences as they were read to the court.

After the guilty verdict was served, Missy was confined to a cell in the Gallifreyan High Prison in the mountain tops. As she hung her head between the bars, a memory entered her mind. The mountains had been where she and her friend the Doctor had played growing up, both free to be who and whatever they wanted, looking out on all of Gallifrey. As children, they knew not of who they would become, or the paths they would choose that would decide their destiny.

One would see the wonders of the universe, and the other would be imprisoned for much of her own lifespan – a waste. But upon reflection, Missy hoped there would come a time she would choose good over evil.

The Shell Game
Rachel Redhead

"I'm bored!"

Judy Collins, survivor of an abusive childhood, critic of shoes, annoyer of saints and complainer about everything, pushed the pile of crystal-bound books slowly off of the librarian's table and onto the floor. The resultant cacophony could perhaps be best described as the sounds made by a deranged glockenspiel.

The Master, in his Al Pacino phase, reminded himself that while he wanted a pet cat, a human was easier in the long term, as he didn't need a background check and a genuine ID to get one.

"We're leaving," he said, smiling coldly at the prim and boring librarian.

He had the book he needed, so the whole planet could safely burn tomorrow now, as fate intended. Not many stars get an exploding Dalek cruiser impacting them, turning them nova. He appreciated the cosmic irony that life was indeed just one big practical joke played on the living.

"There's some books on the floor," said Judy, who was nothing if not helpful. "Hey wait up!"

She walked faster to catch up with her keeper.

***

The Master reproached his underling, once they were a sufficient distance from the library.

"I told you not to touch anything."

"I was bored," Judy replied. "You're not much fun since you shaved the beard off. I once got an award for gymnastics," she pouted, "that was before the accident. Can I help it if my co-ordination's been off since I fell off that climbing frame?" Calling it gymnastics was probably over-selling it, Judy considered, being able to do a forward roll and not get a nose bleed had been worth celebrating, her mother had once told her, before she died.

"What does that have to do with anything? I offer to show you the universe and you just want is to have fun?"

The Master wondered if his pet had outlived her usefulness already.

"Where are we going now?" Judy wanted some fun, some excitement, some adventure. "We never go anywhere interesting."

"I'm a Time Lord," the Master replied as he unlocked the small side door of the city's red stone cathedral, so heavily adorned with statues of blessed types and sacred bores. The door hadn't been there before it appeared today, and it would be gone very soon. "I have things to do."

"What does that mean, really?" Judy sighed as she took off her thin black jacket and put it next to the Master's equally black, but much more expensive jacket. At least that's what he claimed. In truth, he had simply killed the tailor for the garment, stating that it would be unrivalled in the galaxy.

Judy was an expert on fashion and she knew there were loads of jackets identical to the Master's, she was also wise enough not to say this out loud.

"This place is full of junk," Judy observed, not for the first time. She picked up a small bronze statue of an alien god of some kind or other. "What does this do?" she added, shaking it to see if it made a noise.

The Master confiscated the explosive device that had carefully been disguised as a priceless antique.

"Please be careful, some of this 'junk' is far from harmless. These items have been carefully collected from all manner of times and places in your universe and beyond."

"I'm Canadian but I spent most of my life in London, because of dad's job. Now I'm visiting different planets every month or so, does that still make me belong to some arbitrary lines on a map, or am I a citizen of the universe now? Where are we off to this time anyway?"

The Master smiled, deciding to indulge his human.

"You're always needing new shoes, I know just the place in the Andromeda galaxy. Xander V, the commerce planet."

"I always need new shoes."

Judy felt like the Master had no concept of style at all, if it wasn't for her, he'd just wear the first thing he'd find in his wardrobe.

"We do a lot of walking," she continued, "and we can't always wear combat boots to a lavish dinner reception, because one of those times you'll actually want to talk to people, you know, have a conversation and not just shoot them because you're bored, or because they have an accent that irritates you."

"That ambassador had harmonic frequencies in her voice, it set my teeth on edge," the Master explained. "She would not stop talking, an example had to be set to the other hostages."

"Then they turned on me," Judy sighed. It was an old argument.

"You're reasonably cunning, you talked your way out of it," the Master had no time or patience for fools. "I've no idea how the Doctor manages it with two or three of you, one is more than enough for me. Maybe he pits them against each other? I might ask him, after the introductory murders of course. You can never really say hello properly if you don't say it with corpses. It really grabs and holds the attention."

The Master checked the ship's settings, then cleared a space among the weapons of complete obliteration for the tea things.

"You do know how to make tea, don't you? I had to import it all the way from my home in Oakdown to your miserable little planet, just so I could enjoy a cuppa every time I was in the time zone."

Judy smiled.

"My home economics teacher wouldn't let me make anything else, not after the unexpected fire incident. I can't believe she tried to put me up on arson charges. I was just trying to soft boil an egg. It must have been a faulty oven the way it exploded like that."

The Master nodded.

"Such are the injustices of the world. They must be stopped, if you can make a cup of tea then there may be hope for you yet."

He looked at the shrunken bodies of his previous companions, none of whom had matched the sheer chaos and mayhem that Judy caused by accident.

"Do you want lemongrass or raspberry medley?"

"I'll have the Earl Grey I think, hot enough for old Krampus himself."

The Master sat back in his favourite armchair and waited to see if Judy got herself killed by accident with the poisoned needles, but she survived. After taking his first sip of tea, he paused for a moment to see if he could taste any poisons, which he didn't. He was both pleased and disappointed.

"We'll be at least an hour or two, so you can eat or sleep, or whatever it is that you do when you're not annoying me. Be somewhere else, go."

***

"Where shall we go first?" Judy liked to keep the Master in a good mood. He was almost manageable then. When he was in a bad mood though, then it was best to lock herself in her room and wait for his colossal temper to abate. She'd watched him destroy whole civilizations because someone was rude to him. She'd seen him topple insane tyrants, just because he needed somewhere quiet to sit and think. One time they pushed this old guy into a minefield, but that was really just for fun. Who knew that mines were so loud?

"You simply have to get a summer wardrobe, everything you own is so dark and depressing. You've got good posture and reasonable facial symmetry. You need a look that says ruthless power and ambition."

275

The Master looked at Judy like she was more than just a distraction.

"You may be right, what do you suggest?"

"Classy, elegant, sophisticated," Judy pointed across to the self-appointed executive gentleman's tailor. "We can give them a go."

The Master nodded in agreement.

"Afterwards I need to visit one of the local banks."

"If you'd have said that, then I'd have brought the shotguns and ski masks with me. I love a good bank robbery, they are so much fun – watching you shoot the wannabe heroes…"

"After I've let them think they're about to win."

The Master liked to see that final look of shocked disappointment in his victims eyes, when they realised the small candle flame of hope had gone out for good. He had spent a thousand years crushing the tiny dreams of mortal species. If only they realised how pathetic they really were.

***

"Thank you my dear."

The Master poured on the false charm as they entered the bank. He could play the part of the perfect gentleman to great effect, whenever the mood took him. Even back in his academy days he could fool everyone – well, almost everyone, the one notable exception being his onetime closest friend.

Judy was pleased and made a mental note to galactichat her friend, Trudiode, about this. She'd set Trudiode up on a blind date with Violet, who had travelled with her and the Master for a while. It didn't last long – Violet's kleptomaniac ways proved to be too annoying for the Master, despite the fact that he revelled in irritating people as one of his many distraction techniques.

Judy was pulled right back into the moment when a random stranger nearly knocked her over.

"Did you see that? How rude! He just decided to knock me out of the way rather than spend half a second walking around me. It's like I'm not even here! Hello, don't you have eyes? What a jerk, I'm wearing my best top too, some people are just arrogant, entitled jerks. I've got a good mind to report him for something, being an idiot in public or something."

"They'd have to arrest most people if that was a law."

The Master smiled at his own joke because that wasn't the joke, the real joke was much more sublime and had a grandeur on a cosmic scale. The folly of tiny little insects trying to impose their will on a vast and uncaring universe. He knew that striving to create meaning and love made no difference to the cold hand of fate waiting to be played tomorrow. Watching humans fail day after day was the only reason to get out of bed on a morning.

"Once we've finished here I've found jobs for us both."

"I hate working," Judy sighed. "The mundanity of the nine till five, the horrid decay of an unfulfilled life, so small and boring. That's why I ran off to the stars with an alien crime god, I want danger and excitement and being able to shoot people if the mood takes me."

The Master looked sharply at Judy.

"I have a plan and it requires someone else to ensure it goes right. If it's not you then I can always find someone else."

"I'm your stooge," Judy said quickly, "this is just going to be pretend for a while, right? I know you love a good disguise, but the best part of a disguise is always the reveal, right?"

The Master was surprised by how much his pet had picked up from him, perhaps it was best to get rid of her after he'd finished with her part of the plan. He could always get another pet, they were like ants and he loved stepping on them.

***

Deep inside the most desolate hellhole of cruelty and wickedness is a room, and in this room there is a prisoner. The prisoner is a Dalek and every day the Master tortures this creature to within its final moments. Hours of torment and pain cause the horribly mutated being to scream in agony for the amusement of the Master. Why does the Master do this you may ask, well it's because he's cruel and it's his idea of fun. The Master despises the Daleks, not just because they betrayed him, but because they're better at being vicious, spiteful and unrelentingly nasty than he is. He hates them because they don't think they're evil and so he pours his hatred, his malice and his brutality out onto his prisoner every day, until it can take no more. Then, he lets it heal from its wounds and he bounds out of the room eager to find more ways to do the same to the rest of the universe, for the universe is just as cold and uncaring in its regard for those that live within it.

***

"This is boring."

Judy was wearing a skirt suit and she was not happy about being made to look normal.

"I look like I work here!"

She briefly wondered about the large pile of white powder on the Master's desk, but quickly realised it was probably just a hypnotic agent, to make it easier for him to influence people's minds. He didn't need that with her, he'd captured her attention with the promise of crime and fun.

"That's the whole point," the Master reminded his diversion/shield/pet... was it too late to get that cat? "We're here to steal more wealth than even you can spend on shoes and bags and make up. I assume that's what you waste money on, as you don't seem to have stolen any rare pieces of artwork?"

"I tried to get the Mona Lisa," Judy sighed. "You told me it was a fake, which kind of put me off the whole concept of stealing paintings."

"A tragic loss to the world of art theft to be sure," the Master shuffled some papers. "I'm now the CEO of this company..."

"The Malarax Corporation," Judy helpfully prompted the Master. "We had such fun disposing of the body last night – well, I did – you needed some me time in your personal dungeon. There's something clean about dumping bodies into a super massive black hole, elegant even. He hardly squirmed at all as I pushed him out of the door and waved him off with a cheery bye-bye."

"Petty murder is so mundane," the Master sighed. "We have a job to do here, a real job, and when it's over a whole lot of people are going to kill themselves when they realise their magic money tree has been burned down and they're now just like the people they've been oppressing for centuries."

"Since when do you care about social justice?"

Judy was starting to worry that the Master was losing his edge. She knew who he was when she signed up for this gig, it didn't come with any benefits but the chance to learn real crime was worth it. Although why he made her read all those physics books was beyond her, unless that was a form of punishment in itself. Why did she really need to learn about string theory and quantum foam? Why did she even need to learn to pilot the ship anyway? She got their destination wrong every time she tried, though she had managed a three time zone turn that one time.

"You are the new head of marketing," the Master, now going by the name of Ronald Hasteur, informed Judy of her own place in the company. "Products don't just sell themselves, that's where you come in. Sell our products to the consumers and the consumers to the products. If you need me you can set up a meeting through my new PA, Dalia."

"Yes sir," Judy tried not to look at the PA who gave her the shivers, instead she mentally got herself into her new role. She wasn't naturally gifted with talents like deception or cunning, but she made up for both with a vicious sense of spite. "We'll have the best promotion campaign ever."

She hated working, but she loved acting, and she had a flexi-hours contract. This called for an epic early finish and an impromptu works outing for drinks. She wanted to play the nice boss who inspired through rewards. Those who still didn't make it could be cut from the team, at the ankles, into a lake of boiling acid.

Day One.

"I have a dream," said Judy, stealing her intro from the best, "the best marketing campaign in the galaxy. We must allow ourselves to dream up ideas that our competitors would never do… could never do. If we're to put the name Malarax into the hearts and minds of everyone, then we need to do so on an epic scale. I want your best ideas team, today is about big dreams, impossible dreams, from hypnotic lobsters to turning suns supernova. Actually, I think they already tried that in another galaxy, still that's the level we all need to pitch at initially."

Day Eight.

"Are you sure that's viable?" Judy asked Jean.
"The engineering won't be a problem," Jean replied confidently.
"It is a big idea," Jack added.
"We'd better do a limited run first."
Judy was really getting into her role as the bossy, but indulgent team leader.

Day Twelve.

Judy looked at the tech specs for the trial run, it had promise and she'd allowed herself to be talked around to the idea. It was certainly epic, there was no doubt about that, she just wondered if people would understand the concept they were trying to promote.

Day Twenty-Six.

The trial was a success, market share went up by fifteen percent in the local area and news articles spread even further over the data streams.

"We should commence wave one now." Judy said to her team. "Vi'astrox, can you take lead on that?"

Vi'astrox nodded a tentacle in agreement.

Day Thirty-Two.

Meglon Pistachio, COO, looked at Ronald Hasteur. "The marketing division have already spent their yearly budget in just three months… what are you going to do about it?"

Ronald Hasteur paused for a moment.

"I'm assured that they have great plans for a new advertising campaign."

"Campaign, schmapain in my arse! They're supposed to make us money, not spend it!"

Betsy Lynchpin, who won her seat on the board in a game of cards, shrugged. "Perhaps we should wait and see?" she said. "We've indulged ourselves on ventures before and recouped a major profit from it."

"That young marketing whiz, Judy Collins, is a genius," Alan Granter, who had long waited for an injection of new blood into the old company, said to the others, and unknowingly signed his own death warrant. He invested heavily in companies like this, old and creaky, worth billions, and helped himself to a healthy share of its profits.

Day Forty.

Judy pulled some figures together as the board wanted to know how much more the advertising campaign was going to cost them. Not as much as the revenue they'd make, obviously. "Where's your stats at Jimmy?"

"Oh man, I was too wasted last night to do anything." Jimmy had been to the best party on the planet.

Judy was regretting keeping the guy-eye-candy on the team. "Let me have your raw data and I'll analyse it myself."

"Data?" Jimmy was perplexed and then upset, "aw man, I should have been writing stuff down?"

"I am a leaf on the wind," said Judy, starting a meditation mantra she had learned from a pilot she'd met in a spaceport lock up last month.

Day Fifty-Two.

Judy looked at the private account she'd set up to siphon funds out of the company. She wasn't normally one to embezzle a large corporation out of billions, but they'd put her within reach of their finances. She wondered if they'd ever trace the loss of funds, hidden in the vast ledger of the company. She'd taken fractions of a percentage here and there, nothing that would be lost at a glance, but if she was here longer than a year then they would surely discover it in an audit. She couldn't wait to get shot this planet, or, better still blow the planet up – an asteroid impact should do the trick. All she had to do was accidentally nudge it out of its orbit by just a small amount. She'd done it before by accidentally wiping out the dinosaurs, just after they'd survived that mess with the Cybermen.

Day Sixty.

Judy raised her glass "to a successful campaign!" She'd grown to not hate her team over the last three months, though she was more than ready to move on from this heist. The bar was an opulence of minimalism, luxury chic in just enough amounts to be exotic and not tacky. She'd found the local equivalent of champagne and ordered a large bottle of it on ice for everyone.

"Thank you everyone for your hard work, and thank you Jimmy for being there too."

Day Sixty-Eight.

Judy stood up and applauded her creative team.

"This has been the most ambitious advertising campaign ever. Jean, Jack, Jimmy, Vi'astrox, give yourselves a well-deserved pat on the back. We've reached out to markets that we've never tapped before and sales are now coming in from all corners of the galaxy. We're set to not only make back three times our expenditure, but maybe four times, and that's going to make our bonuses spectacular. Giant robot statues walking across the surface of planets, it was a simple dream that I had, but you all made it come true."

The doors opened, and a platoon of security guards entered the meeting room.

"Judith Victoria Collins, you are to be detained for crimes against the Malarax Corporation."

"What?!"

Judy was actually shocked. She hadn't expected the Master to turn on her mid-mission like this, but she was prepared. She always had a plan. Usually it was a bad plan, involving a certain loss of dignity and poise.

"It was all his fault."

She pointed at Jimmy, the slacker, who had done less than ten percent of his allotted tasks. She had only allowed him to get away with it because he was cute and had a nice smile.

***

The experimentation chamber was rather bland in its aesthetic, like a bad hospital set in a b-movie. Judy tapped the glass tank containing the severed head of Jimmy the slacker, just to see if it moved.

"You could really pep this place up with some primary colours," she said to no effect. "At least some flowers or heavy gold ornaments," she added, before muttering under her breath, "ideally, ones that would make a good weapon to use in my escape."

"We use the finest state of the art genetic engineering to turn people into products," Nurse Gimlet said to the annoying test subject. "Some subjects we implant with organs that secrete the raw materials we need for our components, others we simply chop up to see how long it takes them to die.

"I'm not one to complain," Judy lied, "but do you have any fresh pillows? This one's a bit lumpy and what time's tea? I stayed in hospital once with a broken foot and I had tea then."

"This isn't a hospital," Nurse Gimlet replied to the idiotic girl.

"I know," Judy replied and stabbed the nurse in the neck with a very sharp knife she kept for occasions such as this. "You never searched me properly for weapons, just because you can't see them – it doesn't mean they're not there."

She looked around for a handy towel to mop up the blood.

"Oh great, so I now have a dead nurse on me. As if my day couldn't get any worse."

***

The board meeting was boring, but Ronald Hasteur let out a brief laugh during the accountant Perkins' speech on how they should double the prices of all their products, to claw back the money lost in their recent disastrous marketing campaign. "Continue, please, then we can discuss the appointment of the new head of marketing."

"I'm not sure how serious you think this situation is," Meglon Pistachio, perennial wannabe CEO, groused. "We've lost billions off the share index – it'll take years to rebuild that level of commercial trust again."

"Oh, one bad ad campaign doesn't mean losing everything, except for the former marketing team of course," said Hasteur. "I'm sure we have some meaningless glittery sparkles we can throw at this. A public donation always buys goodwill, or a senator looking to secure himself a seat at the table once his term is up."

"Interesting move," Betsy Lynchpin replied, intrigued by the possibility of the company buying more political influence. "Perhaps it's time we had a look around the vault. This company's security is more than just shares, bonds and strategic investments. We've always had the capital to back up our value."

"How exciting," Hasteur smiled. "I enjoy a works outing."

***

Judy looked suspiciously at the three newbies, who seemed to be spontaneously helpful. No-one did anything without wanting something in return. "Who are you three?"

"I'm Saara," the blue girl said with a big smile. "That's Tim, and his girlfriend."

"We were looking for a Stelline outpost, but we took a wrong turn into your universe," Tim explained to the teenage apprentice. "You're not as evil as Hannah's alt, I'll say that for you."

"Who are you people?"

"No time for that now," the unnamed figure announced. "Escape time, Saara if you will."

Saara used her water magic to destroy the nearby wall and a great deal of the various labs and research data behind it. "Oh my, I think I overdid it, I guess I was trying to show off."

"You did the job," Tim reassured Saara, "have a bar of mint cake." He knew that the nervous 'water witch' enjoyed a good sugary snack.

"I'll be off then," Judy said to the trio of implausible people. "I'd say thanks but that would involve there having been some sort of contract between us and I never asked for help. I don't want to get stuck with a bill for it."

"She's not that bad," Tim lied.

"I really was quite the ungrateful little bitch," the other Judy said to her friends, as she looked at her alt history duplicate, "even in a different universe."

***

Ronald Hasteur smiled genially as the security staff unlocked the private vault, waiting his time. The best bit about disguises was the reveal after all.

"This is all so exciting."

Suddenly, alarms started to blare as a torrent of water burst through the ceiling from the illegal genetic experiment pens above. Many dead researchers and their test subjects littered the floor. A couple of the board members used the security staff as human shields. Meglon Pistachio let out a sigh of relief "what the hell caused that?"

"Does it matter?" Ronald Hasteur pressed the final button to open the vault. "Your failure to keep an orderly house is just one more reason as to why this house of petty grudges and banal schemes must fall."

Betsy Lynchpin aimed a gun at the CEO. "Who are you, really? I knew something was up, events lined up too neatly to enable you to open the vault, what do you want?"

"To further my plans," Ronald Hasteur shed his disguise. "I am known as the Master, universally. You can aid me or you can join your former colleagues in oblivion."

"Never!" Betsy tried to press fire but the gun didn't work. "What?"

"I'm a Time lord," the Master smiled. "I move faster that the second hand on a clock when I have to." He took out a dehydrated machine gun and poured just enough water on it to make it viable again. Then he gratuitously used it on the penultimate board member.

"What now?" Meglon Pistachio knew that only the contents of the vault would be enough for him to start over on another colony somewhere. Best to throw his lot in with Master chap today, and do his own thing tomorrow. "We could share what's in there."

"Do I look like someone who shares things?"

The Master shot the idiot, it was for the good of everyone. He walked into the vault and took only what he needed, enough to fill his jacket pocket and leave barely a bump in the fabric. Then he threw a trikillion grenade into the vault, before sealing it up again. The vault would contain the blast, but if anyone should open it again, well – their deaths would be most unpleasant.

Dalia entered the vault room.

"There's a thousand guards coming this way. They're heavily armed."

"Thank you for your loyal service."

The Master opened fire with his machine gun as soon as the first guard appeared, killing his PA for knowing too much. He laughed loudly as he killed guard after guard. He didn't have to concern himself with ammunition since the clip generated new rounds as quickly as they were fired.

Judy was waiting for the Master outside the TARDIS.

"Thought you'd seen the last of me then?"

"I'm surprised to see you, yes." The Master then smiled. "However, I'm pleased too. You've shown intelligence in your problem solving, that bit with the knife was a refreshing sight to see. Know that if you ever try that with me, of course, your death will be the stuff of nightmares. The kind that parents use to scare their children with at night."

"I know too much about parental abuse already" Judy replied caustically. "You're the Master and I'll obey you, but not blindly, unless that's what's needed to do my part of the plan. You're a Time Lord and I'm just a human. I'm not stupid, one day you'll get bored of me and if I'm really lucky I won't feel the blade."

"You understand me as so few do." The Master had some respect for her, even though she was just a human and he didn't want to waste any real affection or sentiment… think of the age gap? He knew Judy was just using him for his criminal mastermind, thinking she could learn all of his secrets and then escape before he realised what she was up to.

He turned the screen on.

"The rioting has begun," he smiled, as the police opened fire at everyone.

Judy smiled too.

"I hope there's dancing. There should be dancing as the world ends." She then looked at the destination co-ordinates. "Mullins World, are we staying long?"

She'd long ago been dazzled by crime and science, but now, after seeing water girl and her strange friends, she'd discovered even more secrets of the universe to use for her own purposes. All we ever have in the end is ourselves, she mused. We must learn to do all we can to stay alive another day.

"Why don't we get a nice meal on the way?" she suggested. "We could stop off – you could wear that nice dinner suit, we could be billionaires at play. You, charming all their gold and money off them, and me, the helpful stooge. They'd only waste it anyway, who needs to buy another yacht when there's the thrill of stealing it from the most secure marina in the universe?"

"Perhaps," the Master sighed and considered indulging his pet. "If you behave and clean your room. You can pay, you stole enough money from my business, didn't you?"

That last dig hurt her the most, he could always tell when he had made the deepest wound and drawn the most blood, metaphorically speaking of course.

Once he'd stolen all the components he needed to get on with the real business of building the biggest doomsday weapon the universe had ever known, and he'd tried to steal several of them in the past. If he could hold the universe to ransom then he'd control everything.

Judy sighed inwardly and tried to think of nothing but the next heist. The Master liked to hurt her, she'd told him about her abusive childhood, and she wanted to believe that in his own way he was being kind by forcing her to grow a thicker skin.

***

"I'm sorry." Judy screamed, as she was shaken about the ship, while trying to make a fresh pot of tea for the Master. "Stop pressuring me. I'm doing the best I can."

The Master struggled over to the controls. "We're headed straight for the centre of a black hole."

"At least we're colour coordinated."

Judy was glad they were both at the emo end of the fashion spectrum.

"I'll try resetting the temporal dampeners," The Master struggled with the ship's controls.

"No, that won't work," Judy called over as she warmed the teapot. She remembered reading about this scenario in the boring book the Master made her read on pain of dismemberment. "You have to use the spatial convergence limiter. It's the only way."

The Master realised his pet was right and pressed the button to activate the spatial convergence limiter.

"Our trajectory will be completely random, we could end up anywhere, any when."

"Kind of like a first date then." Judy handed a warm cup of tea to the Master. "This is so great, a real adventure, instead of those boring old planets where we steal billions from the global economy."

The Master reached for his gun, but would he shoot Judy or use her in the last facet of his plan for universal conquest? Only time would tell…

Viva La Vera
Paul Driscoll

Everyone in the British Isles remembers where they were at five past three on Friday 2nd January 2071. Like the announcement of Princess Diana's death, or the attack on the Twin Towers, this was a day in history that would preserve the personal memories of millions. It was one of those rare 'as if it happened yesterday' moments. For Derek Webb, the day was meant to have been special for an entirely different reason. Later that night he was finally going to propose to Doreen Watson. Since breakfast, his head had been on a constant loop, running through the various possible scenarios. Will she, won't she, should I say this, or should I say that?

That afternoon, Derek needed to be fully focused on ensuring the safety and well-being of his boss, the wannabe MP and party-leader, Vera Daly. This was her big day too, and she had an announcement of her own to make. As her Personal Assistant, it was Derek's job to ensure that everything went to plan in the packed conference room. He should have been making sure she was sticking to her script, not rehearsing his own lines; keeping an eye out for troublemakers, not worrying about what might go wrong on his special date. But Derek wasn't the only one in the room who wasn't completely focussed on the contents of Vera's speech, and he wasn't the only one who didn't care who else was there. As the clock turned three, somewhere in the crowd an assassin was preparing to strike. Would it have made a difference if Derek's mind had been on the job? Probably not, but at least he wouldn't have been left with the guilty thought that maybe he could have prevented it.

He'd worked as Vera Daly's Personal Assistant for three years, sharing all the ups and downs of her meteoric rise from lone-wolf social activist to founder of the grassroots Power to the People party. The great recession of winter 2070 had triggered a call for a snap general election, and on 2nd January 2071, in front of a sceptical and hostile press, Vera was announcing both her candidacy and the formation of the latest party to attempt to challenge the incredibly resilient bipartisan Lab-Con monopoly of parliament.

Vera was known for having a vociferous band of supporters, but they were very much in the minority. Since Brexit and the collapse of the Union, England had become increasingly insular, intolerant and deluded. People who shared Vera's values were largely either dismissed as fruitcakes, or treated with utter contempt. Having risen to notoriety from her direct-action campaigns,

287

championing the rights of the marginalised and the dispossessed, Vera's name became a label of hatred. Those who might once have been dismissed as SJWs and snowflakes were now being called Vera Dalys.

Truth be told, Derek was a hypocrite. He first started working for Vera not out of conviction, but because he needed the money and the position had popped up when he was doing an online job-search. At first, he thought it was a virus or a piss-take when after clicking on the link, a roaming legend of Vera Daly's face filled the screen. He had to click on her left nostril in order to access the job-information. The strangely-worded advert, high on double-entendre, asked for a jack-of-all-trades, but also someone with special skills in online marketing and website design. Oddest of all was the job title, not Personal Assistant, which it effectively was, but Companion.

The salary was incredibly generous, a fact that wouldn't have sat so easy with Vera Daly's genuine supporters. She'd always remained tight-lipped as to where the funds were coming from and Derek had no intentions of rocking the boat by asking. It wasn't all about the money, though. Derek also liked the idea of being seen as a radical; it amused him insofar as it really annoyed his parents. He revelled in the thought of being seen as a hate figure. At best, he was sympathetic to Vera's political persuasion, but in reality he could take it or leave it.

Doreen Watson was the opposite. She had been virtually stalking Vera Daly since the campaigner had first come to prominence when streaking at the 2068 FA Cup final, carrying a plastic Boycott Plastics placard. Love-it or loath-it, Derek knew that if it wasn't for Doreen's embarrassing fannishness, they would never have got together. In his efforts to keep this crazy woman away from Vera's door, he had resorted to escorting her off-premises to the nearest coffee shop, falsely promising to pass on any messages she had for her political hero. It became a 'thing' that every Monday, Wednesday and Friday morning they would meet for coffee. The unlikely couple had fallen head-over-heels in love with each other.

Such was Doreen's passion for Vera and her politics that Derek had decided to pick the day of Vera's historic announcement to pop the question. Partly, it was an act of opportunism – he felt sure it would significantly reduce the chances of a rejection – but the romantic in him thought it would be a fitting gesture, nonetheless. At five past three that afternoon it was looking like the worst idea he'd ever had.

***

Derek's sense of powerlessness as he stood over Vera's bleeding body was compounded by the fact that he could hear the ambulance and police sirens even before he'd had the wherewithal to call for them. The noise of the sirens spurred him into action. Most of the crowd had fled in sheer panic, well before the slow-to-act police had put the building on lock-down, leaving him to push past the more fearless newshounds in order to tend to Vera.

He could feel a pulse, but Vera was bleeding heavily from a bullet wound to her chest. He used his jacket to stem the blood-flow in a frantic bid to keep her alive before the paramedics arrived to take over.

Expecting the paramedics, Derek was both amazed and angered when Doreen, of all people, rushed to his aid. After years of having kept his lover away, here she was, finally stood beside her hero. In the worst possible circumstances.

"How did you get in here?" he said, sharply. "With security this lapse, is it any wonder something like this has happened? I'd been telling Vera until I was blue in the face to hire her own bodyguards, that she can't rely on the authorities... or me, it's not fair."

"I was watching the live broadcast in the café across the road, as close to the action as you'd allow, when the feed went dead. No way was I going to wait outside for news. The police tried to stop me as I pushed my way through the crowd, but I was having none of it. My Derek's in there, I told the two officers at the door..." replied Doreen. She continued to witter on, until the paramedics arrived to take charge.

One of the ambulance crew tended to Vera, while the other tried to make sure Derek was okay.

"I'm fine. I'm not the one who's been shot," Derek snapped.

"You've had a terrible shock. Perhaps you better sit down. Have a glass of water," said the paramedic.

"Come on, love, let them do their job," added Doreen, ushering Derek to the chairs at the back of the stage.

"And I suppose the police just shrugged and let you pass?" said Derek, picking up their unfinished conversation, all-the-while glaring at the paramedic who was still hovering over them.

"That's the power of love for you. But I must admit, they were oddly statuesque and silent."

"They should all be sacked. There's a gunman on the loose, you could have been killed."

289

"You are safe now," said the paramedic, in a vain attempt to offer reassurance. "A police hunt is already underway and a cordon is in place around the building. They will no-doubt want to question you."

"Fair enough, but I'm coming with you to the hospital first."

"That won't be necessary," said the other paramedic, joining them, ashen-faced.

"You mean…" replied Derek, fearing the worst.

"I'm sorry. There was nothing we could do."

***

The horrific events of that day ought to have put to bed Derek's proposal plans, but when Doreen had picked up his blood-soaked jacket, the engagement ring had dropped out of the breast-pocket, betraying his intentions.

Breaking the awkward silence after they had been allowed to return home by the police, Doreen insisted Derek put the ring on her anyway, spouting some nonsense about how they must live their lives together in memory of Vera, committing themselves not only to each other, but to Vera's mission. Derek protested – it was entirely inappropriate and did they really want to forever associate their engagement with the day Vera Daly died? Since he was now out of a job, wouldn't it be better to return it to the store? Doreen's tears, as they so often did, won the argument. Derek, she insisted, must return to work. The party will need his administrative skills and his expertise in running social media more than ever. He could be an interim leader until Vera's successor was appointed. Now she was pushing it.

"Okay, okay… I will marry you Doreen Watson. But don't expect me to work for Power to the People. I'll find something else. I let her down, and I just can't… not yet…"

***

Derek and Doreen married in the summer of 71, on the same day that the police effectively gave up any hope of finding the assassin. Doreen had been right about the job, Derek was still very much needed, and his continued employment ensured that a wedding could indeed go ahead.

But all was not as it seemed.

Three days after Vera's death, Derek had come to collect his belongings from the office. Upon his arrival, he was surprised to find that the locks had been changed. Even more concerning, lights were on inside and he could hear the unmistakable roar of his dying computer fan.

"Hello?" he shouted through the door. "Is that the police? Only, it's Derek Webb here. I've just come to pick up a few things. Is that ok?"

Irritated by the lack of response, he banged on the frosted window panel.

"Look, if you're checking the PC, I can assure you there's nothing dodgy on there. The search history will pull up a few jewellers – I'm getting married you see, but that's the only personal stuff you'll find."

Still no answer.

"Well, if you won't let me in, how about at least handing over my stuff? Top drawer of the desk – I keep that for my personal belongings. I've got a tablet in there, photos, a couple of books, and most importantly the spare keys to my house."

On that note, the door was finally opened.

"Oh, it's only you," said Derek, at a loss to know why Jeremy Spalling, a Lib-Dem defector and one of Vera's potential MPs, had locked the door.

"Good job too. What if it wasn't me here, and it wasn't the Police? Bit foolish mentioning your house keys, don't you think?"

"Speaking of keys, why on earth lock the door in the first place?" snapped Derek, who despised the man he'd always seen as a career politician. He was suddenly struck by a disturbing thought, what if…

"Just following orders," said Spalling in that smarmy voice of his. "Oh, did you think I was here to hide the evidence? That I was in on the assassination?"

"Of course not," said Derek, feeling his cheeks burning and hoping they weren't giving away the truth. "But whose orders?"

"Why mine of course."

Derek's eyes nearly popped out of his reddened face. It should have turned white by now, after all, he was pretty certain he had just seen a ghost.

"What's up, Derek? Cat got your tongue?" said Vera Daly, in a far-from-ghostly voice.

"W–what in god's name. You're – no, it can't be…" said Derek, all-of-a-fluster.

Vera Daly grinned, amused by Derek's awkward facial expressions as his brain struggled to process the encounter.

"After all we've been through to get to this moment, do you really think I'm going to let the inconvenience of death get in the way?" she said, in a sing-song voice. "Jeremy love, lock the door and pull up a chair for our Derek, there's a good chap. Come on, before the poor man collapses."

"Are you sure we should be bringing him in on our little secret?" said Jeremy.

"Oh, why not. The more the merrier, I say."

"This is no joking matter," said Derek, falling into the swivel chair that Jeremy had just pushed into the back of him. "The whole world thinks you are dead. What good is it hiding away here? Your funeral is all set for Friday, for goodness sake."

"Hiding away is the best thing I can do, I assure you," said Vera, sounding reassuringly serious now. "This was always the plan."

Derek could not believe what he was hearing.

"You staged your own death? But the police, the paramedics... the blood?"

"Friends of mine. Even the blood-forms. Well, they were, for one day only."

"And the assassin?"

"That would be me," said Jeremy, proudly. To Derek, that was by far the most believable part of the story.

"You can't hide away for the rest of your life, Vera."

"I have more than enough inside these walls to never have to see the light of day again."

In Derek's book, the whole idea was both preposterous and morally wrong.

"Forget the fact that the world needs you. This is no way to live. It's inhumane."

"Inhumane no, inhuman yes. Finally, I get to be true to myself," Vera replied.

She sounded completely genuine. Derek couldn't be sure, but it looked like she might even be holding back tears – not that she was making the faintest bit of sense.

"What's that supposed to mean?" he said, clumsily.

"As I lay there dying, you felt my chest – and very nice you were about it too. Come now, don't tell me you didn't notice?"

Vera pulled Derek up from the chair. Then, much to his embarrassment, still holding his shaking hands she placed them against her breasts.

"Can you feel them, Derek?"

Derek pretended he could feel nothing, beyond the embarrassment of being seduced by his boss.

"I'm getting married for goodness sake."

Vera was completely oblivious to the social awkwardness of the situation.

"Two hearts, beating slightly out of sync," she whispered, as if being turned-on herself. "The sound of drums. Da-da, da-da... da-da, da-da."

Astonished, Derek tuned his ears into the almost hypnotic double-beats. His own pounding heart had been racing, but it settled as it began to mimic the steady rhythm of Vera's bi-vascular system.

"I think I'm beginning to understand," he said, feeling much calmer now. "You've had some kind of unorthodox surgery to bring you back from the dead… wait, are these animal organs…?"

"And on the third day… No, silly. I was never human in the first place," said Vera, in an almost mocking tone.

At this point, Derek was certain that he must have suffered a bump on the head on the way to the office. This had to be some kind of post-traumatic waking-dream. Had he slipped on that dodgy paving stone just outside the building? He decided that it might be possible to trigger a return to the real world if he simply walked out.

He pulled his hands away from Vera and made for the door.

"Off so soon? Do you really want to miss out on all the fun?" said Vera, sounding frivolous once again.

"I don't know what this is, but it's certainly not fun," Derek asserted.

"You should do that thing of yours, make him forget and let him go," suggested Jeremy, who seemed eager to see the back of Derek.

"The only way to guarantee he won't remember is to kill him, and I'm not that person anymore," said Vera.

"What about the paramedics? Won't they remember?" asked Jeremy.

"Oh they'll be dead anyway by the end of the week. I was most careful in who I selected. One has terminal cancer, the other was about to take his own life when he got the call. Don't worry, Jeremy – you've a good thirty years left in you, unless you really wind me up."

Derek was rather fond of the odd horror flick, but he doubted his imagination was twisted enough to dream all this up. Vera was the one who had gone mad, not him.

"What do you plan to do with me, then? Keep me here forever, too? People will come looking for me, you know."

"You want to make your wifey happy, no?" said Vera, sounding as awkward as ever with the colloquial. "What better way than by helping me make a success of Power to the People. Together we can turn this backward, nostalgia-driven nation into a forward-facing land of welcome. Do this in remembrance of me. She'll be ecstatic!"

Derek would normally recoil at such idealistic twaddle, as he used to call it, but he felt oddly drawn to Vera's biblical call. And yes, it would make Doreen the happiest women on Earth.

Vera held his hands again, tenderly this time, her eyes glinting in the knowledge he was being won over. "You see, precisely by dying, Vera Daly will be master of all."

293

Spell broken, Derek pulled back. She was sounding odd again. Most odd. "Master?"

Vera cursed herself for the slip of the tongue. "Mistress?" she suggested, tentatively.

"That sounds even worse."

"Oh bugger it, you get the gist though, I hope. There's something about a good martyrdom that really gets the ethical juices flowing. It will mobilise my followers and silence the critics. I've calculated that within five years, Power to the People will have control of parliament, the press… schools, businesses and every religious institution."

***

And so it came to pass, exactly as Vera had predicted.

Five years on from that fateful day, and against all the odds, Vera's Power to the People party, represented by three members of parliament, had entered into a coalition government with Labour. Vera had turned from being a figure of hate and ridicule into a sainted martyr. A mood of repentance had swept the country, even if living conditions and public policy had barely changed for the better. There remained much work to be done if this new wave of love for Vera was to go beyond mere words and sentiment, but Derek had never seen Doreen so happy and so full of hope.

At first it was a series of small wins, but the need for Labour to form an alliance with Power to the People just to keep out the Tories, brought Vera the political clout to bring her own good intentions, not to mention her foibles, into law and policy. Some of them were obvious wins in line with her inclusive message – a moratorium on all open asylum cases, the scrapping of NHS-plus, and the writing-off of student debt for low paid earners. Others were eccentric, to say the least. Before Prime Minister's questions, it was decreed that parliament replace morning prayers with screenings of pre-school stop-motion animation shows, on the belief that it would improve the quality of the debate. Most striking of all, the 2nd of January was made into an extra bank holiday – the Holy Daly. On that day, amongst other riotous customs, every British citizen was expected to don a Vera Daly mask, including the Prime Minister.

"Not the first time everyone in England has worn my face," Vera had laughed, when she first handed out the masks to her inner circle – the three Power to the People MPs – led by Jeremy Spalling, and dear Derek; the only four people in the world to know she was still alive. "And it's not the first time

I've been the face of the Prime Minister. This is my redemption, as much as it is your liberation."

Nobody dared ask Vera what she meant. She was often coming out with bizarre statements. In the years since she had confined herself to her office, Vera had grown increasingly unpredictable. At times she was as sweet as pie, but other times, even-so-much-as to look at her in the 'wrong' way would provoke a violent outburst. The four of them worried about her health, but she assured them her alien physiognomy was in tip-top condition and that her mood swings were entirely down to her impatience for seeing her vision for England fully realised.

***

The Holy Daly festivities were in full swing when Derek received the call.

"I'm sorry love. State emergency."

"On today of all days," complained Doreen. "I hope there's not been a terrorist threat."

"Well, if ever there was a day to make a point, it would be today. Don't worry love, it's probably nothing."

Derek hastily threw on his overcoat, folded his Vera mask inside his trouser pocket, and made to leave.

"Aren't you forgetting something?"

"Oops," said Derek.

He yanked off his false beard and hung it over the hat-stand.

"For a party that claims to be the voice of inclusion, that's one act of parliament I'll never agree with," said Doreen. "But it's not worth the risk, you breaking the no-facial-hair-in-public-places law."

"Well, it's a work in progress, my love."

"Try saying that to the Orthodox Jews, the Sikhs and the Muslims. I know Vera was known for her unusual phobia, but that's one tribute too far, even for me. Besides, you look ever-so-lovely in it."

"Can I let you in on a little secret, honey? I shaved mine off the day I first started working for Vera, and without this thriving trade in false beards and taches I'd never have worn one again. As much as I wanted to grow it back after she died, it just wouldn't have felt right."

"You're a sweet man, Derek Webb. But I didn't think we had any secrets between us. I guess I should be flattered if this was the big one. Unless there's anything else you want to tell me?"

Derek forced a smile.

"I'm an open book, outside the remit of the official secrets act, that is. Speaking of which…"

"… you've got to go."

Derek was about to kiss Doreen when she put on her Vera Daly mask. The ultimate passion-killer.

"Viva la Vera!" she shouted, echoing the chants of millions.

"Exactly," Derek replied deadpan. "Bye love."

***

When Derek arrived at the office he was surprised to find Vera alone at her desk.

"What's the emergency this time, and where are the others?"

"There's no emergency."

"But I got the call? I assumed…"

"Everything is hunky-dory with England. There are no immediate security risks, I've made sure of that. Not from outside these walls, anyway."

"Has one of those three snakes defected? I knew Jeremy couldn't be trusted."

"They are defective, like the rest of your miserable species," said Vera, laughing emptily at her attempted humour. "But defectors, no. They'd be better off without me."

"The whole of England is cheering and singing your name, even as we speak – 'Hurray, hurray it's a Vera Holy Daly' – so why so morbid?"

Vera stood up and smashed her fist against the desk. Derek had become used to her occasional outbursts, but they were usually rather comical and tended to quickly pass. Now she was displaying a violent streak he hadn't realised she was capable of.

"This is no fit of depression," said Vera, trying to sound more stern than deranged. "I'm not like you in that regard. When I say they'd be better off without me, I mean exactly that."

Vera pulled out the entire drawer that had once stored Derek's personal possessions and flung it on top of the desk.

"Now do you believe me?"

Derek peered inside and almost laughed at the bizarre sight.

"Voodoo dolls? Can't say I blame you. Don't beat yourself up over it. If it relieves you of a bit of stress then why not? I might have to borrow this one though." Derek picked up a figure with an uncanny resemblance to Jeremy. "My god, they look almost real."

Vera grabbed the figure, took a pair of scissors and proceeded to stab it all-over. Derek recoiled as she squeezed out what appeared to be blood from the resultant punctures.

"Proof enough, or do you need me to carry out a full dissection?"

Derek recognised that voice well enough to know that Vera wasn't bluffing.

"You murdered them? For what?"

"Technically, no. Only the living can commit a murder. But, yes, I killed them. Oh god, I actually killed them. All because they were such awful bores." At first, Vera sounded emotionless, as if murder was of no more consequence than squashing an ant or squatting a fly, but when the extent of her depravity dawned on her, she collapsed into a foetal ball.

Derek was caught in two minds when Vera cried out for help.

She appeared to be in considerable pain, writhing on the floor like a demented snake. His natural inclination was to go to her, but those miniaturised colleagues? What's to say she wasn't about to do the same to him?

It had taken a good few months for Derek to finally accept that Vera was indeed an alien. He had questioned, many times, whether or not she was as benevolent as she appeared, but for some inexplicable reason, he hadn't even entertained the thought that she could be one of many. Now, the doubts were coming in thick and fast. Was he being hoodwinked by the vanguard to a full-on alien invasion? The Power to the People movement wasn't unique to England, with similar grassroots parties springing up on every continent. Did that mean there were multiple Vera Dalys manipulating their way into power?

"Help you? Are you out of your mind? What was it, some kind of alien shrink-ray? Are there more of your kind already on my planet, or is the mother of all motherships on its way? Who else have you killed? Oh god, not the Prime Minister?"

"Stop it! Stop it!" shouted Vera, slithering her way back into an upright position against the wall. "Nobody else has been killed. Yet. That's why I called you here. I need to be stopped. Please, help me make it stop."

Even in the knowledge that Vera had committed the most heinous of crimes, Derek felt duty-bound to support her. Her voice wasn't exactly oozing with conviction, yet the cry for help struck him as being completely genuine.

"What's happening to you? Are you evolving, or is there some kind of alien inside you trying to break free?"

"If it were that simple, I would have regressed or called in an exorcist. This is part of who I am. My old, unredeemed nature," answered Vera, solemnly. "I've been resisting the temptation to revert to type since the day I arrived on Earth. I really thought I'd beaten the old devil."

"Perhaps an exorcist is exactly what you do need then," suggested Derek. "It doesn't have to be a literal demon inside you."

Vera laughed, dismissive of Derek's suggestion.

"The only demons worth worrying about are the ones who stand on the outside looking in; creatures from worlds and dimensions beyond your own. Even my old self couldn't handle them. All the others are mere constructs of your pitiful human imagination, easily dealt with. No, I'm the one who needs releasing here, not some kind of real or imagined beast. I feel as if my hearts have been trapped inside another person's head. Please, Derek, help me put an end to it before I do any more damage."

Vera handed Derek a black, probe-like instrument. He assumed it must have been the shrink-ray gun that she'd used on Jeremy and the others.

"You want me to kill you?" he said, aghast.

"I'd have pulled the trigger myself if I thought that was the answer. No Derek, I'm already dead. Not as dead as those three… but, you know what I mean."

"So what then? Why am I here exactly? You want me to have you arrested?"

"I want you to be my companion. I think that's what I'm supposed to call you. It is after all, your job title."

"Your partner in crime?"

"On the contrary – my redemption-buddy. I need to go home. Back to the place in which I was conceived. This is their mess, not mine. Maybe they can help, but if not, they at least need to know… they need to know that their meddling in my affairs has been to no avail."

"What do you need? A couple of hundred. A grand? I'd need to get to the bank in the morning if it's over £500."

Vera rolled her eyes.

"Your money can't buy me a ticket out of here. I need you to companion me. Whatever that entails. Travel with me to Gallifrey in the constellation of Kasterborous and make sure I don't do anything crazy like try to assassinate the president."

"I'm sorry," said Derek. "I'll confiscate this weapon of yours, but that's it. I need to get back to Doreen."

Vera looked crestfallen, but seemed to understand.

"While I'm away, and in case I don't make it back, I need you to do one other thing for me."

"As long as it doesn't involve using this… thing," said Derek, holding the probe nervously.

"There will be by-elections, we need three suitable candidates."

"I'm sure there are several who would step in. I'd have thought that was the least of our concerns. I mean, how will we explain the disappearances?"

"I've already set the cover-up in motion. Tomorrow's headlines will soon be hastily rewritten. They will be reporting that the PTTP MPs were travelling to one of those international parties being held in my honour when their light-aircraft exploded over the Atlantic. It might even help to further the cause of Power to the People."

"You'd have to kill somebody else to pull that one off," said Derek, immediately feeling somewhat perturbed that he had already normalised the deaths of the MPs.

"There's a pilot in the last stages of bowel cancer who wants to cross the Atlantic," Vera explained. This was becoming a 'thing' now, thought Derek, as she continued. "It's on his bucket list. It's the best way he's ever going to die. There's no need to feel sorry for him."

"And I suppose you've already selected our replacement MPs?"

"In the filing cabinet. Bottom drawer, I keep a portfolio on each of our members. You decide. Pick whoever you like and give them the call. Tell them Vera had personally recommended them before she died. Doesn't really matter who you pick, they will win the vote through sheer sympathy. Choose your beloved Doreen, if you like."

Derek had little interest in following the orders of his deranged boss, but the fact that she might have a file on Doreen was the clincher. He had to know what it said.

He opened the drawer, expecting to find it stuffed with files.

"It's empty, are you sure these files of yours aren't in one of the other drawers?"

Vera sidled up behind her crouching companion.

"Are you sure?" she said. "Let me see."

She opened and closed the second-from-the-bottom-drawer just as Derek went to stand up, knocking him senseless.

"I'll file this one under gullible," she quipped, before pushing him head-first inside the seemingly bottomless bottom drawer.

***

Derek regained consciousness. At first, he thought he was in some kind of hospital. The white and minimalistic surroundings gave the impression that he was in a sterile environment. But here there were no beds. A six-sided console of presumably alien origin formed the centrepiece of the room, complete with a mesmerising column of light with piston-like movements.

"Where have you taken me?" he said, groggily.

"I've not moved you anywhere," protested Vera. "You are still inside the filing cabinet."

Derek remembered now. He had been peering into the blackness of the empty bottom drawer before *everything* went black.

"Don't take me for a fool," he said.

"It's true. Sort of. I mean, I probably should have mentioned that the said-cabinet is a shape-shifting bigger-on-the-inside Time Lord vessel that travels through time and space. TARDIS for short."

"You're planning to make me disappear too, aren't you?"

"Come on Derek. Have you forgotten my shrink-ray device, as you so cutely call it, is in your pocket? I'm trying to put things right. Unfortunately, I can't trust myself to do this alone. I need you. You must be my voice of conscience. If I try anything, anything that might suggest otherwise you have to stop me. And if I don't listen... do you understand?"

She nodded knowingly towards the probe.

The oddly hypnotic column in the centre of the hexagonal console slowly came to a halt, followed by a sudden stillness that betrayed the fact they had been on the move.

"We're here, Derek. After all these years. Home again. Come on, there's no time to lose."

Vera pulled a lever and one of the hexagonal portals that were lining the vessel's walls opened. Ducking, she walked through the exit and emerged from a filing cabinet drawer on the other side.

Derek followed her out of the TARDIS into what looked like a broom cupboard, albeit one with swanky white décor.

Vera was tutting at the incongruous filing cabinet they had both implausibly stepped out of.

"There must be something about the Earth's atmosphere that interferes with a TARDIS's chameleon circuit," she mused. "Either that, or this is typical Time Lord humour. All part of their bid to make me more like..."

"So this is your home world?" said Derek, sounding unimpressed.

"The most advanced civilisation in the multiverse. And the most boring to boot."

"Might as well be the cleaner's office in the commons."

"Oh excuse me for having the small matter of your planet's survival to attend to. I'd have loved to have taken you to Gallifrey's finest beauty spot for a picnic of grilled Grillowfish and Juleberry gin, munching and sipping to our hearts' content on the scarlet mountain grass. I can think of nothing better than to gaze in wonder at the colourful reflections of the twin suns gleaming from the glass citadel, while above us, fluttering Gallimites hum their merry tunes. Unfortunately, we cannot afford such luxuries."

"I'll guess I'll have to take your word for it," said Derek, struggling to picture the scene.

Vera held her hand against an off-white square in the wall, just beside the door. Suddenly, the entire room was bathed in red and a high-pitched alarm was triggered.

A very stout little man, with a ridiculously long beard, entered the room and switched off the alarm. He looked absolutely petrified.

"Please, please. Don't hurt me…"

Derek saw Vera's eyes turn that familiar shade of yellow they went whenever she was about to explode with rage. He held her back and pulled out from his pocket his Vera mask.

"You probably ought to wear this," he said to the stranger, fitting the mask for him. "It's the beard," he added as he rolled up the strands of white hair and stuffed them inside the bottom of the mask.

Vera was visibly relieved.

"I'm sorry Jaygon. It's one of the symptoms. This regeneration is failing."

"But that's impossible," said Jaygon, his voice muffled by his folded beard.

"No," said Vera sternly. "The idea that you can turn the Master good. That's what's impossible. Take the mask for instance. I'm as vain as I ever was. As power hungry as ever."

"No, no, no, no. I'm sure it's a simple fix. Let's get to the records room and we will sort it out. But for goodness sake, be discrete about it. Intentionally raising the alarm? I don't understand why you did that. You had clearance from the High Council to land here."

"I'm not used to coming in peace," said Vera, as they made their way through a maze of uninspiring corridors. "I did it for old times' sake. You see, Jaygon, we have a problem. A big problem. If I report straight to the council, I'll probably poison them all, or something. I'm here to be fixed. I don't want to be that person anymore. Anyway, if I went straight to the top, who do you think will be the scapegoat when they realise the experiment has been an unmitigated disaster? I'm giving you a chance to make good."

"You should have come alone. The human's presence will raise questions."

"Like the Doctor, I'm more dangerous without a companion. Derek here didn't have a clue, bless him, but for years now he's been keeping me on the straight and narrow, just by being around. It's only in the last few weeks that things have really started to fall apart."

"You've been through worse. Quite literally falling to pieces on one of your previous visits, I seem to recall."

"As keeper of the Matrix you don't need to jog your memory. And you should have foreseen this."

"Relax, we will sort it. If need be, we'll call the Doctor. She'll make it right."

"She's a she now? How unoriginal. No, absolutely no Doctor, not any of them – that's the last thing you should be doing."

***

The records room was at least alien compared to the broom cupboard, thought Derek. But despite the clearly advanced technology furnishing it, it looked ancient – like a library in a gothic castle if such a thing had ever existed.

"What do you people do down here?" he said.

"This is where the Time Lord biographers work. Preparing data to be entered on the Matrix. We also use this area to store backups, as well as the provisional and superseded biodata of every Time Lord."

"The Matrix? What's that – the Time Lord version of the internet?"

"It's a little bit more than that. But the analogy still stands," said Vera. "Why are we here, Jaygon? Surely the Matrix itself needs to be accessed if we are to repair my story."

"The Cloister Wraiths are restless. They sense someone is trying to breach the Matrix. This is definitely not the time to be wandering through the Cloisters. We can get the same information from consulting the backup."

"But we can't alter copies. I need full access to the live data," replied Vera. "I was flawed from the moment you replaced my entry with the latest fabrication."

"You've always been flawed. That's the point," countered Jaygon. "That's why we created you as the Master's shadow. The one who embraces the good in him that has always been denied. The biodata will be more or less accurate. Besides, as far as our records go, there have been several replacement versions of you. A speculative historian can access them all and make their own judgement."

"Apart from the ones you wiped."

"And those you stole. The Matrix serves a higher purpose than a history book. Truth is beyond fact when it comes to predicting the future. This is our best hope of finding a cure. We can't change what has happened, not without

302

creating a new bio, and that would need to be cleared by the High Council. We can, however, work out what we can do to fix things."

"I thought that time travel was all about changing the past," said Derek, trying to be part of the conversation. "Not sure how you can call yourselves lords of time otherwise."

"See I told you, Derek. My people are boring, all that power and by default they just sit and watch as the worlds pass them by."

"Not strictly true, though. If we were totally opposed to changing time, all this would never have happened. I did warn them," said Jaygon.

"It's only when you threaten my people's very existence with a Time War that they start meddling," explained Vera. "First the Daleks, then the Doctor – another one of their failed experiments – and now me. So the live bio was compiled after you interfered with my... the Master's timeline to ensure I would be fit for purpose?"

"Yes. We have gone back through the archives, making the necessary corrections," said Jaygon.

"Let's start with my birth shall we and work backwards. We can't rule out deliberate sabotage of the process. Not everyone believes I have the right to be good. Some people simply can't stomach a redemption story."

***

Derek was expecting to listen to an audio recording, or, at the most, watch the 'birth' from a CCTV-like perspective. Instead, the whole room had been turned into some kind of virtual reality environment. They had all been transported to another time and place, to become ghostlike viewers of a moment in history, unseen and unable to intervene, but unmistakably present.

They could walk around the scene and even inhabit the bodies of the various participants in order to experience the events through their eyes. Vera and Jaygon moved freely around the room, between the actors, but Derek stayed in the corner, spooked by the whole idea of being present and absent simultaneously and fearing he might in some way contaminate a crime scene.

It was a convening of the War Council, chaired by President Rassilon. Continuing the medieval theme, the members were sat around a long wooden table, dressed in ceremonial robes that reminded Derek of his catholic upbringing.

"The Doctor has gone dark. He no longer even associates himself with the name," Rassilon was saying. "We cannot rely on his services. It's as if the Valeyard has become a fully-fledged regeneration."

303

"And the Master?"

"We tested him, we prepared him to fight for the honour of Gallifrey, but he saw through our plans. His self-obsession and love of sheer devilry were too powerful – inherent qualities that, side-by-side, could destroy us all."

"So what do you propose to do about him now?"

"The Master's insanity will be his downfall. We will make sure of that. As troublesome as this renegade is, the one who drank from the cup of the sisterhood is more problematic. We need to find someone who can turn the Doctor."

"A companion?"

"It'll take far more than that this time. Only a person imbued with extraordinary levels of suppressed goodness can be the Doctor's brother-in-arms and bring him to his senses."

"Are you proposing what I think you are…?"

"What we need is a Valeyard Master, an aberration of kindness that can only exist between his penultimate and final regenerations."

"The Master has never once shown a good side. He is irredeemable. Even a Valeyard Master would never have the heart to go against his previous incarnations. There simply isn't enough kindness inside him."

"Then we take steps to guarantee that such goodness lies in waiting. We rewrite the Master's history to ensure that he frequently encounters the Doctor. Make him obsessed enough to always seek out his old friend from the academy. The Doctor will chip away at the walls that hold back the Master's capacity for good. The Doctor will fail, he has to, but in so doing, he will have set up the conditions for this new incarnation. The Master must never be allowed to live without the Doctor always being on his mind, and always being just around the corner. This Valeyard Master, uniquely good by default, will control the excesses of the War Doctor. He might also be useful for us in future missions – a reliable renegade ally, at last, in the fight against the Daleks."

"You do of course realise you are proposing a breach of the Matrix?"

"The precedent has already been set, and if ever we had good cause… You should be more concerned with the fact that this plan involves turning the Master into a hero. We all need to be sure that we can live with that eventuality."

Derek watched on in wonder as the gathered assembly entered some kind of mind consultation. It was as if they were doing battle with themselves, weighing up the rights and wrongs of their actions, before coming to a shared judgement.

"What fools," said Vera to a nervous Jaygon, appalled by the scene she had just witnessed. "So my unnatural birth is rooted in the Master's interactions with the Doctor. They manipulated his timelines so that he became obsessed with

304

the idea of being the Doctor's nemesis. No wonder he settled on Earth for a while, even though he despised the place. It was because of Rassilon and the Doctor. Bring us back at once."

Obediently, Jaygon cut the virtual reality feed.

Vera was still fuming about her questionable existence.

"Those monsters in their fancy robes created me to despise myself and to go against all the Master ever stood for. They doctored me, drove me to insanity. I became so fixated on beating the Doctor that it became the sole reason for my existence."

"Was it really such a crazy idea that the Doctor might be a good influence on you?" said Jaygon. "There is plenty of evidence that you did listen to him, especially in his twelfth incarnation."

"I don't need to relive my encounters with the Doctor to know that I was a lost cause. He tried, several times, to save me. But I was beyond help. No wonder this shadow-incarnation is failing. They inadvertently made the Doctor the reason for my wickedness, not the means of my redemption."

"Revisit those times when the Doctor came close. It might help to overcome the fear of failure and the temptation to give in to your old ways," said Jaygon.

"No. The only hope now is to start again. Jaygon, I'm going to give you reason to scrap this bio. I shall make sure that the Time Lords do all they can to keep the Master and Doctor apart. My goodness doesn't need a Doctor to flourish. It needs a world in which the Doctor may as well have never existed."

***

Vera Daly dropped Derek back at the office.

She told him to go and enjoy the rest of Holy Daly with his beloved and apologised – if her TARDIS hadn't been stuck in the form of a filing cabinet, she'd had landed it closer to his home.

She was off to manipulate some ancient Time Lords into making sure that the Master would be forever separated from this Doctor person.

"Do you think it will work?" said Derek. "I mean, whoever this Doctor is, he sounds like a good man."

"And a better woman," agreed Vera. "Whatever happens, it has to be preferable to this. Who knew that trying to do the right thing could be so damn hard?"

"What if you never come back?"

"The same as if none of this had ever happened," replied Vera, mysteriously. "It would be up to you. But tell me this – we did good, didn't we?"

Much to his relief, the Master left before Derek could reply. He had no idea how he would have answered.

He locked the drawer of the desk, too afraid to look at the bodies again, and was about to make his way home when, to his alarm, the door swung open. He felt for the shrink-ray gun that ought to have been in his pocket, but he must have lost it on the way.

Stood in the doorway was another walking miracle.

The right (dis)honourable Jeremy Spalling.

"What are you doing here?" said Jeremy, as smarmy as ever.

Derek should have been used to the impossible by now. But no, once again he had been floored.

"J... J... Jeremy, is that really you?"

"Why of course it is, you mad fool. It's your day off, why aren't you out celebrating with your missus? You don't remember when your wedding anniversary is, but you've always made such a fuss of the day you got engaged."

"I was just here to see Vera," said Derek.

"Very funny," laughed Jeremy. "Now, since you're here anyway... this political party you and Doreen want us to set up, don't suppose you've come up with a name, yet?"

***

Vera Daly knew that she was a freak of Time Lord engineering. She knew that she was born to be good, to make amends for the various atrocities she had carried out in her former lives as the Master. She knew she was expected to stand alongside the Time Lords in the Time War, and specifically to help the Doctor rediscover his goodness. But she had no desire for any of it. The Doctor was an old friend she barely remembered from her childhood. She had more pressing concerns. She wanted to change a world, specifically Earth. And so on the day in which she was created, she ran. She stole a TARDIS and she ran to the one place protected from the Time War.

All the time she was the Master she seemed destined to never cross paths with the Doctor. The Time Lords had made it so after the events known in the Matrix as the war games. She suspected that someone else must have been pulling their strings – after all, surely it would have been in their interests if she and the Doctor frequently bumped into each other? For centuries, it had riled her to know that he or she was out there, somewhere, doing good and getting all the credit for it. She had heard the legends and she made a hobby out of plotting the Doctor's downfall. In fact, she became even more obsessed with him in his absence. When that downfall came so unexpectedly, without her intervention, she could finally lay that particular demon to rest. Help redeem the fallen Doctor? Why on earth would she do that?

Vera Daly knew her limitations. Her head was programmed to be good, but her hearts were never in it. Being good came unnaturally, and she knew that she had to make maximum impact in as short a time as possible. And so she took up a cause. She used her powers of manipulation and her charm to create a band of followers who would at least expose the hypocrisy of those humans the Doctor had been so fond of associating with. The United Kingdom seemed to be of special significance to the old fool, and so after its post-Brexit breakup she chose England as her new stage.

Her hearts wanted power, but her head said no. Without the will to make it happen, Vera Daly never amounted to anything except a figure of ridicule. She wasn't even mad or important enough to make it into her local paper. Even Derek, her supposedly loyal assistant, was only in it to take home a salary. Nobody in their right mind rallied to her cause, only the oddballs like that stalker Doreen.

Hers was a pointless incarnation. All she could do was hibernate somewhere nobody could find her and wait until the next Master emerged. On the 2nd of January 2071 she decided to give up the Earth and her own goodness as lost causes. She phoned in sick that day, leaving Derek to man the shed that doubled as her office of operations. That same night, oblivious to the fact that a filing cabinet had mysteriously vanished, taking his old boss to a new life off-grid, Derek proposed to Doreen. Thankfully, with Vera off work, he'd had the whole day free to rehearse his lines.

***

The Master, now, once again, in his final regeneration, paid another visit to Jaygon the keeper of the Matrix.

"Well, did you replace the bio as I instructed?"

"It didn't quite work out exactly as you planned," warned Jaygon.

"Splendid, dear fellow. That's exactly what I was hoping to hear. Now, about the Doctor. Get down to those cloister rooms of yours and find out where she is, there's a good chap… we've a lot of catching up to do."

THE END

307

Printed in Poland
by Amazon Fulfillment
Poland Sp. z o.o., Wrocław

50965936R00181